SAMBATYON-2

A Documentary Novel

SAMBATYON-2

A Documentary Novel

BY MEIR SIMHA OSTRINSKY

BLOCH PUBLISHING CO.
NEW YORK

ACKNOWLEDGMENTS

Appreciation is due to my wife Martha for having typed and re-typed most of my manuscript, and for her patience and encouragement during the years this book was in preparation. I am also grateful to my son Zvi for his invaluable editorial advice and to my brother Seymour Ostrin for assistance. The bulletin headings for the chapters were selected from the New York Times. The quotations from the Holy Scriptures, Talmud, Midrash, liturgy and Hebrew poetry have been freely translated. The quotations on page 155, are from The Jewish Encyclopedia, volume X, page 564.

M.S.O.

Library of Congress Catalog Card Number: 77-116870

Manufactured in the United States of America by The Haddon Craftsmen

To my wife Martha and our children
Renah, Zvi and Sarah; my sister
Florence Levin and my brothers
Jack and Seymour Ostrin.

Sambatyon, according to its exegetic image in the Midrash and Talmudic Haggadah, is a fiery explosive river beyond the dark mountains, that rests only on the Sabbath. But Sambatyon-2 is a river of hate and violence that never stops. It emerged during the Nazi period and still smoulders underneath the surface. Sambatyon-2 is a man-made river of hate that must be eliminated in order to save mankind from another, even greater, Holocaust.

The Holocaust was the greatest calamity in the history of mankind. . . . Never again shall eyes stare from behind electrified barbed wire. We must be strong and proud Jews. We must never again be led to the slaughter.

Judah G., Si'akh Lokhamim, Tel-Aviv, October 1967

INTRODUCTION

In the spring of 1939, while a student at Yeshiva University, I had a dream that German soldiers were occupying my birthplace. This portentious dream was fulfilled beyond any imagination. After the war ended I began to gather the material for this book. I talked to survivors of concentration camps, young and old, covering every country of the disaster. I made two trips to Israel to interview the survivors from the Polish town where I was born. I read many of the biographical and historical *churban* books, including those from Suha-Vali.* After 20 years of writing, the manuscript eventually ran to 500,000 words, which was cut down to one-third that size for this book.

Many books have been and will be written about the Holocaust. Survivors and authors have shocked up with the incredible cruelty of the Nazis and their collaborators. The statistics and grisly details which predominate in most of the books on this subject do not do justice to the valiant people who perished in the most exemplary martyrdom in the history of mankind.

Sambatyon-2 is the story of Suha-Vali, a small town in northeastern Poland, during the Nazi occupation from June, 1941 until 1944. Only eighteen survived out of a population of 2500 deported to Kolbasin, then to Grodno, and finally to dreaded Auschwitz. But this is not strictly a story of one town: it is symbolic and representative of the cumulative catastrophic events.

There are many unanswered questions. How did all this happen in the enlightened twentieth century? How was it possible for Christian nations, who worshipped the Jewish God, revered the Hebrew Scriptures, sang the Psalms of David, and adapted many of the Biblical laws, Jewish rituals and prayers, to revert to such savagery? Why did the Germans elect and support Hitler as

* Simha Lazar, *Churban Suha-Vali*, Mexico, 1947.
Chana Steinberg, M. Wenchotzker, Y. Levin and J. Zaban, editors, *Sefer Sohovolo*, Encyclopedia Goluyath, Jerusalem-Tel Aviv, 1957.

chancellor after he openly advocated the extermination of the Jews? Why did the Poles, Hungarians, Baltics, Roumanians, Slavs, French, Greeks, and even the Italians, collaborate as officials and volunteers who pillaged, killed, raped, and maimed the Jews in their own ghettos, denied them food and shelter, hunted them down in the fields and forests, and finally helped to round them up and transport them to the death camps? Why did the Roman Catholic Church, through the powerful Vatican, fail to intervene? Could the Jews have resisted? Was their faith in God and man ever shaken?

The Torah, Talmud and Midrash are preoccupied with these eternal problems: good and evil, peace and war, God dominating one kingdom on earth while almost banished from the rest. The Torah speaks in the language of God. One nation, the people of God, has established the dialogue. Floods, wars and disasters have not disrupted this understanding and covenant between Israel and God.

When Rabbi Akiba's colleagues began to weep at the sight of the devastated temple, he was merry. He said, "Now that Uriah's earlier prophecy of Jerusalem's destruction is fulfilled I am looking forward to the day when God will redeem Zechariah's later prophecy that the streets of liberated Jerusalem will once again echo and reecho with songs and salvation." (Makkoth, 24.)

But unfortunately, this chapter of prophecy has not yet been concluded. Arabs, Russians, and their satellites in Communist countries, are waging open war against God and Israel. Today, as in the days of Hitler, we are flooded with deceitful propaganda by Communazi Russians, Arabs and their satanic collaborators who "call evil good, and good evil." (Isaiah 5:20.)

Somewhere along the road of life the Jews who walked with God were separated by the endless raging river of hate and death, *Sambatyon-2*. But like the phoenix, they emerged from fiery ashes to rebuild the Promised Land, Eretz Israel.

They who were snatched from their homes, shops, classes, houses of prayer and study, and even from the cradle, by the wicked shall not have died in vain.

"They shall never again terrorize my people and threaten my holy mountain: for the knowledge of the Lord shall cover the earth as the waters cover the sea." (Isaiah, 11:9)

Meir Simha Ostrinsky.

SAMBATYON-2

June 13, 1941: ALLIES VOW FIGHT TILL WAR IS WON.
R.A.F. BLASTS RHINE CITIES.

*If you fall into the hands of your enemies
they will have no mercy upon you.*

Sotah, 42.

I

THE INTRUDER

The invaders came down upon the town, silhouetted like ghosts
against the clouded horizon. The steel helmeted Nazi hordes
trampled the rye fields as they converged upon the main ave-
nue ...

This apocalyptic dream obsessed David Sokoloff as he returned home in June 1941, after three years. He had been an
engineering student at Königsberg University in East Prussia,
when the Polish army in the summer of 1939, ordered him to
report to his military unit. Hitler's Germany was on the rampage
and war seemed imminent. Germany attacked Poland in September, crushing its army. David was taken prisoner. When the
Germans began executing all Jewish prisoners he escaped to
Russian occupied Poland, which had been allocated to communist Russia as its partitioned share of Poland in the infamous
pact with the Nazis.

David was arrested by the Russians and conscripted into a
forced labor detail. After being detained for almost two years as
a slave laborer, cut off from his family, he escaped again and
made his way, the fourteen kilometers, to Suha-Vali.

How could he warn them of the catastrophe he saw in his
dream? The Jews would never believe him. They had abiding
faith in the goodness of man who was created in the image of
God and therefore rational. It seemed incredible to them that
their erstwhile Polish neighbors and friends of a thousand years
would collaborate with the Nazi forces.

Only a few kilometers separated David Sokoloff from his
birthplace in the village of Suha-Vali. He strained every muscle
over the road that cut through the shadows of the forest. Even

3

when shifting his stuffed sack from shoulder to shoulder, he kept
pace. Now and then stumps and fallen branches appeared along
the road. More and more swaths of naked ground came into
view. The gleaming remnants of old and young trees were evidence of a sweeping scythe threatening the beauty of the forest.

He glanced back momentarily, toward the receding horizon. A
profuse burst of copper rays streamed forth from the fireball sun
setting the western sky ablaze. His head turned, and he looked
straight into the unforgettable nostalgic memories of childhood.
The earth seemed to challenge the sky, just like the wise men
who sometimes challenged God. The lights were in combat with
the shadows.

The town of Suha-Vali came into view, its gable roofed houses
cradling and hugging the synagogues. Everything was the same;
the New Synagogue of squared logs in the center, alongside his
garden; the Brick Synagogue on the square to the left; the shingled pagoda-like ancient synagogue rising majestically on the
right, near the river. Beyond, the twin steeples of the church
reflected the last rays of the sinking western sun.

The quaint old houses with their straw-thatched or shingled
roofs, each one sprouting a clay or brick chimney, looked as if
they were always there and would survive until the end of time.
The forest absorbed all light, but these crude huts constructed
from logs, long, long ago, pushed back the besieging shadows.

He was now past the windmills which marked the outskirts of
the town. It was Friday, he thought; he must reach his house
before the Sabbath.

It was so quiet. He heard neither the familiar echo of the
hammer nor the buzz of the saw. The shoemaker's pounding
was gone. The clank of the blacksmith's anvil was drowned in
cricket song. The last thuds of a wagon's wheels banging over
stones, the hubs scraping against the axle; the lonely moo of a
cow and the muted bark of a dog receded into the darkening
skies surrounding colonies and hamlets.

He removed his cap and lowered the sack. The pale glow of
his forehead set off his dark brooding eyes and wavy black hair.
His eyes stared ahead and his smooth forehead creased. Only the
momentum of a dire dream pushed the young but tired man over
the last stretch over the rye fields and through his garden. David
was determined to slip in before his mother inaugurated the
Sabbath with candle lights.

After crossing his garden he stopped. His heart beat fast. He wondered if he would find everything as he left it. He tiptoed through the hallway to the kitchen. The kitchen door was ajar, inviting and warm—unlike any other door he had ever opened. Opposite the wood-burning brick stove was the big unpainted table, covered with a white tablecloth. David hesitated as his mother, still unaware of his presence, struck a match which burst into flame at the second try. In one instant she gingerly touched the wicks of both candles. The brass candle holders now were proud bearers of light. Gracefully her cupped hands lifted the scarf above her forehead and her lips whispered the blessing, "Blessed art Thou, the Lord our God, who commanded us to kindle the light of Sabbath."

David felt like an intruder. His dream was mere fantasy, his warning an alarm in vain. He told himself, I dare not, I must not. Who am I to profane the Sabbath? He was about to take one step backward when Dinah Elke saw him.

"O my God!" she screamed, "You are alive! David, God saved you." She choked an uncontrollable urge to cry. "My two sons, where are they?" Dinah Elke's tears burst through her mumbling words. "David, where have you been? We were afraid. Papa wouldn't let me speak about it."

Her ruddy face was white as a sheet. Her lips quivered, and her trembling hands reached out to him. She embraced him, held on to him, then sure that he was alive, let go. He inquired about his father's well being, and then couldn't find another word. He was apprehensive that he had returned too late.

"Here David, wash yourself!" she gave him a towel and took his bag. She went back to the living room and put down the family prayer book on the commode. As a final gesture for him to change and dress, she took out an unwrinkled suit, a starched shirt from the closet, and put it on the small round table near the bookcase.

He began to pace the big front room extending over the greater half of the house with the bedroom and the kitchen in the rear, facing the east. He held the prayer book like one about to open a treasure box whose contents were known.

Words, indelible in his memory, and companion melodies, were now released to be woven in the endless golden thread of a timeless loom. The page was open, the words were arranged in a line, grouped in a cluster, waiting to be offered on the altar of the heart.

"Come my beloved, let us welcome the Sabbath!"

To David the beloved meant mother and father; the land of
Israel; the Zionist dreams and activities; Hebrew books; association with Jewish Zionist clubs; and Rachel. "Come my beloved,"
he repeated again. He saw Rachel. All his life he dreamt of
Zion—it was strange that a girl should intrude through all these
moments of reverence. Perhaps she was part of the dream, that
came to him like a longing during worship.

He proceeded. "Those who despoil thee shall be destroyed,
and those who defile thee shall be banished. Come my beloved."
He was still trying to finish the lingering phrases when he heard
voices coming from across Rachel's garden.

David began to race through the pages. He was bowing, bending and stepping backward, as he finished the silent prayer. To
David prayer was a technique, whose pure concentration took
only seconds, but its effect lasted for hours. The eyes and lips
were like a camera that registered in a split second, but the
image remained long after in the heart. Faint echoes of voices
from across the synagogue yard filtered through David's intona-
tions. Shuffling feet on the cobblestones—worshippers returning
from Friday eve services—were now recognizable. The grating
of the door on its hinges as it swung against the jamb, reminded
him that it needed fastening.

The tiny candle lights wavered from the draft of the opened
door. His father Ber Leib froze. Then his warm hand grasped
David's as if to brace his faint voiced, *"Gut Shabbes."* His
bearded round face nodded slowly. The Zionist fund raiser Ben
Zion, tall with an imposing gait followed him. He was less restrained and boomed in his articulate manner, "A real surprise—a
gift—a Sabbath angel." He let his trimmed reddish beard slide
through his fingers.

"David, if your brothers were only here!", referring to one
interned somewhere in Russia and the youngest unheard of since
he was called to the Polish army a month before the invasion.

"Stop, it is not proper, enough—no tears, in honor of the Sabbath!" Ber Leib said. Ber Leib, who wanted to cry himself,
adroitly maneuvered all the tension of his slight spare frame into
the chanting of *Shalom Alechem*: "May your coming be in
peace, angels of peace." Ben Zion raised his baritone voice,
"Mimelech malachey hamlochim, messengers of the most high."

Ber Leib chanted the sanctification in his usual carefully pro-

nounced syllables. The voice was subdued but defiant in its
enunciation. David differed with his father's traditional Messianic conception of Zionism, yet admired his dauntless stand. It
was a revelation—here—this day, where only bullets and the
whip asserted rights and authority, a frail Jew still sanctified the
Kingdom of God, over watery raisin juice, ignoring the outer
world and its terror completely. His own dream of impending
disaster was alien imagination. No, he would not tell it to anyone, not yet.

His father continued, "Blessed art Thou O God, who creates
wine." It was peculiar to bless God for creating wine, when
everything in this world seemed to curse God and men for creating anything. Everything was geared for destruction.

David's eyes were fixed on the silver cup, clasped by the
graceful fingers of his father's right hand. He raised it aloft. It
was only diluted raisin wine. David suspected that it was the
last, for it appeared too watery. Ber Leib reminded God in the
Kiddush that with the very first Sabbath he had established a
new order on this earth. That this cup of wine was the same as
the cup that heralded freedom from slavery in Egypt. Furthermore, that God chose and sanctified the Jews from among all the
nations. Chosen for what? David asked himself. To be the eternal martyrs? Or perhaps to set an example as a model nation
dedicated to God? At what price? He challenged anyone to answer. Why? How?

They were calling him from the kitchen to wash hands. First
the men and then Dinah Elke poured water from a battered
copper tumbler over their hands and into a wooden pail, accompanied by a blessing.

Ber Leib raised the small loaves of rye bread from under the
embroidered cover. It was a meager offering for the Sabbath
over which he made grace, before he scattered a few grains of
coarse salt on his slice of bread. He then cut three more slices,
two of which he handed to Ben Zion and David while holding
the third as he called toward the kitchen, "Dinah, Dinah, Nu-
nu?" Dinah finally appeared, dried her hands, as she wistfully
made the blessing.

"Nu," he again pleaded, softly, "be seated!" Dinah, her
thoughts adrift among scores of plates, pots, smoking wood, a
missing silver ladle, and above all, still concerned about her
skimpy supplies, sat down. She tasted the bread as if it were

cake, almost forgetting to dip it in the salt spread thinly on a
plate, before she swallowed it. All these shortcomings could be
corrected if she were now in the kitchen. "Even the angels don't
help you in the kitchen unless the pots are full," she always
reflected.

While a discussion surged about the holy bread in the temple,
Dinah deftly vanished into the kitchen. She returned with a deep
bowl. David rose from his chair to help, but she quickly emptied
the soup into his plate and then to Ben Zion's and Ber Leib's. She
portioned out—in the same order—scraps of lamb and chicken.

Ben Zion protested when he saw Ber Leib munching a giblet.
The mistress had reserved for herself only a scrawny neck and
the usual sediment of the soup.

"Here mamma," David was furious, and began to transfer his
own meager portion.

"I forbid you, David. I can't eat any more. I have enough! Too
much for me is unhealthy."

"You are not eating, David," Ber Leib reminded him. But
David was in another world.

Dinah suspected that behind all this dreamy appearance
David was intensely disturbed. She did not dare betray her suspicion. Did she not herself shed tears in the synagogue, even
when the text and meditations suggested something sublime and
joyous? Like other women she invoked tears according to her
moods. She burst out with tears when a Halleluya prayer was
recited and remained stoic during emotional prayers.

Dinah tried to rescue him from the shadows that descended
upon him and the holiness of the Sabbath.

"I am more tired than hungry." He tried to reassure her, knowing she could detect the gathering storm within him.

"To be more tired than hungry is very natural," Ben Zion said
clearing his voice and being very deliberate, now that he reverted from singing to his role as a commentator. "I once attended a conference in Warsaw after the 19th Zionist Congress.
We sat in session from early morning to past midnight. All this
time what do you think we had? Only a few cigarettes and
water. We were too occupied with other things."

"Perhaps manna came down from heaven," Ber Leib skepti-
cally eyed him above his glasses.

"Impossible! Don't misunderstand me, I am not discounting
any miracle, though I have always been consistent as a Zionist

not to depend too much on a miracle. Now to return to my subject—if this food came down from heaven, it would have been intercepted or obstructed by the occupants of the floor above us."

Tea was served without sugar, in fact without tea. It was weak as cambric tea, this brew of roasted apple peelings in hot water. David tried to resume his train of thought, only to crash head-long into the presence of an uninvited guest. The dream was pressing to be heard. It was like looking into the mirror and seeing not only his own face, but also a stranger looking over his shoulder.

Ber Leib thought he knew his son. But could he, anchored in a world of traditions, rescue one sucked into a vortex of uncer-tainty? He fingered the pages of the Pentateuch as if in search for a particular, quotable passage. He raised his eyes and glanced at his son. Something within David told him that his son held within him the portent of an alarm.

Perhaps it is better not to probe too deeply into another's hidden thoughts. Only God can unravel the inner mysteries. After all, every young man in such times is bound to be torn apart by the goings on. I took him by his hand and guided him since childhood. All the gates of knowledge I opened for him— everything that I knew. What I didn't know I sent him elsewhere to learn, the Yeshiva in Grodno, and the University in Königs-berg. Now it is best to leave him alone. It will work itself out. Even mountains settle down, and storms—well God alone knows they come to an end. Ber Leib paused, while David talked to Ben Zion.

"What is wrong with the Torah or our prayerbook?" he inter-cepted his son.

"Nothing! You took out the last word from the context. The prayers for our return to Jerusalem are fine, they kept aflame our hope—our Messianic hope."

"David, don't bring up Messiah, don't confuse it with a move-ment—there is good in it—but it is still political, not based en-tirely on the Torah."

"Does it say in the Torah, father, that we must be homeless? Does it say in the Torah that desert tribes, Arabs, must occupy our holy of holies, the land of our fathers? Does it say in the Torah that we must forever be the slaves of every nation, subject to their caprices, dependent on their goodwill, first invited to

settle, then driven out, given protection, then abandoned or even
killed in cold blood? How long—how long are we going to mis-
read such things into our Torah? Remember there will come a
time when Jews will say we were fools not to have listened to the
Zionists." Ben Zion nodded his head vigorously. He felt justified
as a Zionist advocate despite the many frustrations.

"David, I'm not contradicting you. We Jews all believe in
Zionism, except that it depends what part of the Torah you em-
phasize. Remember there are six hundred and thirteen laws and
thousands of derived laws. It is not so simple, just asking us to
return to Israel. If the Torah is our document for repossessing
the land of our fathers, it is equally our indisputable document
for repossessing our faith."

"But father," David countered to challenge him.

"David, it is enough for to-night," he called a truce. He wanted
to rest with the Torah as the mandate for faith and land.

David was aware for the first time that his father had engaged
in his longest discussion about Zionism. There was a time when
he would have evaded such discussions with a remark like: "You
don't know enough about Zion to bring up Zionism," or "Jewish
National Fund collections, drives, clubs, flag waving—these are
all superficial—you need a Moses and a Mount Sinai."

David was glad that the discussion lured them away from the
immediate grim topics that each one faced but avoided bringing
up. He knew that his father was an ardent sympathizer of the
ultra-Orthodox Agudas Israel, which at first was antagonistic
toward Zionism. But eventually the leaders became more sympathetic to this movement, due to the pressure exerted on them by
wiser and younger elements, especially Rabbis and Yeshiva intellectuals. There would have been discussions far into the night.
Now the encounter was brief, but sharp. Ben Zion was a great
diplomat, skillful to maneuver his opponent into one corner. But
David surprised both. He was quite mature even if still a
dreamer.

"Let us say Grace." Ber Leib seized the initiative.

"Nu," he pointed to the kitchen for the 'last waters.' "Nu?" He
again prompted them to perform the ritual of symbolic washing
of their hands. Finally his last punctuated "Nu," in the direction
of David, meant "you are honored to say the Grace."

The lights on the half melted candles began to waver as droplets ran down the sides and cooled into tallow.

"Let us say Grace." He turned in the direction of his father and Ben Zion. "May the name of God be blessed now and forever." There was a pause, as the master of the house recited: "Our shepherd, our provider . . . do not oblige us to get our daily bread from bloody hands." Was it the exact meaning of the text? Perhaps not, but this was what David felt the words meant. He couldn't follow the last paragraphs. Ben Zion began to rise as he finished the last sentence deliberately.

"I was once young and now that I am older I do believe that the just are not abandoned nor do their children go begging for bread." There was no one at the table. Only tiny flames fanned their last lights over the white tablecloth.

She listened to her son's moaning, bent down and put her hand on his forehead. He stirred and opened his eyes.

"Don't you feel well?"

"Nothing!"

"Was it a dream?"

"No! Nothing."

"Your father must be up."

"Please mamma!"

"You make nothing of it. I'll go, but I'll stay awake."

Dinah Elke slipped back to her vigil. Ber Leib who pretended to be asleep got down to investigate.

"Was it a nightmare? I know what you went through the last two years."

"Father, I would rather not . . ."

"David, are you trying to keep this a secret? Not a night has passed since you returned, that you have not had a dream."

"It wasn't a dream."

"What was it?"

"A vision."

"Only a prophet can see a vision."

"It is a warning that the enemy is coming."

"What enemy?"

"The Germans."

"Don't frighten us!"

"I tell you I saw the soldiers in broad daylight, waging a ruthless war."

"David, we are tired of wars. According to our sages, a dream is nothing but the hallucinations of the day repeated at night."

"Two years ago I dreamed that our unit was encircled by a German army. Didn't this come true?"

"David, stop this talk. You were not ordained to be a seer."

"I tell you, the Germans will invade Poland and threaten all of us."

"These are words that Satan put in your mouth."

"No father. This isn't just a dream. The whole world has seen it coming, in daylight."

"David, once you were little and I held your hand. We walked together and shared many things, beautiful secrets."

"Father I am not a little boy any more. I grew up and found a vicious world. We can walk together again, if this awful dream stops pursuing me. But right now I am sure that the terrible Germans will come down upon us."

"David, how can you even for one moment suggest that God will abandon us?"

"It's the Germans—most of them—who will abandon God. The majority of the Poles will help the enemy or turn their backs on us. Who knows how many other nations will do the same. This is what I fear. I saw it in my dreams."

*Even the ordinary in your midst are full of
precepts like a pomegranate.*

Berakoth, 57.

2

SABBATH TURMOIL

Soft voices of the Sabbath morning woke David. The dawning
light burst through the cracks of the shutters. The rays of the sun
had not yet come up from the rye fields behind the synagogue.
Early worshippers were on their way to the synagogue. Pleasant
Sabbath greetings drifted through his shuttered window and
called him to prayer. He could tell by the steps that they were
from the downtown side of the street, very familiar voices, to be
sure, part of himself. That must be Alter Stoliar the carpenter—
why those are his heavy steps and those his sawed-off words
escaping like a high pitched cough. And those measured steps
alongside must be of Beryl the baker.

It was David's custom for many years to recite these prefatory
"prayers of the pious." He had a sudden urge to be there again,
to slip unnoticed into the synagogue early in the morning. He
dressed quickly before Dinah could get a response to her "Sleep
David, I heard only a few footsteps—David! David?" She heard
only the thud of the door closing against the doorposts and the
rattling of the front windows.

"David, David!" an anxious voice called him as he closed the
door on the outside.

"Israel, what is it?" he asked his swarthy boyhood friend
whose military unit never reached the front when Poland collapsed.

"I must speak to you."

"Now?" he asked the intellectual son of the grocery man, who
was so involved in Zionism that he never planned a career.

"Very urgent."

"Sh!" he cautioned him not to wake his parents.

Israel was disturbed by the latest episode. As a militant Zionist and in defiance of the communist regime, he tried several times to guide *Chalutzim* to *Eretz Israel*. Now for the second time within a week several boys were intercepted on the way to Bialystok.

"What can you expect from communists?" Israel was bitter.

"What about Reuvke?" David asked about the grandson of Paltiel the builder and Religious Zionist (Mizrachi) leader. "Reuvke is an architect. He told me that only in Eretz Israel can the Jew plan and build; here it is hopeless." I persuaded Reuvke to spend the Sabbath with his wife. As for Judah, the Rabbi is concerned about his young son. But Judah already made up his mind to break out and get to Eretz Israel."

"What about Kagan's boys?" He referred to the druggist who organized the Labor Zionist Party—*Poalei* Zion.

"They are ready to leave, whenever our boys are ready. You see, David, I don't want Kagan to say that the *Poalei* Zionists will take any risk to get to the homeland. That's why I was so anxious to send off Revisionists and General Zionists."

"Do you think somebody informed?"

"I don't know," were Israel's parting words.

As David turned into the new synagogue yard, the first warm rays of the sun glittered over the dew laden grass. David pushed open the massive door enough to squeeze through.

Beryl, the wispy baker, was on the bench alongside the cold tiled oven, murmuring like a dove as key words came up for breath. His white beard rocked back and forth as he swayed gently. Alter, his closed sinewy hand braced against his cheekbone, waited in vain for an opening to start a conversation, as he fingered aimlessly an old wornout psalm book.

David held his breath while Reb Beryl's melody dipped into a meditative humming. Then abruptly he repeated a passage which escaped him: "That I may never declare the unclean is clean and that the clean is unclean." Could such a corruption ever occur? Can war be peace and can a state of peace be war? Can right be wrong? Can evil be good? Those Rabbis of old, David surmised, were precise in plumbing the line between life and death, mercy and murder, law and disorder. They believed in the principle that all our thoughts must be filtered before we approach God, unimportant as it may seem to us; that a strange thought, an evil thought like a speck of something unclean, can contaminate the pure.

Something from above, gave him a power to warn, to penetrate the cloudy horizon. But he still had the dust of a desperate journey on his clothing. He must not disturb the quiet thoughts of the baker with his unquiet dream. He hesitated, then whispered.

"Reb Beryl!"

"*Gut Shabbes*," Reb Beryl raised his eyes above his glasses and held out his slender firm fingers. David, without any preliminary embellishments, told him about his dream. The baker sifted his thoughts and weighed his words.

"One who devotes himself to the *shira* chapter-song, is saved from many troubles and bad dreams. On the Sabbath we have no time for fantasy, only for thanksgiving prayers."

"But a dream can be true."

"Only a wise man—a Rabbi—can interpret a dream."

The baker's world was well designed and orderly. Its tenants could best appreciate their quarters by tending to their prescribed tasks for man and God.

"What are you up to, David?" Label startled him. "Isn't this too early for you?" He looked up and saw the skinny and excitable redhead barber and part time wagoner.

"Must I report to you?" David resented the communist sympathizer who, it was rumored, was the unofficial commissar over the town.

"Don't be angry. I'm glad you're back. This town needs help."

"Are you furnishing it?"

"David, the two of us share a lot of things. We want to change things and get rid of old fashioned ideas."

"Not exactly."

"Do you approve exploitation?"

"No."

"Do you believe we should fight Nazism and fascism?"

"Of course I do. But this also includes communism; it is also a menace."

"David, why are you afraid of me? I am not an informer."

"What about the boys who were arrested?"

"The Russians don't like Zionists who preach disloyalty."

"Disloyalty? Why who else cares about Jews? Who will give them a home?"

"Russia."

"As communist puppets? To slave, to die, for what?"

"I tell you, you are wrong. It is capitalist and Zionist propaganda."

"Jews unable to leave Russia for Palestine, Jews imprisoned and starved; Russia making a pact with Hitler and throwing the Jews to the devil, is that propaganda?"

"You repeat yourself."

"The truth must be repeated more than falsehood."

"You and I must get together. If Russia is in danger we are all in danger. I must leave now. I've got something important to do. I may be back."

David was surrounded by worshippers and yet he was alone.

The sun poured forth from the tall rounded windows. David stood there unable to move to his seat. His eyes were fixed to the windows, the fields beyond. Birds shot up in pairs playfully or in courtship. Others scampered to the ground, striking now and then at an earthworm wiggling through the crust or peeping through the grass. All around the courtyard, the Sabbath quiet prevailed. He knew it, as if he were outside observing all this. He was again within and yet beyond the walls. He saw faces and exchanged greetings and yet he knew that none of them shared his dream. Somehow he was drawn toward his own seat alongside his father.

It was a world at prayer, a kingdom of priests—garbed in praying shawls—each free to express his own thoughts and interpretations.

Prayer to David was always personal. He even wondered whether being versed in Hebrew was not more of a deterrent than an inducement. Noske the chanter's voice was now warmed up and his swivelling head and rolling eyes synchronized with all his gyrating throaty chants. Still he couldn't concentrate. His father beside him, who communed so amicably with the angels that minister to the soaring prayers, now draped the *talis* over his head to concentrate. David was lost, a stranger among his own, frantically trying to bind the torn threads of the past. His was the only discordant tones. He demurred as he listened to everyone's fervent convictions.

"Only he proclaims wars and dispenses justice," Noske continued. Justice and war, David professed, are incompatible. There was no justice even in peace under the Polish regime, only a Polish brand of anti-Semitism, not as blunt as the Nazi brand but subtle and equally crushing to Jewish hopes in Poland. Now it is all war with no justice under the Russians and even something worse under the Germans, poised a few miles away under an uneasy truce with Soviet Russia.

"He creates cures," the voice said. Cures for what? It must be a sick world. Only a few seats away, Reb Jacob Zaban, the Talmud instructor in modulated baritone syllables, jubilantly proclaimed, "He in his goodness renews constantly the work of creation." Reb Koppel the learned innkeeper and timber merchant voiced his challenge, "Every day?" Reb Koppel turned his leonine head in the direction of the instructor who smiled benignly and replied with the next line, "His mercy endures forever."

"Every day, every day," Elyeh, the shoemaker nodded; his fingers moving over the rough table as if making sure the wooden nails secured the sole to the last. They called him the *"latutnick,"* the patcher. From God he wanted a more perfect job, a new, a better world, not just one patched up and ready to burst from the seams.

Chaye, the *zadekes*, the good and pious above in the gallery, dared not look down upon the empty seat of her husband Melech, now an invalid. "For the sake of Gedaliah make him well *Oi Gotenu*," she addressed him intimately, sighed and then regretted. It was forbidden to utter sadness.

Ber Leib was aware that his son was weaving his own thoughts amidst the prayers. He was more than amazed that David could skip over so many thoughtful prayers, whose meanings were so profound, in a few minutes.

"Work of Creation," Alter the carpenter examined the words which after floating between Jacob Zaban, and Koppel soared to the ceiling. Examining for a thousandth time the beams and the white washed ceiling, slightly out of line. Maybe not perfect— but who can make perfect work? His horny fingers were fondling the prayerbook, so delicate, so strange and full of magic formulas. "Work of Creation," he bellowed. Only God is a perfect craftsman.

Hershke, the miller, added his hoarse wind-whistling voice, "Blessed art Thou who creates lights." The prayer for wind and rain was, according to ritual, suspended after Passover. "Now how can a prayer for light help me in June when I need wind and others rain? If we have lights we'll also have winds and rain," he dared to comment.

Noske the chanter sensed this symphony of prayer surging above his own interpretation. He must assert himself over all other voices. He is the *shatz* delegated to officiate, to compromise all their independent and divergent renditions.

Gradually climbing up from the 'valley', he held onto a high pitch. Abba Dunsky, the wistful Hebrew teacher, glanced now and then through thick horn rimmed glasses toward the *talmidim* of the *Beth Hasefer,* favoring the Hebrew instead of 'students of the Hebrew School'.

In the far end corner of the eastern pew, Ber Leib found himself overwhelmed with problems: his textile store was confiscated by the Russians, he lived on his last savings and worried about David. Now that the morning service was concluded, he made the last minute preparation to read the Torah.

This morning, however, he couldn't remember one word of its proper intonation. No matter how many times he looked it up— it became elusive. He finally recalled it—but stuttered as he moved his lips. His clever eyes looked ahead away from the page. There was something unusual; Label, the only fanatic communist sympathizer in Suha-Vali, was in view.

Label usually came to the synagogue, if he came at all, toward the end of the service, during the round-robin discussions in the rear or in the yard, during the pause of the Pentateuch reading. To-day he was much earlier. Nobody noticed him, but there he was, walking proudly among the worshippers.

David sensed that although Label's eyes were sweeping the worshippers from wall to wall, his gaze was more tense and deliberate whenever their eyes met. Is Label suspicious about his return from Grodno? His papers are in order. Perhaps Label will accuse him of plotting to smuggle out young men to Israel?

There was an electrified silence as the ark was opened. The scroll was lifted and held by Noske the *Schochet,* tenderly, like a beloved child, in his bony but firm hands. The entire congregation rose to its feet at the call of the ages: "Hear O Israel, the Lord is our God, the Lord is One."

Momentarily Label's face was lost as they responded in unison:

"One is our God; Great is our Lord; Holy is his name." Noske hesitated before calling on David—for the traditional honor of

being among the first seven or more called up to the reading of
the week's portion. Although David was not attentive—lost in
another portion of his own world—he summoned him to witness
the reading of the law and to offer a thanksgiving blessing.

Label sat proudly up front as if saying, "You always regarded
me as a poor barber, a communist, troublemaker. You never invited me to your meetings. If I spoke up you ignored my words.
Now look at me. The whole city is now at my command. I'm not
going to be hard on you except for a few. I would like to see
some of you sleep on the stone floor; see what it feels like."

Label almost expected an answer. For he was quite agitated
and in a mood to hurl aimless darts in all directions. For a
moment he stood there as if addressing the worshippers in a
bitter language of his own. Paltiel, the *gevir* (rich), stood erect
behind his stand, his blond beard turning silvery gray, blended
perfectly with the *atorah* ornament on the rim of the shawl
arching over his forehead. "You," Label almost blurted as he
singled him out for his phantom tirade. "You, you look fat and
satisfied; you enjoy all the good things in life. How would you
like your family to be in rags and starve, not even potatoes and
black bread." Label had an urge to come nearer to Paltiel who
swayed majestically as if intoning every word and syllable with
every movement of his bones and joints. Label had learned to
wait for the proper moment. Timing and surprise was part of his
ideology. He, Label, must exemplify the best of communist leadership. Revenge is too blunt—there are other methods, but one
must control oneself. You are afraid of me. He now turned his
attention sideways.

Noske tried to catch his breath as if something was stifling
him, and preventing his words from reaching his listeners. Young
children were dangling under the *taleisim* as if seeking protection from some danger beyond.

Why are you afraid of me? I'm not an informer. Some of you
are still rich; you bow down to me; you want favors. Don't
worry, we'll take everything away from you. We'll find them.
We have very persuasive methods. Paltiel, I want your house.
My house near the river is too damp. You better cooperate before they'll confiscate everything, and deport you, Daniel the
brewer, and other wealthy people to Siberia. It's not my idea—
it's theirs. They are a little busy on the front, but it's coming,
remember!

He eyed Rabbi Kalir, as he supported his forehead with his

white slender fingers. He always regarded the Rabbi as a holy
man. Holiness was a 'reactionary' invention to enslave mankind.
Still Rabbi Kalir was 'holy', different.

Suddenly Label bolted from his stalemated indecision. He
walked straight to Koppel Magid the innkeeper who was busy
thumbing a Talmud folio to verify a commentary he recalled on
a particular verse.

In a moment heads were raised from the scriptures. They
beheld a shocking sight; Label arrogantly summoning Reb
Koppel to follow him to the rear. Ber Leib hesitated as he tried
to continue reading in the midst of murmuring and whispering.
The sexton pounded with his open hand on the scroll table for
silence.

Label and Koppel went into a conference behind the oven.

Curious children pressed toward them, followed by elders who
pretended to shoo them away while catching a few words or
phrases from the converstaion.

"Get back to your seats!" Label angrily commanded. A few
obeyed. He turned to Koppel, "Did the peasant ask you many
questions?"

"Which one—you mean the one who asked to be served beer
late on Friday eve?"

"Yes, yes, tell me everything."

"Nothing to tell," Reb Koppel, more perturbed by the inter-
ruption than by the cross examination, continued, "You know I
don't sell beer. I deal with lumber and besides there is none to be
gotten—no deliveries from Grodno—nothing made locally."

"Never mind about beer," Label grew impatient.

"What is it you want to know?"

"Reb Koppel, don't you know that in wartime there is no beer
unless you sell contraband?"

"Oh no, absolutely no! Every peasant knows that a Jewish
place is closed early Friday eve," Reb Koppel's suspicion was
now also aroused.

"Must have been a stranger. Yes, he did ask many questions."

"A stranger from a strange land, maybe on a strange mission?"

"It could be—fishing for information—but he looked more like
a peasant."

"A good spy would look like a peasant. I need your help."

"What shall I do?"

"If he shows up again call the police."

"I can't suspect everyone. I was trained to respect."

"Times are different. This is all. Forget about this kind of talk. There is treachery all around us. Who knows?"

"Only God knows," Reb Koppel whispered.

"Batlonim!" he challenged all gaping at him as he made his exit. He meant they were too naive and deeply rooted in religion to suspect that an ordinary peasant could be connected with treachery.

Outside excited children began to follow him. The faster he walked the more were those who joined them. Without turning he warned them, "Away! Stop! Go back!" Ignoring his protestations they pressed on past the old Brick Synagogue where a new wave joined them. "A thief," one cried. "A robber," another suggested. But the majority ran just for the sake of expecting the unusual on a tranquil Sabbath morning.

Label now deftly cut across the lower market place hoping to shake them off behind the wooden fire house. He now turned sharply to his left, between the church gate and the priest's parish. He ran alongside the stone walls encircling the church like an island in the market place.

Several wagons were parked. Their horses munched from feed bags. Label eyed warily one young peasant who seemed more nervous than his two companions. They were all alike in their shabby homespun outfits; there was stubble on their faces. He faced a surprised middle aged peasant.

"Where are you from?"

"Ledinchine."

"And you?" he turned to the second peasant.

"Pokosne."

"And you?" he eyed the youngest.

"Agustowa."

"That's near the German border, East Prussia."

"Not quite."

"How are the Germans?"

"We don't bother with them."

Label was at a loss. He began to search the wagons but found nothing but bedding, hay and some empty sacks.

"What have you got in there?" He pointed to the young one.

"Potatoes."

"Potatoes from Agustowa?"

"For barter purposes—nobody accepts money. It's worthless."

Label was so certain of his suspect that he forgot to point out that spreading rumors against government money is a crime.

Meanwhile two Russian *gendarmes* alarmed by the commotion rushed to his aid.

"Any trouble comrade?" they addressed him casually.

"Arrest this spy!"

The young one first protested, then cursed Label. "Can't a stranger come into this town without being set upon by a hooligan?"

"Don't call me a hooligan; you are a treacherous spy—it's all over you."

But he still couldn't prove it. Although the *gendarmes* could press out the truth in a few hours, he wanted some credit as a loyal and a skillful communist comrade.

The young peasant began to adjust the feed bag that slipped down the horse's neck. Label yanked it off abruptly, ran his fingers through the oats but found no clue to his suspicion and accusation. Desperately, he now slipped his finger under the collar snug over the horse's shoulders.

Like every horse collar it was well worn, only the lining on the edge was strangely loose as if pried open. He forced his forefinger and felt something unlike leather. He wedged in two fingers and pulled out thin papyrus paper with map-like markings.

"*Poydom,*" the *gendarmes* gripped the arms of the suspect. Label stood there alone, not knowing whether to be apprehensive over a spy sent by a supposed ally. He glanced back as he saw them lead away the spy. He was not even invited to testify. It was something private and secretive.

It was now well after the Sabbath noon meal. Jewish families, with empty chairs for missing soldier sons and fathers, sat around frugal tables, and blessed God for His grace and His bounty. Jews had a blessing for all occasions of joy and of sorrow, but not one for torment.

"Bim, Bim Ba-bim-bam", Ben Zion hummed a Chasidic tune. The Sabbath was again in their midst. He repeated it several times until David raised his voice lustily, Ber Leib tapped his fingers and Dinah sighed to the tune. Her vigilant glances seemed to say: "It was my fault—a little more meat—meaning a few bones, a handful of beans, a few potatoes and the table would have burst with food." She left the table. Minutes later he heard her say:

"Here is a hot cup of chicory." It was watery and tasteless, but it warmed him up. "I'm saving this for winter," Dinah explained as she returned with an uncovered dark green earthen jar. She ladled out a spoon over a slice of bread. It was cherry jam, a rare delicacy reserved for sickness, colds, coughs and assorted ailments. As he bit into the jam-covered black bread, his revived appetite made him think of his mother. Her kindness was genuine without being dramatic and demonstrative.

His father understood his mind, but his mother his heart—the earthly one that needs food to banish hunger and affection against mounting pressures, as one of the dividends of a mother's inexhaustible love. He was certain that his father, now reading the Mishnah in low tones, had the same feelings for him. But like most men, he tried not to show it.

Ben Zion continued to hum a Sabbath tune. David picked up a few notes—a voice without a heart is a muted melody—and then retreated into his privacy. He left an opening for the one who shared more of his anxieties than he cared to reveal.

"Mother," he wanted to speak intimately and tenderly. "Mother, I know what is in your mind. You are worried. I am too. It is about my sister, her husband and the children in Grodno. I brought no regards from them. I did not want to get them in trouble when I left my job. Communists make every one in the family accomplices."

"You are through with this trouble and more trouble is on the way; a mother is never unburdened. You haven't received any letter from your sister in America, your brother in South Africa, who desperately tried to get us passports. All the letters and telegrams from across the ocean never reached us; now we are cut off, and are being closed in from all sides. Your other sons— one vanished with his interned unit in Russia and the other was drafted like myself in the Polish army—why was I luckier, mother, they were such good sons?

"I better not ask too many questions. The milk—the earthen jars, are empty. You must be selling the milk or maybe the cow is dry. It can't be in June. Dearest mother I feel so guilty to speak like that—only I know that you are so much better, a thousand

times. You keep it all in within yourself. But your sighs give you
away. I can even tell whenever you start to cry in the synagogue behind the curtain."

"David, what are you thinking or saying?" Ber Leib suddenly
jarred him.

"Nothing!" he blurted out as he tried to assemble an explanation.

"Nothing! Eh—I thought you were praying, but you seldom
pray by heart, so—"

"Father, there are a lot of things that come up."

"A lot of things, eh?" Ber Leib repeated. "The world is full of
worries and troubles. There is not a house without trouble."

"Father, sh—Ma is listening."

"I'm only repeating what she says—only in a different language. Do you think it's easy, to hear her crying in the middle of
the night?" He lowered his voice. "*Oi Ribeno Shel Olom!* Help
us Lord of the Universe."

"All mothers cry."

"Yes, but there must be a limit."

"Women have a special understanding and a mother senses
danger. It is a warning just like a dream."

"Suppose it is so, what can she accomplish? As for a dream, it
is just a dream. Only a prophet's dream can be taken seriously.
Life is full of worries and troubles. That is why we have the
Sabbath to interrupt this letdown. A pious Jew always reckons
the days of the week: the first day after Sabbath, the second
after Sabbath and so on. We are under the spell of this holy day
three days before and three days after. This is all we have
left."

His father was insulated from the restless and violent world. It
was a world that was deaf to a prophet, callous to a mother's
tears and contemptuous to a dream and a dreamer. Why was his
own father indifferent to his dream?

That was probably one of the longest intimate utterances he
heard from his father. He seldom spoke at length. Ber Leib was
only aroused by family or religious emotions. But it was all measured—like an old wine. He employed it only like a sacramental
cup, for a purpose. Dinah did not waste tears in the presence of
such an understanding husband. It was enough for her to merely
indicate that she was on the verge of crying. Ber Leib, rather
than face the threat, yielded submissively.

"Please don't cry. You are only going to sadden yourself and all of us."

Ber Leib didn't say it exactly, but Dinah interpreted it as such whenever he intercepted her vaunted tear-weapon with a pleading sigh, followed by vigorous nodding. Dinah triumphantly complied.

Ber Leib, with a cursory look toward the kitchen, was satisfied to the point of relaxation. Dinah began her preliminary thumbing of a *Tehinah*—prayer book whose tender phrases and ardent comments were gateways to her own grief.

He put away his Mishnah and pretended to enjoy this Sabbath rest. He had diversions. Some he could pursue in the pages of the sacred books, but the others demanded his attention. Was it proper to engage in problems which were speculative and disturbing on a holy day? he asked himself. He was certain that no violation was involved. Only the Almighty was capable of judging what one should do or not do. David did not tell him anything about his experiences. Perhaps his dreams were nightmares of privations? He had no heart to question him.

Voices and echoes came from the outside. He walked out through the back. He looked across the synagogue courtyard to Rachel's house. Her brother was outside.

"Avreml, is Rachel in the house?" he asked him.

"No, she went for a walk."

David returned to his room, more restless than ever. Although it was only the first day at home, he felt that Rachel should have come over to see him, or at the least call him from across her open window or yard.

For some time he paced his room, listening and waiting. Again he opened his door.

"David," his father called him back.

"What is it father?"

"Why don't you talk to me?"

"Talk?"

"Maybe I can advise you, if you have any problems. You were gone for two years, and you never told me . . ."

"Not now," he was abrupt when he heard Rachel's voice.

He crossed over to her at the very moment Zechariah the dairyman came out from the side gate of her garden.

"Rachel!" he said and stared at her.

"David, I . . . I'm so glad," she said.

Petite and more beautiful than ever, with her raven hair in braids, she appeared to be nervous.

"I'm very . . . it's so good to see you."

"So many things have happened since you were gone," Rachel said.

"Yes," he said, unable to find the right words.

"Nobody knows . . ."

"Yes . . ."

"Even here, this morning, was it really a German spy?" she asked him trying to divert him to another subject.

"Yes, he probably was a spy."

"What will happen?"

"He'll be shot. But nothing else."

"I don't understand it."

"Stalin," he looked around, "made a bad pact with Hitler and unleashed him against the nations. He wouldn't listen to any intelligence reports that Hitler would double cross him, and that Germany would attack Russia any day. I heard in Grodno, that officers of high rank who reported such information were shot. Wasn't that Zechariah who left your house?" his tone changed.

"Yes."

"Why?"

"I don't want to talk about it."

"Rachel, I would like to see you tonight near the windmill."

"I can't."

"Are you and Zechariah . . . ?"

"David, I don't want to discuss it," she ran into her house.

David was shaken by the sudden realization that Rachel somehow avoided him. No it couldn't be. Rachel and Zechariah, they were worlds apart and so different . . . It was a good thing his parents didn't notice anything. His father advanced to the second stage in his nap, intermittent snoring. Then having reached the climactic and methodical "wood sawing," nobody could have disturbed him. This is how he remembered his habit in normal times.

Meanwhile in the kitchen his mother's head rested over the table. Her left palm was stretched over the opened prayer book, nested inside the larger *Tehinah*. "Wait a minute," it implied, "I have to read something." It was a batch of letters from her far flung children. He surmised that she read and reread every one of the loose bundle. First she read the letter, then pressed into the *Tehinah* or prayerbook, as if belonging there like a missing page. Then with tears clouding her eyes, she pressed each one, to kissing lips.

She was now talking in her uneasy sleep. "Joseph, Jacob," referring to her sons, "David is here." "Joseph, my son! Jacob, my son! Where are you? Are you alive?" It was cruel to allow her to torment herself with the memory of his brothers lost in the now shattered Polish army. He must wake her—no it may be worse if it comes like a shock.

"Every time," she breathed deeply, "I see a soldier, a captive one led like an animal, in rags and hungry, my heart leaves me. Are you prisoners? Where? Where? I'll get there, I'll go now, this minute. Joseph! Jacob! Why don't you answer? Maybe you were wounded. Forgive me, O God, I could cry and cry. Look at my prayer book—all the pages soaked with tears. God, O, God, how can you?"

"Mamma, mamma, what are you saying? It's me, David, what are you doing?"

It was a familiar question to which he resorted like his father to arouse her from her obsessions.

"Nothing," she responded. "I can't cry. I have no more tears and I can't dream because—."

"It's better."

"Better what?"

"If you don't worry too much."

"I don't understand you. I am worried about you."

"About me?"

"What is going on, you and Israel, whispers and secret words?"

"Nothing!"

"David, I heard you talking to him this morning. You are not planning to leave us again?"

"I returned, didn't I?"

"You changed. You moaned in your dream. What is troubling you?"

"I didn't change."

"You changed. What are you holding back from me?"

"Mother, please leave me alone."

"David all we have left is you. My heart tells me. I feel it for my children who are scattered and need me. Your father may be calm but he suffers too. It is too much for a mother to bear. It is too much for all of us."

There was nothing for him to say or to promise. She sensed the
troubles about her and he foresaw it encompassing all. Yet he
couldn't walk away from her without soothing her.

"Mother, why think about it—what can you accomplish with
your worrying? Why look for trouble?"

"Trouble? Why, worrying is like crying. I like to cry, it helps
me. My mother worried and cried and my grandmother did the
same."

He stood before that long buffet table near the book shelf.
Everything, the books, the periodicals, newspapers and opened
letters, waited for the master who now returned. Notations on a
Hebrew magazine attracted his attention, for on the soft cover
was a notation: "All Jews in Poland and in Europe are Zionists
who must be saved from—" He remembered that he hesitated
because he didn't want to spell out a word of doom.

Dinah now resumed her position except that she opened the
Tehinah while she fondled the letters. The noon sun fingered
her rays through the front windows. From the cobbled street
came the never ending echoes of children's voices, hefty and
ringing with eternal bliss. The soft whispers of noonday strollers
and the measured gait of pious men returning to the synagogue
lured him outward. He began to open the hall door cautiously,
making sure that she was asleep in the chair.

David was frustrated and bitter. He came to warn of something terrible only to find his own beloved estranged from him. A
girl could be mistaken. But these people should have been more
responsive to his warning of danger. Outside he saw the wise
innkeeper.

"Reb Koppel, I had a dream," David recovered his thoughts.

"Dreams are either romantic, meaningless or frightening."

"My dream was different, like a warning."

"A warning to whom?"

"To all of us, that the Germans will invade our town. The
Russians are bad, but the Germans are the worst."

"What is your proof?"

"I don't need any proof."

"David, I can't—none of us can—believe that the dream you
had will happen."

"Do you believe the rumors about the terrible things happening to the Jews in Poland?"

"Incredible. Only God knows."

"I am certain that it is true, and it could happen here."

"David, do you claim to be a prophet?"

"No!"

"Then it is only your imagination."

"I tell you the Germans are coming to kill us."

"God forbid! Don't repeat bad news."

"I'm telling the truth."

"You have no right to tell everybody that terrible things will happen to us. I just can't believe it. Nobody wants to believe that God and all the nations and people of the world will allow it to happen."

Far into the afternoon, more and more faces pressed against the window panes or ventured to peek out through the opened windows. Curious eyes picked up the strollers within their range while they in turn inspected for the thousandth time Hershke's ripening gaping orchard, Ber Leib's bench occupied by a new shift, Sarah Beile Novor's flower decorated windows, Baba Zippe's clay caulked walls, the swinging boot-shield of Elyeh Schuster hanging from a birch cornice on his house. Now all eyes were turned to the recently arrived *Yeshiva Bochur*—who alternated to study between the New Synagogue and the Brick Synagogue. Velvke arranged days for him. This Sabbath it was at the old Melamed Reb Isaac. But Chazkel Schneider made a request to eat one day a week in his house. Was it Hadassah? She was only fifteen? On such rumors were built speculations or vice versa.

It was the same for many, many years, and was destined to be the same for many more years, if left alone. They were hungry and happy. Some were looking forward toward a tomorrow of work, others to hope; some to good news from afar, others to the same routine; some were restless, others were content to have faith in God. Only David found it difficult to merge the old and the new. Here it was Sabbath while the turbulent *Sambatyon* who always rested on this day, was defiantly on the march, closing in from all sides.

He was alone, but his thoughts strained to the lush world beyond. His feet were now treading upon the grass footpaths, sprinkled with dandelions and blue corn flowers. Like a green ribbon it cut through the fields and extended to the dirt road on the eastern horizon. It linked the windmills on the right and the Tatar's village on the left, alongside the river.

God created every plant for its place in the sun and every
blade for its particular location. The Suha-Vali fields were rotated with different crops every season. Some were fallow and
rested like Jews on the Sabbath. But there were always rye fields,
bending and bowing their proud heads toward the synagogues.

They were neat and orderly, each section belonging to a particular farmer. So it was for many hundreds of years. The villagers owned hay fields in the meadows, and barley, oats, maize
near the forest and woodlands.

In the nearby fields or in their own gardens they grew flax,
potatoes, beans, peas and lentils. Farmers who nestled close to the
river raised on the black rich soil cabbage, tobacco and vegetables. But it was the barley and wheat fields, stretching endlessly
—first up the high ground where the windmills stood and then
rolling gently up and down toward the forest on the right and
the isolated colonies in the center—that enchanted David.

It was now twilight. Inside the synagogues the Sabbath Queen
was courted with prayer and song on the eve of her departure.
Velvke the *gabai*, charity collector, led the spirited singing in the
red Brick Synagogue. In the New Synagogue, Beryl the baker
with the silent whispers of a dove, went through the very painful
weekly experience of parting with the Holy Sabbath and going
back to the every day, with its yoke of "uncertain" bread, rumors
and forebodings. Only the weapons of faith, prayer and Jewish
bitohen could repel these besieging forces of insecurity.

The conglomeration of people that filled the red Brick Synagogue uptown became restless, as they caught glimpses of flickering stars from the ever darkening skies, through the high
domed windows. The shoemakers, tailors, oil pressers, carpenters
and blacksmiths had nothing to await them but endless toil into
the late night. Maybe a smoke, a cheerful word at home, or good
news about the end of this horrible Nazi war beyond would
break through the unknown that faced them. Merchants, especially those dealing with grain, were tense and eager to venture
once more into an occupation outlawed by the communists.
They had no alternative if they wanted to live.

In David's New Synagogue and in the Downtown Synagogue,
whether rich or poor, those awaiting the conclusion of the Sabbath were more patient and sedate. But in all synagogues, long
tables seated with sages over the soul stirring words of the
candle lit pages, would carry on to hold back the darkness.

June 16, 1941:   RUSSIA ORDERS GENERAL MOBILIZATION.
                 GERMAN SOVIET CRISIS. . . .

Because of my love for you I shall abandon my
abode in heaven and dwell in your midst.

                                    Tanhuma, Naseh.

3

IDEALISTS

David planned to stop and see his old teacher Reb Isaac, Chazkel's neighbor—he already visited Rabbi Jacob Zaban who first
taught him Talmud and would see him again at the Hebrew
School. Smoke was curling straight up from the chimneys, and
the houses he passed on the cobbled rise to the red Brick Synagogue had not changed much. There was a clear voice from the
inside. A Yeshiva *bochur* (seminarian), he thought.

Over an open Talmud volume, sloping on the standing lectern,
the student's slender frame swayed in intense motions. His lean
face and dark fiery eyes moved now up and down now sideways
as the morning rays from the tall window sprayed his back and
glanced off him into the sun lit page. If he could only bring back
those happy days in the Yeshiva, when he too was captivated by
a saintly world.

Velvke, who had a hardware store, was on a bench near the tile
oven to the rear of the synagogue. As the affable charity gabai he
helped the needy, especially Yeshiva students. Like an older version of Chagall's Jew in flight, the slight, silvery haired *gabai* was
also carried away by the words and the rhythm. After a while he
began to write:

                    Sivan 21, 5701 (June 16, 1941)
                    Portion, Shelah L'cha
Ezekiel ben Yitzhak Halevi,
          By the Grace of God
Honorable benefactor, lover of Mitzvoth—deeds, charity piety. The
Ben Yeshiva and Ben Torah known as Elchanan, will grace your
table for one day. May the Holy One blessed be His name, grant

31

you with children Bnei Torah and wisdom and blessings from
heaven.

With Torah Greetings,

Zev ben Matithyohu, called Velvke.

"David," he called out as he put away his pencil and began to
fold the note in two and then in four. "I didn't know you were
here. A fine young man, I wish I were a Yeshiva *bochur* again, but
you could . . ."

"Velvke, I wish too, but . . . !"

"Who is upstairs, come down," Velvke looked up curious at the
movements of high heels in the women's gallery. "Would it be
too much if I ask you to deliver this note?"

"Let him be in our house."

"He was, the Sabbath before you arrived," then turning
around, "Oh, it is you, Hadassah. What were you doing upstairs?"

"Watching."

"Whom?"

"Him," she pointed to the unaware seminarian.

"Aren't you . . ."

"Too young?" she cut him off, "I'll be sixteen a year from
today."

"And twenty one six years from today," then to David, "Where
did you intend to go?"

"Somebody, a good friend, Potocki."

"Be careful! Good day."

"Good day," David said.

"I'll just give this note to her and join you," Velvke said.

"Why don't you send him to us, Reb Velvke?"

"Here is a note to your father. Don't read it now and remember . . ."

"To stay away four cubits from him and make sure there is a
third person present." Hadassah giggled and then stopped when
Elchanan momentarily distracted, turned around to glance at
her.

"It is a bright day and good for learning," Hadassah snuggled
up to the pew behind him leaning on the bannister of the Bimah.
He kept on reciting the same page, then one page back.

"If his father did not teach him he must teach himself."

"Do you like Suha-Vali?" she addressed him again. But he
continued on the next page, somewhat shy with his voice but his

eyes still in complete contact with his theme—a father's duties to his son.

"To take a wife for him . . . To teach him a craft. And some say to teach him how to swim. Rabbi Judah said: He who does not teach him a craft . . . is like teaching him brigandage."

"Why don't you speak to me? I'm only a girl."

"It makes no difference," he finally answered, without looking up.

"I'm four cubits away from you."

"Diversion knows no limits."

"Am I a diversion? Look at me!"

"You are a girl, I know that."

"That's all?"

"I have to study."

"That's all? Why don't you come to our house?"

"Why should I?"

"My brother went to a Yeshiva too."

"He did? I'll come to talk to him."

"That's all?" She began to open the note, first squinting then shaking her head at the Yeshiva bochur, who resumed his stance and sang, and finally putting her hand against her mouth to restrain her laughter on the way out.

"Oh, what is the name of this volume you are studying?"

"*Kedushin.*" (marriage)

"That's interesting. Does it tell how? I mean what does it tell, that you have to spend so many days to learn, and you yourself are still single?" Without even changing his swaying the student kept up his learning."

"You didn't answer me."

"There is no answer to such a question."

"Then you are married."

"No."

"Engaged?"

"No."

"That's good!"

"What are you talking about?"

"Oh," she shuddered as she read above his shoulder, "A woman is bought, is that what you are learning?"

"Don't be silly."

"I understand Hebrew—that is what it says."

"It does not."

"Does not what?"

"On the contrary it is a sacred obligation when one marries. The same expression is used in the relation of God to Israel—one of love and responsibility."

"I see—don't forget to come to our house."

The next day—after Israel Grodzensky came to call on him —David joined the library committee. For a long long while every one was busy leafing through books, magazines and newspapers. Ever since the turn of the century when it was organized by four young men, the library became the clearing house for all literary mediums. If the synagogue with its duplicate role as a Beth Hamedrash—the house of study—was the gateway to the Hebrew culture of the Holy Scriptures, the Talmud and rabbinical literature, then the library was a second door to the secular cultures. All available books that could be collected in Yiddish, Hebrew, Russian, German and Polish were catalogued and neatly filed. During the first World War it became an invaluable source of reference, in addition to cultural enlightenment, for the ideological identities of the Zionist organizations subdivided into General Zionist, Religious Zionist (Mizrachi), Labor Zionist (Poalei Zion) and Revisionist Zionist (Betar). The Bund with its socialist Marxist leanings attracted the smallest number.

"We are waiting for Kiva Kagan," Israel Grodzensky spoke up, "he is collecting for the *Keren Kayemeth* (Jewish National Fund)."

"Our parties remind me of the fire—the big fire when half the market square was burned down—each group and each one tried to save a different house or do according to the pressure of the moment," said Zeidel Stuzinsky, the brewer's son who like David was neutral in the inter-party strife.

"What you are saying is that if the parties were united under a central leadership they would accomplish more," Chaim Schneider, the teacher, said.

"I have to agree with Zeidel; there is room for everybody who wants to work and build. But in time of crisis the national need must take over. For the present let each party organize a colony in Eretz Israel and put to practice its program," Shmuel Leiser, who helped his father in the wool processing plant said. "We General Zionists are the most tolerant."

"I disagree with any party or ideology that confines you to its own limited viewpoint," David said. After being away at the University he became disenchanted with the inter-party rivalry. Although by instinct he favored the religious, by the emergency of the times he was inclined to the Betar and from practical consideration he felt that labor would play an important part in the rehabilitation of the homeland, but when a fire—which he could see as yet smouldering but soon would ignite into a conflagration—was threatening everything Jewish, it was no time to quibble about such things.

"I for one agree," Israel said. "Suppose we could fulfill the rebirth of Judea through militant revisionism. Isn't this preferable to divisive parties?"

"Labor Zionism is not only a means to restore a home to our homeless people but also to build a state—a socialist state—according to the vision of our prophets. This is our solution, the Poalei Zion solution," Kagan countered.

"Then perhaps the religious Mizrachi and Agudah Zionists have the strongest argument to rebuild Zion according to the Torah," David implied that no party by itself could fulfill the dream of Zion. "Let us concentrate on urgent problems."

"If you mean the Hachalutz, we all agree," Shmuel Leiser said.

"What do you say Kiva?" David asked.

"I say there is a good possibility for a number of our Hachalutz members to go through Riga and maybe through Copenhagen—reach England and then to Palestine. But the risk is great."

"We must take the risk," Ruvke Rosenberg the young fair haired architect who looked to Israel for approval, insisted.

"The roads have narrowed," David responded with an ominous phrase, "what I mean is that we have to follow our proven contacts and the gates to Eretz Israel that are not yet shut—Rumania."

"What about the N.K.V.D.?" Abba Dunsky, who joined the group, asked.

"It is not so much these 'four letters' that give us all the trouble, but also the 'Yevseksia' informers," as David referred to the hated small clique of Jews collaborating with the communists in Russia against Zionism and religion.

"Thank God they got through and inspired the continued ex-

istence of this wonderful group," Kagan observed about those in
a group picture of Chalutzim pioneers who made their way—
legally with certificates and illegally as *Ma'apilim*—to Palestine.

After a while they changed the subject. They were discussing
the latest rumors about the uneasy peace between Russia and
Germany, the first black reports about wholesale shootings of
Jews in Poland and elsewhere, the concentration camps, the
ghettos, the collaboration of Poles and other nationalities with
the Germans, and the strange silence and impotency of the allies,
the free nations, the Vatican in Rome, Christianity and all other
religions.

"Are you following the discussion?" Abba asked David.

"Leave him," Israel defended him.

"Is it a dream—a day dream?" Ben Zion who had just returned
after a futile search to get through the boundary, added "Let it
be a good dream about a *'geulah shlemo'*—a complete redemption."

By noon the group began to disperse. Although this Monday
was designated by the Communist regime as a day of rest, they
still felt safer at home from the prying eyes of the Russians. Only
David and Israel remained.

"This dream everybody is talking about," Israel prodded
him.

"Whatever it is I don't want to talk about it," David rebuffed
him.

"I wish . . . time is short, danger is all around us. We've got to
be practical."

"Don't I know?"

"This is no time to dream but to act."

"How?"

"Let's get out of here, you too."

"Not yet."

"Why?"

"I promised. I can't abandon my parents. They'll be helpless."

"And with you they won't be helpless?"

"Israel, stop it and shut up!"

"I have made up my mind."

"It isn't just to save ourselves, we must do something to save
all."

"Show me the way, David."

David walked away, turned and looked at Israel who left. He was alone again. He had returned to warn to alert everybody to the greatest danger that faced them. Yet his vision of the inevitable was not taken seriously. He paced from wall to wall, from row upon row of books, seemingly silent witnesses. Yet he felt that here among his friends, people and books he would recapture his own balanced perspective.

David always believed that the Jewish people were a valiant and dedicated nation to the ideals of the Torah. A nation must have a territory. It was in foreign hands. But the Jews always lived there, never gave up their claim and now were in the process of regaining it. A nation must be united by one culture. The Torah was the unifying force. A nation must be disciplined. How could it be done when the Jews have no means of enforcing obedience, no army to defend this minority surrounded by hostile neighbors and aggressive invaders beyond. Compared to most nations with vast territories, ample resources, large populations and governed by force, the Jews deprived of these, did quite well for themselves. They constituted an empire of God.

Some intellectual Jews expressed doubt in Jewish survival. The Jewish youth was splintered into parties, some maintained. Cultural assimilation would eventually engulf the Jewish people, others said. A few radicals even suggested that a classless society based upon the socialist formula of Karl Marx would eliminate the causes of racial and religious hatred. This could be accomplished by the abolition of religion and narrow nationalism.

If David was in doubt about other things, he was certain that the Jewish people followed a proven chartered course. The trend of the parties, was on the contrary a manifestation of Jewish democracy. The ideal of social justice was codified into law by Moses and the prophets. The Jews were not just a minority. They had a unique role to play, as witnesses, ambassadors and teachers of God's empire on earth. The totalitarian shades of communism could not solve the ills of society. Communism—exemplified by Russian excesses against its slave subjects and acts of cultural genocide and other animosities against Jews—was incompatible with a free society and free enterprise for all nations and cultures.

Jewish students and Jewish youth read all books in many languages. David was amazed by the variety of subjects and the

scope of opinions expressed by different authors of many nations
in books, periodicals and newspapers. Yet he knew that notwithstanding the avalanche of new ideas in the secular books, the
Jewish way of life as formulated by the famous academies of
learning from Yavneh and Pumpaditha to Wolozin and Slabodka,
were sound. Jewish morality, law and culture were unsurpassed
by western civilization.

Now just before the war—all their energies which was demonstrated in organizing the Zionist groups, was now poured into
'Hachalutz'. It was the crown of their achievement—this movement to prepare young men and women, including teen agers, for
the hardy life of a pioneer in Eretz Israel. It was the equalizer
between the old fashioned flimsy segregation that existed between the uptown and downtown elements of the older generation. All were equal—it was an ideal long rooted in Judaism. It
reached back all the way to the beginning—an example set for
all of mankind.

When the tabernacle was planned in the desert on the way to
the promised land, offerings were asked from the Jews. It was to
be given willingly. The Jews responded, admirably. Men and
women gave up their ornaments, golden bracelets, earrings, rings
and jewels. Not only that, but others who had only silver and
brass, skins, tapestries and needlework were equally exalted. The
only qualifications were a willing heart and ready hands. Nothing is mentioned about offerings for more food, dress, shelter or
even the war effort. Now again their limited wealth—due to
intense competition of stores sponsored by the Polish government
and oppressive taxes—was channeled for education, Eretz Israel
and charity.

"Aleh Chalutz," he read one of the banners on the wall. It
meant wake up, rise up, ascend, redeem yourself and rebuild
yourself, get out before it is too late. This is what it meant, this
call to enroll as a pioneer and undergo training in Bialystok,
Lodz, Wilna, Danzig, Grodno and Kieltz. These were distant
training centers for trades like masonry, electronics, welding,
mechanics, shoemaking, tailoring, carpentry. Here at home they
were quite successful in agricultural training and general man-
ual labor. He was proud to have completed such an 'Hachshara'
training course on the Potocki estate.

Who would ever have imagined that these intellectuals,
dreamers, students and even those who already underwent voca-
tional training in their fathers' carpentry, tinsmith, shoemaking,

tailoring shops and other establishments would now load manure, plough, plant, harvest, dig potatoes, chop wood and do other back-breaking work all for the privilege of being qualified to migrate to Israel? In practice the hardy and lucky had to fight and smuggle into the Holy Land. For England, guided by its obdurate colonial policy and truculent Arabs, never granted to the Jewish agency the immigration certificates demanded by the thousands.

"David," it was Rachel speaking to him. "David," she spoke to him again. He was in a trance even more now when he longed to talk to her and she with him.

"David, there are so many things happening, I don't know myself," she didn't finish.

"It is the times, war and—but we have to go on."

"It is so difficult. I'm happy that you returned."

"Now we can be together again."

"We are now."

"I mean you and me. Nothing changed?"

"No, I will always admire you and like you."

"I don't want to be admired."

"What do you want David?"

"I want you as you were before, mine."

"I wish I could give you an answer. Things have changed."

"Did anything come between us?"

"No, except . . ."

"What is it, is there another man? Is it Zechariah?"

"Please don't say another word," Rachel turned her head aside and abruptly changed the subject. She told him that while he was away, the 'Hachalutz Hatzair' was organized to absorb the demand of the young boys and girls to be trained as pioneers for Eretz Israel.

"You remember when we were young children and we dreamt of participating in the dramatic plays staged at Tevel Stuzinsky's brewery?"

"I remember, Rachel." He wanted to add I wish it were the same world. Why did it grow up so prematurely like a monster?

"Then it changed to Zionism and 'Chalutzioth'. Now what are we to do, David? The Hebrew school is forbidden. We are cut off, aren't we?"

"No, not yet, Rachel. I suppose you conduct a small class secretly."

"Yes, we assembled at Hennie Rachel's, under the excuse of

teaching Russian, but they are watching. We have to move to a
new place every week. But it is possible—the commissar told me
privately—that they'll relax as long as we teach most subjects in
Russian. We'll have to make sure when the committee comes to
test the classes in secret on Saturday that we watch out for
snoopers."

"Rachel, I want to see you."

"You are seeing me now!"

"I mean, we could meet, for a walk or just be together."

"I—I have to do certain things like teach the children. My
mother needs me to take care of the twins and Avreml when she
is out. Last week she travelled to Grodno. She still hopes that we
can make contact with an American consul and maybe travel by
way of Japan to America. We sent a letter to our father asking
him to send us the papers and money. We hope and wait for an
answer."

"I wish you luck."

"We all need luck." Rachel smiled at him and then just departed by saying, "I have to go now."

She was changed, everything changed. There was something
she wanted to say to tell him, that something new—like an invisible separation exists between them. Could it be true that she is
engaged to Zechariah Handler?

Two days later David went to see his friend Graf Potocki.
Potocki wasn't just a customer who bought textiles from his father before the war. His family was related to the legendary Graf
Potocki, who was converted to Judaism as Abraham ben Abraham Potocki. It was never verified, even by Potocki himself.

The early morning sun projected into view the wooded hill in
which was nested the Potocki mansion, its stables, kennels and
other houses that made up the Potocki estate. It was hidden from
prying and curious eyes by walls of trees. The Potockis kept to
themselves. The family's contact, outside of their immediate personnel, was the circle of landed gentry scattered along the East
Prussian border. On special occasions they visited friends in
Warsaw and Cracow.

The road that wound through oak and pine lined on both
sides, now neared a grove of birch which was a sort of a bright
welcome to the estate. Even before he reached the gate of the
half moon driveway, he heard the barking of dogs. As he came

closer, a man with three dogs straining on a leash moved toward him, growling with their muzzles through the iron grating.

"Denikin, a friend!" he heard a girl's voice.

"A friend?"

"Yes, a friend! Call them off!" the girl spoke firmly to the caretaker taking orders from the Russians who seized the estate. She leaned out through a dormer window above a stable and directed him through the gate.

"Panie Sokoloff," the squire greeted David warmly from his wheel chair as he came up the stairway through the lower floor now housing an old coach instead of a car.

"How do you feel, is your back better, Panie Potocki?"

"Much better, you know I am supposed to be called Potashkin —Grisza Potashkin—this is how it reads in my papers. Grisza sounds Russian, now that this—all this is owned by the Russian state, Basenko my former valet is a manager for the state. This is communism—a servant becomes a master and a master is supposed to be . . ." He did not finish, but lowered his head.

"Have you seen a doctor?"

"Not since I was examined by Dr. Lev last March. I don't trust a Russian military doctor. He'll ask questions and I'll be imprisoned."

"Is there anything you need?"

"No, no, I have my memories and my books. Clara,' 'he called his young daughter, "get some cherries for our guest. I have to thank you for what you have done for me." He referred to September 1939 when he, with a bullet lodged in his spine, along with others, including David, was captured after the German invasion of Poland. David helped him to escape from a prisoner of war camp in East Prussia across the Polish border town of Agustowa which was under Russian control. He did not mention his wife and older daughter who were stranded in Warsaw while visiting friends.

"Can I get you anything?" David felt that he was helpless.

"No, no, I have food, a table, two beds—and all these books. I borrowed them from my own library through the courtesy of a bribe to Basenko. I have nothing left. They took away my Mercedes-Benz in exchange for the old coach. They want me to become a peasant. I don't know how. I have been reading a lot, especially our history. We, the descendants of the *Szlachta*, despised the peasants with their work habits. Later some

of our kind joined peasants and agitators to wrest all the
Jewish enterprises which the Polish leaders encouraged many
years ago in order to introduce commerce and industry into a
backward Poland."

"We were probably the original settlers, or we owned our
houses and gardens before the peasants were given land. Our
synagogues were all built before there was even a church in the
market place. To tell you a secret we even helped to build the
church. It was small and three miles from here. We wanted to
attract the churchgoers to our town, shops and stores."

"Yes, you are not strangers in Poland," Potcki nodded.

"The Jews settled in Poland a thousand years ago. The old
synagogue is over three hundred years old. Our history as freedom fighters with an exemplary religion and culture; our patriotism, contributions and accomplishments have been forgotten.
We found Polish society run by task masters of slaves, serfs and
peasants who never learned to read and those who can read
today have been poisoned by bias and propaganda. What are
you reading?"

"History, literature, sociology, the Bible and a little of everything. There is much to be learned which we failed to learn. I
understand it now. Yes, yes," he sighed. "Everything that followed turned sour. The French Alliance, Pilsudski's coup in
1926, and the regime of the colonels from his successors from
1932 to 1939 under Josep Beck who erringly made non-aggression
treaties with Soviet Russia in 1932 and with Germany in 1934,
took Teschen from Czechoslovakia in 1938—and this is where
we are now."

"Did you ever see a Jewish officer in the Polish army?" David
pressed the indictment.

"No, perhaps one or two."

"Don't you think if Poland encouraged the Jews, with their
ability, industry and willingness to help Poland that things could
have been different?"

"Yes, Poland would have been stronger and more just. Our
army—with its cavalry regiments against tanks—was preoccupied with the Jews instead of the enemy. Our leaders suppressed
all Jewish ability and our church incited against the very image
of the Jew, and thus undermined our name and everything that
once made us great." Potocki paused then said:

"Panie Sokoloff, I promise you that I will remain a friend."

"This is what I have been waiting for. There are rumors and anything could happen."

"What could happen?"

"They are not just rumors—they are rounding up Jews in Warsaw, in Lodz, in Lublin, in every town and village, and sending them to prisons, concentration camps, slave work—and Poles in the local places are collaborating to the bitter end."

"God save Poland if her sons shed innocent blood—how could they—how could they," he mumbled and just clutched with his fingers the arms of his chair to which he was confined helplessly.

When David returned to town, through Yanowa Street, he met Velvke who seemed perturbed as he spoke to him.

"David, you must help me!"

"How?"

"You see it is about the Yeshiva student."

"You can assign him to our house to eat and sleep as long as he wants."

"That's not the problem."

"What is?"

"He is at the Schneider house right now, but Elchanan insists that he cannot come there again to eat on Friday, including the Sabbath."

"Let's go."

As they came up the steps of Schneider's battered house, Hadassah ran toward them and with glee in her voice, "They are eating," and then waved them away.

"The Yeshiva Bochur too?" Velvke was surprised.

"Yes."

"You want to see my kittens? Come! I'll show both of you."

"Not now. Is this such a pressing *mitzvah*?" Velvke was politely amused.

"Maybe it is, come on." But only David reluctantly followed her in the yard. There under planks near the barn she introduced them. "This is the grandmother, Her Majesty," she pointed to a beautiful black cat with a white spot on the face, and dots under chin and above her paws. "This is Panther, her daughter," who seemed friendlier than her suspicious mother. "These are Panther's older children and these little ones are only a few months old." She identified the frisky kittens who pawed, chased each others' or their own tails and stalked or shadow-moused. They practiced their mother's subtle lessons, who merely wagged her tail briskly on the ground daring them to catch it.

"You want to know their names? This is Squeaky, Punchy and Lonely."

"Isn't Squeaky too big?" David asked.

"No, he or she is from a previous litter. She takes care of her sisters or brothers, just like a nurse."

"Isn't this wonderful?"

"It is, and don't believe that cats are dumb. Why, Her Majesty can smell danger even better than we."

"Why is she limping?"

"Somebody hurt her leg, maybe a boy or man, and ever since she doesn't eat until every one goes away. This Panther is very smart, she knows when we cook and she wouldn't eat anything until we give her that which has the better smell—like cooked meat. She can smell good food and tell us when anyone is bad, and likes those who are good. You see she doesn't run away from new faces. But she likes him best." She pointed to Elchanan through the window.

"We can go inside," Velvke called David. Hadassah followed them inside.

"Why do you bother them?" her brother, the teacher, admonished her.

"I merely told them that these cats understand."

"Yes, she is right," Elchanan shyly remarked while glancing at her from the corner of his eyes. "King Solomon understood the languages of all creatures."

"You see, I told you."

"Now Elchanan, David is here," he took him aside, "he once studied at a Yeshiva too." Velvke coughed for privacy and the father, son, his wife and Hadassah joined their mother in the kitchen.

"Elchanan," Velvke lowered his voice, "it is not right to insult the hospitality of this man. I know he is a hard working tailor and can't give the best of foods."

"On the contrary the meal was the best and so was the company. Chaim the teacher once studied at Mir and later at Telz, quite learned."

"Yes, he is quiet and dedicated," David praised him.

"Then why do you refuse to accept his invitation?" Velvke pleaded with Elchanan.

"It is a great injustice for me to take away their food. I can see how they give me a piece of meat and for themselves just flavored potatoes with a bone. They said something about diet, but I found out it is not so."

"But Elchanan," David glanced toward the kitchen, "if you refuse you will hurt them—remember you are welcome into our house without an invitation." Velvke frowned at him, as if saying, "You are upsetting my *mitzvah* project."

"We must find a solution," Velvke smoothed out the creases on his forehead, conceding that sometimes a *mitzvah* deed has to be performed judiciously.

"There is a way," David called Velvke to speak to him in privacy. "I'll get food from Potocki with his note, that it is a present for something he intends to fix."

"Will Schneider believe it? He is a patcher; for new garments they go to the more fashionable tailors."

"He is an honest man, and when he sees an honest note, why should he doubt God's will?"

"God's will," David conceded Velvke's ingenuity; "that's different."

*The world survives as long as children are
free to play and study.*

Sabbath, 119.

4

SONGS AND THUNDER

Late Saturday afternoon the Hebrew school committee began to
assemble in the red Brick Synagogue. The children drifted in one
by one in order not to arouse the suspicion of the Russians. They
were to wait until after sunset and *havdalah* before going to the
classes for the open examinations. It was time to depart. David
felt honored to participate in the monthly examination of the
Hebrew School children. He wasn't sure how he would react in
Rachel's class. Outside a motorcycle moved by as if in pursuit of
something. The Russians were secretive. To all questions they
always replied *"Charisho,"* everything is in order. David wondered, as he forgot about his own emotional involvement with
Rachel, whether everything was in order. All along the way to
the Hebrew School these and other problems assaulted him this
early June day.

The Hebrew School or *'Beth Hasefer Amami,'* as it was called,
was located in the courtyard, behind the red Brick Synagogue,
opposite the spacious square. It was the only brick structure that
was built in Suha-Vali since the war. The *'Landsmanschaft-
Vereins,'* from New York, Chicago, Detroit and Philadelphia,
provided all the expenses, including the well stocked library
room in the rear.

Nobody built in Suha-Vali, at least not recently. All the
houses, excepting five of white-washed brick, were made of
wood, mostly pine. They were made of squared logs, joined at
the corners by dovetails, and packed with forest moss in the
cracks. Timber was always plentiful and inexpensive, only a few

47

minutes away from the edge of town. But money was scarce.
Besides, every family learned to be content with whatever it pos-
sessed, be it an old rickety house, rough furniture, straw mattresses, or brick ovens that were smoky in summer and wood
hungry in winter. The school structure was the only luxury that
offset all the other shortcomings. It had a center hall flanked by
eight classrooms on both sides, with the library and social room
serving as additional classrooms to accommodate over three hundred children.

By an unexplained miracle—political expediency, others said
—the Hebrew School was left alone by the Russian regime. With
German armies poised on her sprawling frontiers, communist
Russia had to contend with more pressing problems than the
suppression of Hebrew culture. Nevertheless the education
committee took no chances with the unpredictable Russians and
arranged the examination for Saturday night, after the services.

On the raised terrace in front of the doorway, Paltiel the
builder, *gevir*, (rich one) jovial and in high spirits, dominated as
usual whenever Religious Zionism was on the agenda. It was
basically a non-partisan committee. Israel Grodzensky, who was
by conviction and affiliation a militant Revisionist Zionist, skill-
fully detached himself from any ideological controversy.

"Prayer was not a special occasion. Young and old always
came to the synagogue. It was a habit. How did they get the
habit? Let me answer, let me finish." The genial Paltiel, who
master-minded the merger of the religious and Zionist schools,
recounted nostalgically the transition.

"We were taught by *melamdin* (teachers) in a room next to
the kitchen. A chicken, a cat and sometimes a goat crowded us
for space and air. Do you know how many hours they taught?
They taught from eight to eight by candle-light. There were no
such subjects in their curriculum as geography, history, arithmetic, botany and not even the spoken Hebrew. You wanted
young men and young girls promenading in the woods and over
fields, conversing in Hebrew."

Paltiel was now out of breath. Koppel took over. He considered
it a duty as surrogate for the Rabbi and defender of the
melamdim to launch his counter-attack against the neo-educators.

"Tell me Paltiel, did you ever study arithmetic or higher
mathematics? Yet you kept books. You, Menashe," he turned to
the willow-limbed owner of the beer parlor, "did you learn geog-

raphy? No. Yet you always found your way to any city in Poland
and Russia whenever you got tired dodging the police. You even
made your way to America. It was not your fault that at Castle
Garden they found something wrong with your passport and you
were sent back.

"You were getting along, at least until the war. Tell me
Menashe, does it require any knowledge of chemistry to make
your vodka?" There was a restrained chuckle.

"Anything important we learned and made a habit; religion,
prayer and Hebrew. Unimportant things like arithmetic, geography, and even a language, we picked up here and there. Hebrew was not a mere language, it was a bridge to holiness.

"But take the Germans. I travelled there. It was big business,
selling timber in the millions. You, David, you were there as a
student for a few years; tell me if I am wrong. They have many
schools, universities, libraries, museums. Every young man wears
a special student cap. The solid citizens—*Bürger*—want to belong to a beer house or be accepted in a *gemütlich* company of
silent, singing, marching or rioting mob.

"Every German wants to belong to something, to be ordered
by somebody, to be regimented somehow, to march somewhere.
They believe in order and discipline—but it is all like their military marching—a goose step. Did you ever see goose feathers?
They're just carried aloft to nowhere."

For a while they stood there motionless, still under the spell of
Koppel's magnetic motions and vibrant voice. To David it was a
genuine, if painful, revelation. He always shunned everything
that seemed old and quaint. But now he was convinced that the
old coin which he found in Suha-Vali was valuable. The greenish
film of age only proved that it was genuine.

Koppel appeared to him like a merchant of rare antiquities
whose price was greater than anything new.

"It is not so, David?"

"I agree with what you said about the Germans."

"Anything else?" Koppel prodded him.

"Everything you said about education is also true. Maybe we
discarded our traditional methods and sources in our haste to
leap over the centuries. We can always return."

"If we return to the ways of our forefathers."

"Right now we have to look ahead, not behind. Something is
coming down upon us."

"Is it real or just a frightening dream?"

"Whatever you call it, I see it coming."

"David if you were to tell this to the Russians, do you know what they would do to you?"

"I can guess. Jews always had prophets in their midst to warn them of the invaders."

"The period of the prophets came to a close long ago, as you well know. A wise man is better than a prophet now."

"I don't claim to be a prophet nor a wise man, but I saw it . . ."

"Only God can reveal the future. . . ."

"The Rabbi is here," someone interrupted.

"Let's go into this class. The children are singing," another suggested. They were now in Rachel's class.

She signalled to curious cherubic eyes. Her long-sleeved hands dipped and rose gracefully in harmony with the high-pitched big clear voices.

> Sleep and slumber my son,
> Harken to my melody
> Long, long ago, far away,
> There was a city, a tale of glory.

To David, Rachel appeared now lovelier than ever. She was poised and unaware of herself, innocent yet purposeful in her dedication. There is no greater charm or beauty than that of a girl in the midst of a task. To some there is an attraction in coquetry and sheer femininity. But to Jews, especially to the young men with a tradition of reverence for an idealistic girl, Rachel was enchantment.

"Beautiful, a beautiful song," David whispered to Koppel who caught David's furtive glances toward Rachel.

Gedaliah now rose to sing the solo. His small face, pale and vivid, was animated with an innocent smile. In a surprisingly firm voice he intoned:

> A day will come and from the nation,
> Like a lion will rise a leader.
> From every corner, from every station
> Exiles will rally to the call of the redeemer.

Rabbi Kalir paused as thunder-like rumblings came from somewhere in a far distance. "Maneuvers," Alter the carpenter suggested.

"Maneuvers in wartime?" Koppel Magid wondered. Once more the class joined in the refrain.

Gedaliah raised his bell-like voice and sang another stanza from the "Cradle Lullaby":

> Then like a roaring lion a voice will call,
> 'He who is faithful, follow me'
> Then from the multitude a voice like a mighty call;
> 'Long live the Messiah, the hope of the free.'

"Do you hear anything?" Koppel asked a boy. The student shook his head.

"I understand you started the second book of Moses. You are now learning one of the five books of the *Chumash* (Pentateuch). This is the most important part of the Holy Scriptures, which includes all interpretation and is called the Torah.

"What," he asked, as he scanned the eager yet reserved faces, "does Torah mean?"

"Torah means learning, also wisdom." A boy in the back stood up.

"I know," another boy in front waved frantically, "all the Jewish laws, what is good for us and what is bad for us."

"Very good," Rabbi Kalir beamed as he extended his right hand to Koppel Magid and the others in a graceful gesture that meant "now you may ask some questions, please do!"

"Now children," Koppel Magid acceded to the routine catechism, "there are books and learning among all nations, even laws about good and bad. In what way is our Torah different?"

There was silence. "Don't be afraid," he appealed to the cherubic Gedaliah, almost hidden by bigger children in front of him.

"They, the gentiles, have books and laws, but sometimes, like in wartime, they don't count."

"What do you mean, they don't count?"

" 'Don't kill' and 'don't steal' are laws the Germans don't obey. They kill Jews and steal from Jews."

David, who was so conscious of Rachel, was tempted to challenge some of the opinions. But he realized that they were examining themselves and probing their own minds for so many unfathomed and unsolved questions.

"In the 'Shema Israel' the text reads 'Hear, O Israel, the Lord is our God, the Lord is one.' Rabbi Kalir stated his question:

"Why must Israel hear it, why not anyone else? Do you understand, children? Israel means the Jews—why must the Jews hear it first?"

"I know—because—" Gedaliah stood up.

"Yes, yes," Rabbi Kalir embraced his enthusiasm.

"Because they tell lies and gossip about us; they call us bad names. We deny it three times a day openly. To prove it we say Israel was and still is the first nation that believes in our kind of a God."

"Excellent, excellent," Rabbi Kalir repeated his compliments until all faces turned.

"I'm sure I heard something," Koppel said aside to Alter.

"Now children, you have gladdened my heart. What is the meaning of 'Thou Shalt love the Lord thy God with all thy heart and with all thy soul and with all thy might'?" the Rabbi asked again.

"It means, it says—I mean," a boy hesitated, "to love like you love your mother."

"And the father?" Rabbi Kalir prompted him.

"The father too, only——"

"Can such a love—with all your heart—be between two people?" David rephrased the question.

"A boy and a girl?" The boy smiled quizzically.

"Yes, this is how life is. Two must love one another with all their hearts."

The Rabbi fidgeted and Rachel blushed. David continued.

"It is told in the Bible how Jacob worked and waited for his beloved Rachel. And the Talmud tells us, how Rachel—another Rachel—waited many years for Rabbi Akiba. This is the way true love is and should be."

"What is the meaning 'with all thy might'?" the Rabbi resumed.

"Children, what does the Hebrew word 'meod' mean?" Rachel emphasized the key word of the rabbi's query.

"Very much," all chorused.

"Very much," David repeated. "Suppose in order to love one must give up possessions, convenience and even life, do we still love?"

"Yes we do."

"It is true that love is a good thing that you can't see?" Koppel asked Gedaliah.

"God is good and man can't see him." Koppel and the Rabbi nodded with admiration.

"One last question, if you can't see a good thing, how can you prove that it is really good?"

"We can't see the sun—I mean straight, and yet it is good for the fields. It gives light and keeps us warm."

"It is written 'Thou shalt love the Lord thy God with all thy soul'" Rabbi Kalir emphasized the last words as he smiled at Gedaliah.

"Our teacher told us it means sanctification of the Holy name."

"What do you think?" Koppel turned to the class.

"We must always be ready to die for God, to love Him," a girl's clear voice came from the back.

"Is it easy to love?"

"Not everything," she replied.

"Leah," David acknowledged Rachel's sister, "why can't you love everything?"

"Well, we are supposed to love everything, not just a boy or a girl or parents—even non-Jews, but it is sometimes hard because they do bad things."

"Suppose it is hard to love, like a whole group of people, a different nation, is it right to make war on such a people, to destroy them?" the Rabbi pressed on.

"No! No! That is what the *goyim* do—the bad nations," voices vied with each other.

"Is it correct if I say that to 'love with all thy heart' means even a neighbor, good or bad or——?"

"Yes, yes," the class thundered.

"Even if your senses tell you not to!" Rabbi Kalir interpreted.

"Correct!" the class roared.

"'With all thy soul.'" Rabbi Kalir returned to his favorite theme. "Now you said before, even to die. Suppose bad, very bad people, cause us suffering—like in our history—there were many times when Jews were martyrs at the hands of their neighbors. Do you still think we should love God?"

"Yes, yes," they shouted.

"With all thy might, if, God forbid, it comes to that where Jews have to sacrifice everything, home, family, birthplace, do you still love God—Jews did it at all times."

"We too, we too," the voices overwhelmed everyone.

"This is a little too deep for the children," David was apprehensive, lest their tender feelings be aroused by something too near and too real for such discussion.

"This is an age," Koppel defended the realistic approach of

Jewish history where young children get old before their time
and older people wish they were young to forget. "Who knows,"
he whispered to David, "maybe they understand more than we
suspect."

"I hear thunder, the sky is clear. . . ." Koppel said to David.

"No, no!" David shook his head in disbelief.

HITLER BEGINS WAR ON RUSSIA FROM
ARCTIC TO BLACK SEA.

*Whoever persecutes Israel is elected by evil
people to be Head of State.*

Gittin, 56.

5

THE COILED MONSTER

They sat in tensed silence, an imminent threat suspended over
their heads. Reb Koppel the wise elder, who summoned the
committee to his house at this ominous hour past midnight, was
right. The rumbling thunder and lightning on the far horizon
spelled out something sinister. The naive Russian commissar told
the apprehensive inquirers minutes ago that there was no cause
for alarm, it must be maneuvers. Whoever heard of maneuvers
on Saturday night and so close to the border? What the wise
elder sensed with his incisive logic, David foresaw in a dream.

"We must have *bitochen*—faith and trust," Koppel opened the
meeting.

" 'Pray' we are told," the Rabbi set the tone, " 'for the welfare
of the kingdom'—its uninterrupted continuity; 'otherwise one
kingdom would swallow another'. When Leviathans start swal-
lowing one another then it is—it is a calamity."

David listened quietly. The mere mention of Leviathan revived many stories from his childhood days in the *Cheder* classroom of Reb Isaac. One, how the Leviathan, tail in its mouth, is
coiled deep in the oceans around the world. Should it ever stir to
pull out its tail, the whole world would be deluged. It was a
story repeated by Reb Isaac year after year during the short
winter days, when shadows danced around the flickering candle
late into the night. They never tired of hearing the story, for it
seemed real and terrible.

"The Leviathan," Rabbi Kalir began slowly.

"Is this the time for a Leviathan story?" Alter the carpenter
protested.

"Leviathan is a noble creature," Rabbi Kalir said, "but today it

55

is a monster flooding the shores as it rises from the deep with its claws poised for something—something only God knows. It is not a fairy tale. We are also told 'do not become alarmed from the sudden calamity spawned by evil men'."

Label, who could no longer control his Marxist temper, dropped his fist on the table.

"You are the supposed leaders, where is your plan? What are you going to do? The Russians are preparing to evacuate. Let us follow them."

Ben Zion, took up the challenge. "I'm a Zionist and you belong to a different world, but I'm willing to consider, even support any sound plan you may offer."

"My plan is this," Label was direct, "that we accept the advice of the Russian military leadership. We must even offer sacrifices."

Koppel, who was very familiar with most of these platitudes, interrupted him. "You mentioned sacrifices. What sacrifices and by whom?"

"Russia has saved us from the Germans, and is the only one who can save us now. But we must help her in return."

Alter chimed in with "Good! Good! How can we help?"

"There are certain tasks that even civilians can do; like sabotage behind the enemy lines, destroy communications, ambush troops, and keep the Russians informed of all military movements. There may be some among us who will join the red army or drive the supply wagons—now," Label paused, "who will be the first one to volunteer?" There was no response. "I'll be the first one to volunteer. Will you follow me, David?"

"I don't think that it is proper to ask us—certainly not you—to offer ourselves on a strange altar," Ben Zion said.

"You asked that we accept Russian leadership, offer volunteers and sacrifices," David summed up Label's emotional appeal. "Mother Russia wants our town—the baby—to lay down and die just for the privilege of calling her Mother."

"A few may be misled by false idealism and follow you, Label," Rabbi Kalir faced him. "But how can you ever atone yourself if you persuade young men to follow you? What will happen to their abandoned families; parents, wives and children?"

Now that everyone had spoken Abba seized the right moment to make a 'resume'. He was careful not to offend anyone but to confine himself to the simple, direct and methodical language of the school master.

"Number one," he peered reflectively through his thick glasses, "whatever we decide, it must reflect our unity. History teaches us that strife is the worst enemy.

"Number two, let us not get panicky, or alarm the rest. The enemy will probably be here within a few hours. I therefore suggest that a committee await them on the high road with bread and salt.

"Number three, we must tell our people to remain in their homes."

"Bread and salt for fascists?" Label protested. "How about crowding into the synagogue, opening the ark, praying, you know?" he taunted them.

"Label, enough," David pointed his finger at him. "Must you drag in the synagogue to provoke us?"

"Who provokes? I'll tell you the truth. You can't escape to Palestine. England and the Arabs won't let you. America is far away and also closed. The Christian countries, including their center in Rome, are silent. Only Russia can help the Jews."

"How can we depend on Russia? She established Biro-Bidjan not to save Jews but as a synthetic homeland and diversion from Eretz Israel—this is the correct name, not Palestine. Even if some Jews make their way into Russia, and it seems impossible since the Russian army on the frontiers is itself trapped, how will they exist as Jews? The Jews in Russia are like prisoners. Russia has, since 1917, imprisoned all Zionists, closed most synagogues, and all Hebrew Schools, and has, with rare exceptions, prevented Jews from migrating to Eretz Israel or any other country."

"Repetitious propaganda, not a word of truth," Label shouted.

"Communism is the enemy of truth," David glared at him.

"Children, let us not quarrel, at a time when the enemy is at our gates. Our salvation can come only from God and from decent people who can summon God through good deeds and hearts." The Rabbi leaned against the wall in prayer like King Ezekiah in time of distress.

It was dark when David returned home. The after-glow was still etched over the horizon and the top of the trees. Sounds and echoes mingled as solos into the harmony of this June night. As

usual he thought of the window shutters. He took several deep
breaths of the cool air, walked inside and made no effort to
fasten the shutter's brace with the spindle through the eyehole.
It was a subconscious slip of his own forebodings.

He listened to the strained snoring of his father and the half-
asleep half-awake shifting of his mother. He heard steps—or was
it his heart pounding. There was that familiar steady tick, tick
from somewhere on the wall—it could be a cricket or a misplaced watch.

He turned from side to side on the stuffed straw mattress. All
through the long seconds and age-long minutes he geared himself
against slumber and sleep. There was no plan. How could there
be a plan? What kind of plan? How many. . . , how many could
be saved?

He heard again the sounds and echoes of the night. They were
the dispersed notes now drifting aimlessly in the moonlight. He
recalled their haunting call whenever he was away from Suha-
Vali. He had returned to rendezvous with them for an unknown
destiny. He heard once more the familiar sharp metallic sounds
of the cricket, as he furiously stitched together, in short bursts,
the wandering shadows of the darkness.

From across the river, barking dogs exploded in alarm. Nearby
in the garden, cries of tom-cats, like suspended cries of babies,
pierced the still attuned voices of the sleepless night. The lonely
owl, perched on the chimney above the synagogue's roof,
sounded the hunting call with its mournful cries. David raised
himself on his elbow as he strained his ears to strange far away
echoes. He thought he heard the rolling rumble of thunder. If it
was thunder, he should utter the blessing, "Blessed art thou, O
Lord our God, King of the universe, whose strength and might
are everywhere." Soon hard rains would fall; the river would
overflow, flooding the rye fields. But no, it was not thunder.

It was long past midnight. But David's eye lids were heavy
and would not close. He tiptoed to the curtained entrance of the
bedroom. Ber Leib breathed heavily, and Dinah, as usual, turned
uneasily, as if witnessing the pressure threatening to burst
through the walls. Both sensed the danger from which he tried
to shield them. If sleep would only grant him reprieve for the
remainder of the night, he could somehow allay their suspicions.

He moved closer to the shuttered window and heard the
steady vibrations of telegraph wires. What did they mean? He

wanted to know. What were their frantic coded messages? Were they from a friend or a foe?

He sat down, his elbows on the table and his head couched in their embrace. He wanted to elude all these relentless visitations. He could find refuge in books. They would barricade him against the intrusion of tormenting images. Waiting to embrace him graciously were Holy Books, *Mishnahs*, *Gemaras*; also secular books in Hebrew, Polish, Russian, Yiddish—and German books which repelled him in the corner—on the bookshelf, on the dresser, almost everywhere. Magazines and newspapers in these languages, that he saved since his teens from Grodno and Bialystok, Tel Aviv, Warsaw and Berlin, were piled up on the floor.

Drowsiness pulled his head and it slumped over his elbow, limp on the table. He saw a strange vision. The courtyard of the synagogue was filled to capacity. All eyes were turned toward a wedding canopy. Underneath the scarlet and gold embroidered tasseled covering, a veiled bride—the face of the groom was under a helmet—faced the Rabbi. It was at night, but there were no stars. Children were everywhere, wide awake as they pressed forward or climbed on fences to get a better view.

A wind lifted the canopy and the four men of honor who held the shafts steadied its swaying motions. The chatter of carefree children stopped as the Rabbi in a mellow sonorous voice began to rhythmically recite the benediction. Candles to drive away the darkness glowed and flickered. Suddenly they were flung to the floor. The canopy began to sway violently until it was carried away by a storm. The groom was snatched away. The bride fainted. There were weird screams.

David was choking. Furiously he strained to free himself from his paralysis. He wanted to warn the girls and boys to hide in the woods, to run, to escape. But he could not open his jaws.

Dinah, who was aroused by his moaning and gnashing of teeth, was at his bedside. She patted his sweating forehead.

"You must have had a dream," she soothed him, careful not to say "a bad dream". "Does anything hurt you?" she asked. Her voice pried open his jaws, his lips relaxed and his gummy eyelids opened up. Before him was his mother. He knew it was a dream. "Mother, go back to sleep," he reassured her. But he knew that sleep would not come again.

Sporadic explosions faded in the distance. Whirring sounds of motors came closer. He pressed against the window. Cautiously he released the bolt from the eyelet of the elbow iron, until the shutters flung open. The iron bar swung freely, creaking and grating against metal and wood.

He was startled, and froze as he gazed at grim helmeted faces silhouetted against the gray darkness. Lorries packed with soldiers; half-tracks with mounted mortars; trailers with special equipment. Now and then a driver's hand signalled through the cab window. Two armored cars with heads above the trap doors completed the line. It must have been a reconnaissance unit. The main invading column was probably bypassing the town on the military highway.

He knew that in every house, young and old were by this time wide awake. Yet they would have to suppress all signs of alarm.

It would be useless to expect help from their Christian neighbors. A wolf pack coming out from the woods and stealing through the gardens with their gaping jaws and shiny eyes would have aroused everyone to fierce retaliation; but not these seemingly heroic men. The farmers, after a tranquil sleep, were now on the way to their fields. The church bell rang at the usual time.

Dawn began to tint the gray with a light blue. It was quiet again. There were footsteps outside. First came the light steps of Beryl the baker. David could almost catch the words of his 'morning confession' which he uttered within sight of the synagogue door. It was a savory prelude to prayer, like the zest induced by freshly baked bread. Both finished products were the result of good ingredients blended with the warmth from man and God.

Alter the carpenter shuffled along in his heavy boots. Like Beryl he slipped through the gardens, then cut across. Elyeh the shoemaker's hurried steps came from across the street. There was scraping on the window pane. Only the sexton ventured to wake him in this manner, when he was needed to be the tenth man required for congregational worship. But it was always accompanied by pounding.

"It is I, Koppel."

David wanted to cry out, "You shouldn't have done it!" For he knew that he had to cross the market place, and soldiers, especially if they are German, will not hesitate to press the trigger in sight of Jewish civilians.

David hurriedly put on his jacket over his open-necked shirt. As he followed behind them, he hesitated momentarily. There was a light in Rachel's window. The mother and the children must all be frightened. Why didn't he notice it before?

The crisp voice of his father Ber Leib who followed him into the synagogue interrupted him, as he intoned "Blessed be he who said let the world be created. . . , Blessed be he who has mercy upon mankind." Within less than half an hour, the worshippers finished their tension filled prayers and returned to their homes.

Windows rattled as armored cars piloted a long column of vehicles. It was probably a regiment from the main invading army that detoured from the military highway into town. The trucks slowed down as they passed the stone walled Jewish cemetery before the rickety wooden bridge.

Soldiers in field green-gray uniforms from the lead truck jumped down. One who was checking the bridge's approaches with a mine detector signalled to the others to follow him as he carefully inspected the entire span.

It was only routine. For the Russian army at this point, only a few miles from the East Prussian border, was quickly overwhelmed by the surprise invasion; its squadrons of planes at Agustowa were smashed on the ground, and its defense forces were caught off guard. Engineer units went to work to reinforce the bridge's capacity under the heavy strain of movement and tonnage.

Several companies with fixed bayonets were in the middle of the column where the cobbled street dipped between Liverant's water mill and the blacksmith shops. They were now past the *Mikvah* (ritualarium), bathhouse, and the little square facing the big pagoda-shaped frame and shingle synagogue. Here the street —identified only by outsiders as Synagogue Street—began to rise again. Field kitchens, signal units and light tanks completed the column.

As it swung past the New Synagogue and then the Brick Synagogue, where the street enters the market square, the regiment split in two. One, the main unit, continued diagonally past the walled church into Karpowitz Street which rejoins the highway in the direction of the Fort Ossovetz and Bialystok. The second unit bivouacked on the square to regroup for military police duty in Suha-Vali and outlying towns.

As if by a prearranged schedule, military police headquarters were established by noon in the red frame house alongside the parish house, across from the church. As far as one could remember, the Russians (Czarist), Germans, Poles and Russians (Communist) respectively employed it as the residence and seat of police, army and now under the direct control of the black uniformed S.S. command. It was strategically located on the west side of the square.

It was the heart of the city, as Koppel Magid pointed out. The town had the shape of a man; its head was Long Village extending from the upper end of the square to the south; its two hands were Yanover and Karpowitz Streets pointing east and west; and its two feet Synagogue and Church Streets stretched to the smaller down town square. Both continued their parallel course but to different destinations. The first bypassed the old synagogue across the bridge to the highway and the second lost its footing in the scattered hamlets and sands dotted with willows.

In normal times the heart—the imposing Brick Synagogue, the Hebrew School behind it, the Rabbi's house and library alongside on the eastern side of the square—functioned well and in the right place. On Thursdays it became a teeming market and on Sundays it was crowded with worshippers who came to church and afterward came for a snack or a drink in the inns. But in abnormal times, like war, the heart was stricken. The malady spread from the police station across to the church on the western side, and was aggravated by the headache, the Polish rowdies from Long Village.

Before evening, without any warning, a truck of soldiers parked near the Brick Synagogue and began to transform it into a hospital. The newly constructed school building in its rear and supported through the generosity of American 'Landsleit', was spared from the same fate, temporarily.

A motorcyclist raised a column of dust as he roared across the market square. He dismounted in front of the soldiers removing tables, benches and stands from the main chapel and vestries of the synagogue. They were awed by the black uniform of the S.S. man. The cyclist pulled out, from a leather bag suspended from the saddle, a printed sheet, and posted it on the wall. It was the order of the day. He sped away, to post the same, on the New Synagogue and on the Old Synagogue, and its adjoining *Beth Medrash*.

Before long, men, women and children began to crowd around the notices which announced, under the dateline June 22, 1941:

1. The German army demands complete cooperation and order from all citizens.
2. All weapons must be turned over to the police within 24 hours.
3. It is forbidden to hoard food or merchandise.
4. All stores and shops must be opened for German soldiers and personnel.
5. A curfew will be in force from 9 p.m. to 9 a.m.
6. The community must offer dwellings, services and all necessities for use of administration.
7. All violations will be punished severely.

They were too stunned to react to the vague but fateful decrees.

Skura, the son of a poor Polish horse skinner, who volunteered his services as head of Polish police, was on hand.

"Don't worry, Jews," he taunted them, "there are a few more surprises for you." There was uncontrolled laughter by his men as they mimicked the Jews.

"Quiet!" he suddenly shouted. "You Jews must deliver wagons and men to cut wood and deliver them to headquarters. Thirty men every day for the forest. Also girls—don't laugh!" he sneered, "girls about ten, to nurse the wounded soldiers in the synagogue hospital. Don't forget," he reminded them, "I, Bogdan Skura, am in full charge of the auxiliary police."

They walked away, distressed, but oblivious to the insults and shouts of the renegades. Abchik the aging druggist, substituting for the ailing mayor was as usual on the spot. But he was a silent witness, assaying the situation before committing himself. He was deliberately ignored by Skura, his cap tilted to one side and his hand resting on his revolver.

Abchik hurried to Koppel's house. It was an unofficial office where he received information and advice. Each in turn, Paltiel, Ben Zion, Israel Grodzensky, Abba Dunsky, Shmuel Leiser and David Sokoloff transmitted grave news. Confiscation without warning of the few trucks owned by Jews. Seizure of grain, flour, meat—by house to house raiding, with Skura and his gang acting as open informers. No public assembly of more than three persons . . . Pending arrests of collaborators with Russians.

"This never happened in my lifetime," Abchik said. "Skura and his hooligans would not have laughed in our faces and threat-

ened us unless they got the nod from them." He pointed in the
direction of the red house across the left upper corner of the
square. "We have no alternative but to obey," he paused after
each phrase. "Let us not give them a pretext to catch men in the
streets or from their beds. We must act and do it as one unit."
His sensitive lips were quivering as he gazed around the room
and eyed everyone, expecting approval.

Koppel leaned on his forehead in a meditative mood.

"Let us be careful whatever we do," David began in his deliberate manner. "Now let us see . . . they want men. We could
choose them by lot. But it may fall on the wrong man—say, one
sick or old. Then again, we could appeal for volunteers. This
would be the best plan. But only God knows if this will satisfy
them. Are they asking us to contribute hands for work or is it
something else? I recommend that Abchik appoint a committee
to handle this difficult task. Above all, remember, we must never
surrender our daughters to these debauchers."

"Who knows? Who knows what is in their minds? These are
different Germans from the ones we knew in the first World
War." He looked around cautiously to doors and windows.

"Reb Koppel," someone suggested.

"Let us hear from the younger men," he declined graciously.

"Of course, of course," Ben Zion seconded.

"In Suha-Vali," David's voice was tense and vibrant, "the voice
of our elders has been always respected because they understand
and respect our youth. Now greater things than respect are required from us. Are you aware that Skura went to the vodka inn
and spread the rumor of the raids hours before they took place?
How else was it possible for the Germans and these low characters to get together in such a short time? It was planned many
days ago. How? I don't know. The Nazis are experts in these
things. They promised them a free hand. One of the drunks
blurted out "The Jews are in our hands."

"No, no, impossible," cried out Abchik.

"We must not allow it," Koppel shook his head in utter disbelief.

"You say impossible," David faced Abchik. "The Jews are
naive, too honest, they don't know this nation, these people,
these soldiers, these creatures. But we must not and will not
allow it to happen," he turned to Koppel.

"International law, Geneva convention," Ben Zion suggested.

"Letters to London, Washington, Rome," Abba tried to raise his voice.

"We'll try, appeal everywhere, and if we are abandoned and betrayed we'll fight the best way we can," David spoke resolutely. "We will never surrender nor bow nor beg mercy. We'll fight with our bodies and souls and if the worst happens, the blood be upon the heads of those who stood by so long and did nothing."

After long seconds of silence David was remorseful. The burden of his vision was too much. Its mounting pressure began to show in his ominous decisions and doubts.

"It is all in the hands of God; what else can we say." Koppel yielded to fate.

"Not quite!" David demurred.

"Do you question this truth?" Koppel eyed him with surprise.

"I don't, except that God is in the wrong hands. Since many nations claim God as their own, he becomes, according to them, a silent partner. They commit all the crimes and bloodshed in his name."

Koppel did not respond. He could not deny it nor affirm it. "There is something else," he finally said.

"Not now," David was impatient. "We have before us difficult decisions and we are responsible for all the Jews. This committee will draw up the details for all voluntary labor requisitions, food distribution to the needy, emergency funds ..."

"I have an important announcement," Koppel cut in. "There will be a wedding."

"Who, what?" They were curious. David froze. Oh, my God, he thought, this must be the disrupted wedding I saw in my dream.

"Rachel is the Kalah and Zechariah is the Chasan," Koppel answered.

"When?" they shouted.

"This week, it cannot be postponed."

David stood alone, numbed and speechless. He sat down, not knowing what to do next. This was a nightmarish thunder that struck him.

"What is it David, don't you feel good?" Koppel asked him.

"But she is so young," David protested after he recovered somewhat.

"She is seventeen, but very intelligent and mature," Abba startled him.

"Rachel is only a child—a beautiful child," Ben Zion steered a middle course. "The beautiful and the good sometimes sacrifice themselves for others. How could her mother, cut off from husband in America, feed her children?"

"Who knows what is best?" Koppel mused. "Our mothers married at a young age and it turned out right. War either postpones marriage or requires a prompt marriage. Eighteen is a marriageable age for a boy but a girl can be younger. Rachel had no choice, and consented."

"Consented? Never, never," David exploded.

"It is the will of God, to save her." Koppel faced David.

"Will of God? I don't believe it. How can anyone even think of marriage at such a time?"

June 24, 1941:   GERMANS PENETRATE 80 MILES INTO
RUSSIA. VICHY AID TO NAZIS PROVED.
. . . HAIFA ATTACKED.

> *When the wicked enter the world, wrath
> follows.*
>
> Sanhedrin, 113.

6

TAKE OFF FOR VULTURES

They were waiting for Colonel Johann Kristus Von Preissig, the newly appointed Kommandant of Suha-Vali. S.S. Captain Messer and S.S. Lt. Schrecke, who rose from the citizenry of Frankfort and Oberammergau to this rank in Nazidom, were to be his aids. They were instructed by the Gestapo to keep an eye on this Junker officer.

"Did you see the cellar?"

The hatched-faced lieutenant pointed to the narrow stairway descending in the rear corner of the room.

"Not yet," the portly captain replied, still foraging for something to decorate his own room. It was next door, formerly the Polish public school, and before the Hebrew School. At last he spotted a miniature spinning wheel, hanging over the wooden bulletin board on the hallway wall. "Maybe good for a lamp."

"It's about eight meters wide." The lieutenant paced across the front office and then estimated with the trained eye of a farmer. "And twenty long. The room to the rear is for the Kommandant. Below us is the wine cellar. Do you think the Kommandant drinks?"

"Whatever he drinks, we drink something stronger than wine. Did you see those things in the steel closet?"

"No."

"Polish handcuffs, Russian shackles; primitive stuff—we'll add our own improvements."

"I get you." The muscles on his thin face flexed as his lips tightened in agreement. "A nice room," he said to the captain who was examining the scribbling on the board.

"Russian, German—1916," Captain Messer strained to read, "Polish and Communist Russian—I studied a few years in the gymnasium, and I learned enough for my purpose at the Gestapo school." He meant to put his assistant in his proper place. I'll write over the funny Russian 'Heil Hitler.' "

"I'll do the same," Lt. Schrecke said. "Was that German script of the older generation?"

"Now, now they were young husbands as you are, and fathers of children like I am; they got old and we too—who knows . . ." He began to fill cognac glasses which he unpacked from a duffle bag. "Oh yes, tell Sgt. Todt or Murad, when they return—they are collecting gifts from the *verfluchte Juden und Pollacken*—to call on the Kommandant." He clicked his heels, stiffened his body and half saluted, all in the same motion of suggestive envy and derision, "I think he is coming—there he is . . ."

"Heil Hitler!" both said.

The Kommandant Col. Johann K. Von Preissig echoed the "Heil" half-heartedly and raised a feeble hand.

"Herr Kommandant," Capt. Messer was now eager to be pleasant even if it was synthetic, *"Wir trünken,"* he handed him a filled glass and poured one for himself and the lieutenant. "Heil Hitler!" he smacked his lips after he downed the cognac. He refilled his and Schreke's goblet and watched his superior only tasting it and then putting it down.

"I have been travelling since early in the morning, heavy traffic all the way from Grodno." He reacted to the Gestapo team correctly but icily.

"Yes Colonel, the roads are heavy with our victorious soldiers marching on Russia."

"Also the wounded."

"How else?"

"Also other incidents, some unpleasant."

"I say, victory and death to our enemies," he prodded Von Preissig's patriotism. "It's good to be here," he put out his hand for a glass, "where history is made."

"What do you mean?"

"This is an important post, a forward position, not far from Tannenberg. Certain things will be tried here first, I know it from an official source." Messer stopped to gulp down his drink.

"Yes, I presume it is," Von Preissig's flat tone reflected also the unmilitary behavior of his supposed subordinates.

"I ought to know, I was in the thick of it; by the way colonel, where were you in 1923?"

"I was still in the military academy, my last year."

"Well, I was in the beer academy, my first year. Don't laugh Fritz, you were a baby then, a hungry baby. Do you recall the Munich beer hall putsch?"

"I do, it was one year after Mussolini marched on Rome, and it didn't——"

"You are afraid to say it—it didn't succeed. Many arrests, I was put behind bars for trying to free Germany from the Versailles disgrace—only for a few weeks—I was lucky. The Führer," he pointed to the newly hung portrait on the wall, "was also sentenced."

"Yes, he wrote 'Mein Kampf' there and in 1933 the great general Hindenburg made him Chancellor of Germany."

"He was great only for this."

"Captain Messer!"

He addressed him for the first time by his rank, more in reproof than acceptance. "The German people have the highest regard for the great hero of the fatherland. Anything that does not reflect admiration is an insult."

"This is a new age and a new order."

Captain Messer tried hard to be polite to the colonel and not to threaten him with something worse than back talk. "Generals today have to serve the fatherland—you know what?" His speech and temper began to show the effects of the alcohol, "We give orders to generals, yes we do. You know something else; I was close to him," he pointed an unsteady finger at the face in the frame, "I could have been way on top."

"Why aren't you?"

"I got drunk; I lost out. You know to whom? To Frank, the Governor General of Poland. He knew how to play the piano and bowed well, and I didn't."

"Was it your midsection?" Lt. Schrecke, who was bored, asked him.

"Stop, you swine, Goering is much heavier and he almost got to the top. *Wir trünken,*" his mood changed, "we'll all get to our right places."

"Some day," Von Preissig said and raised his still filled glass.

"They are here," Ludke the orderly announced.

"Come in, Sgt. Todt and Murad! What have you got for the

Kommandant?" Captain Messer raised his voice above the clatter and movement of furniture.

"A desk, a bureau, lamps, radios, fur coats for winter and even
a guitar—see it plays—for our parties," Todt said.

"Good job, well done!" Messer complimented them. "The desk
is for our Kommandant, take out the one the Russians used, it is
all marked up. I'll take the bureau and a few things." Messer
spoke openly.

"Do you know where we got them?"

"Yes Sergeant." He replied, aware of Todt's tactics and ser-
vility.

"From the brewer near the power station. There is more in his
house and in others, and plenty of beer. It was hidden underneath the empty barrels."

"You are a regular bloodhound; sniff, sniff, sniff. You'll come in
handy," Messer said. Then turning around to Von Preissig he
spoke formally: "Oh yes, I almost forgot to tell you, we are
expecting Col. Schwarzhund—you know very close." He pointed
again to the portrait, "Gestapo, be nice to him, eh Colonel."

"I have a schedule you'll excuse me," Von Preissig was glad he
did not say anything incriminating, for the S.S captain was more
cunning than drunk. It would be rough going with such rude
company and its barbed remarks.

Von Preissig walked through the doorway to his office. The
desk was in front near the bay window. The view was interesting. On the desk was the detailed map—house by house—of the
city, furnished by the main Gestapo office in Warsaw, and he
could check its accuracy by comparing it to the square. The
massive red synagogue with red bricks showing through the
chipped stucco, was straight across; the wall enclosed twin-
steepled church on his near right, and to the left the fire house.
Most arresting was the movement of vehicles and the removal of
goods from the Jewish houses and stores. War is war; at least he
could sit at his desk with his back to the square.

As a Roman Catholic, he would probably pay a few token
visits to the church. But it would be best not to mix God with
war. Meanwhile he could reflect on the men around him. Todt
knows how to get things done. A nice desk and a beautiful table
for his bedroom. Even the paintings look authentic. He will
mount his own, his family portrait in the middle.

But how would he spend his days? A Junker officer was trained for duty and the proper social and sporting events. The formal dances, with lavish, ornate and resplendent uniforms, staged by the officers in Berlin and Leipzig, was now a thing of the past. His riding habits—where and with whom? Messer is a butcher boy from Frankfort, a parvenu despite his ready smile— he always disliked those who smile too easily and bow anxiously. He made inquiries about this Gestapo underling. He drinks and his face becomes crimson, like many of the pushy Nazis when confronted by a ranking officer of the Reichswehr. Schrecke is frank and brutal, a farmer, a mechanic and even an actor of sorts, from the town of Oberammergau near Munich, famous for the Passion play in which all the townspeople participate. He seems out to get his hands on everything and his quick temper can be triggered by a nod, or who knows what. You can't trust them—they are not officers. Todt is a bloodhound, very useful, up to a point. There are the Gendarmes, Ludke the orderly, and Ratten the cook;—they are simple and obedient. But once covered with a uniform and away from home, there is a little animal— dormant until now—that takes over inside their skins. Who knows which one of these is keeping an eye on him. Gestapo never tells in advance, and when it does it is too late to do anything.

But wasn't everything that preceded the unpleasant the same? The monotony of grinding study at the academy, the officers' barracks, field maneuvers—and worst of all his demotion by Gen. Von Graber from field commander to a menial job, at the behest of Goering or Goebbels, for failure to pursue and drive into the sea a retreating British Brigade at Dunkirk, and later for being human to Russian prisoners. He much admired his uncle Maj. Gen. Stulpnagel, who told him: "At the front, the disciplinarian who wins battles becomes famous. Behind the lines, with all the cruelty of the riffraff, you have to be different to distinguish yourself." Should he tell his uncle about his idea what to do with the Jews? Meanwhile he must think of it as a job—an important job—even though it was a demotion to serve as Kommandant. This functionary existence behind the lines is much worse than war—all its tensions and risks without its thrills and glory. He'll have to be correct and even overlook all the cruelties. He is primarily a soldier, not concerned about its morals. As an officer of the Reich he must obey all orders from those on top.

These German books that Todt got him—presented "to David
Sokoloff—by Rachel Novor for study at Königsberg University"
—quite interesting. It's stuffy, where do you go from here?

"Herr Kommandant, is there anything else you need?" Ludke,
who moved in noiselessly while the colonel pondered, stood at
attention.

"You will place everything in order," he anticipated by habit.
"My portfolio is on a rack over there," he pointed to a double
shelf near the outside corner, "you can put the books in the
bedroom; make sure there are curtains—it's got to be presentable." As Ludke disappeared into the bedroom he called after
him, "One more thing, call Sgt. Todt."

There was movement in the hallway from the veranda. A truck
and a wagon bulging with household goods snatched at random
by "persuasive" means, as Todt and Murad described their raiding, were waiting to be unloaded. The sergeant, flustered and
puffing from shouting directives to the sweating Polish and Jewish movers, encountered Ludke on the steps of the porch. He
cupped his ear for the orderly's faint voice, in the presence of the
Kommandant.

"Sgt. Todt, my compliments for your discretion," Von Preissig
appreciated his procurement service.

"Plenty more . . . ," he said, but did not add to be gotten from
hundreds of houses, not yet inspected.

"This will do, just fine, but you could help me locate an estate,
with riding stables."

"I can get you all the horses and estates."

"What I mean is a country place where I can relax, with or
without horses."

"Yes Colonel, I get you—I heard something about an establishment, a rich landowner with a riding stable and a kennel—
real bloodhounds—for fox hunting or whatever else."

"Excellent, *sehr gut!*"

He approved the sergeant's readiness to comply with his
needs.

Von Preissig checked his wrist watch; it was three in the afternoon—long past lunchtime—and Ludwig Schwarzhund, the Gestapo Colonel, had not yet arrived. Perhaps it was a deliberate
delay on the part of the Gestapo to put a military man in his
place. While waiting he could either go over his papers or take a
nap—except there was no sofa. He forgot to ask Todt to get him

one. On the other hand, if he should go to bed in the afternoon it would seem odd. There was a rapid knocking on his door; he opened it.

"He is on his way; he stopped on the bridge or near the cemetery," Ludke announced.

"Who?"

"The Colonel from Gestapo, an inspector. . . ."

"Yes, yes, the colonel," he pretended to be casual. "Prepare cocktails for two and dinner settings for four."

The minute that Ludke was out of the room, he could not restrain his anxiety as he tried to identify through the partly open window the bursting roar of a motorcyclist and then the passenger car coming into view near the Brick Synagogue. The staff car and the motorcycle came to a sudden stop in the yard. Von Preissig now hurried back to his desk, made last minute adjustments of his impeccable uniform and waited for the Gestapo colonel. The inspector entered, walked straight toward the Kommandant, who stepped forward from behind the desk to exchange salutes. Although the colonel half bowed and smiled, Von Preissig could discern that it was mechanical and rigid like his angular face. There was something about him, the fine clustered veins in his cloudy eye corners, that told of frequented ports, on an aimless journey.

"Shall we drink?" Von Preissig put him at ease as he sensed the colonel's roving eyes trying to size him up by his minutest gestures.

"Heil Hitler!" he made an effort to down the glass.

"Heil Hitler!" Von Preissig obliged in a monotone and added, "to victory—*sieg heil.*"

"*Ach mein Herr, das ist unzer granzen leben,*" he responded and then abruptly, "*nein, nein,*" when offered a second glass. Simply fantastic—our victorious army—and do you know why it is so? Because the people and the Reichstag gave my Führer power. From that time on—fantastic military conquests.

"So far."

"So far?" The inspector was taken aback, "This will go on. It is paving the road for the right moves in the right directions—the final conquest. Did you get the latest news?"

"Not yet, the short wave radio has not arrived yet. The sergeant who is a good mechanic is fixing up a local radio for me."

"Then you can't know how well we're doing. Everything going according to plan."

Von Preissig studied the inspector's rehearsed gestures. It was not the language of a military man, or the appraisal of an historian, but rather that of one who threw around phrases and terms he picked up in the company of the Nazi crowd. For the first time he saw himself almost parroting the same undercover of detached professionalism.

"*Ja, ja,*" he grudgingly agreed.

"Do you have any doubt?" the inspector was amazed.

"Not exactly—it depends."

"What is it that you doubt: Germany, the Führer, our victories?"

"None at all."

Col. Ludwig Schwarzhund listened intently as Von Preissig spoke of the progress of the war. Was Von Preissig really candid and outspoken? He detected quite a few deceptive phrases. Was the Kommandant perhaps setting up a trap for him, the Gestapo agent? Who knows? They told him to keep an eye on the Kommandant, but a trap can also be set against the trapper. "It is something else if we analyze it from a different angle," is how it sounded. One moment he heard Von Preissig say "The Fuhrer justly denounced," but before that was another moment —was it a slip? "Germany mounted a violent propaganda campaign." Does he listen to the B.B.C. broadcasts? Has no radio— maybe he's got a hidden radio. He would find out eventually. Has he got a connection with somebody among the higher ups— he is too brazen even for a Junker, unless. . . .

"Are you related to Goering?" he asked him.

"Certainly not," he was emphatic, "besides I am so thin." Both exchanged glances but kept the humor to themselves.

"Are you from Prussia?"

"No, no—the name? Way back there may have been a Prussian in our family. In fact there was a mutual ancestor for the Hindenburgs and the Von Preissigs. But our family for many generations had its roots in Bavaria. I was born in Heidelberg. It is famous for its climate, people and culture."

"A university town, eh, the student prince operetta locale, not far from Munich," he stressed his own association with the name.

"Yes, but . . . ," Von Preissig rejected the comparison, it was not the same image that they shared of the city; the reference to

Munich was particularly disconcerting. Was Heidelberg a good neighbor of Munich or Munich a bad neighbor of Heidelberg? They were interrupted by Sgt. Todt who began to tinker with a radio in the front office, with the door opened as an invitation to approve his mechanical know how.

"Very good, a Polish name but of German manufacture," Col. Schwarzhund who inspected it remarked.

"What is the range?" Von Preissig asked.

"Within range of our victorious army, let's listen!" The inspector tuned it to the Propaganda Ministry station that was now blaring throughout occupied Europe and beyond.

"Tuesday, June 24th, 4 P.M."

"Our conquering German forces will save Europe and the world from the Bolshevist clutches . . . The Spanish Falangist paper 'Ariba' declared yesterday that the exorbitant spending by the Red Cross for food and medicine, for so-called refugees, is a Masonic Jewish and Liberal plot . . . Brest Litovsk has been occupied . . . mopping up at Grodno and Bialystock . . . 5000 prisoners and 300 planes destroyed . . . Alfred Rosenberg expressed view that the world should welcome attack on Russia . . . Raids by British planes repulsed over Hamburg, Bremen, Coblenz, Frankfort, Stuttgart, Magdeburg and Kreutzbach . . ."

"Isn't this wonderful?" Col. Schwarzhund said. "Can we get a station from Switzerland, sergeant?"

"I'll try. Very faint signals from Berne."

"Turn on full power." The inspector was also eager for the latest news, even oblivious to the source. There was whining and crackling until the hoarse sounding voice came across with clarity.

"Russian army of over 600,000 around Minsk, totalling twenty-five infantry divisions, ten cavalry divisions and fourteen tank brigades, is retreating toward Pripet Marshes . . ."

"What does that mean, Col. Preissig?"

"If the bulk of this army with its heavy equipment," he gave an expert opinion, "did not succeed to escape behind the marshes —which I assume it didn't—it faces disaster; because our attacking army with very mobile armor moves faster than the retreating Russian army, which is by now disintegrating under the 'Blitz Krieg' tactics of the surprise attack. Now," he opened up an attache bag and unrolled a map, "if the German army will fan out around the Pripet Marshes, it will trap this entire force."

> *Even when the sword is thrust against a man's
> neck, he should pray for mercy.*
>
> Berakoth, 10.

7

BRIDAL CANOPY SNATCHED BY STORM

For almost two weeks David experienced the heartaches of romantic disaster. He survived a war, a prison camp and slave labor under three hideous regimes. But he felt crushed now that the girl he loved was lost to another man.

Meanwhile the news of German victories was shattering. The German army was a hundred miles deep into Russia. Two well equipped Russian armies were trapped between Bialystok and Minsk; they suffered 500,000 casualties. Haifa was attacked by the Italian air force. Graf Potocki got the news from his former caretaker Denikin who overheard it from the boasting Germans. Col. Schwarzhund was so sure of future victories that he asked Todt to install a short wave radio at Potocki's former mansion where he and his aides gathered to hunt and celebrate.

One news item however, seemed like a miracle. Potocki sent word with Clara that a snowstorm was impeding the Nazi advance toward Lwow. A snowstorm in July? God was still around. Maybe his bad luck with Rachel would change. How? He was never a good loser in soccer games and he certainly would not concede victory to Zechariah. It was a painful thing for him to wish Rachel *mazel tov* on the eve of her marriage the following day, on Saturday night. But to show he was a sore loser would seem even worse. Come what may he'll see Rachel.

Sarah Beile was excited and almost cried as she saw David. She was in the midst of preparing for the Sabbath. Rachel's little brother and sister, the twins Leishke and fair-haired Lea, wrapped themselves in the curtain over the entrance to the kitchen, and their curious eyes peeped out. Avreml ventured to cross the threshold, but retreated quickly when Rachel first glanced at her brother reprovingly and turned around to greet David.

"Come in!" she said, somewhat flustered.

"I——came, to wish you happiness. . . ." He didn't know what else to say.

"Thank you, thank you, David . . . I just don't know. I hope it is for the best."

"Yes," he said.

"It was not easy——I mean, to make a decision."

"Yes, I understand, but why did you do it?"

"There was no other way." She began to sob. "We haven't heard or received money from father since 1939. Who is going to feed my mother and her four children? You went away to study and never said anything. You were drafted by the Polish army. And never a word. How long were you gone—a year, two years, a lifetime——and never a line for me? I lost track of the time. You were captured, you escaped, you worked under the Russians, you never sent a letter, David." He was silent. "David, why didn't you write to me?"

"Letters, at such a time?"

"Didn't you send letters to your parents?"

"No. You can't imagine what it means to be working for the Russians. It was worse than slavery. Every one is a slave in Russia, and the Jews are worse off than any other nationality. I missed my family and you, I escaped."

"David, if . . ." Rachel tried to say something. Then she turned away from him, sorry but unable to change anything.

"Rachel all these years I've been thinking only of you. When I was recalled from the University almost two years ago and mobilized I had no time even to say good bye to you. Then came the German invasion. We were on the run day and night for two weeks. We were without artillery support. We were bombed and strafed continually. Men dropped like flies. The dead were unburied and the wounded were unattended. We were surrounded and taken prisoner.

"Jewish soldiers were separated from their Polish comrades. Some were shot on the spot. I and others were herded into a barbed wire enclosure without food or water. Every day scores were taken out into the woods and shot. I and two others escaped. After two days of wandering I came across Potocki who was badly wounded in the back. He joined us and at night we crossed into Russian occupied Agustowa.

"The Russians sent us to Grodno. Potocki was released immediately and the rest of us were locked up. Did Potocki report this to my parents?"

"He just told them you were a prisoner of war."

"It was better. I was really a civilian prisoner in Russian hands which meant they could have sent me away to any part in Russia or even Siberia. Not many came back in good health from such incarceration. I vowed that if I would survive and return. . . . I love you."

"Oh, David, why didn't you tell me? I mean how you felt about me . . . ?"

"I had nothing to offer you——not knowing what the next day would bring. I could not stop. . . ."

"Stop what?"

"Stop everything and think only of us. It would be like setting up a bridal canopy in the midst of a storm. I could never face my *chaverim*, who have given up so much."

"David, you and all of us have been in love with Zion for a long time. But our love was young, and it was cut off. Now it is too late."

"Don't ever say it again. It is never too late."

"I made a promise."

"You had no right to. I mean it was ordained in heaven before we were born, that only the two of us. . . ."

"How can you be so sure?" Rachel began to cry.

"One mistake and we are separated. Don't we forgive? Don't we repent and declare a new year? Why can't we start all over again?"

"We can't. There is no other way."

For a long eternity David stood there. He rubbed his forehead, and stared off into space. He must have been selfish not to have known Rachel's predicament. Her mother began to sell her jewels to keep alive. What else was there to sell: the broken furniture—the last few copper pots hidden away from the Russians and the Germans? The three growing children went to sleep hungry. His mother left food at Rachel's door. But it was not enough. His own family was impoverished. The Poles ruined his father's textile business. The Russians confiscated most of it and the Germans took away what was left.

Why, why? he thought, is there no other way? Why must one always accept doom in such a sudden and humiliating manner?

He didn't know which blow was greater, Rachel's inevitable marriage or the threat of the Nazis.

They stood there, trying not to read in each other's eyes the truth that each could no longer hide from the other. Voices from behind the front door preceded the well-wishers who suddenly overwhelmed them. It was no longer a secret: that Rachel, with whom David was in love, was now engaged to Zechariah, the son of the rich dairyman.

The room was now full of young people, especially giggling and blushing girls who released their emotions strained by the war. They looked forward to the wedding tomorrow night after the conclusion of the Sabbath. David was in their midst and yet completely detached. David suddenly turned away and walked through the doorway on the way out.

From the doorway came the jarring thud of spurred boots. More steps scraped against the threshold. Two soldiers with fixed bayonets stationed themselves inside the doorway. They saluted smartly from either side as an officer, followed by aides, passed between them.

He was resplendent in the uniform that covered his slender body. He wore cavalry breeches tucked neatly into polished boots. A silver winged insignia flashed across the crested crown of his garrison cap. The lacquered visor tilted rakishly over small caustic eyes. He stopped in front of the *bimah* and spoke in low tones to the sexton. The sexton, who guided the lines of the scroll with a silver hand, whispered something to Ber Leib, the reader. Ber Leib, after a quick glance in the direction of Rabbi Kalir, continued the reading.

The sexton led Von Preissig straight to Rabbi Kalir. The officer motioned to him to remain seated when he saw the Rabbi rising to greet him. The Rabbi extended his hand, the German grudgingly gave him his gloved hand. After a brief exchange, the Rabbi pointed his finger. The officer saluted Rabbi Kalir, then turned his clanking steps toward the opposite corner. He sat down near David.

It was evident from the officer's relaxed response to David's fluent German that he knew quite a good deal about him. It was the policy of the German administrative units of every occupied city and town to to assemble a dossier of "special personnel." This category included men of wealth, professionals, organizers, merchants, suspected communists, former soldiers, beautiful girls and intellectuals. The Gestapo had long ago laid down the law that anyone learned, gifted, healthy, and able was a potential enemy. If he could temporarily be useful or exploited, his liquidation would be deferred. For eventually all the Jews would be doomed.

The reading of the Torah was almost concluded. Von Preissig, who inquired about David's university education, suddenly stood up and whirled his hand. A soldier, carrying a camera mounted on tripod, responded. It was quickly adjusted. He began to turn the handle just as two worshippers were summoned by the *gabai*—one to lift up the Torah, *"hagbah,"* and then sit down holding it, and the other to roll together the scroll, fasten it, and slip on its maroon velvet jacket, *"gelilah."*

"Fortsetzen sie das gebet," Von Preissig ordered, aware that Jews had a fair understanding of German. At his direction, the focus of the camera was trained on himself and then on the Torah being carried to the ark, and finally at the swaying and bowing Jews draped in white and black striped shawls.

Von Preissig had no qualms about this intrusion into the sacred privacy of the Jews. It was "mild" in comparison to what others were doing. At least he was not one of those "S.S. rogues dressed in black to fit their acts," in the words of his uncle General von Stulpnagel.

The service was now at an end. *"Bitte zich zu melden morgen,"* he turned to David, who resented the brusque episode. David was also suspicious of the *"bitte"* (please) preceding the command "report tomorrow."

At the Sabbath meal, David could not lift his voice to sing Grace. Somewhere in the rye fields he sought to find the spirit of the song which had abandoned him. He paced hurriedly through his garden, alongside the massive wall of the synagogue. He climbed over the fence and he was shoulder high in the midst of rolling, glistening soft waves of golden rye. To his left was the dirt track that bypassed the town on the way to the woods beyond the bridge. It was near but too exposed to the prying eyes of German and Polish police.

It was so quiet that he could hear the creaking wheels of a wagon churning the rutted road someplace alongside the river to the north. Ahead, a peasant's figure, bowed down by a sack, plodded toward the windmills, which were at rest on this Sabbath day. As David passed in front of him, he noticed that the peasant was barefoot, his boots slung over his shoulder. A crow took off, flopping his wings and sounding the alarm with long caws.

He was now beyond the mills, where the sandy road led into the big forest. First came the stumps on the parapet, then the young saplings, and finally the tall, aged pines and firs forming canopies of green over his head. After a short distance, the sun broke through again in a clearing. It was the oval-shaped meadow. Its daisy-sprinkled grass was walled off by the dark tree trunks. David sat down, and after trying out several reclining positions, fell asleep.

Some young people strolled singly or in pairs to the meadow. Zionist and religious clubs convened there from Sabbath to Sabbath in this enchanting forum. What could be more fitting for this hallowed day than a domed sky above, emerald carpeting below, towering walls of pined banners encircling from all sides, the elusive echoes of joyful birds, and innocent chatter magnetized by laughter?

David was awakened by the sound of voices of a group coming toward him. He eyed them glassily until they became familiar. Chantze Abchik's, willowy and pert, waved at him with a rolled-up pamphlet. Abba Dunsky blinked through his glasses. In Chantze's presence, he always withdrew into a mental tent from which he was ready to burst out at the merest call. Shmuel Leiser (the mechanic who preferred to be an unpaid librarian) was, as ever, ready to join any discussion or any action. Israel Grodzensky, the revisionist-Zionist, scanned the slanting rays from the southwest as they picked off the steady stream of young people converging on the meadow. If the Germans would make a surprise raid, there would be only two directions open for escape —deep into the forest east or south. He always planned ahead, concerned and alarmed.

"I have something good to read," Chantze said, turning around until her glance rested on Abba's pale face.

"Yes, it's the best thing for us," David, fully awakened, added.

"Is it classical or modern?" Abba inquired, with the pedagogue's curiosity.

"It is Bialik," Chantze unrolled the soft-covered "Anthology of Hebrew Poetry."

"Bialik is both," Israel projected his voice.

"Read it, Abba." She handed it to him. He read:

> Let me walk upon the fields
> To hear the voice of G-d,
> Humbly I behold the glorious rye field,
> My hands did not toil
> To cultivate your seedlings,
> I did not give you my strength
> Nor will I bind your sheaves.

Abba raised his head, to await the effect of the last key line. "Chantze, please help me finish it," Abba pleaded and handed her the opened book.

"David, you always read for us. Continue from this line." She pointed. He was distracted by the sight of Rachel perched on a low saddle trunk and leaning against Zechariah in front of her. He did not expect to find the two on the very eve of their marriage at this Sabbath rendezvous.

"Yes, yes. What shall I read?" he recovered.

She smiled benevolently as she traced his stare, and patiently prompted him to continue.

"Yet you are precious to me." He stopped, the page slipped from his fingers. Momentarily he lost the place. Chantze flushed and, concerned with the secret she now shared with him, turned the page for him. This time his voice was strong and even.

> Yet you are precious to me.
> So many times precious to me.
> For you bring back to me
> My far away brethren
> Who toil in the land of our fathers,
> And raise their voices from the hilltop
> In response to my heart's blessing.

"Good, very good!" voices of approval came from everyone.

"Bialik is a great poet—but I like the new novels from Eretz Israel," Chantze stirred the dispute.

"If not for Bialik and other Hebrew poets, there would be no novels," Abba rebuked her.

"This is not one of those novels?" David pointed to a thin pamphlet which her closed hand tucked under her balloon sleeve.

"Oh, no, this is different. Label asked me to read it for an opinion."

David put out his hand and Chantze hesitated as she handed

him the yellowed folder. He read the title out loud, " 'The Communist Manifesto' by Karl Marx. Get rid of it!"

"It is not safe. Why look for trouble?" Abba pleaded.

"What trouble? Do you think these Germans care about manifestos? They want land, whole countries, maybe the entire world, and all its people as slaves," Chantze was nettled.

"What you say is true, but why blow a trumpet if it will arouse the snake from his lair?" David spoke quietly.

"Don't suspect me of being a communist. I want to find out for myself."

"There is nothing to find out!"

"How about you? Aren't you? And aren't the Germans trying to find out something from you?"

It came like a bolt; David was rankled by its suddenness.

"I don't know what they want from me."

"Are you going to the wedding tonight? Do you think it will . . . ?" Chantze didn't finish.

"I don't know. I hope nothing happens."

"What do you mean?"

"I don't know. I wish her the best of luck . . .", his voice trailed off.

David was now swelled with anger, but he was glad that in the presence of all it looked more like a personal exchange. For he felt that it would serve no purpose to incite them and himself with impending crises.

The meadow was now like a beehive. The flower of Suha-Vali youth was now on its shaded turf. Some were whispering or laughing in couples or in groups. Others just enjoyed the serenity of the Sabbath and the open sky.

Birds began to settle down for the night. Broods in their nests were snug and ready for slumber under the winged warmth of their mothers. Crows sent out their last frantic calls for their tardy scouts to return to their colonies, perched on the trees. David with hesitant steps walked home alone.

The sun began to dip below the peaked windmills. Long bands of shadows lanced through the latticed frames of the windwheels. Everyone lingered for one more speechless stroll; another whisper, one more look into someone's flashing eyes; to hold a hand, to push back the night of Sabbath eve.

David could almost see the echoing prayers making contact with the winking stars. But his own prayer was adrift—he lost

Rachel. He was also concerned lest the Jews be deluded by this temporary calm. The flash of a distant light in the synagogue soon set off twinkling lights in many windows. The Sabbath would soon depart and Rachel would be married within a few hours. Darkness began to settle, first like a clear mist and then like a heavy veil over the fields and roofs of Suha-Vali.

"Russia defies Hitler. He can never win the war. . . . Vice Commissar of Foreign Affairs, S. A. Lazovsky, declared Russia could mobilize another ten million men . . ." There were steps outside.

"Anything wrong with the radio?" Todt surprised Von Preissig as he knocked and in the same instant partly opened the door.

"No, no, just static. I'll change to the other outlet. It is all right now." Todt is very considerate, Von Preissig reflected. Still, one has to be careful, even if it isn't Messer or Schrecke or even Ludke, and maybe Ratten. Ludke particularly hangs around the door and glides in like a ghost. Ratten is just a cook, and Todt is a mechanic. Both are good and simple. But aren't many of the uniformed Germans good and simple, yet doing dishonorable things? Both are in uniform and, like the rest, are not above suspicion.

"Hitler cannot win . . ." Von Preissig flung his hand toward the radio and changed the station, as the door opened.

"Great news," Colonel Schwarzhund bounced in with hearty greetings in preparation for tomorrow's excursion to the Potocki estate.

"Yes, yes, the German army is deep in Russia," Von Preissig casually remarked.

"Do you think this is all true?" Then, after listening awhile, he asked, "What's this, a Russian speaking German, Lazovsky? Must be a Jew!"

"What's the difference, let's hear it."

"Capture of each Russian city weakens instead of strengthens the Germans."

"A Russian joke, eh?" Schwarzhund scoffed at the very thought of listening to enemy propaganda.

"As a military man, how do you assess it?"

"I don't."

"Why?"

"I am not in command or authority."

"Suppose you were."

"I don't speculate."

"You have an opinion."

"I do, only in a non-official capacity," Von Preissig said.

"We are winning the war against Russia, isn't it so?"

"Not quite. We are defeating the Russian army, not its people. Right now, I have it from reliable sources that the military is implementing a novel plan. General Vlassov, a captive Russian general who defected, has been entrusted with the task of recruiting an army from among the military prisoners and defectors."

"Russians fighting Russians?"

"No, Russian units are going over to our side and fighting alongside our army because we promised to liberate them from oppressive communism and not to take over as new taskmasters."

"Do you think we'll succeed?"

"No."

"Why?"

"Because we are getting some negative results—*natürliche fortsetzungen.*" He was cautious to avoid saying "We are reaping the harvest from our provocations."

"What?"

"Don't you know about the scorched earth policy of the victims?"

"Why, why are Russians doing it?"

"Desperation. When word gets through that our army hangs and starves civilians and prisoners alike, they destroy everything in the path of our soldiers, and even fight when encircled."

"But we—they—are doing it only to Jews."

"The more Jews killed, the more atrocities. And there is no guarantee that Russians, Poles and others will be spared. All these things turn the neutrals against us. Do you want to listen to news?" Von Preissig casually asked him. Colonel Schwarzhund nodded, then turned on the same station from Berne, which a while ago the Kommandant had turned off as a precaution.

"Russia is sure of America coming in. . . ."

"That's bad," Von Preissig said.

"Lies, lies and more lies," Colonel Schwarzhund's anger vexed him to the point of explosion as he cut off the broadcast with a nervous snap.

"Herr Kommandant," Colonel Schwarzhund changed his tone.

"Captain Messer tells me about permission you granted for a wedding."

"Yes."

"Isn't it strange, to allow them to worship, promenade in streets, fields and now have a wedding?"

"Jews are strange beings—optimists."

"I mean for us to grant them permission."

"I have permission from the highest authorities to keep things normal, up to a point. I intend to have the wedding filmed."

"To study them?" the inspector sneered.

"To know them and use them."

"What is there to know about them?"

"Bayonets can never secure our victories. Think of the scorched earth policy."

"You are entitled to your opinion."

"I am in charge."

"And I am to inspect and advise," Colonel Schwarzhund reminded Von Priessig of the Colonel's backing by the Gestapo. "I instructed Captain Messer not to let it get out of hand, and to remind the Jews of our presence. Do you object if we also invite the Polish Police?"

"No." There was very little he could do to prevent it at this point.

The courtyard of the New Synagogue teemed with excitement on this Saturday night. A wedding was not an ordinary occasion in Suha-Vali. In war-time it was especially unusual. They were coming from all sides; from the fields through the rear; across the gardens from the sides; but mostly through the front.

Everyone was there—from the sage and blacksmith to the baby on her mother's arms. There were those who crowded nearer and nearer to the canopy now being readied. Maidens measured their hushed phrases. Mothers turned their eyes skyward to repel the evil eye, and fathers prayed for God's protection. Young boys were agitated and full of expectations in their darting movements and carefree shouting to one another.

Inside the synagogue, near the Holy Ark, Rabbi Kalir waited anxiously for the wedding to commence. In front of him was an open volume. It was *Sanhedrin*—all about meticulous justice by the great Sanhedrin in Jerusalem. He did not know why or how it came that from all the folios on the shelf in the rear, he selected this book. But he could not concentrate. Something

roused him to apprehension. Was it David whom he saw on the
way, walking alongside Elyeh and his wife, withdrawn and
somber? No, it is something else. But he must banish all disquiet-
ing thoughts.

"You know, Koppel," he finally gave up the struggle with the
page in front of him. More faces leaned closer. "It was all pre-
destined forty days before they were born." But why did G-d
choose this year, this week, and this night, he ventured to ask,
but did not dare openly. G-d must know better, he concluded.
"G-d himself was the matchmaker," he attested.

"I would say it with reservation," Koppel Magid was dubious.
"It is a good thing that G-d is the *shadchan*, otherwise we would
continually blame friends who introduce girls to boys. Parents,
of course, would be condemned for urging their children's mis-
matched marriages, by persuading a son that a bride was more
beautiful than her face, and that a groom was a greater provider
than his earnings showed. The greatest abuse would be heaped
over the heads of the *shadchonim* for meddling into the occupation of G-d."

"The *Chasan* and *Kalah* are coming," someone shouted
through the doorway. "Bring in the *Kalah*," Rabbi Kalir relayed
to Abba, who repeated "the *Kalah*—yes, bring her in, for the
unveiling." Rabbi Kalir rose and walked to the rear of the Synagogue.

Rachel was escorted through the doorway by her mother
Sarah Beile. The teachers of the Hebrew School, Rabbi Jacob
Zaban, Abba Dunsky, and Chaim Schneider, followed. Avremel,
her brother and the twins Leishke and Lea trailed behind.

She gathered her long satin dress and sat down on the bench
in front of the long table. It was her mother's, and was oversized,
but she was proud to wear it. It soothed her and protected her
against all those strangers—the police and soldiers waiting outside.

"Where is the *Ketuba?*" the Rabbi remembered.

"I have it," Abba responded, as he unrolled it.

"Reb Koppel and Reb Jacob—you be the witnesses." While
they were signing the marriage contract, he realized that no one
had brought the glass to be shattered at the end of the ceremony.

"Avremel, run fast and get a glass—a small glass—any glass
and wrap it up in something—fast, very fast," he ordered.

"Zechariah the *Chasan*—where is he?"

Zechariah pushed his way into the ring of people surrounding the nervous but charming *Kalah*. "Cover her head with the veil," Rabbi Kalir instructed Zechariah. Like all strong and muscular men, his hand was limp and awkward as he lowered the veil over Rachel's face.

The Rabbi intoned as he blessed her:

"Our sister, be thou the mother of thousands of myriads. God make thee as Sarah, Rebecca, Rachel, and Leah. May the Lord bless thee and keep thee...."

The Rabbi, preceded by his aides, now led bride and groom from the Synagogue to the canopy outside.

"Clear the way, clear the way for our Rabbi," the sexton shouted in a hoarse voice. Reb Shepsel found his way through the flowing mass of people. Alter the carpenter kept on shouting, "Make room for the Rabbi, for *Chasan* and *Kalah*."

David was only a few paces away from the canopy. Ber Leib and Dinah Elke were in front of him. As parents, they were unaware of the pangs that seized their son on the eve of his beloved being irrevocably given unto another man. He avoided their backward glances, for his eyes would have given him away. The canopy seemed blurred. Or did he imagine it? Or did he see it in a dream? Where is the gold Star of David? It is supposed to be on the canopy. His thoughts were interrupted by ignited flaming combs thrown skyward by spirited boys. All the people had dressed themselves in their Sabbath best. Some wore threadbare and patched garments. But for the moment their hearts were full of the overwhelming rejoicing of a wedding, and there was not room for thoughts of war.

How could she—raised in the school and youth movement—find happiness with one who was so different? No, it was not right for him to be envious. He took her for granted—he hesitated, while Zechariah was ready to do anything—to help feed the entire family. David saw the canopy buffeted by a gentle breeze. He recognized the Star of David.

Girls screamed every time a flaming comb came down in a trail of sparks and smoke. The resinous odor was cleared by the ever-increasing wind. Clouds began to snuff out some stars above.

Friends and families were now stationed around the canopy. "The glass," Rabbi Kalir whispered and everyone turned around. "The wine in the cup?" The sexton nodded his head.

Dinah Elke pushed forward to greet Sarah Beile and Rachel. She wanted to cry now, so that she could smile later. Sarah Beile deserved *nachas*. She had to support a hungry brood by herself. "David, David," she sighed, "—Rachel. If God will some day grant him one like Rachel."

Two fiddlers and a flutist approached. Young faces beamed and a few elders frowned. "War time! Not now!" their voices rumbled. "A wedding is a wedding," Rabbi Shepsel Kalir ruled, with an authentic gesture of his hands, uplifted in the manner of the priestly blessing. He followed it up by directing them with a graceful bow to proceed with a wedding march. G-d bless all who came to gladden the bridegroom and bride, he said to himself.

"Call out the *Chasan* and the *Kalah*," he pointed his finger at Abba. Somebody whispered to him that Gendarmes and Polish police led by Skura, and rowdies armed with clubs had arrived. Where was Avremel with the glass? "Who has the ring?" he called out loudly. "Oh yes, it is in my vest pocket," he said.

Abba led the procession of the Chasan Zechariah Handler and his parents. They were pressing from all sides, as if alerted by an oncoming storm. "A groom is like a king," Koppel Magid exhorted them. "Make way for him and his bride." Zechariah's face was perspiring and his pale features were drawn together, pinched with hunger; he had fasted. At last he shoved his way through the crowd and stood facing Rabbi Kalir on his right.

He was greeted with *Baruch Haba* (may he who cometh be blessed) and then the Rabbi, his voice attuned to a higher pitch, sang

> He who is supremely mighty.
> He who is supremely praised.
> May He bless this bridegroom and bride.

All eyes now turned toward Rachel. They strained forward to behold her radiant form weaving her way gracefully through the crowd. Some were delighted, others were amazed. There were those who thought she was an angel descended into the world; others were indifferent—but all wished her well. For it is written: those who partake in the rejoicings of a *Chasan* and *Kalah* dedicate a holy sanctuary unto God. But also present were the unsympathetic piercing eyes, of the uniformed soldiers, astigmatic with images of lust and demolition.

Rachel, her face absorbing all the candlelight, stepped up softly on the right of Zechariah, whose face showed the strain of the delay. At last, Avremel, pushing through the crowd, held aloft a glass and waved it.

Rabbi Kalir acknowledged his signal with a nod, and lifted the cup of wine to recite the betrothal benedictions. There was a silence as he blessed the wine. The stars above blinked in unison. Scattered clouds feebly challenged them from below. A gust of wind lifted the canopy, but the youth leaders, who were given the honor of holding the poles of the canopy, steadied it. Two cursing Germans knocked down people as they pushed nearer.

Rabbi Kalir raised his sonorous voice under the great canopy of the deep blue sky. "King of the universe," he intoned. Every word became an angel, every tone a cherub in swift flight, heralds to the domed throne of the Almighty.

". . . And hast commanded us concerning forbidden love." A strange murmur came from somewhere. "And hast allowed us only those married through solemnized betrothal." Skura began to shove forward.

"Blessed be thou O Lord who sanctifiest thy people Israel through solemnized betrothal." Israel Grodzensky, who held one of the poles, gesticulated in the direction of the Polish auxiliary police, straining to get nearer.

Rabbi Kalir held the cup firmly as he located the ring in his vest with his left hand. He moved the cup first to Zechariah, who swallowed a mouthful, and then to Rachel, who took one sip. Rachel's eyes stared wistfully through the sheer veil. The color of the red velvet canopy was reflected on her face. Zechariah, rigid and tense, took the ring and began to repeat after the Rabbi, "Behold, thou art betrothed to me with this ring, in accordance with the law of Moses and Israel." Zechariah began to place the ring on the forefinger of her right hand. Suddenly Skura, the leader of the Polish police, came up to Israel Grodzensky and punched him in the mouth. Israel lashed back at him. A raging peasant moved toward Rabbi Kalir, but Alter Stoliar knocked him to the ground with one blow. Skura and a German began to pull Rachel. Zechariah fell to the ground with the German soldier, while David exchanged blow for blow. More Germans and Polish rowdies joined what started as a fracas but now began to take on the appearance of a pogrom.

Alter the carpenter tried vainly, with the help of David and

the men around, Reb Koppel and Hershke the miller, to hold
back the onrushing wave. Two Germans now rushed up to Israel,
who was standing over the fallen and bleeding Skura, and began
to batter him with the butts of their guns.

The burly Captain Messer, his hands clasped behind his
back, calmly observed the momentum of swirling fury from the
steps of the Synagogue. But his aide, Lieutenant Schrecke, uneasily shifted his bony frame. He smelled violence and was excited by imminent action. The Captain preferred the neat job
that the brown shirts performed back home with lead pipes and
rubber truncheons.

"A Jew hit me," a Polish hooligan screamed, as he lunged
forward and fell in front of the canopy.

"Help, help," he called hoarsely. His cry was picked up and
relayed by frenzied voices in the rear, "The Jews are killing one
of ours." In an instant a flying wedge of hoodlums rushed
through an opening made by the club-wielding police. They
knocked down every one in their path, chanting "Kill the Jews."

The shafts of the canopy wavered from the massed pressure
around them. Rachel, Zechariah, and the Rabbi were pushed
back. Momentarily the Jewish guard closed the gap, but German
soldiers led by Lieutenant Schrecke broke up the resistance, hit-
ting and punching young and old, men and women.

The mob now overwhelmed the bridal canopy from all sides.
They snatched the velvet coverlet from its felled shafts and flung
it over the heads of the people. A strong draft caught it, flapping
it downward, and then lifting it soaring into the star-lit blue
beyond.

Rachel, who had fainted, was revived by David and Zechariah. They fought off German soldiers who were attempting to
drag her away, but before long David was surrounded and
beaten mercilessly until he collapsed. Zechariah, bleeding profusely, was dragged away with two uniformed thugs twisting his
arms behind him, and a third choking his neck with a strangle-
hold. Meanwhile, Burka Mazik, the horse dealer, and Zorach,
son of Alter the carpenter, crept through the picket fence surrounding Rachel's garden, which adjoined the synagogue. David,
in bad shape, crawled behind them. Lieutenant Schrecke began
to shout orders, but the situation had gotten out of hand. He
fired point-blank into the crowd. Those who were trapped in the
courtyard surged to get away.

David saw an opportunity to save Rachel when her captors turned away from her unconscious form to hear instructions from the Captain. While Zorach screamed eerily in the dark, and Burka Mazik engaged a hoodlum to distract attention, David carried Rachel away. He made his way through the thick growth of the potato gardens. She came to and moaned, "Zechariah, Zechariah." Lest he be pursued, he put her limp body down in a quiet corner of Zechariah's big garden.

More armed men, mostly from the local recuits, began to carry out instructions from Captain Messer, who now was in full control. He now began to rub his twitching little finger, but it felt numb. He barked commands, cursing in undertones because the whole mess dragged on too long.

"*Verfluchte Juden*," he shouted angrily. "Take away this swine," he pointed to Israel, who tangled with a Pole. "He'll be shot like a dog any day."

"Why, why?" Rabbi Kalir and Reb Koppel began to plead. They were joined by David, who now returned and demanded, "By what right do you do this? We have permission from the Kommandant."

"Take them away too. Arrest all these swine who resist our Glorious Führer and Reich."

"Disperse. One, two, *geschwind, eraus!* No assemblies. No weddings. Punishment for all of you!"

*The sword and the Book came down from
heaven wrapped as one. God warned mankind
if you observe the Torah, you will be saved
from the sword.*

Leviticus Rabah, 35.

8

THE SWORD VERSUS THE BOOK

It was before dawn three days later when David's painful, unconscious slumber came to an end. His fingers reassured him that neither his nose nor any other part of his body had been broken or fractured. He felt lumps and swellings on his face and legs. Who else was in this dark and dank barn behind the police station of the military headquarters.

Abba touched his hand. Without his glasses and with a blackened eye, the teacher seemed at a loss to recognize him in the dark. "David, David. "It's me, Abba." He could hardly raise his voice.

"You are not hurt, are you Abba. No? Thank God. But Burka needs help. He is soaked in blood."

They found Burka propped up against the wall. "It's nothing, David. It's nothing, believe me."

"Who else is here?" David asked in a whisper. They heard steps. A guard leaned close against the wall. With the butt of his rifle, he called them to attention. *"Donnerwetter!"* he commanded. "No more talking."

The uneasy sleep of the arrested was disturbed by a fierce looking SS man, whom David recognized as Captain Messer. He pointed his revolver menacingly and screamed, *"Auf, auf, Schweinhund."* When his words drew no response from the half-drowsy and terrified people, he sank his boots into the spent, helpless bodies stretched on the floor. *"Zum Kommandant,"* he shouted and within a few moments all of them stood in the office of Johann Kristus von Preissig.

For a moment David thought himself in another office, a provincial but very German office. On the wall, between the two
windows, was an oil painting of three figures. He recognized
only the central one, which resembled Frederick the Great. It
was flanked by a recent war photo and a World War I group
picture. The last one was dominated by an officer wearing a
sword, epaulets and spiked helmet; the soldiers behind him were
standing, the ones on either side were kneeling and two in front
were stretched out with a water-jacketed machine gun.

A runner on the red-painted floor led to an improvised desk,
behind which sat Johann Kristus von Preissig. He was adjusting
a cigarette in a gilded holder. He struck a match, drew the
smoke passionately, and then released it, letting the smoke curl
upward against the painted trilogy on the wall behind him.

It was familiar and yet strange and unnatural in that singular
frame. After a long draw, and a cough, Von Preissig placed the
holder in a cylinder. He casually turned to the corpulent Messer.
"Are these all the accused, Captain?"

"*Jawohl*, except two who were taken to the clinic." He almost
jumped to attention and bowed.

"Rabiner Shabsi Shepsel Kalir!" Von Preissig read from a
paper. "You are accused of stirring up the population to disorder.
Was sagen Sie?" Von Preissig coldly fixed his eyes on the patriarchal figure, and ancient hatreds within him began to detonate.

"God is my witness. I only performed my duty. We—I mean
the whole community—are loyal and peaceful citizens."

"God is not a witness; the witnesses are soldiers and representatives of the Third Reich. As for your religious duties and
peaceful intentions, that is questionable."

"But Herr Kommandant, it was only a wedding."

"A wedding is what I expected; but it turned into a riot." Von
Preissig pointed his cigarette holder like a king pointing a
scepter.

"Herr Kommandant," Rabbi Kalir pleaded. "God bid us, it is
written in the Torah, the Holy Scriptures, which you also, as a
Christian, hold sacred."

Von Preissig enjoyed his role as interrogator and prosecutor
more than the actual questions asked and answers given. "You
may go on, but—" He shook the ashes and flipped his wrist,
implying that none of Rabbi Kalir's arguments would change the
present situation of the Jews in Suha-Vali.

"We are—we Jews have lived in peace for hundreds of years in Suha-Vali. We respect our neighbors and they respect us. With a few exceptions there was never any bad blood between us. God is our witness."

"Leave God out," he commanded the Rabbi, whose train of thought was now jarred.

"Zechariah is a man of peace. He is honest and hard-working and pious. I can vouch for him. His bride is pure and kind and innocent. Her father is in America. Her mother, cut off from his support, has to provide her four children with food and minimum necessities. What else could I do? I had to sanctify the marriage. It is a holy union—we Jews have practiced it for thousands of years. It is the basis of civilization, the solemn union of two in wedlock. Our rabbis tell us that God himself blesses every marriage."

"That's enough! I am not concerned with religion, or the history of marriage, but with an act of military violation. I have come here to establish order in the name of the Führer. Anyone who dares to question or defy it must suffer the consequences. We Germans are impatient with *Schweinerei*. Keep them under arrest until further orders," he commanded the guards.

"You!" Von Preissig suddenly pointed his finger at David as he was leaving. "You failed to keep the appointment."

"It was impossible, since I, as you see was under arrest."

"That's exactly my point. An appointment means preparation and discipline. If you were properly trained, you would not have been involved in acts of treachery."

"But Herr Kommandant," David protested. "It was a wedding, a religious ceremony. No hostile act was involved."

"You Jews survived under other regimes because, being weak, they tolerated you. We are strong and do not have to resort to the morality of the weak. We are here for the next thousand years to purge this world of nationalities. There is room for one master nation only, the Germans. All other nations will be given the choice: to qualify by generations of servitude as Folk Germans or to perish. We will rid this world of our greatest enemy and obstacle—the Jews." Von Preissig's thin lips were now drawn tight as his personality adapted itself to his tirade. "You will not crucify me," he shouted with venom. "I will crucify you!"

"Do you still want me?" David asked the morose Kommandant

who stared downward mumbling incoherently. Without lifting
his head he said, "Get out! All of you get out! Guards, throw
them out," he screamed. "We can arrest them any time."

The summer rain saturated the gardens and orchards of Suha-
Vali. Hershke the miller looked out through his back window.
Droplets of water were suspended like pearls from the glistening
leaves. The old apple tree was proud, for its blossoms had borne
fruit, and tiny apples cuddled close to their stems. They withstood the heavy downpour and summer storms. They were
secure in their clustered togetherness and would soon ripen into
the first fruits of still another summer.

The plums were firm, and looked like purple heads nailed to
every plum tree. The tender raspberry shoots pointed to their
root-like quills, recording on parchment the blessing of the early
rain. A few lonely surviving cherries on top of the tree proclaimed the orderly transfer of the fruit crown from one species
to another. The house was exalted to be enshrined by all this
beauty.

From the front window, looking across the rye fields, he saw a
different vista: The wings of the windmill stood still, their sails
were rolled and lifeless. Rain was good for Hershke's orchard,
the gardens, and the fields, but not for his mill. Stray winds gave
life to the mill, but these same winds uprooted trees and tore
chunks of yellowed faded straw from thatched roofs.

Everything was good in its time; wind for the mill, and rain for
the fields. As for himself, he had to work hard and to be patient
with God's winds and rains.

Hershke thought nothing of working alone in the windmill.
During the long winter nights, he sometimes rose at midnight,
making his way to the mill through howling winds and snow
drifts. Roaring gusts of wind spun the windwheels, which in turn
rotated the flour-grinding stone. The smell of freshly-ground
flour was good company.

But he never liked the idea of being alone with his thoughts.
Just turning over in his mind those unseen, unheard and drafty
speculations was unsafe. Motke, his son, always brought along
books. He talked about the shores, where ocean and wind are
locked in deadly combat. But then Motke was a poet, a dreamer,
not a good miller. It is unsafe to open one's self up to speculation. It was all right to pray alone because the words were fixed,
like the mill. Still, he preferred to pray in company.

There were times when he trudged straight from the mill to the synagogue. His face, reddened by the wind, would be caked with flour, from his eyebrows down to his gray-black beard. His hat and coat were powdered. Even his boots were chalked. His very appearance was a sign of good tidings—bread and work. The community respected him, and he was proud of his role. Only when he came near the learners and scholars did his proud body bow in humility.

It was now time for the evening prayer. Maybe it is unsafe to go to the synagogue? No! Hershke was never afraid of the wind or the dark nights.

He crossed the threshold of the synagogue and brought an offering—his lonely thoughts. He stood alongside David, who continued to turn pages of a Gemara. Nearby, Rabbi Shepsel Kalir rested his forehead over his right hand as he hummed softly. David still turned the pages. It was a frantic search for something forgotten; then he found the lines:

"All occupations provide security only during one's youth. In old age, one is exposed to hunger. But the Torah not only sustains one when he is young, but also gives him hope and dignity in later years."

"Very good," Hershke agreed. "What is the use of learning if you can't make a living?"

"What is the use of an occupation without Torah?" David answered. "It will lead to brigandry. A father who does not prepare his son for a useful occupation is the same as a father who prepares his son for banditry. This very day we have the best examples of occupations without Torah. Nations without Torah resort eventually to Nazism, fascism, and even communism, with all their criminal consequences."

The evening service ended, and soon the synagogue was empty. Empty, that is, except for David and Rabbi Kalir.

"You know, David," Rabbi Kalir broke the silence. "Every volume of the Talmud starts with page two. Where is page one?" Before David could answer, the heavy tread of boots resounded in the synagogue.

Two dim candle lights reflected the harsh faces and the stinging eyes of von Preissig, accompanied by gendarmes, SS men and Skura.

"Is anybody else here?" Von Preissig's shrill voice bounced against the walls.

"What are these books?" von Preissig inquired.

"These are our cultural treasures, our heritage," Rabbi Kalir explained in halting German.

"Are they all ancient or modern?"

"They are timeless, like our Torah."

"What is this book—what do you call this?"

"This is a volume of the Babylonian Talmud, explaining the 613 laws of our Torah."

"Babylonian?" Von Preissig was inquisitive.

"It was compiled by the editors of the Talmud in the fifth century, in Babylonia."

"What is in it?"

Rabbi Kalir hesitated as if to say, why do you ask? Is it sheer curiosity? Or is it something with an evil-savoured design?

"It is called 'Kedushin': marriage—holy marriage."

"Holy marriage!" retorted von Preissig, "quite interesting. But how could they make marriage laws fifteen hundred years ahead of their time? This is a different age and a different order and we need new laws for Jews too."

Rabbi Kalir began to explain without fear or hesitation. "Brides wear different gowns and veils. The outward style may have changed a little but the inward style is the same. We Jews live by the law of Moses. These laws are sound, beautiful and modern."

"You impudent Jew!" von Preissig suddenly erupted. "How dare you defy me? There is no law of Moses! Only the laws of the Third Reich, handed down to us by the Führer."

"Herr Kommandant," David interceded, "our Rabbi interprets the laws of the Five Books of Moses and the prophets."

"Then why do you need these big books?"

"These books of the Talmud explain the laws to which only brief reference is made in the Bible. For instance, 'an eye for an eye' does not mean to punish with blindness one who accidentally blinded another. It means compensation."

"Is it really so?" von Preissig inquired wryly. "Are you telling the truth?"

"You are free to go," he said to Rabbi Kalir. After the Rabbi left the synagogue, passing the lounging police stationed near the door, Von Preissig turned to David. He opened his mouth to say something to David, then changed his mind and turned away, to gaze at the interior of the synagogue.

David felt that this visit by von Preissig to the synagogue and his detention would only add to the suspicion of Label, that David was being taken into "their camp." It was a horrible thought.

"Would you allow me to go home first?" David pleaded.

"As long as you Jews will obey, nothing will happen. We are more interested in Jewish culture than the Jews themselves." Von Preissig now paced toward the Holy Ark and mounted the first step.

Suddenly, after some hesitancy, he mounted the second and third steps and stood before the "throne of Elijah," the symbolic chair of Elijah the prophet, who will herald the coming of the Messiah.

"What kind of a chair is this?"

"It is the throne of Elijah. He will proclaim the coming of the Messiah who will bring peace on earth."

"Why doesn't Messiah come now?"

"He can't come as long as there is suffering." David inserted his own philosophy about the coming Messiah.

"We'll put an end to your suffering—I mean the suffering of mankind. Are you sure the Messiah hasn't come yet?"

"Every religion has its own interpretation. God would certainly not send down the Messiah and then allow bloodshed to continue as before."

"The Messiah hasn't come yet? Your Elijah will come before him?"

"Yes, he will herald the Messiah."

"What kind of a man will he be?"

"It is not just the man. It could be more than one, even a whole nation."

"If it is not a man, then it is not Messiah."

"No, no. It's a man who will represent a new era or influence, a new movement, an age of peace, a world where God's commandments will prevail."

"Not a bad explanation." Suddenly losing interest in his discussion with David, Von Preissig turned to the guards at the door.

"Come on, men. We Germans have work to do. Let the Jews speculate. We shall establish order. We won't need a Messiah, but maybe we'll have a chance to dictate who he will be."

There was a distorted smile on Von Preissig's face as he fol-

lowed the men out the door. For a moment, the corner of his
mouth was twisted and cruel; then, regaining his composure, his
lips tightened, and his face again became an impenetrable
mask.

Colonel Von Preissig's first encounter with a Rabbi was a revelation. Von Preissig hated him for what he represented. At home
and in school; in books and sermons; the Jew, and even the
Rabbi, was presented in a villainous image. Yet he had moments of doubt now that he came face to face with a Jew, a
Rabbi.

His thoughts now shifted to his competitors. Ludwig Schwarzhund appeared to von Preissig as an "intrigant." Rintzler
emerged as a ruthless savage who looked and acted like Himmler.

Von Preissig removed a letter from his coat pocket, and after
lovingly and carefully examining the envelope, he finally opened
it. He read it slowly to make sure he didn't miss a dot, slant or
hyphen.

I am very proud of you, and so is my class and school. Only they
asked me questions. Isn't the front further east toward Moscow?
I explained that staff work, like ministries, are not near the
trenches. Could you send me some pictures, real pictures of action?

Is it true that a snow fell on July 4, and it caused havoc to the
enemy? How could that be? The pastor told us Sunday morning
that it is a Freudentag, because God is on our side. *Gott ist mit
uns.* Is not this the same slogan of the First World War? Was He
really with us? Mother cried when I told her about the snow and
Aunt Cathy said we can't go against God if he makes a decision.
What decision? Which God? It is all so confusing.

Heidelberg is more of a secondary school town now. All the
university students are either in the army or about to be inducted.
A few returned—they look bad. Of what good is an iron cross to
a crippled soldier? Do you think they'll need me if the war goes on
for a few more years?

For a long time he struggled not to succumb to tears—not
even one tear. An officer does not cry. There was nothing he
could do or undo.

Soon Ludke the orderly would knock on the door, and he
would be relieved of the piles of papers he had signed: draft

details—old men, young men, wood cutters, carpenters, street and stable cleaners, cow and swine herders; jobs and supervision; discipline and punishment. He thought of the refusal of the young maiden, Rachel, to work for him in the library. Jews don't seem to trust their women to non-Jews. The Jews hold women in high esteem. It seems a part of their life. What was that word? *Kedushin*—holy marriage. "We Jews live by the law of Moses," the Rabbi told him. He had learned a great deal about the Jews in the last few days, Von Preissig mused. Do the Jews really have such a great culture? Von Preissig tried to put that unwelcome thought out of his head. It is important not to become sympathetic with them, he told himself. He must be strict, aloof, German—like the rest. He must prove it.

July 11, 1941:   REICH LISTS THOUSANDS OF RUSSIAN
                  PRISONERS.

                  This is the Law when a man dieth in a tent.
                                              Numbers 19:14.
                  *The angels asked God: Is this the reward for
                  Torah?*
                                              Berakoth, 61.

9

COVENANT

Dawn came early to Israel Grodzensky that Friday morning.
After his release from jail, he was ordered to report daily for
herding ducks and geese. He remembered the order to appear
sieben uhr scharf. His mother Fradel was preparing his lunch,
two slices of bread spread with oil. Mendel, his father, was praying deliberately, while Israel hesitated as he adjusted his phylacteries: first on arm, then on head.

"Father, these are different times. We Jews spend too much
time praying," Mendel recalled his son saying. His grocery store
shelves were empty, and troubles were all around. He differed
with his son's views, but respected his convictions. Nevertheless
Mendel was concerned when word was relayed to him that
Israel made a heretical statement that the straps of the phylacteries could be put to better use as whips and weapons against
the enemy. Some even said it was outright atheism.

Israel's challenge to the opponents of militant Zionism was, "Is
there anyone in his right mind who believes that the Jews will
ever get a homeland in Eretz Israel by diplomacy or *shtadlonus*
and *krechzen.*" He had great faith in Jabotinsky's advice, "The
Jews must learn how to shoot." It was meant against the Arabs
who terrorized the Jews with Arab-style pogroms. Israel protested even against the word "pogrom." "No, not in Eretz Israel.
It can't happen there, what happened in Russia, in Poland and
now in Germany. In the Holy Land Jews will have the means to
fight." Of one thing Mendel was certain—that his son's remark

105

about the phylactery straps was not atheistic. When twenty-four
Yeshiva students were killed and mutilated with typical Arab
savagery, Israel had spoken out at the meeting of the Zionist
party, the last meeting he attended before he joined the Revisionist party. "They should have kept revolvers under the Gemaras—and if they didn't have guns, they should have fashioned
sling shots out of the phylacteries."

Mendel didn't think that Israel was impulsive, but rather that
he was very brave. "Your uniforms of the Betar group, your
militarism. How much and how far can you get with the one gun
you possess?" he told Israel, who was in uniform on the eve of a
modest field exercise.

"Father, this gun is merely the symbol of our own confidence
and strength." What his son said may have sounded too blunt,
but it expressed something that everyone believed.

Fradel came out from the kitchen still drying her fingers on
her apron. She was up very early, aroused by motherly premoni-
tions.

"Drink your tea, Israel," his mother pleaded.

"I'm full," Israel answered placidly. The drink consisted of hot
water flavored with a little milk. His sisters admiringly followed
his movements from behind the curtain that draped the entrance
to their bedroom.

Israel put away his praying shawl and phylacteries on top of
the dresser, below group pictures of his company in the Polish
army and the uniformed company of the Betar Club on district maneuvers near Bialystok. It was time to leave.

Skura and the local auxiliary police were already in the police
station's courtyard, ready to assign duties to the Jewish men.
Since it was Sunday, he wondered whether they should have
first gone to church. The priest, Anton Slovenko, rebuked the
absentee youths. "It wouldn't be correct for the Germans, some
of whom are Catholics, to see the local Catholics become transgressors of the Sabbath."

"It is too late for church," Skura told the police.

When most of the Jews had arrived Skura took command.
After lining up the group of seventy-five young boys and men, he
began to call the roll from a list, and then assigned a group of
thirty-five to take the geese to the pasture. Twenty were to clean
the stables, farms and pig pens, while the rest, including David,

were told to cut wood, mend the fences, and draw water. David
was exempt from these chores, but he thought if he volunteered
von Preissig would perhaps not force Rachel to work for him.
Also, it would impress the Jews that he sought no privileges for
himself.

The men were marched off to their respective tasks. Skura felt
relaxed as he lowered his carbine and cracked the air with his
knotted leather whip. He was particularly elated to single out
Israel Grodzensky for the pig pen. His blood rushed to his eyes
and face when he recalled how he was beaten at the wedding of
Rachel by this Jew.

While Skura schemed to get even with Israel, one of the
policemen brought back the first reports.

"They don't like this work, especially washing the pigs. I told
Grodzensky and Sokoloff that if they clean and wash the pigs,
they'll become kosher." Skura burst into a hysterical laughter.

After washing the pigs, David, Israel, the blacksmith's sons,
and seven children swept the yard, weeded the garden and piled
the manure on a wheelbarrow, dumping it in the ravine down
the slope beyond the picket fence. Germans do not raise cows on
manure bedding, Von Preissig instructed Adolph Murad, the SS
man. Once outside the barn, the manure must not become a
breeding place for flies, Von Preissig said, as he recalled his
school lessons in the Red Gymnasium. Flies breed germs and
germs bring disease and death; and Germans believe in order
and cleanliness, in order to reduce sickness and prolong life.

It was past midday, when Murad with the pock marked face
pompously blew a whistle and shouted, *"Mittag, fünfundzwan-
zig minuten für essen."* David, who was hungry, and exhausted
by the insults and the work, started to walk to the well to wash
his hands before eating. From the other side of the shed came
threatening shouts and curses.

He turned around near the fence, pretending to munch a slice
of bread. It was Israel, kneeling over a turned-over wheelbarrow
of manure. Skura, cursing and maddened by his own violence,
lashed furiously with his fists at Israel.

Now Schrecke the lieutenant and Murad rushed to the scene.
"Donnerwetter," the first addressed him, as the second followed
with the familiar, *"Verfluchter Jude!"*

Skura responded to the cue with the crack of his whip over the
lean body of Israel. Skura moved in closer and began to hit him

over his head with the handle. Israel fended off some of the
blows; and then, his eyes swollen and closed, he desperately
caught the whip in his grip and yanked it out from Skura, who
sprawled head-on over the wheelbarrow.

Now Murad threw himself at Israel and began to batter him
with a gunstock. Israel rose instinctively, but as he tried to upright the wheelbarrow he lost his grip and more manure fell to
the ground. Murad pointed to the manure. *"Mit die hent!"* He
kicked at Israel, waving away David and the children, who were
ready to clean it up.

Israel was groggy and almost out; he was hurt badly, but he
stumbled and tried pitifully to lift handfuls of dung into the
wheelbarrow. The Germans and the Polish police stood by, jeering at Israel, who wiped with his sleeve the free flow of blood
from his face. *"Geschwinder Jude!"* Murad was enraged at the
Jew's dazed movements and kicked him violently. Israel tried to
rise, and mumbled, *"Was wollen sie um Gottes nomen? Mensch-
lichkeit,"* he appealed as he thrust aside the butt of the gun that
came down upon his stomach.

Stung by this daring response of the victim, Murad leveled his
gun and aimed it at Israel, who was still talking defiantly as he
tried to stand up. The explosion from the gun hurled Israel back
to the ground, where he lay kicking until the ground absorbed his
last warmth and life.

Appalled by the crime, the detail could not move a limb until
they were driven back to work. David now saw confirmed what
he always feared: that sooner or later the Nazis' methodic plan
and thoroughness would erupt into brutality, and the day would
come when the hooked cross would unshroud itself and the ugly
death mask would grin over innocent bodies.

Baba Zippeh adjusted the blue polka dot kerchief over her
head. It set off her egg-shaped, wrinkled face against the pine
boards leaning against the wall. "Golden hands, like your father
of blessed memory," she complimented Alter. Baba was proud
indeed of her son's skill as a carpenter. She tugged her wig of
hair inside the kerchief and watched her grandson, Zorach, who
was busy marking off a piece of wood with a flat pencil. By
steadying the frame saw against his left thumb, he began to push
and pull the saw in the ever-deepening groove.

Baba Zippeh shuffled out like a whisper to her house, which

was joined to her son's house but had a lower roof and clay-covered moss in between the log spaces. Koppel Magid called it the "clay house." She was always well supplied with the gummy, red clay used for sealing the oven on Fridays, and for filling cracks in the outside walls. The rain always washed the clay down the walls in brown zigzag streaks. But inside her oven, this same clay, shaped into a variety of clay pots, performed Sabbath miracles for the table.

Baba's face was all aglow in front of the brick oven which crackled with bursting heat. It was ready to perform the weekly miracle whereby a few potatoes, beans, water and a bone would simmer overnight in these earthen bowls, transforming into a most tempting meal by the next morning.

All the pots were now in. Drops of water sizzled and exploded as the intense heat embraced the cold pots. The wooden door and the lump of clay were now in the tired but willing hands of Baba. Chaye the Good beamed as usual, except that she was a bit tense as she announced her Sabbath eve mission.

"Wait, only a second. Even the holy Sabbath is willing to wait for a Mitzvah. Let me—I'll do it for you," she pleaded with Baba. "It is Fradel's pot I recognized."

"*Oi rebonah shel olom,*" Baba sighed as she uncovered it and nodded her head sideways. She gingerly pulled out a fat-bellied pot and removed a sizable chunk of meat, which she put into Fradel's pot, and replaced it with a large potato from another pot. "May God forgive me," she said and sealed the oven door with clay.

"Baba, God is pleased, you are helping Him." She stopped for a moment in the doorway and beheld Baba standing with regal grace as she raised her hands to perform the blessing of the lit Sabbath candles. Chaye the Good left the door a wee bit open; myriads of Sabbath angels visiting Jewish homes had not missed Baba's clay house.

The candle lights stood still for a moment, then wavered as the door opened and a draft preceded Ben Zion Solomon.

"Ben Zion! God bless you. I knew you would come and not shame my table."

"Baba, God grant you more than blessings. Do you know what I am going to do? I could still make it to the synagogue. But I am going to pray in your corner. I'll even use your prayer book. This is my synagogue tonight."

"I know. I'm not worthy, and many *balei batim* would vie to
take you home, but please sit down. I have everything ready:
chalah, fish, soup and meat. Here is your chair waiting for you,
and David will join us, and maybe others."

Ben Zion, who never shunned company, now welcomed privacy. He was glad to be in this house. He remembered her husband Uri, who went around collecting money for Eretz Israel at
a time when people still frowned on collections. It came back
very vividly: Uri had asked him what to reply to those who were
full of doubt and asked, "Uri, Uri, do you think you or I will ever
see it come true in the Holy Land?" He had told Uri the story of
the sage who was planting a carob tree when passers-by stopped
him and said, "Grandfather, do you known that this tree will not
bear fruit for another seventy years, surely you don't expect to
see it ripen in your lifetime." And the old man replied, "I found a
carob tree planted, someone planted it for me and for you. I can
do no less than to plant for a future generation."

Uri had been delighted with Ben Zion's parable, and since
that day his house was open to Ben Zion whenever he came to
town in behalf of the Palestine Fund. It was more rewarding to
spend the Sabbath in Ber Leib's house or in Koppel's or at the
well-set table of Abchik Optaker, the druggist. But here Ben
Zion could recharge his thoughts; while Baba was preoccupied
with her prayer books, he could retrace his steps and plan ahead.

After Ben Zion finished the Sabbath meal, he settled back in
his chair and began singing Sabbath melodies, *zemiras*.

"Ah," Baba Zippeh sighed, "if Messiah would only come, we
would all be in the Holy Land."

"We are the Messiah. Yes, Baba, every one of us, like every
part of the earth, has a spark of God within him. We can collec-
tively bring the Messiah to earth. We can all be in Israel."

"Ben Zion, becoming lyrical, spoke feelingly, until he noticed
the tears running down Baba Zippeh's face.

"Baba! Baba! It's Sabbath, Baba! We will bring Messiah to
earth."

Then she began to wail. "Why? He was so young. He passed
by my window every Friday, but not today. I know why. He is
dead. They killed him. Israel! Israel!" The arrival of guests interrupted her outpouring of grief, and she brushed away her tears.

"Good Sabbath, Ben Zion." It was repeated successively by
Koppel, David, Abba and Shmuel Leiser, the handsome me-

chanic who devoted his executive ability to the library and the *Hachalutz,* pioneer training for Palestine.

"You have traveled a good deal," David said.

"Not much, lately. Traveling to me means in behalf of Zion— to collect funds is forbidden; to transfer funds is forbidden; the German currency on hand is almost valueless."

"Ben Zion, you are taking risks. How did you get here?" Shmuel asked.

"There are ways—even if they are fraught with danger. It is here that. . . ." He did not finish; for all his life he propagated the Zionist doctrine that the only safe refuge for the Jews is in their own homeland.

"You know, Ben Zion, I don't always agree with the Zionists. What are we to do? Just put on our coats and fly away to the Holy Land? But one thing I have to admit, you are above the ordinary fund collector and propagandist for Zion. You told us the truth, and we did not want to face it." Koppel averted the whole painful episode of the slain Israel Grodzensky and the greater catastrophe that it implied.

"We Zionists," Ben Zion spoke in a low, even voice, "always hoped to be redeemed by our timely—I repeat, by our timely return to the land of our fathers."

"David, you better tell him what is taking place," Koppel said.

"The Germans refuse to return the body of Israel to his family."

"I don't understand," Ben Zion said. "Tomorrow will be three days since he was shot."

"I don't want to, but perhaps I'd better go to Von Preissig. I am appalled even at the very thought of being in contact with Von Preissig. So far the only ones with whom he negotiates are myself and Shmuel."

"Did you say negotiate?" Ben Zion was inquisitive.

"It's not that," David said.

"How do you explain it," Koppel turned to Shmuel, "that only you two were received by him?"

"I fix radios—someone informed him; one of Skura's men I think."

"He—Von Preissig—wants me . . ." David fumbled for words. "I just don't know. It looks like he has some designs. He mentioned translations from Hebrew. I just don't know what he is up to. All I know is that he wanted Rachel to act as a sort of secretary. I volunteered in her place."

"Did you succeed?" Koppel asked.

"No."

"Very strange."

"Do you want me to get out of this?"

"No, on the contrary, stay. Find out everything you can. But remember, it is dangerous."

"What about the burial?" Abba was concerned. "It is not according to Jewish law for the remains of Israel to lie unburied in the market place."

"They have their own laws," Koppel answered.

"And their own designs," David added. "Von Preissig said, 'We don't intend to pickle the body—it will be buried officially.' "

"Officially?" Ben Zion asked.

"That is the word he used."

"What could that mean?" Koppel was concerned.

"I don't know. I'll try again tomorrow night."

"Does the Rabbi know all this?"

"I don't think so—he doesn't."

"Then we better see him at midnight; will you join me, Ben Zion? It is better that just the two of us go. The night patrols are on the lookout, especially for young men," Koppel said as he left through the rear door.

"Ben Zion." David had something on his mind. "You could have left for Israel. Why didn't you escape before it was too late?"

"To tell you the truth," Ben Zion answered slowly, "I had an opportunity to join my family and go via the underground railroad to Paris, and from there via a southern port to North Africa, and so on. It was not easy. David, you are in charge of guiding local Chalutzim to get out from here. Why didn't you escape yourself? I only wonder why I allowed my wife and children to attempt the impossible. I only pray to God that my family is safe—wherever they are. You know, I sometimes feel guilty: did I do the right thing to try to save them when there are so many others to save? You and other young men stand a better chance."

David unburdened himself. "Some of us could escape at least from this. Yes, from this slow suffocation. But we can't leave behind our people. We must stay together."

Two helmeted soldiers rounded the corner of Velvke's white-washed two-storied house. They kept step as the thud of their boots struck the cobbled stones with precision. Koppel and Ben Zion, crouching furtively on the opposite side of the square, followed with their eyes as the soldiers passed the church and went up the steps of the police station. Within seconds another pair began their night patrol. It was the change at midnight.

They turned left near the bakeshop opposite Paltiel's house and stepped into the vestibule of the Rabbi's house. Ben Zion hesitated; maybe they were intruding. The Rabbi must be worn out from all this, and perhaps he was sleeping.

"He must be up—he never goes to sleep when people need his advice. Listen," Koppel said as he pressed his ear to the door. "I can almost hear him talking—or studying out loud." They entered the anteroom and almost inaudibly politely greeted the household with "Good Sabbath," to announce their presence.

"Come in, come in!" Rabbi Kalir's voice carried from the kerosene-lit room behind the double curtain of the wide doorway. Someone came forward and parted the curtain for them to enter. It was Paltiel. At the massive table Rabbi Shepsel Kalir sat on his high-backed chair. Next to him, on his right, was Rabbi Jacob Zaban, his closest friend from the days of the Yeshiva at Wolozin.

"It is the year 5701 since the creation of the world—July 11, 1941 according to the secular calendar. Last Saturday," Rabbi Kalir continued, "we read the fourth book of Moses, *Bamidbar* (Numbers), the portion of *Chukath*. *Bamidbar* means desert; *Chukath* means law. You know the meaning of these words without my interpretation. But there is something that intrigues me—and it should enlighten you."

" 'Speak unto the Children of Israel, that they bring thee a red cow without blemish'." He quoted from *Bamidbar*.

Ben Zion marveled at his dignity, but reflected sadly that it was an anachronism to depend on mere wisdom or law, in the face of the terror that was spreading throughout Germany and its occupied countries.

"Now, this red cow, has aroused much derisive comment. Yet this red cow—has it ever harmed anyone? Did we ever try to force it upon any people? A few verses later we read, 'This is the law when a man dies in a tent.' Resh Lakish explains it thus: 'The Torah cannot be fulfilled except if one is willing to die for it.' "

"Correct, yes, yes." Jacob Zaban anticipated something more than an exegetic gem.

"But—and may God forgive me if I am a zealot for our people —is it right that one man die for the Torah, while others do nothing? Is it justice that one nation die for the Torah while others do nothing?"

Koppel Magid held his breath. He himself had been very personal with God, even questioning certain aspects, but it was his private opinion. This was the first time he had heard such a challenge from the Rabbi, a renowned authority in the rabbinate. He wondered what it was that prompted Rabbi Kalir.

"Now, I said before that *Bamidbar* means 'in the desert.' Three thousand years ago, our people wandered in the desert for forty years on the way to the Promised Land. I ask this question. Are we not here also in a desert? Don't we want to get out of this desert? Aren't our persecutors as wicked as our ancient enemies?"

Then and now vindictive enemies obstructed the victims of oppression to find refuge in the Holy Land. Then and now the Jews were plagued by fiery serpents. Who were these fiery serpents? Our sages hint that they symbolize the evil tongue, propaganda against us. In every generation we were confronted by a satanic nation and creed that instigated other nations against us through the deadly serpentine propaganda. This terrible serpent that bites, not to still hunger or thirst but only to satiate its lustful hatred, threatens us. It emerged long ago in the image of Amalek during Exodus after he went out of his way four hundred miles, to harass the Israelites. It reappeared as Edom to deny water and innocent passage to the weary Israelites.

In recent times we were plagued by this monster in many Euopean countries: Czarist and communist Russia, Poland, Hungary, Rumania, and fascist Italy. Nazi Germany is now heir to Satan's conspiracy against us. It is the prime instigator. And now God forbid, this monster is before our very eyes. We must arouse the nations to face it and overcome it. Otherwise we will have to face it alone, in the tent of our Torah."

Rabbi Kalir rose from his chair like one freed from bonds, for he had never spoken so openly. They always took him as one who mediated between God and man; now it appeared that he thrust himself between his hard-pressed people and God, not in a pleading role, but as a challenging figure. It was strange. Reb

Koppel—he had many doubts about God's supervision, but now he found an ally who went beyond his own daring sallies into this very occult and precarious realm.

"Get an appointment with the Germans," the Rabbi concluded, as he bade goodnight to them. "I'm ready even now to go wherever you want me. It is not merely Israel's interment that must be given immediate attention. There is more—much more that we face. God have mercy on us. . . ."

*He who destroys one Jewish life, Scripture
condemns him as if he destroyed the whole
world.*

Sanhedrin, 37.

I O

ELEGY FOR A ZIONIST

Sgt. Todt gloated over the fact that while appearing as a drone
to the others, he held in his hands the fate of all these men—
particularly the former Junker general, now the Kommandant of
this town. His fishing line was in active waters, and the main
catch—Colonel Von Preissig—was worth waiting for, even if it
meant boring days and constant repair of radios, or procurement
of household furniture and goods for his superiors.

He could tell that Schrecke, whose face always showed lines
of anger, wanted to get through with the war. The lieutenant
was impatient to do his bloody share and rejoin his hard drinking
cronies at home. For it was there, he boasted, in his theatrical
roles of the Oberammergau Passion Play, that he was acclaimed
and lionized. Todt was quite certain that Lieutenant Schrecke
would one day crack under the strain of too much drinking.

Messer, the former butcher from Frankfurt, liked food and
easy living. He was a *gemütlich* type that could be used. How
Messer earned the rank of captain was something he could never
figure out, but after seeing Rintzler, a former rapist and convict,
put in charge of the Grodno Ghetto, he was ready to believe
anything.

Ludke, the orderly, and Ratten the cook, were small-fry, but
the Junker Colonel Von Preissig, a demoted general, was something special. He couldn't quite size him up. There was one thing
that especially intrigued him. Why would a ranking officer be so
careless, and leave himself open by listening to broadcasts from
forbidden sources?

Todt turned on the shortwave radio: "Our glorious forces in-

117

flicted heavy damage on the enemy . . . 223,898 prisoners . . .
captured and destroyed 3,332 tanks. . . . Soviet air force lost
6,233 planes."
"Leuna Werke, near Bitterfeld, heavily bombed. . . ."
It hit him like a bolt. That was his home town, where his wife,
three children and his old mother lived.
"It can't be true. Lies. All lies." He turned off the radio.

Elyeh did not go to the synagogue for the afternoon Minha
service. He was in a trance: he recalled the time when Israel
came to have his boots fixed.
"Your boots, Israel, wear out fast. Good soles, cured like before the war, are hard to get. The soles we have now are like
cardboard. A few splashes in the mud—and we got plenty of
it—and they become soggy and peel off. Where do your feet
carry you?"
"There is work to do."
"Work in the store?"
"No, not in the store. Nobody comes to buy. We have nothing
to sell. The Germans took everything away."
"What can we do, Israel?"
"The best way to fight the Nazis is to stay alive. I mean alive
as Jews. We must keep our school going; the library must be
kept open, and our hope for the land of Israel must ever be in
our hearts. We've got to be unafraid. Well, I've got to go to meet
David." Elyeh's vision of Israel disappeared, and the bitter realization that Israel was dead dawned on him.
"Why, why, oh merciful and great God? I don't understand. I
am only a plain shoemaker. From dawn to midnight, except
when I dash into the synagogue for a morsel, I sit humped over
torn shoes. Who can afford new shoes? But my work becomes
sweet, because of the young ones. They join hands and clap.
Their songs speak of the valleys and hills of Eretz Israel. Now he
who was called by its name is dead, and I don't understand."
"All these years I have prayed and prayed. I, who don't even
know what a ten-year-old student knows. Yet I prayed with my
humming and my hammer, the awl and the pliers, the spit on the
wooden nails, the swish of beeswax over the thread, and my own
forbidden whistling. Now more than ever, merciful God, grant
me a son. He will be another Israel. I will send him to a Yeshiva, the biggest in the world, in Wolozin. Then he will come
back and sit before the big Gemara. He will raise his voice, and

point to any page and know what is in it. Then he will sing his special tune as he studies and I will listen and just nod like this, and maybe hum a little. Merciful God, hear my prayer."

Elyeh began to chant softly a tune he had once heard from a Yeshiva student, but was interrupted by moaning from Malke.

"Elyeh, comes here—it is here."

"What is here?"

"The baby is about to . . ."

"Impossible."

"Everything is possible."

"But it is supposed to be coming in two weeks—why, Chaye the Good pressed her hand against your belly and said so."

"Elyeh, it is the pain."

"What pain?"

"The labor pain. Call Grune."

"So suddenly on Saturday noon—and tonight I have shoes to repair."

"Elyeh!"

"Yes, I'll get her."

From noon till twilight Grune, nurse and midwife for the Jewish community, administered ice packs and drugs to ease the labor pains, and Chaye the Good was in charge of the household. Sarah Beile and her daughter Rachel were on hand to do anything that was asked.

Elyeh was lost. He didn't know what to do or say. He stood against the wall and sighed for Israel. At this very moment Grune the midwife pulled out the baby, tied the umbilical cord, and smacked it on its back. It began to cry with the lusty voice of a boy.

Rachel came out of the bedroom.

"Hot water! Make a fire!" she told Elyeh.

Make a fire? It was the Sabbath. Then he understood. "Yes, yes," he assented. It was permissible according to the Torah to violate the Sabbath in a life saving emergency.

After a few minutes, the fire was crackling on the clay hearth in the kitchen. "The water is on the fire," Elyeh called out to Rachel. "How does she feel?"

"She is doing well but is weak and worried."

"Shall I get Dr. Epstein from Bialystok?"

"No, it is not that dangerous. Besides the Germans have drafted him for the front."

David entered. He was followed by Abba.

"It is time to put on a light, Elyeh; the time is thirty minutes after sunset," David said.

"What is the hurry?" Elyeh asked. But much as he disliked working on Saturday night, especially after the miraculous birth of his first-born son, he knew that he would have to get some work done, so he quickly said the *havdalah* prayer to usher out the Sabbath. With the Sabbath officially over, he was now able to work. He uncovered his work bench, climbed up on the stool and stretched out his hand, touching every bag and dusty piece that had been there for years. He then pulled out a neatly folded package. He opened it and recognized the patent leather lasts for the boots which he had promised Malke that he would make for the newborn baby.

"We need a wagon and men and a horse." David turned suddenly to the problem at hand. "They promised to release the body," David continued, "but we must be ready to move it."

"There is only one friend from Ledinchine, Franik—I'm making a pair of boots for him." Elyeh patted the unfinished boots as a confirmation. "He owes me a lot of favors. Maybe he'll give us a horse."

"Good. I'll get Burka and the Smith's sons," David said.

"I'll go over to the Grodzensky house," Rachel volunteered. "Mother is there now. Chaye the Good and your mother will surely be there." She faced David.

The door opened and Velvke the gabai entered—his call—if not for charity—was usually, a message from the Rabbi.

"I came to tell you in the name of our Rabbi, may God prolong his days and give him strength, that the military command refuses to surrender the body. The Rabbi, Koppel Magid, and others are in Israel's house now. You can join them later, but please do not all come at one time. Germans are suspicious."

"That means that—God beware," Elyeh hesitated, "that they deny him a Jewish—"

"A Jewish burial," Abba finished.

Rachel began to weep and then in a lamenting voice said:

"Only God knows what will be the end. My own Zechariah—a good man. They took him away from under the canopy. I didn't even walk one step with him, or say one word to him as his wife. God of our fathers, how can you look down upon all this?"

"What is happening?" Malke moaned. Tell me what's happening. What kind of a world did we bring out child into?"

The lone mirror in the house, over the table, was half-hidden by books, and the top was draped with a *talis*. It was Israel's *talis*, that had been presented to him by the library committee.

Mendel rose as Rabbi Kalir entered. He did not speak. Only Fradel locked her fingers while her two daughters huddled close to her on footstools, as if to cushion the sorrow that almost strangled her. She wanted to cry but there were no tears.

Only the eyes of Rabbi Kalir turned toward her. He wanted to cry like a child, but how could he in the presence of all? He turned his chair nearer to Mendel's stool. David and Abba sat on chairs alongside. Burka Mazik came in and whispered to David about a sack of potatoes that he emptied into the Grodzensky cellar. Label said something about giving Israel's family some of the meat smuggled into town at great risk by Leibchik the butcher, and getting money from the community chest. Rabbi Kalir's lips twitched and moved but he could not speak. There was so many sayings of condolence that flashed through his mind: all the reservoir of learning was before him, but it was locked and sealed. "Our father in heaven," he uttered to himself, his eyes open but unseeing to everything before him.

Colonel Schwarzhund was very pleased. "A little violence at a time," he said. "It keeps them hoping. A little appetizer of violence, and then we sit quiet and wait a while, pass more meat. Yes, and we'll send a lot more meat to the front, when things are settled here."

Von Preissig was startled by Schwarzhund's phrase "a little violence at a time." He remarked, "Yes, the supply of meat can be increased. It is only a matter of efficient requisitioning. More wine, Emil. All Poles are good cooks when they prepare and we eat."

Messer roared with laughter. "Poland will be a good country if we can first get rid of the Jews, and then take care of the Poles too."

"Comrades," Von Preissig stood up, "a toast to the invincible German Army." Everyone rose. Schrecke straightened his uniform, wearily lifted a glass, and cried out, "Heil Hitler."

"*Kaffee, ach die gute schwarze kaffee,*" Colonel Schwarzhund said. "Are there cigars?"

"Here." Von Preissig offered him a cigar.

"Ach, what's going on there?" Von Preissig pointed to the market place.

"*Der verfluchter Jude,*" Schrecke answered. "We know how to deal with a Jew who had the nerve to resist us. We shot him like a dog and buried him right in the center of the market. When a German reads the marker over it, he'll be full of anger."

"Anger over what?" Von Preissig inquired.

"Because the Jew resisted the German Army."

"But it was a police action," Von Preissig said.

"We all serve the German Army," Schrecke snapped.

"The German Army has traditions, it cannot be involved with anything like that," Von Preissig protested.

"It's all the same," Messer stoked the coals of the squabble. "We do the dirty work, and they get all the glory and the iron crosses. Let's all share responsibility. Aren't we comrades from the same barracks?"

"Responsibility, yes, but we can't share it, if that is what you mean. It may spoil all our carefully laid out plans," Von Preissig said.

"What kind of plans? It's no secret that the inspector is here to check your plans, and also . . ." Messer almost blurted out the mystery man from Grodno and the details of a confidential briefing. "Let's kill them now—why do it according to plans?"

"Captain," Von Preissig was irate. "As a German officer, I command you not to interfere with my administration. That's all."

Colonel Schwarzhund said nothing. He rose from the table, saluted Von Preissig, and seeming hugely amused or hugely contended—or both at once—turned abruptly and left the chamber.

The telephone rang just as Von Preissig was about to light a cigar. It jarred his nerves.

"Hallo, Kommandant Von Preissig."

"Kommandant Rintzler," a laconic voice identified itself on the other side. "How's it going in your place?"

"According to plan."

"Good—any incidents?"

"Nothing unusual."

"That is boring—I like action."

"If the plan works, why. . . ."

"Nothing works," the Monch (Monk) from Grodno, as he was ironically called by his admiring henchmen, cut him off, "unless there is action. Action, I say, on the front and behind the front, otherwise what are we doing here?"

Von Preissig could almost see him, a double of Himmler: the

puffed eyes with two pin points peering through thick glasses, a baby face and a soft voice. As Kommandant of the Grodno Ghetto, Rintzler boasted of the fact that he had liquidated smaller ghettos and transported them to Grodno. Finally he dispatched them to Auschwitz and Treblinka.

"Are you there?" he taunted.

"Yes, I am listening," Von Preissig answered reluctantly.

"You must improve your methods!"

"Yes."

"You may expect me as your guest one of these days, yes?"

"Yes," he answered feebly. There was a click and a dead stillness followed on the telephone. He looked at the dead instrument for a moment, then replaced it on its cradle. Why had he been servile?

"Come in," Von Preissig answered, after repeated knocking.

"Where is my orderly?" He asked surprised that it was the radio mechanic, Todt.

"I forgot to bring along tubes. I sent Ludke to pick them up," he replied. Before he had time to reprimand Todt for violating an officer's prerogative, he was cut off by Todt's recounting of his woes.

"I am worried, Colonel, about my wife and family."

"Your wife—where is she?"

"In Bitterfeld."

"Bitterfeld, yes, near the Leuna Werke."

"You know about it?"

"Who doesn't? What I mean is, any German officer knows that the I. G. Farben Industrie is there. But is there anything new going on there?" He pretended not to know about the latest bombing.

"They are bombing certain places in Germany, the few planes that get through."

"A few? Then it's not so serious."

"It is, Colonel."

"Why?"

"If they bomb the Leuna Werke, then Bitterfeld is under fire."

"Perhaps."

"Why the Leuna Werke?" Todt was seeking reassurance and at the same time authentic information.

"It is a military secret." Von Preissig did not care to divulge what he knew from various sources: that it was producing the much-needed synthetic oil and its by-product, nitrates used in explosives, from the plentiful, inferior brown coal lying close to the surface.

"Do you think there is danger for my family?"

"There is danger for all our families."

"But we are winning."

"There are still many battles ahead."

"Is your radio working?"

"I do not have too much time. There is much work. Many details and a great responsibility." Von Preissig ushered Todt out just about the time his orderly returned with tubes.

"Here are the tubes, Kommandant." Ludke bowed saying, "You sent for them?"

"Oh, yes. He told you," Von Preissig responded. He had a hunch that Sergeant Todt had deliberately sent Ludke away so that he could surprise him listening in to forbidden stations. "Leave the tubes here, Todt can fix the radio tomorrow. You may leave now."

Alone, Von Preissig settled back in his chair and gazed contemplatively at the ceiling. Once more he saw himself, in his grandiose day-dreaming, as the "conqueror of man's soul, ferreting out the secret of a people." That's it, ju-jitsu! Using the enemy's strength was a grand idea. Rome failed because it couldn't inherit the soul of Greece. The Mongols failed because they only conquered with swift horses. The German empire could not be eternal unless it could secure a captive inner soul. The Jews had it; he would become a savior by grafting the Jewish soul into the German body. Von Preissig stood up and looked in the mirror, admiring himself. A sergeant knocked on the door. "A delegation from the Jews to see you."

The delegation filed in silently. There they stood before him with hats in their hands. This is it, Von Preissig thought: the laboratory in which to develop his theory of "conquest by psychology" and "subjugation by spiritual ju-jitsu."

"Herr Kommandant," David began, "we want permission—the Jewish community—that is, according to our religion, the body has to be buried."

"It was buried." He casually lit a cigar.

"But not in the right place."

"In the public square." Von Preissig gestured with the cigar. "It is unique."

"Herr Kommandant. Soldiers pass by and read the sign for 'Resisting the German Army' and they beat the Jews—they even broke into several houses."

"It is unbelievable," he waved with the cigar. "There must be a mistake."

"Right now they are abusing the Jews in the market place."

"It is only curiosity. Nothing more."

"But we have a cemetery and we want to bury him there," David pleaded.

"That's different," he pretended to yield. "You can bury him tonight at midnight. Only the grave diggers and the family can attend. And no crying! You might arouse the soldiers from their sleep."

He signaled to the sergeant, who dismissed them.

Strains of music came from the house across the square. There was also singing, the kind induced by drinking. Fradel and Mendel, with their daughters, controlled their tears. David held on to the spade while Burka and Shmuel adjusted the improvised stretcher for the third time. At the sight of the disturbed grave first Fradel and then her daughters broke out into a choked weeping. Their bodies were chilled, and shook to the tempo of their chattering teeth.

Lights went on and off, and then a flood of light burst out from an opened door. Two uniformed Gendarmes were coming toward them from the direction of the house. As they drew near, they were joined by Skura and five men of the Polish auxiliary police.

Lieutenant Schrecke checked on all present and warned, "Absolute quiet."

It was very quiet; only the steps of those who carried the burial crib were heard. It was like carrying an ark—like the ark that the Jews carried in the desert after the exodus from Egypt.

The procession moved on. "Justice will walk ahead of you," Abba whispered. A German guard turned around at the head of the procession, but he did not hear. Rabbi Kalir began to move his lips. "Do not be afraid of terror by night . . . and pestilence that walketh in the darkness." His mind lapsed into reverie. There were two arks after the exodus; here, only one ark, containing the bones of Israel. The second ark, that of God, is in the heart. They can shoot us, torture us, humiliate us, but that which we carry inside the heart they cannot touch. He mouthed again with soundless lips, "Nor shall any plague come inside thy tent, for he will put angels in charge over thee."

David felt a straining pain on his left shoulder and Abba began to show signs of fatigue and weariness. The pain increased but the sharp glances of the German guards restrained him from calling a halt to rest and change shoulders.

As they passed the New Synagogue yard, it seemed shrouded in prayers clinging to its doors and windows. A small *yahrzeit* candle on the sill of the memorial pane struggled against the darkness outside. A bead of sweat ran down David's eyelids. The candle light was suddenly transformed in his mind, reminding him of Rachel left standing alone under the canopy, surrounded by flames.

They were now in front of the two birch trees whose stately glistening whiteness contrasted strongly with the low, drab house which Israel had converted into a command post for the *Betar* cell and an academy for revisionism. "Israel, you are home!" Mendel said softly. "All your life you dreamt of *Eretz* Israel and now. . . ."

"Halt," the Germans shouted. Lieutenant Schrecke swung his gun from his shoulder, clutched it with both hands in front of his body, and fixed his eyes on something stirring behind a fence. "*Ach du verfluchter hund,*" Lieutenant Schrecke's voice expressing disappointment that it was a dog, and not a Jew, that ran across the road just as he was about to fire.

"March," he suddenly commanded, and the procession resumed, until they were clattering on the boards of the bridge in front of the water mill.

The sharp commands of Lieutenant Schrecke drove on the pall-bearers over the last sandy stretch. Beyond loomed the walled enclosure across the river, and the little forest ahead stood guard. Crude stone markers stood vigil over the remains of countless generations, prayers, and memories.

They were now before the gate. The procession halted. The German guards instructed the Polish militia to supervise the last act, and then turned back toward headquarters.

Skura took over. As he handed Burka one shovel he growled, "remember, it's got to be finished before daybreak." He felt cocky and proud to be in command over both the living and the dead.

Below the top scrub layer, the earth was loose and fine; as he dug deeper it was hard packed with gravel. Yellow sand drifted in from the rim of the pit.

"We need more boards to shore up the sides. It will cave in," David said.

"There is not enough time," Skura snapped. "Lower it and get it done."

Rabbi Kalir protested that it was not deep enough.

"Come on, Chlopzis, we'll do it if we have to ram the corpse down with our boots."

Rabbi Kalir foresaw the desecration and gestured to David and Burka to lower the body before the drifting sand, churned up by the continuous gust, filled the bottom. The Rabbi took the little bag filled with sand from the Holy Land, opened it and carefully scattered it over the remains of Israel.

"Who dares to say, 'what doest Thou,' " he began to intone in Hebrew. "Thou who promisest and fulfillest, show thy gracious mercy to us . . . hearken to our prayer." He took a handful of earth and painfully let it drop into the grave. "Dust to dust, holy dust to holy dust. May your soul rest in peace." "Thou who dwellest on high," he continued, "grant perfect rest among the holy and pure."

"*Yisgadal, Veyiskadash*—Glorified and hallowed," Rabbi Kalir recited with Mendel Grodzensky. His voice slowed as he came to the words "Praised be He who will resurrect the dead . . . and establish His kingdom during your lifetime and during the lifetime of the whole house of Israel, and let us say Amen." "Don't cry for the departed, cry for the living," the Rabbi added as he turned to leave.

Fradel bowed low and let one tear fall over the fresh grave. A light breeze fanned the pine trees and solitary needles dropped like tears, drifting helplessly over the sand until they were lost in the scrub grass. The mourners turned their steps back across the river, but paused a while on the bridge, as fine sand obliterated all traces of the burial.

"Move on," a shrill command echoed in the night.

*The sun is in eclipse on account of a betrothed
maiden who cried for help in the city and there
was none to save her . . . The eclipse of the
sun is a bad omen for the wicked.*

Sukkah, 29.

I I

FESTIVAL OF FIRE AND WATER

Hoary fingers of the night touched David's shoulder. He turned
over and they tapped his other shoulder. He quivered and sank
his face into the pillow. It was something that hovered from
beyond time, ahead of time.

There was neither sun nor moon. There were many fallen
trees. He fell over the stumps on which no light played; stumbled over lopped branches on which there was no sun, no moon.
There was no sound of birds, no voices of crickets nor the shrieks
of animals. There were shadows, but no light to cast shadows.
The trees were not swaying, the leaves were not rustling. There
were boughs but no breeze to lift them. The sky was not blue.
He couldn't remember any sky. It was silence without an echo. It
was silence that flooded everything. It was everything about him
being carried away by fire. It was everyone running to the river.
Someone's clothes were on fire. Or was it a flaming *talis* draped
around a tree. Or was it only the sun in his face? There was no
sun.

What had he forgotten? He could not remember what he had
forgotten. Remember! Yes. What was the prayer that one said,
when God sent the sojourning soul across the river? He could not
remember. He had lost it.

He was running with Rachel. Others were falling down, then
floating out of sight. He couldn't see or hear; she couldn't run or
move. The place was unfamiliar, and the road that stretched
before him receded into nowhere. The faces were blank. The

129

houses were shuttered and the streets were desolate. Ahead of him a lifeless doll rested atop a heap of charred books and parchment, staring at him with its glassy eyes.

Burka Mazik tip-toed to David and whispered in his ear. One head after another popped up and stared at the squat horse dealer. Burka ordinarily attended the downtown synagogue. His sudden appearance here was something special. David forced himself to appear calm by concentrating on the pages. He began to turn pages, holding the bunched pages and letting them slip from his fingers as if in search of a forgotten passage.

The quiet of the synagogue was suddenly jarred by loud shouts.

Commands were heard first in German then in Polish. The door was forced open amid harsh-sounding voices, and Skura's men appeared in the doorway.

Rabbi Shepsel Kalir ascended the Bimah, lifted the Torah and intoned, *"This is the Torah which Moses set before the Children of Israel, by the words of the Lord."* He sat down and held on firmly to its rollers. Koppel grabbed its upper handles, rolled up the parchment and covered it with the velvet mantle. Rabbi Kalir held it to his bosom like a baby.

"Do Palestina," cries were heard. "This sheepskin will make a good pocket book." Skura advanced and pointed to the Torah embraced by the Rabbi.

"Give us your money, Jews," the chorus began to chant.

"Don't you know to-day is Sabbath, the money is not in their pockets?" Kopka, a former apprentice of Elyeh the shoemaker, explained.

"Where is it, Kopka?" the mob shouted.

"It's in their bellies."

"Let's get it," cried the chorus, and the Polish guards surged forward. On their heels were peasants with knotted canes, leather whips, weighted belts, and knives.

Rabbi Kalir, guarded by David, Alter the carpenter, and others who barred the way to the threatening mob, resumed the singing.

"It is a tree of life for those who put their faith in it and for those who uphold it are made happy."

"Let's teach the Jews a lesson!" the maddened mob shouted.

"Zabitz Szidoff, kill the Jews," a shrill voice urged them on.

"Its ways are ways of pleasantness and all its paths are peace."

Rabbi Kalir led the procession to the ark as blows rained from all sides.

"Do Palestina Zidzi," they chanted as the frenzied mob began attacking the Jews.

" 'A pillar of fire and smoke will accompany you,' " Skura cynically shouted. "Bring the hose with gasoline!"

The Jews opened the ark and struggled to place the Torah inside, when the command "Halt!" froze them in their tracks. Suddenly two German Gendarmes pushed through the crowd, Col. Von Preissig appeared, followed by two cameramen. At the swing of his whip, which he employed like a baton, they began to turn the cranks of the cameras. One cameraman moved forward to take a closeup shot. "All faces look toward me!" the cameraman shouted. Von Preissig, showing flashes of the Junker General that he was before his demotion, rattled off directions. He pointed to Beryl the baker, who stood there moving his lips inaudibly, his eyes almost closed, clutching a prayer book in his hand. Von Preissig then noticed little Avreml, his eyes wide open and frightened, seeking protection on the comforting lap of his godfather, Velvke.

Von Preissig signalled for a different angle. He liked this particular setting. His artistic eye favorably envisioned the result: Velvke, with his silvery beard framing rosy cheeks, holding an open book and reassuring young Avreml.

The cameraman then focused the lenses to the women's gallery, above in the rear of the Synagogue. He was attracted by the spasmodic weeping, choking and coughing. But Von Preissig swung his whip, dismissing the cameraman's efforts with a curt *"Halt! Keine alte Frauen."*

David tried to approach Von Preissig, but was discouraged by two bayonets pointed at him. He retreated toward Rabbi Kalir near the altar steps. Von Preissig, with a last elated glance, flagged his hand up and down and all activity stopped. The cameramen began to fold their tripods and pack up their cameras. In no time the spectacle was over.

Von Preissig steepped into his Mercedes and sped away. Schrecke, the S. S. man, remained in charge. At a pre-arranged

signal, the doors of the synagogue were closed and Germans and
Poles were stationed at every window. A flamethrower was
moved into position and its furnace-hot flame caused the wooden
walls to smoke and then burst into flame. The multitude, com-
prising the Polish camp followers, the rabble of the town and
nearby villages, started to shout in glee. One of the two cameramen, stationed in the yard, began to film the conflagration.

But before the flames could envelop the entire structure, a
water pump of the local fire brigade appeared, manned by Jews
and Poles. A wagon filled with barrels of water was pushed up to
the synagogue by Jews, who began to draw pails of water from
the barrels into the pump. The spray of water played back and
forth over the flaming walls, but the supply from the barrels was
soon spent. When they tried to fetch water from the nearby
wells, Messer, acting on Schwarzhund's instructions, stopped
them.

Elyeh's wife broke through the crowd and tried vainly to open
the door, crying, "Elyeh!"

"Mercy! Mercy! We will all burn," Elyeh cried, and rushed
frantically to his wife's cries, but he was beaten back.

Now Skura jumped forward to push her away. She cried
"Murderer!" He struck her with the butt of the gun and a German kicked her. She fell bleeding.

The flame grew stronger and was whipped by a breeze, the
kind that always lurks in ambush whenever there is a fire. A German on a motorcycle raced into the yard, clearing the way for
Von Preissig, who had returned upon seeing the blaze. The car
came to a roaring stop in front of the excited crowd, whose
tempers rose higher and higher at the smell of smoke and fire. He
signalled with his hands to Captain Messer, "Nein," pointing to
the straw thatched roofs surrounding the synagogue.

Captain Hans Messer grudgingly yielded to Von Preissig's
order to put out the fire and stop the pogrom. He ordered Lt.
Schrecke to open the doors. Men began to rush out, some falling,
some bleeding and some following with enough strength to enlist
for fire fighting. David and Burka asked for permission to bring
pails and shovels and recruited an entire brigade of volunteers.
From somewhere in the distance a bugle sounded the familiar
fire signal.

A German medic bent down to examine the victims, but
stopped when he was called back. Inside, Elyeh lay on the floor,
badly beaten and holding his head. He tried to raise himself by

climbing to the altar, but he collapsed on the first step. He began
to repeat verses from the Psalms.

"Elyeh, let's escape."

"No, we can't. I can't, it is too late." For thirty years he had
given his strength to make boots and shoes. Now he wondered if
he would live to make the boots for his newly born son.

"O great God! At last a friend! Kopka, please help me! Kopka
it's me, Elyeh Schuster, help my wife and child! Help these
people!"

Lt. Schrecke peered through the window of the synagogue,
then turned to Kopka. "Do you know him?"

"He was my boss, I learned a little shoemaking from him."

"Well, Kopka," Lt. Schrecke laughed out loud, "your troubles
are over. You'll be the boss now. Get yourself an apprentice."

"But he is my boss. I want to do something at least for him."

"Kopka, you are a soldier, a *Volksdeutscher*, you have a job to
do." the Lieutenant winked to him.

"Just one favor."

"It's granted." Lt. Schrecke said. "Here is a revolver, finish him
off."

"Is this an order?" Kopka stuttered. "I, I—can't do it. Let me
shoot at him from a hiding place."

"There, stand behind the camera, *geschwind.*"

Kopka shrugged his shoulders, and aimed shakily at his master. For a moment Elyeh's good natured face pleaded hopefully,
then it disappeared from the shattered window.

Elyeh crawled back to the altar. He pulled himself up on the
steps; he touched the feet of Elijah's throne. With one last lunge,
he raised himself and gripped the velvet curtain over the ark. His
weight pulled it down, the doors sprang open, and the scrolls of
the *Torah* were now visible. He looked long and steadily at the
Torahs, trying to pray for the holy scrolls. Lt. Schrecke whispered something to Von Preissig. After shaking his head somewhat reluctantly, he approved the next step.

With Von Preissig's approval, Lieutenant Schrecke ordered all
the Jews, except the few still busy putting out the fire, to march
to the market place. A special escort accompanied Rabbi Kalir
and those around him. Lt. Schrecke snatched a pail from Skura
and ceremoniously placed it on the Rabbi's head. Beryl the baker
tried to remove it, but was knocked down. He lay there helpless.

"The Germans," Von Preissig addressed the subdued Jewish

population, "are interested in Jewish culture, more than in the Jews. But the Jews need not be alarmed. A culture always survives a nation. We Germans have inherited the best from every nation. Out of the cultures of Greece, Rome and Israel we will mold the greatest nation on earth. Yes, we will have it all. We take what we need and what we can't use we destroy. The Jews, I repeat, have a great culture. Ah, but they lack discipline. Witness the disturbance that took place today, because of your fanatical resistance to subordination. I shall have to teach you a lesson in obedience. The first lesson is how to march. Guards and special police, please preserve discipline!"

Within a short time the Jews were being dragged from their synagogues and homes by armed Germans and Polish police and brought to the square. They were aided by hundreds of instant collaborators who harbored long-repressed hatreds for the Jews. It did not matter that the Germans were sworn enemies of the Poles and would attend to them too after the Jews. This was an invitation to kill, rob, and rape—sponsored by the government.

Roving bands ravaged from street to street and from house to house to herd all not yet apprehended to the square. Even Isaac the Melamed, the old retired Rabbi and teacher who was ill and could not attend synagogue, was knocked down from his bed by Skura's men. His wife, who could hardly walk, was temporarily left alone. He was subjected to insults and obscene remarks all the way to the square, but he was oblivious to all the taunts. He always believed that if there were no sins, there would be no sinners. The sinners laughed in his face. Something was wrong, but not with his innocent faith. He could hardly stand in line. He closed his eyes, his silvery pointed beard heaving up and down with his heavy breathing. The line wavered when bystanders broke through and pommelled him and many others. He faltered, fell to one knee and got up. Zorach, his former student, held him up.

Skura's eyes blinked as he looked in the direction of the sinking noon sun above the steeples of the church, and he exchanged glances with S. S. Captain Hans Messer. The last mass in the church would soon be over, and the pandemonium that would erupt would meanwhile not disturb the worshippers. Once they came out of church they would coalesce with this Sunday crowd as easily as they had fallen on their knees in the pews.

Paunchy Captain Hans Messer leaned against the south wall of the church. His lieutenant, Fritz Schrecke, was handling the Jews and he arranged for the mob to participate.

The crowd was now like the crowd at a soccer match, excited and glad that this game was crooked, pegged in advance. He was always on the winning side. It was a set-up, Captain Messer reflected, with thousands of potential victims, to whom he could do as he pleased. To get their loot he would need Schwarzhund's approval. Kommandant Rintzler gave orders to Schwarzhund, who, in turn, had the upper hand over Kommandant Von Preissig. All he had to do was to select the orders from either one that suited him best, after handing over a modest share of the spoils to both.

Would it not be a good idea to settle down here in one of those well-located houses, like Tevia Stuzinsky's, Koppel's or Abchik's? In Frankfort he faced competition from the other butchers; here he could command many customers.

In the marketplace, David was guarded by two Poles, his face swollen, his shirt torn and his tousled hair soaked with blood. When he had seen Skura taking away Rachel and Sarah Beile, with Avreml crying alongside her, he struggled with Skura and his men, but he was overpowered and beaten until he was helpless. He feared that she was taken to Von Preissig's office.

Abba's body could not absorb much punishment. He had forgotten to put on his glasses when they surprised him in his room. He was concerned about Chantze. "Run, run away" she told him. "This is what I am going to do." But where can one run, when all the roads are blocked, and everyone is an enemy.

"Follow your Rabbi" the mob chanted, and pelted with stones his pail-covered head. "Follow your Rabbi on the square, sing, dance on all fours." New faces, in a festive mood after having attended church, took up the maddening chant. The Jews were stopped repeatedly and then marched in circles. Alter Stoliar, who continually circled around the Rabbi, shielded him from many a blow which he deflected with his muscular arms. But he could not protect his own head.

As Rabbi Kalir led the slow moving circular line of Jews, they were pushed, punched and abused from all sides by the taunting mob. Captain Messer ordered that the Jews form a column. The Jews were now driven to the lower corner of the square. Cam-

eramen were posted on the terrace steps of the Brick Synagogue.
They were to wait for Col. Von Preissig to film the last march.
Schwarzhund conceded this part of the spectacle to him. No
sooner did the column reach the entrance of Synagogue Street,
when Messer shouted "About face". This was repeated for several hours until the final command to march down to the river.

Alter started to sing but all he could remember from the many
psalms he recited and heard from others were his favorite verses.

He saw Koppel Magid mouthing words. Was he talking to
God? Demanding an explanation? Right next to him, Reb Jacob,
the teacher, was on the verge of exhaustion. A girl student held
him up. Noske the chanter fell to the ground. Elchanan, the
Yeshiva student, raised him. A *Gendarme* punched him for holding up the line. Hadassah tried to stem the flow of blood from his
mouth.

"*O God, thou art my God; early will I seek thee: my soul
thirsteth for thee, my flesh longeth for thee. . . .*" He was unable
to finish. The words hung and withered like fruit on a parched
tree. He moved closer to Rabbi Kalir and repeated this second
verse of the Psalm.

"*In a dry and thirsty land, where no water is*", Rabbi Kalir
rescued him. "Without Torah there was only famine."

All eyes turned in the direction of Synagogue Street. Young
rowdies beat on plundered pots and pans, while others drained
the last drops from bottles, as they escorted Schneur Zalmen and
his two young sons. He was the only Lubavicher *Chasid* in
town.

"Make way, make way for the Jewish Messiah," a red-faced
peasant shouted.

"Now look at him, he's got curls," another man shouted. Then,
pointing to the *Chasid's* sons, he added, "And so do they." Two
young peasants began to pull their curls. Notwithstanding the
pain, he remained calm and retained his dignified composure. He
was dressed in the *Chasid's* princely garments: a wide brimmed
hat, a long open coat over a white wool *talis koton*—a praying
shawl worn as one of the inner garments—and short velvet pants
tucked into knee-high white socks.

"Follow the Rabbi to the square. Get in line."

"Do you know what this bandit tried to do?" the local laureate
shouted in a more literary Polish.

"What did he do, the bandit?" a dull-faced drunk muttered.

"The nerve of him, he tried to break down the door of the

women's floor of the New Synagogue to save them, he said. Here he is."

"Kill him!" they shouted in frenzy.

"Kill him? Yes, but slowly, as he, the Jewish Messiah, deserves. Hey, *Chlopzi*."

"Sing, sing, sing and dance; sing and crawl; sing and jump; up and down; and down and up—all around." They poked him with sticks and jabbed him with pocket knives as they formed a circle around him.

"Inside the circle, sing louder, sing, sing."

"By the rivers of Babylon, there we sat down, yea, we wept, when we remembered Zion. . . . How shall we sing the Lord's song in a strange land?"

The bell of the church tolled the afternoon hour. Packed wagons, men and women who were on their way home after mass, turned back. Something special raged in town, and they didn't want to miss it.

Meanwhile, Von Preissig fretted in his office. He was to return to the square to supervise the final filming of Jews drilling and marching. But he was delayed waiting for a call from Kommandant Rintzler. The call from Grodno came through earlier but he missed it.

The sudden ringing jangled his nerves.

"Yes Kommandant, *heil Hitler*, I want to apologize. . . ." Von Preissig unconsciously saluted as he talked on the telephone.

"What are you doing?" the voice from Grodno crackled after a staccato burst of stinging words.

"According to plan," he replied to the Gestapo chieftain who was empowered to oversee the liquidation of the local ghettos.

"Colonel, are they jumping?" Rintzler asked. There was no reply.

"Are they down on their knees and are you carrying out my orders?"

"I'm performing my duties," Von Preissig finally answered.

"Good! Don't coddle them! I'll be there. Good hunting."

"Good hunting," he repeated sheepishly the sinister phrase.

One never knew when the bespectacled Gestapo chief with the slit eyes and wicked grin would show up. But he had to be ready for him with the right answers and facts. Col. Schwarzhund reported everything to Grodno.

He was in a tight corner. The spectacle of "fire and water" now

that Schwarzhund took charge of it in the name of Rintzler was
more violent than he expected. He was especially worried lest
some Jews escape.

He called his orderly, Ludke, and dispatched a note to Captain Messer to summon the Judenrat. Kiva Kagan, the handsome
druggist with a red gash on his forehead, and Paltiel, the community leader, his good suit in shreds, were picked out from the
marching line in the square. Messer backed them up against the
Brick Synagogue.

"Where is Shmuel Leiser and the others who escaped?" Messer
demanded. "I warn you," he shouted and raised his fist, all Jews
who escape or are in hiding must report immediately. I will hold
the members of the Judenrat responsible for their return. Otherwise, many hostages will be shot before nightfall."

Meanwhile, Shmuel Leiser slipped in behind Paltiel after a
futile attempt to see the priest. First he was told that nobody
could interrupt him during Mass. Then there was a baptism and
later a wedding on his schedule. Finally, the priest was ill. When
he wanted to see for himself, his aide threatened to call a Gendarme.

"Where is your leader?" Messer asked.

"The Rabbi," Shmuel replied, "is here."

"No, the young man Sokoloff", he demanded.

"Get him and bring him here immediately," Messer commanded. Before he had finished, Skura's boys dragged in David
and kept knocking him down.

"He resisted, shall we kill him?"

"No"—Messer hesitated, "we'll get to him." He did not care to
reveal to them that Von Preissig depended on David for his
eccentric library project. Otherwise, there was no reason to keep
David Sokoloff alive. For it was no secret that when the Germans
captured soldiers, Russian or Polish, they did away first with the
officers and the bravest. This recalcitrant Jew was continually in
their way. First he broke down the door of the Synagogue and
released girls who were about to be assaulted and then when overpowered, he fought back.

Rintzler arrived at headquarters late in the afternoon. He
passed by Von Preissig who came out to greet him and said:

"Everything is going well. I hear you have very interesting films to show me, not now." and crossed to the ante office. Rintzler went over the rough details with Col. Schwarzhund. It was to disregard any interference by Von Preissig. He told the sweating Messer that this was *"Ein versammlung für belästigen und belustigen—"* a gathering for trouble and amusement.

"Sehr geschickt." It was very clever.

"Was?" Rintzler's slit eyes brimmed with bile.

"Ja, ja" he saluted him and then as he departed mumbled in admiration," *der Schuft,* the rascal."

Now Michalski, the *Starosta* of Long Village whom the Germans raised to Bürgermeister of the town and Haupt of the task force, stood aside as he talked in a whisper to Skura. He returned and announced "All communists step forward." No one answered or made a move. For there were no communists. The only one with sympathies, Label, was in a daze after the beating he took when he tried to protect his younger sister. Michalski repeated again "Communists step forward." When there was no answer, Messer and Schrecke huddled with the Bürgermeister and Skura.

Paltiel, the leader of the religious Zionists, stepped forward.

"There are no communists in our midst."

"Do you hear that Chlopzi?" Skura shouted. He crept behind Paltiel and began to search him. "It is not in his pants or in his beard. Maybe it's in his belly, let's open it. Give me a big knife" he called out, "and I'll slit it open, maybe somebody is hiding there." They rocked with laughter. The Germans enjoyed this barbaric stage play.

"I was their teacher," Reb Jacob now addressed them.

"Ah, ah their teacher," a chorus resumed, "and what about this one?", two peasants screamed and lifted Label by his ears.

"I taught him myself, he is as good as anyone of us."

"Then you are all communists," they shouted.

"You, you also must be a communist," they pointed to Burka Mazik, "You stole horses, so you must be one."

"I was his teacher," said Chaim Schneider. The frames of his glasses were bent and the crystals were cracked. "He doesn't know anything about communism. He is a poor man, supporting his mother."

"You hear that Chlopzi, let's make a collection for him."

"O teacher, maybe you are a communist," Skura grabbed him by his tie and tightened it until he began choking.

"Let him go," Kagan, the druggist, intervened.

"Then you are, you are a communist."

"Where is your sense?" he said. "How stupid can you be? Didn't many of you buy drugs from me? Did I ever turn anyone away? Do you recall", he pointed to a sandy-haired boy, "when you came to me for medicine for your mother, and you had no money, didn't I give you the medicine?"

"That's enough!" Messer said.

"*Verfluchte Juden Kommunisten vorwärts*".

Without waiting another moment, Messer turned to Michalski and his strong arm Skura and screamed, *"Pflücken sie aus die banditten"* (pull out the bandits).

Whoever carried a grudge against Jews, owed them money or disliked them generally, invented a pretext to start working them over. Patriarchs and young men, women and young boys and girls, were beaten mercilessly with clubs and truncheons.

They belabored the Rabbi, removing his pail and pounding him over his bare head. A drunk came forward with scissors and shouted, "Let's cut his beard." He clumsily clipped and pulled strands of hair and flung them in the faces of the Jews who were held back at bayonet point.

"Now resume the exercises. Left turn, right turn, turn around . . ."

Ben Zion complied in order not to attract too much attention to Noske. He shielded him from their anger since he did poorly in calisthenics. Hershke the miller, managed, under extreme provocation, not to strike back. But it was in vain; they were singled out for special attention.

"Come here" Michalski addressed Noske. He had already carted away a wagon load of plundered Jewish goods after he downed a few glasses when he broke into Branfman's cafe. "Are you a capitalist?" he asked and removed his watch from an inside pocket.

"Why did you hide it? You must be a communist or a capitalist, or both."

"Are you a communist too?" He pulled out Hershke, who instinctively resisted and was slashed across his face with a knotted cane. Noske next to him gave him his kerchief.

"So you are a helper", he said to Hershke in a mocking tone.

"Can you help me with gold?" and switching to Noske asked, "Where is your liquor?"

"I have none."

"You are a liar. Give me vodka or I'll choke you to death."

Hadassah broke through. Where was Chaim, her brother, and where was Elchanan? "*Tate*, Father," she cried. "Mamma," she was in tears. Skura seized her to take her picture and have her pose. But she broke away and ran straight to Elchanan, who received blows for shielding her.

The long column was being marched away down synagogue Street toward the river. Avreml located David and fell in line. If anything bad had happened in town, Avreml reflected, people would always run to the synagogue and offer prayers. They would then rush to help the victims. Why don't the Poles who had lived in peace with the Jews, run to church to pray and stop the Polish hooligans?

"Let's run away after dark", somebody in the line whispered.

"I can run a day and a night and I won't get tired," he told David. "I can hide very deep in the forest, even at night. I won't be afraid. I'll say my prayers. Then I'll come out in the morning and pluck some green peas—I know the patch, on the other side, after the sky touches the earth. I can also pick berries, where there is moss and the big ants won't bother me."

"We must stay together" David gritted his teeth. "This is what they are waiting for to hunt us down, to corner us into a death-trap."

Meanwhile, after a long huddle with Messer, Michalski and Skura arrived at a decision that would yield each his due share. They understood perfectly what Messer meant:

"We have done our part, you do the rest."

It was outright sanction to provoke more than a pogrom: an open season to steal, plunder, rob whatever they could find and do with every living Jew whatever they wished. Michalski assigned the rough work and the details to Skura. He, himself, immediately commandeered wagons and took along with him townspeople and friends to go through the Jewish houses and take whatever their hearts desired. Skura now took charge. Men were separated from women. Some were taken away for special work to clean latrines, or ordered to sweep and pluck the grass from the streets, collect beer and liquor, or do anything which would humiliate them. Others were ordered to clean up the market place, remove the wounded out of sight, and bury the dead.

The rest of the men were now taken away and locked up in the Polish school and in the Brick Synagogue, while girls and women were locked up in the women's gallery of the New Synagogue.

Rabbi Kalir knew immediately what was taking place, when he saw David breaking away, followed by Burka, Kagan, Shmuel Leiser and Zorach the carpenter's son—all of them were fearless against blows and butts; workers and scholars, Zionists and teachers, and the old sages. But would they be able to prevent the inexorable defilement of their wives and daughters and sisters? He cried out in his helplessness, but without tears.

Soon he heard their frantic cries fill the square. Cries for help, the wailing of women, the shuddering shrieks of girls became more prolonged, more desperate. Some of the men hurled themselves at their captors, trying to break free to rescue their wives and daughters. They were beaten down. There was a long piercing cry. Then all cries stopped together. There was only silence and a few more bodies crumpled to the cobblestones.

Rabbi Shepsel had great difficulty walking upright. Every time he raised his head, the pail began to slip.

"Who is holding up the march?" Schrecke was fuming.

"The Rabbi!" answered Skura.

He began to make faster strides with his new-found strength, amid the cracking of whips and abusive words, which set into motion little hammers pounding his head to the beat of his pulse.

They were being driven to Synagogue street. Both sides were lined with Polish onlookers, rowdies, Gestapo men in civilian clothing, German women, speculators, merchants conniving for Jewish wealth, servants, loose women and thieves, who were waiting for the Jews to pass through the gantlet. It was almost like the intoxicating *"Sieg Heil"*, as a chorus of voices screamed "Hang them! Kill them, drown the Jews!"

"We are Germans, we do things our own way." Von Preissig reminded Michalski and Skura who were now in command of the Jews. "There is to be no riot, only an orderly march down to the river." He was ready to supervise the filming of the last episode from a standing position in the rear of his Mercedes that would move ahead of the column. Messer and Schrecke would be on hand to enforce non-interference with the Polish conclusion of the march.

The Jews were reassured. Rabbi Shepsel Kalir sincerely believed him. He did not dare to doubt. Did not the Rabbis say "Even on the threshold of Gehennam, one must still have hope."

The lines were ordered anew. The Rabbi and the leading citizens were placed up front, and then the others, according to their rank, as designated by Polish police. David had no doubt as to their intention. The Poles carried knotted sticks, and one of the Borowski brothers held a scythe under his arm. Abba tried to think hard and fast. Perhaps he should address Von Preissig and explain that once the Poles were left in charge a pogrom would begin.

"Herr Kommandant," he suddenly stepped forward with hat in hand. Before he could even finish the first sentence, Lt. Schrecke hit him square on the face. He faltered backward and sagged on his knees. A camera began to grind feverishly, as David and Rabbi Kalir helped him to his feet.

The bell on the church tower began to toll and spirited commands were issued. The procession began to move behind Von Preissig's automobile. They were now passing the red Brick Synagogue, on the left side of the square, almost opposite the church.

Some faces appeared in the windows alongside the march, but stones quickly drove the women back into their imprisonment. Their husbands, sons and brothers, sisters, even mothers were led away. There was no time for grief.

A barefoot waif threw sand in the Rabbi's face. He wiped his eyes. But there were no tears. Tears were luxury. Jewish tears were orphans. No one cared. More barefoot boys from the Long Village, now joined the spectacle of the Jews being marched down their own street to the jeers of hostile strangers. Someone was throwing stones in the direction of the Rabbi. They bounced off the wobbly pail over his head. There were deeper debasements.

Michalski, with the hoarse voice and Kopka, with the bass singing voice, impersonated Jews at prayer, by swaying and shouting detached phrases.

Rabbi Shepsel whispered a prayer as the pail pounded his head. He was almost dazed by the rough voices. But he was calm and dignified as he thought he heard voices from the sages.

Elyeh, the shoemaker, called Kopka, his former apprentice, for he was now delirious, but he was held up and dragged along on the march. He murmured unconsciously "Kopka, mercy!"

"The Lord is right unto them that are of a broken heart."

"Where is he now?" Rabbi Kalir himself now dared to question the Lord. " 'Thou hast caused men to ride over our heads: we went through fire and through water.' Were these men or demons?"

"Is it day or night?" Rabbi Kalir stared into the hollow of the bucket, now tipped on one side, now on the other, his ironical crown of spiritual leadership. And then he said:

" 'Blessed be the Lord my rock who teacheth my hands to war and my fingers to fight.' This should have been stressed more in a world where we encounter demons," he added.

They were now almost to the bridge, but the weary column was barred. David held the arm of Rabbi Kalir, who prayed more in his heart. His eyes turned neither to the left nor to the right. Suddenly there were voices.

"All to the Synagogue!" said the imitating voices, in the familiar tune of the town crier who alerted the Jews to cease work, close shop and go to the Synagogue before the sun set on the eve of the Sabbath.

"Into the water!" the voices continued.

And the refrain was repeated: "Into the water." "Cup and wine!" and a voice repeated, amid laughter, "Cup and Wine."

"Drink wine? No wine!" a chorus answered.

"Let them drink water."

Suddenly David felt a sharp blow, he was falling reeling over the bridge, into the water, sinking. It was painful, yet so pleasant, so dark. Only he had forgotten something. What was it? The prayer thanking God for returning the soul after its sojourn of sleep? What was it, Quick! Time stopped, his heart stopped, the sun stopped, all movement stopped. No more voices, no more curses, no more blows.

No! The pleasant dream had gone on too long, too dangerously long. Somehow he would have to return. Quick! Remember to return!

Crows were making their last frenzied flights. Their raucous calls echoed in the sky above the trees. The night was settling down, and the black crows merged with the gathering storm.

July 20, 1941: RUSSIANS REPORT NAZI DRIVES HALTED.
SOCIALIST LEADER WARNS CALAMITY IN
BOLSHEVIST SURVIVAL. AHMED HUSEIN,
"LEADER OF FASCIST YOUNG EGYPT
MOVEMENT," ARRESTED.

*Woe unto the wicked and his collaborating
neighbor.*

Sukkah, 56.

I 2

ENEMIES AND COLLABORATORS

Dawn finally came, after two nights, to those who escaped across
the river. The hens were more alert than usual. It was still dark
when they began to crow. The wounded were so wracked by
pain after the ordeal that they hardly slept at all during the two
nights. The bruised were so spent that they couldn't even wake.
Crows greeted the horizon, turning into a warm hue. The river
received the first rays on its glittering wavelets. The first steps of
the morning touched the earth. They must have been the peasants', who impressed the soil with their bare feet. For the day's
work began when the peasant girls brought in the cows from the
pasture for milking. Now that the sun was out, they began to
unroll the soaked linen for bleaching.

"Gen Dobra!" David was startled by a man's voice. He looked
up, it was Malinoski who greeted him.

Malinoski, the kind grizzled handy man, his legs bowed inwardly by age, lowered his head. He said only, "The *chlopzis*
disgraced us." Malinoski recognized and greeted each one in his
usual manner. He took out his pouch of tobacco, folded a piece
of rough paper, rolled it, sealed with his tongue and tapered its
ends before he put it into his mouth.

He was about to take out his flint to light it when he shook his
head: "Smoke is not good. It may flush out the wrong people."

"There is a baby crying in the synagogue." Malinoski's watery
eyes blinked in the sun as he spoke slowly. "It may be a trap."

Before the others could volunteer, David and Malinoski de-

145

parted. They walked from the rear, stopped to look around and inched their way into the synagogue.

Inside it appeared like the aftermath of a satanic devastation. Jagged glass and chunks of plaster were strewn over half burned and mutilated books on the floor. The pew benches were charred and overturned. A pall of acrid smoke billowed sluggishly toward the smashed door and broken windows.

The altar was untouched. The throne of Elijah was still erect. But the curtain of the ark was hanging like a flag at half mast. The doors of the ark were open, as if in desperation someone had opened them to pray before the undamaged scrolls.

Below the scrolls' closet, was the cabinet in which coverlets, silver crowns and breast plates were stored. David opened the door; the silver and velvet mantles were gone. But deep inside, Elyeh Schuster's baby was huddled in a corner.

Malinoski was about to go down on his knees and remove his cap. But he realized that it was a different altar. Here submission was in the mind and in the heart.

Is Elyeh alive? Is there anyone left to care for him? How did the baby get into the ark? Somebody must have placed it here, but who?

The baby sighed and squirmed as if finally realizing that they were real friendly voices. But it drew back its pudgy fingers at the touch of strange arms.

Suddenly the door opened. It was Skura leading a hound on a leash accompanied by two of his police.

"Where is the baby I put it there myself to sleep?" Skura demanded. "So you tried to hide it," Skura teased him. "You are under arrest, Sokoloff, or shall I call you Panie David Sokoloff? Your parents must be dead," he spoke to the baby, "I'll get you a new mother to take care of you, baby."

"But this is a Jewish baby," David protested.

"Take the baby from him and take him away."

"By order of the Kommandant, all Jews who rioted on Saturday are under arrest, as hostages. They will be detained until there is evidence of good behavior on the part of the Jews of Suha-Vali." Lt. Schrecke read from a paper. "The Germans," he continued, "will not be responsible for a repetition of the chaos which followed the march. It is to be avoided for the Jews' own protection." The heavy bolted door was closed. David looked around and saw in the damp darkened Stuzinsky brewery that those who escaped with him and many others were confined within its drab walls.

The stone foundations of the brewery were also the walls of its basement. In winter it was filled with blocks of ice from the river, for refrigeration of the beer in summer. In good times it served as the theater for the Theatrical group *"Hashmal."* Now it was, in addition to the regular prison, a big house of detention. Big empty vats, raised above the dirt floor, lined the walls. Only stale beer fumes remained. Their beer was several weeks ago drained into smaller barrels and carted away to military head-quarters. This and other "voluntary" contributions were collected either for local use or for the *"Heimat."* The last referred to packages of food and valuables dispatched to their own families.

The brewery floor was covered with slumped bodies half sprawled on the dank clay floor. They stared at the shafts of light that penetrated the spaces between the logs. The dried moss that once filled the cracks had long ago been removed by those who wanted to see the plays presented by the young actors of *Hashmal.*

On the platform that had served as a stage, empty barrels, sacks of hops and clusters of bottles were stacked on shelves on the wall above it. Through the small barred slots near the ceiling, boots of guards were seen. From time to time one of them bent down to see that nothing suspicious transpired among the sixty prisoners.

In the right corner near the platform, alongside stacks of empty sacks and canvas, Rabbi Shepsel Kalir spoke softly and in measured phrases.

"Wise men be careful with your words." Originally it cautioned Rabbis against hasty judgment and severe verdicts, Now, bereft of his usual Talmudic and Biblical quotes, he cautioned them against panic.

"Rabbi, Rabbi," he heard voices of the wounded and the crushed. If words could be balm for their agonies and revive them to hope, then it was perhaps better that he let each one speak. He scanned the small barred slots, the cracks in the walls and said, "Do not fear the terror of 'reshaim'."

"Our history is full of encounters with barbarians," Abba, his face ashen gray and bloodied, said, "It should all be written down, if only I could get my letters out." He came over from his corner and sat down.

"Kagan," the Rabbi pointed his finger to the druggist on the floor, "have you . . . ?" Kagan shrugged his shoulders. He had no medicines with him. He tore off a strip from his own shirt and patted Abba's bruised cheeks.

Heavy booted steps descended the steps to the cellar. The German soldier who was accompanied by Skura pounded with the stock of his gun against a barrel and shouted angrily, *"Ordnung, keine schweinerei!"* He tightened his lips and shook his head like a skeptic. "I thought you Jews were praying what with all the noise you were making. You are our prisoners."

For a long while Rabbi Kalir's lips quivered, unable to speak. To whom could he turn—God? How would he know—know what? Perhaps God was disturbed. How could anyone dare to say it? David and Abba were in bad shape. The cries of the maimed—and the worst of all—the wounds of the assaulted girls and women distressed him. There were bruises all over his body especially under his eyes and all over his face.

At such times the only contact the Jews had was with God. Was it possible that the unclean separated them from God? If so Satan was in charge, and that was incredible!

The prisoners were ushered in. Their clothes were disheveled. Rabbi Kalir who led them, stood out among them. He retained his dignity, though his face was drawn and his eyes were drowsy. It was like the conclusions of the great fast day on Yom Kippur. He stood before the throne of Judgment. But it was unlike the court in high heaven. Here there were no angels at attention. Neither a reasonable prosecuting angel nor a zealous defending angel. There was no book of life, nor was any other book brought forward to reveal both the omissions and merits of daily deeds. Von Preissig examined documents while all waited. No one can escape sin. Maybe I did commit errors, he began to think, as fatigue and exhaustion gave way to strain and agitation. Perhaps I wrongly admonished my people. I called them uncharitable, and transgressors—when all the time I knew in my heart that they lived frugally, and most in poverty. They favored the rich with honors in the Synagogue; yes it was wrong. There were poor and hungry Jews, but it was much worse among the Gentiles. A few were quarrelsome, not all were perfect. Oh yes,

sometimes they violated the Sabbath, especially the young people.
They smoked cigarettes. They went on hikes to the forest and
carried food along. They played football on the meadow. But they
repented. God forgive me if I speak irreverently. But in all
these years that I, Shabsi Shepsel ben Levi Yitzhak served them
faithfully if not always wisely, ever since the eve of the first
World War, they never killed nor maimed a single Jew or Gentile.

"Attention!"

"Burka or Berl Minsky—what is your occupation?"

"A trader."

"A horse trader?"

"Yes."

"Stolen horses?"

"No."

"I don't believe you—if you are ever brought in on a charge,
you will be sent away to the district prison or even worse."

"Abba Dunsky—a teacher," he read from the dossier.

"Ben Zion—a fund raiser. What funds do you raise?"

"For Palestine, I used to. Not now."

"Let me warn you, if there is any collecting, you collect for us.
The Jews have hidden away gold, silver and diamonds. I appoint
you to be in charge of voluntary collections. Any Jew who refuses to hand over his valuables will be shot."

"Koppel Magid—what is your occupation. It says here you are
or were a lumber merchant."

"That's correct—also an importer of German chemicals."

"What else?"

"I used to import textiles, but I discontinued it when it became difficult."

"Aren't you an innkeeper?"

"It is only temporary."

"Any other business. You seem to be a man of a hundred occupations."

"I tried to make a living. My son sent me from America . . ."

"America is an enemy country," he cut him off, "we have no
contact with it, but if you have American money, turn it over to
us."

"I have none."

"There will be penalties, let me warn you, there will be many
penalties for holding back from us all forms of currency."

"I have none."

"We shall see."

"Rabbi Shepsel Kalir—you are not to instigate the Jews. You see what happened when the soldiers and even the Poles are provoked."

"I worship God and guide my flock."

"How do you guide them, against us?"

"Not against you or anyone else—I—we are all guided according to our law."

"This is a new age and a new law—the German law," he raised his hand dramatically. "Shoemaker, tailor, blacksmith," he read then stopped. After a while he turned to the Rabbi:

"You will report to this office every day until further orders. Make yourself presentable. Trim your beard. You need not wear this outlandish Prince Albert coat, dress modern!"

It was difficult for Rabbi Kalir to restrain himself, though it was dangerous to argue.

"I have been wearing this mode of dress," he ventured to reply, "since I became a Rabbi—my beard too." Von Preissig looked at him with the eye of an artist—it was indeed a picturesque figure and patriarchal in appearance—the more reason to denude him of this dignity.

"The soldiers don't like the archaic dress of the Jews, and the Poles—well, you saw how they acted. You owe your lives to us Germans. We saved you from a bloody pogrom. I can't speak for the future. It is up to you," Von Preissig concluded.

The prisoners were all dismissed on condition that they pay a heavy fine. David was all alone with Von Preissig, who was now somewhat fatigued. The two were facing each other; the master and the prisoner; the prosecutor with a thousand weapons at his command and the defender, with his soul as his only shield.

"You speak German rather well, where did you study?"

"In Königsberg. I was a student of engineering, but I didn't finish."

"Too bad, or who knows—do you care to smoke?" Von Preissig opened his silver box and extended to him a cigar."

"No thank you—I haven't smoked for a long time."

"We should be able to get along and understand each other. As for the other Jews, that's a different matter." Von Preissig lit the cigar and blew out the match with the smoke.

Von Preissig rose from his chair and began to pace the floor as if dictating to a secretary.

"Jews are our greatest challenge," he said and shook the ashes from the cigar. "Take the Czechs, we assured them of an undisturbed life, and a little church going. Now they are well adjusted and tame. Premier Hacha is an old lady.

"The Poles, well we destroyed their army, we bombed their cities, we killed and imprisoned enough to make it impossible for them to venture anything beyond a little underground activity.

"The Russians are holding on—there are so many of them." But our mighty army finds the wide open spacious steppes to its liking. We made a big mistake. Instead of freeing them from communist slavery we began to shoot them down and treat them like animals. Now they'll fight us with even more determination. We have our mighty panzer divisions. But you can't conquer a world with steel and explosive gadgets—unless you want to rule over a desert.

"For the Jews, conquest and enslavement is not enough, we've got to do something which is epochal and final. Did you ever read the story of Faust?" he asked David in a friendly voice.

"He sold his soul!"

"I don't mean that—we wouldn't go for that—you can't coerce a soul—we'll therefore work together, help one another. It may save the Jews from a fate much worse."

"But what can I do?"

"You are lucky to know me. I am not just a colonel in charge of a back province. I have an idea, a great idea, and you are going to help me."

"I still don't understand. What do you want me to do?"

"This is a scientific war. We've got tanks, aeroplanes, bombs—but we are not interested merely in conquering space. We want to conquer time, history, the spirit that unites, moves and creates history. Your religion contradicts our aspirations and your God denies us the image of a conqueror. But since we control you physically, we must also control you spiritually. We are conducting great experiments. Whoever controls the minds of mankind will win this war, and we are about to get complete control of everything living and breathing on earth, if you help us."

"We are a humble people. We live according to our own traditions. We are a peaceful people. God's name is the prince of peace."

"*Drang nach Osten,*" Von Preissig obsessed by his mania continued, "means, not only our need for territory but also to spread

our *Kultur*. We need land; we need markets; and the English
control the seas, and the Americans control the purse strings of
the continents. And the Jews control God, and we must conquer
all three, because you stand in our way." Then in a savage voice
Von Preissig cried out: "You will not crucify me, I will crucify
you. We don't need your God."

David was frightened. He had long been familiar with rumors
about the mistreatment of prisoners: experiments being con-
ducted by injecting camp mates with deadly viruses and air
bubbles, skins removed from Jews, Poles and Russians and
grafted to the skins of Germans who suffered burns. He heard
stories of slow tortures by immersion in frozen ice water, slow
death by experimental starvation and the repeated rumors of
methodic massacres of Jewish towns.

Von Preissig lit a new cigar. He bit into its fresh end and
continued to spawn his dark thoughts, which gradually assumed
a form of a deadly web, to ensnare and trap its victims.

"In science we employ laboratories. We might as well admit it.
Some of the best discoveries and inventions came from war,
otherwise all the sacrifices would not be worthwhile. We can use
guinea pigs, mice and rabbits. But there is no reason why we
can't employ other plentiful species for the sake of science.
However it doesn't have to come to that. But you must be willing
to help. Here is what you can do. Classify, translate and assemble the best of Jewish learning. Reveal all its secrets to me. If
you need help, I'll get you all the scholars in the world. I want to
know your innermost thoughts—what the Jews are up to. Anything of value, we must know."

"Why don't you use Christian scholars?"

"A master's painting cannot be copied by another and claimed
as original."

"I can't do that."

"What do you mean, you can't. I am ordering you!"

"I can't become a traitor. That's what you are asking me."

"You are not realistic," he eyed him sardonically. "Well you
are free to go. We'll treat you as you treat us. The Jews must
learn not only to obey but even to offer everything for the good
of the German Reich. Be ready when I call you."

The news from the front was bad. The Russians withdrew their
forces from Smolensk. The Germans claimed they were two
hundred miles from Moscow. . . .

David did not yet fully recover from the Saturday pogrom. Dr. Epstein began to treat the wounded, but he was recalled by the Germans and sent to Grondo. Dr. Lev preceded him a day before to treat the many wounded from the Russian front. Rachel was still detained as a hostage. He saw Von Preissig twice but each time the Kommandant gave a different excuse for her detention. At first it was for her own safety. She was beautiful, and some Germans including Schwarzhund had eyes on her. Finally he hinted that unless there was more cooperation, either one of them or both would be detained indefinitely. The Kommandant told him bluntly that he could resort to force, but he would prefer not to deal with servile slaves.

When the Rabbi sent word that he planned to see Potocki, David was ready to accompany him. Abba wanted to go along too. Chantze who made several attempts to deliver his letters via couriers, had left for Bialystok with a *Chalutzim* group. He hoped she and her group would succeed to reach Eretz Israel. Abba persisted to believe that somehow one of his letters would reach the outside world. Potocki was now his best hope.

"I am ready!" David said.

"I'll call Burka, we may need him," David said as he closed the door, while Rabbi Kalir went into the bedroom to see his son Judah, whose broken arm was put into a splint by Dr. Epstein.

When David returned with Burka, it was late in the afternoon. The brooding chestnut trees in the churchyard began to wall off the last rays of the day.

"I'll go ahead and let Potocki know that you are coming! There are dogs," Burka explained to them, while Rabbi Kalir tried to reassure the Rebetzin standing over Judah.

"If you mean the caretaker Denikin's dogs, they are under control. Call Clara, Potocki's daughter," David said.

"What about Basenko?" he asked about the former valet who managed the estate. "Hasn't he got trained bloodhounds?"

"Those are hunting dogs, for special events."

"Special, ah, and they recognize Jews?"

"What do you mean, Burka?"

"Only the other day Zeidel Stuzinsky, who was pursued by Skura's men into Lendinchine, passed a big vicious dog belonging to Mikulak the bad one. He was dressed like one of them, in peasant clothing; he carried his own suit wrapped up in a potato sack. The dog looked him over and almost let him go by, when

he sniffed the sack, began to pull it and when he recognized a
certain color he showed him his teeth, bark and bite."

"What do you mean, Burka?"

"It is simple—these dogs have been trained to know that one
dressed in homespun garb or a sheepskin is a friend, but one in a
black or cut suit is an enemy. Prince, Leibchik the butcher's dog,
always accompanies Jews wearing Prince Alberts all the way to
the synagogue. This is a respect that comes from his boss."

"One more thing," Burka called David aside. "It will be too
dark to go through the forest. You'll have to go through Long
Village, but be careful when you pass by the *Starosta's* house,
three houses down from Skura—there is a cross mounted on the
gate—don't stop to gaze at it—make believe you don't see it."

Late at night, the Rabbi and David arrived near the birch
grove. Up on the hill the manor stood out, shrouded in darkness.
Only the two windows above the stable glowed warmly. There
was a restrained bark and then a command.

"Quiet!" It was Clara with Burka alongside her, who now came
forward to greet them. "Good evening *Panowie*, father is waiting for you *Panie* Rabin," she turned her attention to Rabbi Kalir.
David stared at Burka whose face was swollen and more marked
than before.

"It is nothing. I tried the short cut through the forest, somebody stopped me near the crucifix. He told me to show respect
for the Lord or God or something. I said, 'Why don't you show
respect for women and children and old men, you murderer.' 'So
you are a Jew!' he answered. He cracked a whip at me. I grabbed
it from him and gave him a taste of his own medicine. He ran,
screaming 'Ayesus.' There were others with him. I did not care
to test my luck."

"Come, I'll clean your face," Clara said to him. "You are
brave," she whispered to him.

"Brave? The Rabbi and all the Jews—they are brave—to stand
up to all this—with only God inside them."

"Clara!" her father called her, "please bring some food, milk
and bread. You are my guest, *Panie* Rabin, my honored guest."

"No, no—I . . . Thank you . . . I can only speak for myself . . ."
He realized that he had no right to deny food to others.

"I don't know how to begin," Potocki, who sat on an improvised wheel chair, spoke slowly. "*Panie* Sokoloff knows my feelings."

"We have solved so many problems. We discovered God and know how to obey him through the laws of our Torah. We have established the Sabbath to make man holy; attained freedom to ban slavery; advocated peace to put an end to war. What did we not do to make man a partner to God in creation and in a just society. We have even overcome the fear of death through resurrection. But we can't escape the murderers who are after us; because people who are supposed to help us, help them." The Rabbi spoke grimly.

"These walls will never betray you."

"Yes—these walls are like the walls that cry out for justice and the answer shall echo from the rafters."

"But Graf Potocki, all this anti-semitism didn't happen. It was planted on Polish soil long ago."

Abba strained his eyes, and adjusted his glasses over his broken nose as he introduced a document.

Since Poland has but lately joined the fold of the Christian Church, it may be apprehended that its Christian inhabitants will make the move easily, yield to the prejudices and evil habits of their Jewish neighbors, the establishment of the Christian faith in the hearts of the believers in these lands having been of such a recent date. We therefore emphatically decree that Jews living in the bishopric of Gnesen shall not dwell together with Christians, but shall live separately in some portion of their respective towns and villages. The quarter in which the Jews reside shall be divided from the section inhabited by the Christians by a fence, wall or ditch.

Abba looked up after he finished the quote from paragraph 12 of the ecumenical council of 1266.

The pagan Poles were tolerant and fair to the Jews, but now came the bearers of God's word, with Jewish scriptures on their lips, teaching their new converts not love, but hate, not justice but abrogation of the law, not goodwill but malice, envy and hypocrisy. They erected the first wall and ghetto in Poland.

Jews were ordered to dispose of all their real estate holdings in Christian quarters; they were forbidden to appear on the street during church processions; they were restricted to a single synagogue in any one town; they were to wear a special cap to distinguish them from Christians; the Catholics on their part were forbidden under the threat of excommunication to invite Jews to feasts or social events; they were ordered not to buy meat or other

provisions from Jews lest—they were intimidated—be poisoned.
Jews were not allowed to keep Christian servants, collect taxes or
customs duties, nor to hold any public office.

These regulations of the Breslau ecumenical council were reaffirmed by the Council at Ofen in 1279 and anointed with another
infamy. The Jews were forced to wear a red badge.

Abba finished and rolled up his papers.

"Sinful, *rishes*," Rabbi Kalir said, and added, "and every day
we confess our sins, on Monday and Thursdays, and on fast days,
and on the Day of Atonement we condemn ourselves for transgressions and pray for forgiveness. Who sinned all these centuries and who should confess and ask for forgiveness?"

"This is where the Russian Communists got the idea of one
synagogue per city," Abba added.

" 'Nuremberg laws —they had good teachers and well prepared lessons from the thirteenth century and on." Rabbi Kalir
traced one of the origins of Nazi-fascist ideology. "Why, why did
they make the pogrom and violate the honor of our women?"

"They are hooligans," Potocki denounced them.

"How was it possible, that for two days, on Saturday and Sunday, no one came to inquire, to help, or even to express regret?
Their screams roused the dead, their cries were heard around
and in the church. For two days, not in a jungle or a cave—right
in the city in front of all the people who walked to church. They
passed by or dipped their hands in our blood, while we were
killed and maimed and marched to fire and water, and our purest
and noblest were defiled. Am I perhaps saying anything out of
place Panie Potocki?"

"No!"

"Against your faith?"

"No!"

Rabbi Kalir had finished. David felt it was his turn to speak.

"Now Panie Potocki, the Jews of twenty seven hundred years
ago resided in a small, poor land. They were farmers and shepherds who contributed one tenth of their produce to the priest-
hood in Jerusalem, and they reserved special allocations for charity. Their land was cultivated only for six years, and the seventh
was a sabbatical. They endured droughts and locusts, and above
all, rapacious neighbors, gangster nations who devastated their
land, sacked their cities, cut down their forests, burned their
temple, robbed their reserves of foods, destroyed their irrigation

systems, until the land turned to dust bowls; ravaged their women, sold their sons into slavery, and exiled the remnants that escaped from hunger, plague and sword. Are these not the people whom your preachers denounced wrongly for hundreds of years in the name of prophets? They who withheld a few bushels of rye, and dried grapes from the tithe? Did they go out to invade or conquer their neighbors, kill innocent men and children, or violate strange women?"

"I wish to God I could do more than just agree," Potocki said.

They were all silent. David did not forget to remind the Potockis that Rachel was still in a cell or a room. That he'd advise her to come here if it meets with their approval.

Abba was patient, with his letters still in his pockets, waiting for the last minute when he would shyly bow and hand them to Potocki, to be dispatched to all the capitals that could be reached. When Clara finally said, "I'll help Rachel," he handed her a pack of letters saying: "Send them, mail them, do anything. Maybe one of them will reach the outside world."

When they finally parted late at night the Rabbi carried in his heart an image of another just Pole, besides Malinoski. Graf Potocki who gave each some food to take along, proved that though in a wheel chair he sat on the throne of the just.

"You may go," Von Preissig finally released Rachel on Saturday evening, one week after her temporary arrest. "You are fortunate that you were in my custody."

"Am I?"

"I wonder if you understand," the colonel was annoyed.

"Understand what?"

"That it could have been worse."

"What could be worse, tell me?"

"I mean for you."

"Oh, just me." Rachel was aware that he was only concerned about her, whatever that meant.

"You'll excuse me. I have to attend to certain things. Here is a pass, a peasant's garb, and a cross. You may be molested but not killed, unless you start talking. Then you'll be in trouble."

"Danke," she said as she slipped out of his office; then to herself, "thank God." She threw away the cross and rolled up the peasant's dress and tucked it under her arm.

At first she wanted to return home and find out about her family, to locate David and the others. But there were so many casualties. The Germans detained the two Jewish doctors in the Grodno army hospital. The mob emptied Abchik's drug store. The mourners needed comfort and the wounded care. Jewish women and girls were assaulted by Polish ruffians. Her last resort was an appeal to the priest to stop it. But how could she get to his house adjoining the police. She must ask Graf Potocki to see the priest. It was now late at night and the roving bands were for the moment celebrating, resting or carting away their loot, as they have done for the last week.

A patrol stopped her as she passed Velvke's house. A dim light shone from the window. Were they attending to somebody who was hurt? She thought she heard moans from another house as she was about to enter Long Village. Polish police with armbands, unsteady on their feet, called her first politely, then in vulgar language. She ran through Teviah Stuzinsky's yard all the way back to the brewery, where huge barrels and vats needing repair were stacked against the wall. She squeezed herself into a narrow space between barrels, changed into the peasant dress, folded her own and dropped it through an opening into one of the barrels. She thought she heard breathing and movement from several of them. She then climbed over the rear fence and across several railings of gardens and she was again in the open, on the sleepy tranquil street of Long Village. She heard a few barks; and then a villager came across, checking the arrival of the wagon master, who unloosed the horse collar, shafts and harness. Was he one of the murderers, looters or bystanders?

"Hey *panenko*, watch out for your old man and better tell a good lie." He tried to engage her in conversation as he came toward her. She kept on walking and rebuked him while bypassing him, *"Pashol*, you smelly goat." It was an unpalatable experience of words, tones and manners for her. But it was better than flashing a cross.

Late after midnight she arrived at the Potocki estate. The main house was lit up. Col. Schwarzhund, the S. S. Officers and his staff were there to celebrate. They were confident that German victories and Jewish incidents would continue uninterrupted till Christmas and New Years; hence many more celebrations. These *'feier abendan'* were a means of relaxation and driving away boredom.

Somebody was coming toward Rachel from the rear of the mansion with a barking dog on a leash. It was too late to run. Finding herself trapped against the bolted big stable door, she began to pound it with her fists. The barking became more furious. The dog pulled the man on the other end of the leash toward her. The window above opened and closed instantly.

"Who is it?" she heard a girl's voice from some one running down a stairway inside.

"Help me! Rachel! Open!"

While not recalling the name, since it wasn't a man's voice, she opened the door. "Over there, hide!" she let her in and pointed to storm windows and doors leaning against the stairway.

"Ah, Clara!" Denikin, the caretaker who followed within seconds called out, "I thought I saw somebody."

"It was me."

"But you have a night dress on."

"And you saw a darker shade?" She rebuffed him.

"Yes." He wanted an explanation.

"I took a night walk; went upstairs and changed."

"Late at night?"

"You are up!"

"That's different."

"Anything special?" She casually sought information.

"Lots of parties. Many officers. Women. Eat. Drink till morning. Happened many times before. Fall asleep on floor."

"Well, good night Denikin, I'm tired."

"Good night. Only funny, dogs don't bark at you."

"Maybe they mixed up smell," Clara said as she closed the door behind her.

"Maybe," Denikin said to himself, scratched his head in bewilderment, then having figured it out, departed.

"You must be the Novor girl," Clara recognized the petite beauty with the dark intent eyes peering from a pale drawn face.

"Help, we need help," her voice quivered.

"I and my father will protect you."

"It's the women and girls who must be rescued. We also need doctors and medicines."

"What can I do? Father is in a wheel chair."

"Go to the priest."

"We are being watched."

"You must!"

"You can't stay here," her voice tensed as she stopped to listen. "Denikin knows his dogs, he sniffs like a dog himself. He'll inform Basenko and they'll come to search here."

"What shall I do, tell me?"

"Here, put on this *babushka,* you'll look like a real peasant girl. But don't speak, your Polish is too literary. I'll go to the priest before dawn."

"And the doctors?"

"They are here—there was an accident, one of theirs was attacked by the dogs." She went to the window, opened it slightly. "I think someone is coming. Out this way," she guided her down the steps and opened a trap door for her that led to the shallow tunnel underneath the stable.

"What about the dogs?" Rachel was apprehensive as Clara opened for her a screened opening through which she climbed out.

"Without the dogs there is no warning, it is a surprise. Hurry, I must return to engage Denikin. Be careful, avoid patrols, don't talk to anybody. I'll be there early."

Clara could not return to sleep. Denikin was still lurking in the circular driveway of the mansion when she called him.

"Denikin, take me into town!"

"Now?"

"It is almost dawn, I have to do something."

"On Sunday? So early?"

"I have to get medicine."

"The doctors are here."

"It is a standing prescription, and I have to see the priest."

"That sounds better." He seemed unconvinced. "I can't use a car."

"Take our coach and harness one of the horses."

Dawn was late, and the night tarried too long. When she arrived in the ravaged city, she heard a blood chilling scream race from roof to roof, into the trees. The birds withdrew their beaks from their feathered slumber, blinked into the shadows, and returned to sleep. The cry raced down Synagogue Street, over the river, bounced off the woodlet opposite the cemetery, and returned through Church Street and dashed itself against the massive stone wall, surrounding the church. Fragments of sighs were scattered in all directions.

Clara bypassed the guards who rushed from the red house to question her.

"Zu Priester," she said in German and incoherently made motions.

"Eine dumme aber schöne mädchen," (a beautiful but dumb girl) the scraggy faced soldier remarked.

"Ich weine wenn ich daran denke," (I weep when I think of it) the roly-poly one shrugged it off. It wasn't worth a damn to him. Womanhood was a commodity exploited by the German civilian and soldier. Thousands of drafted women from occupied countries were supplied as slave labor to German factories, farms and homes. Thousands of girls were snatched from their homes, tattooed *Feld Uhre* and dispatched to army brothels.

Clara knocked on the front door. When there was no answer, she went to the rear and banged furiously on the door, until an old servant appeared.

"What do you want?"

"They are killing the Jews. You heard that cry?"

"I heard nothing, there are many screams at night."

"But not such a wailing cry."

"A scream is a scream."

"Where is the priest?"

"He is sick."

"Speak to him."

"I can't."

"Let me speak to him."

"You can't."

"Why?"

"He can't speak."

"What is wrong?"

"Lost his voice."

"A stroke?"

"Yes."

RUSSIANS PUSH NAZIS BACK.
SWITZERLAND IS GAY ON 650TH
BIRTHDAY. ISLAND OF PEACE,
NEUTRALITY . . .

*The wicked do not repent even at the gate of
Gehennam.*

Erubin, 19.

13

IDOL-GODS EMERGE FROM SAMBATYON

While Sambatyon erupted with fire and water during the day
and its searing effects would penetrate every Jewish house,
prison and refuge during the night, the bloody sunset in the
country was idyllic. The peasants were done with the day's
duties. The fields were abandoned and the gardens were left to
the care of night-dew. The rye was tall and full. The potato
clusters in the ground were now full sized. The rich black soil in
the gardens were carpeted with patches of big round cabbage
plants, ever spreading their big green leaves to absorb all the
sunshine by day, and catch the precious dew at night. Slender
onion shoots drew flavor and salt into their firm tubes. The morrow and after tomorrow would be busy and well spent. And then
there was a happy harvest of the fields and the busy days in the
garden. Wagon loads with sheaves, potatoes and all kinds of
vegetables would fill the barns and the cellars.

And then the short winter days and long nights. Big bowls of
steaming potatoes and tangy cabbage soup, and pork and lard
from the inexhaustible family barrel. And sleep and more sleep
and on Sundays to church and drinks. And good suppers. And
spinning for the women and smoking, drinking and idle gossip
for the men, holiday gifts and games for the children; and then
the church bells ringing in the night and more sleep.

There was a knock on Von Preissig's door, then another and
another. The orderly was outside on the lookout for Kommandant Rintzler.

"What is it? You look worried," he told Todt.

"I sent a letter to my wife—about three weeks ago. I mailed it on the night of July eleven," the mechanic said.

"Yes three weeks—it's war and mail is slow."

"Do you think it was a heavy raid?"

"I don't know," Von Preissig said guardedly.

"I mean confidentially."

"It is restricted information. I'm quite certain you'll get a reply," he told him.

"Is the radio in good order?" Todt asked.

"Yes," he replied to the mechanic, whose probing questions disturbed him. "I have an appointment," Von Preissig cut the interview. Presently Ludke knocked on the door and announced: "Company had just arrived." He waited for them in his office, he was in no mood to entertain them in the more spacious reception room in the rear.

Colonel Schwarzhund greeted him formally as he entered and introduced the Kommandant from Grodno, Rintzler:

"Have you met before?" he asked the host.

"In a way." He referred to the telephone conversation on July 12, and added, "Yes, we met before." Rintzler could not recall the occasion. Neither cared to recall the July 18 meeting.

"Would you be my guest for supper?" Von Preissig invited Rintzler, but he was not insistent.

"No, I've had a busy day at the hunting lodge. Yesterday and this morning too."

"Any worthwhile trophies?" he asked and observed that the inspector squirmed.

"A sporting event to me is not for trophies, but action and excitement." The Kommandant now readily agreed that the name "Monch" (Monk) fitted the copy of Himmler perfectly. His button eyes blinking from behind his glasses, his inscrutable face, faded skin, puffed eyes and low voice, gave him the appearance of an introvert average citizen or clerk found in many a German office, factory or shop.

"Did you have any action?" Von Preissig asked him.

"It was quite exciting until the accident."

"Accident?" Von Preissig heard it from Messer who was a witness. One of Rintzler's aides, a giant but dull-witted man, was attacked by the bloodhounds, particularly one, and was badly mauled. Drs. Lev and Epstein were called in to save him late Saturday afternoon at the height of the bloody spectacle.

"I regret that I couldn't be there both days," Schwarzhund, who was quiet spoke up, "I have to attend to my duties."

"Then you saw the entire action," Rintzler prodded him about his observation of the 'disciplined action march', as Rintzler referred to it.

"Yes this took place on Saturday two weeks ago."

"Oh yes. I recall the date. What do you think of it?" Rintzler sounded out his host.

"I can't say it was my idea, but I carried out orders," Von Preissig said.

"I give you credit for being frank. And you?" he spurred the inspector to speak.

"I was very much impressed," he answered and repeated his theory. "Germany takes a step at a time, then watches the reaction. This is how it will work with the Jews: first we'll take a few towns at random. We'll create a few incidents; then confiscation and drafting of labor. A small ghetto, a bigger ghetto after protests. Two families in a house, then four and five, and even smaller towns moving into larger towns and all the time the vise will be tightened; less food, less freedom, less medicine, more and harder work conditions, tighter and tougher experiments; punishment will label them in the eyes of the non-Jews as open for attack, as different. By being different, by being reduced to skeletons, even the mostly docile Poles will become predators, unaware that in the end they'll be hunted down too. Are you interested; I can tell more?"

"No," Von Preissig answered. He resented both the commentator and his theories.

"Bravo!" Rintzler commended him. His lips parted, half smile, half venom, half cynical, half beastly cunning. "You forgot the conclusion," the Monk reminded his adopted disciple.

"What is it?" he looked up to him.

"Ah, these will be implemented according to time and circumstances, but it will be beautifully finished, without a trace of clumsiness. My car is waiting, and much much work, final decisions. Good hunting. You'll hear from me," he said, saluted mechanically and departed.

"What is the purpose of all this?" Von Preissig reversed himself in order to ferret out secret Gestapo plans.

"The purpose, my good colonel, is to spread rumors, and wait
for international reaction. Should we be reprimanded by the
Geneva convention, the neutrals or even the Vatican, we could
easily counter with news releases and broadcasts that the rumors
are Jewish-Bolshevik fabrications, and atrocity propaganda. Always combine Jewish Bolshevik and atrocity propaganda, the
latter worked in the last war for the Allies and the first in this
war for us. So far so good, we haven't heard anything to be
afraid of from the Red Cross, the neutral diplomats or the religious bodies, including the Vatican. Only the usual Jewish protests. Now and then a trade union and a few writers will release
a few lines to the press. Nobody pays any attention to them."

"Then what?"

"The next step—the first large scale shipments of Jews to concentration camps—will be the turning point. In between we'll
schedule a mixed cargo shipment of anti-Nazis: communists,
socialists, liberals; also Slavs, Dutch, Scandinavians, perhaps,
yes, even gypsies."

"I don't get it." Von Preissig pretended naivete.

"If after the mixed cargo there are the routine war bulletins
sub-headlines, mild protests and backpage press coverage, while
the headlines are blazing with individual exploits, sport events,
inventions, speeches, mass protests, crimes, scandals and benefits
—we'll sneak through during all this maze with the second shipment of Jews. We'll wait to appraise our results from our listening posts in London, Paris, Rome, Washington, the Vatican and
Cairo. The second and larger shipments will be staged as punishment for resisting us—we can always say resisting: we did
away for the same reasons with tens of thousands of Polish and
Russian prisoners. It will take place simultaneously in Poland,
Germany, Hungary, Roumania, Czechoslovakia, Bulgaria,
Greece, France and Russia, and even the fascists in Italy, will do
the same, and the Pope will keep quiet. Did I leave out any
country?"

"Is that all?" Von Preissig was now impatient. He had heard it
so many times, that it seemed incredible that one would repeat it
with such intensity, as if all of Germany's future and victory
depended on this.

"Now," he continued without a letup, "if after this second
shipment of Jews from the bigger ghettos and concentration
camps, there will again be only Jewish demonstrations and pro-

tests; columns and leading editorials in allied newspapers, long pronouncements by the Pope, with vague phrases about our Jewish heritage, we'll go ahead with the final solution."

"How far have you already gone?" he now wanted to find out something which came to him unverified.

"Quite far. Within a year or two it will all be finished. The all clear signal to liquidate the Jews will depend as much on what we do to them and what the Allies fail to do for them. Then this will be the terrible end."

"Did you say terrible?"

"I meant final, terrible for the Jews and Allies."

"It is terrible," Von Preissig remarked. He got up, looked in the window and sat down again evidently depressed by the fact that he would be a cog of this machine, his dream of trying to salvage a part of Jewry as robot slaves of Germany was evidently not even considered.

"Why are you upset, it didn't happen yet?" Colonel Schwarzhund asked.

"Because of what happened."

"Only an incident."

"You call this an incident, killing, burning, rape? As a German officer I am responsible."

"Your responsibility is for the Führer and the Third Reich."

"I thought . . ."

"That you could experiment with your theory to save the Jews as slaves for Germany. We have plenty of slaves, Poles, Russians, many others will follow. We want to get rid of them, get their savings and properties, resettle all these cities with Germans. With millions of German shopkeepers, merchants, artisans, mechanics, importers, exporters, professionals, administrators, executives, colonizing these countries, all supervised by our government—why we'll own Europe, all its resources and people. Did I say people? I meant slaves."

"We'll be held accountable if we go too far."

"Why should you?"

"Because."

"My dear Colonel, you are not practical. All we do is carry out orders as Kommandants, inspectors. We build ghettos . . ."

"Did you say build?"

"Call it designate."

"We transform cities into ghettos."

"Whatever it is—we manage and govern it—we provide work."

"Provide or conscript?"

"Don't be so technical—we even supply man power to local and distant industrial complexes—all for the war effort. In a sense we are administrators who take orders from high above."

"Aren't you afraid of this future?"

"The future is ours."

"Suppose . . . ?"

"It isn't, you mustn't say it or think it!"

"I didn't say anything, suppose some day you will be held accountable for all this."

"Accountable again?" the inspector was irked that this *"verantwortlich"* was flung at him twice. *"Die ganze Welt ist verantwortlich."* (The whole world is responsible.)

"You can't tell it to a court," then realizing that it was a rash utterance retracted, "What I am trying to say is, we have to protect ourselves."

"Now you said it," he snatched from the Kommandant the last phrase which he could have meant 'to protect ourselves' against charges of excesses, "I am preparing for that. You must know about it—did you ever hear of Swiss banks, South America, Argentina particularly?"

"Perhaps."

"Well what do you think of it?"

The telephone rang, it gave him an opportunity to cut off this dangerous dialogue with Colonel Schwarzhund. He wasn't a functionary educated simpleton as he thought at first. He appeared to him crafty, and with good connections to higher ups. He could be dangerous. It has reached a point where everyone is dangerous.

"Yes," he intoned a worn-out greeting into the telephone and waved limply to the departing Colonel Schwarzhund.

This was not a game any more. It was getting entangled and he was caught in a web. As a Kommandant he had to be firm; he was up against a rogues' gallery. No officer of the Reich was going to be outsmarted by such characters, but how? What about his plan for the Jews and one special Jew who would serve as—as what? He was a front all by himself. How could he resolve all the conflicts between his duty as the Kommandant to liquidate this town and his own plan to exploit the Jews as slaves?

Von Preissig was virtually paralyzed with inaction after the confrontation with Rintzler and Schwarzhund. He dressed and sat on his bed, trying to figure out what move to make.

Von Preissig listened to the radio reports on his short wave set. It was a period of decisive German victories on the eastern front. The panzer divisions and the Wermacht broke the backbone of the Russian army. The shadow of the German front was leaping kilometers nearer to Moscow. There was glory and fame for generals in command, and he a relative of General Von Hindenburg was hibernating behind the front. It was not even a rail point, just a town along the highway midway between Bialystok and Grodno.

It was humiliating for a military man to squander the best career years as Kommandant of a forgotten town. It was depressing and driving him to the brim of paranoia. He should have been at Von Hindenburg's funeral. He would surely have been marching right behind the caisson of Germany's dead president. He missed his opportunity. Adolf Hitler the former corporal who succeeded him as Fuehrer and Reichskanzler would perhaps have thrown something his way. Now he can't even get an appointment to see the Fuehrer.

As a result he had to contend alone against his superior the sinister Kommandant Rintzler from Grodno and his local overseer Col. Schwarzhund and the henchmen Capt. Messer and Lt. Schrecke. These S. S. men would watch his performance as subjugator and liquidator of the Jews.

Resourceful great men however always emerged on top no matter where they found themselves. General Paul Von Hindenburg won his fame on the Mazur marshes of East Prussia, Guderian excited the imagination with his lightning tank thrusts in Africa and Von Paulus with his swift advance on Stalingrad.

Von Preissig, too, had his plan. He would have to accomplish it against the greatest of odds. In war he employed forces and weapons to attain his objective. Now he had to generate his own power and tactics. He grappled with something unconventional. How to attain the same end by first reducing the Jews to slaves before finally eliminating them. Perhaps there could be a middle phase-power; to exploit the invisible Jewish power. He would concentrate on the first phase: put them to work, exploit their talents, divert all their means, possessions and energy for local and distant projects on the farms and factories. If he succeeded here his plan would be adopted for all of occupied Europe, with him in charge. It was too early in the morning for such a nebulous plan. For it involved not merely the physical capacities of the Jews, but also their spiritual potential.

He went over his schedule for the day: arrests, confiscations, punitive measures and memos from Rintzler with notations to check with Schwarzhund. Right now he was very eager to see the films of the "Fire and Water," episode.

"Are the pictures in order?" He was referring to the movie reels, that were being developed at extraordinary speed by Gerhardt Swarcz, the all around cinematography expert who operated the projector for Von Preissig's private amusement. Little did Gerhardt realize that these private showings of 'pictures in the raw,' as he called them, were invaluable to his master's carefully hatched plan.

"They are ready," he answered.

"Then proceed," Von Preissig ordered. He began to sip his somewhat cooled coffee as Gerhardt covered the windows with blackout paper.

Gerhardt was now ready with the projector. Von Preissig was amused and flattered by his own likeness on the screen. His face was pale but photogenic. The lines on the face, the wedge-like nose, the small gray eyes, were all lost in lights and shadows. His face, against background of a well cut uniform surrounded by black garbed S.S. men, stood out as important and authoritative.

"Well done," he paid a compliment to Gerhardt in an undertone.

The preliminary tidbits were now on the screen. They were labeled for "export" to fascist agencies and neutrals; for home consumption and beer halls; and trimmed even to satisfy the fastidious prying of the Geneva Convention. There were the usual S.S. men in uniforms, presenting loaves of bread to civilians. Shots of headquarters and crowds receiving inoculation. Polish guards training to put out fires, and peasant girls presenting them with flowers in front of the church. All these preceded the main feature, as yet untitled. Synagogue Street came into view; children, first curious and then running away into the yard of the synagogue. Then came the young men walking in and out of the synagogue. The pictures taken inside the synagogue were excellent. The morning light illuminated the close-ups. Again Von Preissig saw himself in the mist of patriarchal figures, covered with praying shawls. Some were standing, others leaned or gazed intensively into Hebrew books. Instinctly he reacted with a wry smile at the swaying worshippers and the gesticulating bearded men in a corner, in friendly dispute about the text. A Jew ascended the *Bima* and another one descended. That was interesting. The uplifting of the scroll of the law appeared like a painting. A still picture would be grandiose, Von Preissig thought. But there was nothing so far amusing about the Jews in their general behavior. They were unafraid and unbowed in their own house.

He fumbled for the box of cigars, changed his mind and called out "Ludke, cigarettes!" Why were they unafraid, he asked himself. They marched and suffered horribly on the market place. They struggled violently to free their women from abuse. Yet they showed contempt when faced with death. Power—the Jews have great power and conspire to destroy us, we were told. But where is that power? They can't overcome us physically. But neither can the French, Russians and all the others with all their formidable weapons, mighty armies, navies and air forces. He lit a cigarette.

Then why do we fear the Jews? They are reputed to have a destructive power against us. Didn't they help to defeat us in the first World War? So the Nazis tell us. But this is nonsense. Jewish soldiers in German and Austrian uniforms fought on our side. Then this fear is against something invisible. It is a spiritual power with which the Jews threaten us. Suppose we win over the Jews on our side, or at the least extract from them the secret of their power—whatever it is—then Germany would eventually win this war.

No, no, Germany cannot conquer by arms alone. He lit another cigarette and began to pace the floor.

"Shall I stop?" Gerhardt asked.

"Proceed!" he waved his hand in disgust at being interrupted.

Even if Germany conquers all her enemies, exploits their wealth and reduces their people to serfdom, it is still not assured of a permanent victory. Europe is at Germany's feet. But in the midst of all this, there is the problem of the Jews. It is the strength of the Jewish people which cannot be broken, no matter how many are starved, shot and gassed. Gassed? We don't even gas the soldiers of the enemy. It is forbidden. What is forbidden?

"Power," he mumbled as the films demonstrated amply the

thrust of the bayonet, the butt of the gun, and the lash of the whip against the Jews. But this is not real power, eventually. Egypt could not enslave the Jews, nor could the Roman legions conquer them. What is the mystery of this Jewish power?

It is an unknown quantity, but vital to perpetuate the one thousand year reign of the Reich. The Jews have it in them. Didn't they accomplish the impossible, invent a God that everyone believed existed but that couldn't be located? Didn't they cleverly impress upon the world this formula, through their own scriptures? It wouldn't do for the Germans to accept a substitute for God, a son. Especially, since he was handed down to them unconditionally. No! The Germans must have a hand, even in the shaping of God and his satellites. They will not accept a religion that considers them only followers. The new Reich religion must make followers and satellites of all Christians. But how, by what authority and primacy?

The Jews—their best minds were now in German hands. Great religious minds are not heralded nor publicized while they are alive. They are learned but simple, humble individuals. Suppose he could locate such a simple Jew with some knowledge and background, convert him psychologically and then through his captive soul advocate a surrender not only of the Jews, but of Judaism itself.

David is the ideal subject, but he is not so simple. To win over David, that would be the key to this plan. It would unlock the closed gates to the inner secrets of Jewish power. If David could persuade the Jews—why not? It could be done.

There was no choice left for the Jews or David. If they accepted his plan, he might even succeed in saving them from further annihilation. It was not yet perfected in his mind. But through research based on a recruited elite of the best minds—young Jews with a German education—it could be accomplished.

It was too early for such visionary plans. It was as yet unclear in his mind. But it agitated him to lay the ground work for this experiment in the ghetto.

The orderly knocked on the door. He was allowed in by the guard. Von Preissig awoke from his reverie.

"What time is it."

"Twelve. Your lunch, Kommandant," the orderly said as he placed a linen covered tray on the desk. He forgetfully turned on the radio. The same grinding voice, or so it seemed. For the hundredth time it denounced Winston Churchill, Roosevelt and the International Jewish bankers. He turned it off. The orderly set before him his favorite lunch. The Berliner Tageblatt was neatly folded as usual. He opened it, glanced at the headline then his eyes caught an item on the inside page. He swallowed chunks of food. He was like a tourist at a provincial inn impatient to get away from its dreariness and back to the main highway.

"Good shots," Gerhardt remarked as Von Preissig sipped his coffee and then added, "Very interesting."

He put down the glass. The last word sounded strange: Death, food, and "interesting?"

"Repeat the second part, the fire," he ordered Gerhardt.

Even at the sight of the fire, they were not panicky—they were aware of danger. German soldiers ran in panic when a shell exploded in their midst. He remembered a frightened soldier who crawled into a trench and refused to leave. Of course he had to be shot. But these Jews—what is this? Here is the march, no one fell to his knees "kissing the German boots." Well, the next scene would be different. No! Men and young boys, even the old, led by their dignified Rabbi, were marching in good order. Some were praying, but all looked straight ahead, ready to meet the worst with a prayer. What stuff are they made of, these Jews, unafraid of death?

But wait, the water would make them look ridiculous. There they are forced off the bridge, some disappear, as they are driven like cattle, some swim and are shot. Rabbi Kalir is now at close range. Two limping Jews are at his side. He holds them up. One falters and falls and the Rabbi summons a Jew behind him and they carry him off. A boy paddles along frantically like a duck with a broken leg. There were more boys. Too bad they couldn't swim. The Jews are still calm, water is dripping from their hats; the Polish guards and the loose women jeer at them.

The S.S. men appear frantic; they would like to machinegun them and get it over. Captain Messer has abandoned all authority to Lt. Schrecke who fires a machine revolver in all directions, like a boy a toy pistol. He is the only one who appears himself. The Germans and Polish guards' faces, are twisted and poorly focused. They appear like cattle drivers and the Jews like saints.

Maybe that's the reason the Germans want to murder them.
They are witnesses. No trace must be left of the things we are
doing. The Mongols killed every living thing in the path of their
invasions, so that no alarm could be given that the Mongol
hordes are coming. The Germans would kill not only those
within sight, but everything that bears in its soul the voice from
Sinai "Thou shalt not kill!"

For a fleeting glance he sees the mother—Malke Schuster and
her child, its face contorted by crying. A German is bending
down, picks up the baby, but it cried even more fearfully. The
soldier puts it down near its mother. The baby is tugging at her
sleeves, pulling at her friendly but lifeless face. The baby is now
terrified by a dangling swastika or cross that a soldier swings in
front of its face. The baby is crying bitterly.

Now this was a discovery—a mother—like a statue, prostrate
and helpless. Yet its child was alive and kicking in its defiant
crying. Death giving birth to life. "Hold it!" he signalled. Before
his eyes was a strange revelation, a Jewish mother whom he had
actually murdered, and yet he was full of compassion for her and
hopeful for the child. He himself had only one son.

His wife was always sick and promised him that after the war
there would be a house full of children. But who wants a house-
ful? Here is one to be claimed. A Jewish child. But how could he
love a Jewish child? Germans had been hating Jews for centuries, nevertheless they worshipped every day in their churches,
a Jewish mother and child. But this would be even more epoch
making. The revelation of life emerging from a damned world.
The Jews were doomed. If he could save them as slaves, even a
portion of them, this in itself would be a great achievement. It
would be greater than just worshipping a Jewish mother and
child, while murdering or hating the rest of the Jews. But how
far could he go? Not one German officer or authority has so far
dared to deviate from the Fuehrer's genocide policy against the
Jews.

The reels were all finished, the curtains were opened wide,
and a diffusion of light swept into the room. He was now relaxed
and lit a cigar.

Von Preissig stood up, looked in the mirror, adjusted his uniform and tie, switched his cigar to the left side of his mouth and
with his teeth gripping it tightly, casually asked Gerhardt, "How
does it appear to you?"

"It depends what you want to see and what you desire to show," he gave a professional opinion.

"I want to see them as they are—conquered, helpless and guilty characters."

"The camera plays many tricks. It sometimes reveals everything. They were not panicky."

"In other words, it was not according to our script."

"Exactly, in fact they wrote their own scenario, winning the sympathy of the audience by emerging as martyrs."

"Martyrs, martyrs, that's the last thing I had in mind. A whole religion was made by a few Jewish martyrs. No martyrdom for them, whatever happens to them. Martyrdom is *verboten*."

"We can counteract this unfortunate impression by editing the films as we did in Bialystok." Gerhardt added as he slapped with his notebook on his leather jacket.

"Oh yes, I recall that film, a cameraman held back the Jews going to the synagogue on Saturday for special shots, and the caption read 'Jews Welcoming German Army.' "

"And do you remember the scene when Jews were forced to bury their own dead whom the Germans shot, just to terrorize them? The caption read, 'Volunteer Jews Dig Trenches for German Army.' "

"That was almost comical. But there is one scene, the child embracing the dead mother," he reverted to his technical observation—"it steals the show."

"I thought about it. I haven't yet come to a decision. Meanwhile do not tamper with it until further orders."

The proud dignified faces of the Jews intrigued him. All his life their very image had been impressed upon him as that of villains. In the dark recesses of his disturbed religious training, he saw them as Christ killers. But he always wondered. How can they be killers? They were a peaceful people. They didn't recognize a Jew as a Messiah. He was not the choice of the majority. He defected from their struggle against Rome and was unlike the prophets, vague about Zion's redemption. It is all wrapped up in contradiction and mystery. How can one hate the Jews and yet worship a Jewish mother and child? How can Christians respect the Jewish religion and accept only the parts suitable for their own biased interpretation?

As a cadet in the academy, his mind was saturated with military science. He was guided by the theoretical lectures as well as the experiences of his teachers in actual combat. It was based on the mastery of weapons, tactics, strategy, intelligent planning and execution. But now he explored an uncharted field with neither stars nor compasses to point the way.

September 21, 22, 23, 1941:   POPE REFUSED TO DECLARE
WAR AGAINST NAZISM A JUST
WAR. JEWISH NEW YEAR
SERVICES: APPEALS TO JEWS
TO ACCEPT WITHOUT
GRUMBLING SACRIFICES
NECESSARY TO SAVE WORLD
FROM BONDAGE.

*There is no peace, said the Lord,
unto the wicked.*

Isaiah, 48:22.

*It is permissible to wage war
against the wicked.*

Megillah, 6.

14

DEFENDER AND PROSECUTOR BEFORE
HIS THRONE

For three weeks Moshe Davner, the sexton, roused the Jews of the
New Synagogue to the pre-dawn *Selichoth,* supplications. On the
third Saturday they assembled for midnight services. Thus the
month of *Elul*—the month of spiritual maneuvers—was concluded on the eve of the new month. *Tishrei* ushered in the new
year, two days of *Rosh Hashonah* on Monday and Tuesday
and was climaxed after nine days of penitence on *Yom
Kippur,* the first of October. It was always a delight to look
ahead to these first ten days of the seventh month, *Tishrei.* Were
they not days of awe, judgment, confession, repentance and re-
examination of man's destiny and purpose on this earth? They
were, but they were also days of expectation, the joy of giving
birth to a new year at a time when the autumn leaves were
breathing their farewell before the oncoming cold rains, lashing
winds and the bleak days of winter.

On this second day of *Rosh Hashonah,* the Jews were permitted to assemble for prayer after the stoppage on the first day. It was a long day—the prescribed two days to mark the new year—as God wanted it to be, two days to solemnize one full day of a better and blessed year. No one—not within memory—has ever dared to slice it in half, as the Germans did by blacking out the first day, the first half, from this earthly kingdom emulating the heavenly kingdom.

The first sounds of the *shofar* reaffirmed the covenant between God who transmitted the Torah to Moses, and the Israelites after receiving it from this foremost prophet. They pledged to uphold it with all their hearts, souls and might. It was significantly right after the reading of the Torah, that the coronation of the *Malchuth Shomaim,* the heavenly kingdom, was reenacted through the *shofar* sounds. This humble ram's horn symbolized the ram offered on the altar in place of Isaac. Throughout Jewish history its reverberating echoes pierced the threatening clouds above them and shattered the siege walls around them. Now its alarm signals became the only means of communication from their valley of despair to the unobstructed exalted heights of the King of Kings.

The multiple blasts for the second time, re-established not only communication with God, but also activated a covenant of mercy through the medium of *Zichronoth,* remembrance.

Finally, for the third time, during *Shofroth* of the afternoon *Musaf,* additional service, the shofar blasted through the barrier of the inimical besieging hostile nations, and satanic incriminations to seek acquittal through zealous and merited defenders in heaven. The Jews always got along quite well with God. He was their father and they were his children to love and be loved, to be reprimanded and to ask forgiveness. They guarded zealously their commitments to and mandate from Sinai. They invoked his promise to redeem them from atrocious pagans, to return them to the Zion of Torah and to restore Jerusalem as God's capital for all free and just nations.

The Rabbi began to recite the preliminary "Hymns of Unity," in the New Synagogue. Though three different readers were to chant the prayers, he was to be the accredited ambassador, *Sheliach Zibbur,* of the Jewish community to the heavenly kingdom. He geared himself, beyond mere supplication, for a relentless dialogue with God.

There were things that forewarned him of a master plan of

unheard cruelty, to be perpetrated by men masquerading as the just, the pious, the religious church worshippers.

O God, what can I tell my people? I heard the bad news: one hundred men—boys and elders—drafted for Strassenbau, on the Yanowa-Sokolke highway, another hundred at the work camp of Novidvor-Dombrowa, an additional contingent of one hundred at Shtraflager of the firm Kirchof and still another one hundred at Agustowa. Is there no way to impede the Nazi plans? The *Judenrat* committee refused to comply with Von Preissig's request at the behest of Col. Schwarzhund. What good would it do? Who could select the Jewish children who now slave under cruel guards? The children are beaten and starved, until they wish death to rescue them. Girls toiling for peasant taskmasters pad their dresses with rags even on hot days to withstand daily beatings.

Does it not say in the scriptures that 'The Lord your God is he that goeth with you to fight for you against your enemies to save you?' Therefore it is up to God and we can do nothing. But this was indeed idolatry, employing God's name in vain by violating the commandment, 'Do not stand by while your neighbor's blood is shed.'

But the Rabbis know that man, not God, must safeguard justice, prevent murder, and unite all to go into battle against an enemy embodying evil. For it was written that an anointed priest should empower, justify, and arouse all to fight against an enemy!

"What is that sound?" Col. Schwarzhund asked the Kommandant.

"It's from the synagogues."

"How do you know?"

"I gave them permission to sound it."

"You did, to hunt—or what is it?"

"To proclaim a New Year, or frighten away bad spirits like the Chinese with fire crackers."

"Are you sure?" the Colonel Inspector was skeptical.

"If you doubt my words—why . . ."

"Let us not quarrel about our doomed subjects. To me a horn is a hunter's call. It certainly sounds funny when one is not hunting," the Colonel Inspector was on the verge of a snicker.

"It's not funny at all. It is an awakening."

"Ah, ah, you are an expert on the Jews."

"How did it go yesterday?" Von Preissig was anxious.

"Very smooth, according to plan. We took away the Jewish livestock and rounded up more Jews for work camps. We even collected brass and copper pots for the army and a few odds and ends for distribution."

"Distribution?"

"Colonel! If we didn't take it for our families the *verfluchte Pollacken* would have stolen it."

"Any incidents?"

"No. We padlocked the synagogues and they had no place to go. They sat in their homes and mumbled."

"This is how they pray. Yesterday was to have been their first day of New Year."

"First?"

"Two days in the Jewish New Year."

"Two?"

"One for God and the other for themselves."

"How do you like that, everything different to spite us."

"They were the first to celebrate New Year as a religious holiday."

"And now they are last?"

"I don't know. They were barred from the synagogues and prayed in their homes. They even sounded the *shofar* at a great risk in order to proclaim their New Year."

"Are you as a German officer sympathetic to these condemned people? How come you know so much about them?"

"As the Kommandant I am realistic. As a German I have learned something about this enemy."

"Enemy? The Jews are as good as dead."

"I am not quite so sure."

"I am. If you must know, Kommandant, I give the orders. Rintzler from Grodno and the territorial Kommandant Heriles back me up."

"I am not disputing authority."

"Do you have any doubt in our policy?"

"Do not put words in my mouth!"

"I might as well tell it to you now. You will be responsible to deliver every last Jew in this town still alive to Grodno when the time comes, and soon."

The orderly interrupted the exchange and handed a telegram

to Von Preissig. He tore it open as soon as Schwarzhund left and read:

> Sept. 23 S.D. Eastern Front
> Colonel Johann Kristus Von Preissig
> Flying east. Stopping over.
> General Werner Von Stulpnagel.

At first the cryptic words alarmed him. Was it an ominous hint of a problem or even trouble for either one? He was aware that Gen. Stulpnagel was attached to Admiral Wilhelm Canaris, Chief of German Intelligence.

On the ninth day of repentance, Rabbi Shepsel Kalir, who planned to pray in the uptown Brick Synagogue on *Yom Kippur* and in the shoemaker's *minyan* at *Neilah*, was so immersed in the preliminary prayers that he was totally unaware of worshippers coming up to greet him or of the congestion of men, women and children in the courtyard.

"Master of the universe! Father of mercy and forgiveness. . . ." He began the long prayer of 'purification', as a preliminary devotional adaptation before reciting himself, as one delegated by the congregation—*Schatz*—the solemn *Kol Nidrei* declaration, in the New Synagogue.

"Thou hast given him two inclinations, the good and the evil, so that he may choose . . ."

According to Judaism, man had been left free to choose or reject *Zedaka* (justice), tempered by charity; *Chesed* (grace) governed by love; and *Rachamonus* (mercy) determined by compassion.

My son, my son Judah, you sit beside me yet I know that one day you will leave me. If you can escape to the Holy Land I give you my blessings. Last year before *Kol Nidrei* you opened your heart to me. You had some doubts about these people who committed transgressions and errors. They who asked year after year for forgiveness, promised to change and yet remained the same. The *gabai* still favored the rich with honors. A certain impudent man talked back to me, apologized to me, confessed to God and still remained the same. Did the neighbors help the orphans, widows, and families whose providers were drafted in the army or were overseas? I responded: Did anybody since the beginning of this town ever kill or maim a person, rape a woman, steal a house, torture in a cell, set a synagogue on fire, loot and rob in daylight, or terrorize families and a community? Perhaps a storekeeper overcharged. Did not one confiscation of Jewish property, inflation of currency and default of savings by government banks, not to speak of pogroms, killings and robberies by gentiles under the administrations of Russians, Germans, Poles and communist Russians, overweigh these comparatively minor infractions?

Yes Judah I cannot absolve them of their deliberate transgressions unless they promise not to repeat them. You are silent now, for at such times I cannot indict them, although the law makes no exceptions, except to save life. Whatever you want to say, I understand. Do you understand me?

"Thou hast endowed me with a mind and a heart . . ."

During such a confessional prayer, Rabbi Kalir always reviewed past actions, decisions and sometimes mistakes. He was deeply troubled by David's overt love to Rachel. Zechariah was taken away by the Germans from under the bridal canopy. No one knew whether he was alive, or God forbid . . . Halacha law is averse to speculation. If Zechariah did not return, Rachel would have to wait ten long years before she could marry David. Why should this happen to a granddaughter of the *Dayan* Rabbi Eliezer Novor, of blessed memory?

"Thou hast warned us in Thy Torah:
That you go not about after your own heart and your own eyes."

Is not the symbol of this month *Tishrei* a scale? Perhaps David was misled by the eyes and heart of emotion. This unbalanced scale could only be righted by a mind controlling his heart. Love versus law, David was persistent in his love versus the law. Was the law itself infallible? Perhaps the marriage was not consummated—not completed under the canopy.

"Thou hast endowed me with ears, in order that I may listen to the Holy words and to thy Holy Torah."

But there are cries outside—curses of the wicked, uttered in German and Polish. Stones are showering glass right behind me and above me. Let us defy the criminals with our prayers, our devotion and confessions.

"Thou hast distinguished man from beasts."

See, my God, our God, God of all mankind, what they have done. David bears scars of blows, ever since he defended Rachel and my own body. For my soul suffers no humiliation at the hands of the unclean. But my people. Oh Lord, if they dare not—I do—to speak in their behalf.

"I have carefully examined all the members of my body and found them crippled."

Burka's eye is swollen and it pains him to control himself against those whom he calls cowards and thieves. Schneur Zalmen Lubavicher is swaying like a *lulav*, and his two young sons cannot understand why their father is praying in a plaintive voice, and not singing out triumphant melodies in the true *Chassidic* manner. So many with bandages, so many wounded and every one is pained within.

"And I poor and wretched . . . the toil of earning sustenance."

This is true of Sarah Beile and her four children, and Alter the carpenter. And Elyeh Schuster—where is he?

"We are ashamed and abashed to raise our countenance unto thee. How dare we open our mouths and raise our heads."

Yes, we dare. No, we are not ashamed for our deeds. What is Koppel thinking? His wife is fading fast and his son never returned from forced labor.

"We have been abandoned . . . into a wilderness, a place
   of impurity and evil spirits.
For I delight not in the death of the wicked, but
   let him turn from his ways and live."

Ben Zion, you are right enough. Your family is lost somewhere, yet you are concerned that we escape to Zion, to which Amalek in our midst bars the way.

"We have already been chastised by being subjected to the oppression of governments; by the infliction of bodily pains, by poverty."

Chaim Schneider, how silent you are. You spent your youth, days and nights for Torah.

"And the sorrows of raising children."

You teach under task-masters, you guide children without bread and without hope; you struggle daily together with the other teachers, to keep the eternal flame burning brightly. Your own flame is their bread and their hope.

"Have mercy upon us and command thy Holy Angels . . .
to purify us of all our sins."

Is not Chaye the Good an angel? She, whose only son Gedaliah gets feverish every time he is drafted for work. He is so delicate. Then there is her sick husband, to whom she is so devoted and returns daily after errands of mercy.

"Cause us to be clothed again with the robe of holiness."

Hershke, come nearer, don't shy away. Perhaps you have hidden a few things for your own family. It is all in vain. Whatever you have, share with us, as we share all our little mistakes—yes, little. But I am not commanding you to do this. This is private between you and God.

Beryl the baker, I understand your whispers, your supplication, your insistence. You who never ask for anything, are now demanding. This too I am reciting before God.

"Restore unto me the joy of thy salvation,
and let a willing spirit uphold me."

You do not speak of yourself; you and I are both praying for the House of Israel.

"Create in me a clean heart, O God . . ."

Elchanan, Yeshiva student, are you in the shoemaker's Minyan, to pour out your heart? Your prayer has been answered:

"And pardon shall be granted to the whole congregation of Israel, and to the stranger who sojourneth among them, when all the people transgress ignorantly."

Without explaining to any one, the Rabbi summoned Noske Schochet the, chanter.

"You will be the *Schatz*."

"What is wrong, Rabbi?" He was amazed that the Rabbi would stop at this climactic point and not resume the major part of the *Kol Nidrei* service.

"I belong there."

"Where?"

"I should be with them."

"With whom?"

"At the shoemaker's *minyan*."

He did not elaborate. But since Elyeh Schuster lost his wife on the first black Saturday, Chaikel Farber the *Baal tefilah* from the burned down big ancient synagogue was ailing, there was no one to chant or take charge. He sent Elchanan, the Yeshiva student, to lift their spirits, but there must be someone to lift up his voice in their behalf.

As Rabbi Kalir, accompanied by his son Judah, David, Chaim Schneider, and Burka, made his way through the courtyard, he was greeted by whistling and cat calls from the Polish guards and civilians, as well as some of the *gendarmes*.

Three faces were illuminated by a single candle. Chono Latutnick was draped in a long *talis*. It was a gift from his father when he returned from the Yeshiva to help him patch shoes. He kept up his studies at the New Synagogue and every morning at his father's *minyan*, behind his house. Half a day was for work, and half a day for God. But even at work, his mind was on Torah. Now he stood there, forehead still bandaged, his sad eyes searching the world—the beautiful world of learning— which was curtained off by the unclean. On his right was Rabbi Kalir, and on his left Elchanan, and Chaim Schneider encouraged him in his own modest way from his corner. He began to chant the words of *Kol Nidrei*.

"All vows and self prohibitions, vows and abstinence and promise . . . from this day of atonement unto the next day of atonement . . ."

Chono remembered. All the vows he made not to return home before he attained a Semicha Ordination. He recalled the vows of self prohibition, whereby he denied himself meals by day, and sleep at night. He had only one goal: to return home and help his father and mother. As a son of a poor shoemaker, he paid a big price to be admitted into the world of Torah. It was a world where no class distinction existed. Only the status attained by *hathmoda*, dedication, self sacrifice and love of learning counted. Nobody came to learn a profession or a trade in a Yeshiva; no one came to acquire business skills or the means of self aggrandizement. A Yeshiva was a source of life, a Yeshiva was a foun-

tain of wisdom. This was his world. All the days of hunger, all
the nights of sleeping on a hard bench; all the lonely and
sublime hours as he drove his body to quench his thirst for learning, all the humiliations he suffered as a slow student, and the
renunciations of all the pleasures of this world, were fully rewarded. Days and years of atonement were finally redeemed.
How much more could he ask? The Rabbi, the Yeshiva bochur
from Stabin, David and Chaim Schneider, who himself studied
in a Yeshiva and found his salvation in teaching, honored him. It
meant so much to him that they had come. For now even his
fellow shoemakers along with his father, were convinced that the
gates of learning were open to all, even to a son of a poor shoemaker. They watched Rabbi Kalir embrace him and nodded.

The following morning at the Yom Kippur service, the Rabbi's
dialogue with God—his protest and attempt to attain final confrontation, did not abate. The dreams of David, whereby he
visualized the inevitable catastrophe, which he—at least out-
wardly—discouraged and deprecated as dangerous and provoca-
tive, now obsessed him. Reports of arrests, beatings; men who
disappeared in the middle of the night, came to him every day.

The ark in the Brick Synagogue was now open after some
delay. They waited not for the privileged or the learned, or the
sages, but for those who returned broken in body but not in
spirit: boys and young men, aged and men on crutches or supported by children or by parents; women too, with benign faces
and intelligent eyes reflecting the horror and shock confronting
them on this Yom Kippur day.

"Our father our King, help us for the sake of them that went
through fire and water for the sanctification of thy name."

It already happened to them for three long months; the fire of
the twenty-fourth of *Tamuz*, when the New Synagogue was set
afire with Jews locked inside, and on the same Saturday when
they marched the children to the river to drown them.

"Our father, our King, avenge before our eyes the blood of Thy
servants that was shed."

It was not limited to the past; the present and future were
even more terrifying. The ark was now closed.

Chaim Schneider, the tailor's son, was honored to read the chapter of the Prophets, after the reading of the portion. It was an honor reserved for teachers. When Meir Noskes left for Eretz Israel, Dunsky was next in line, and after him Rabinowitz. Reb Jacob Zaban, the Talmud instructor, was already accorded this distinction on *Rosh Hashonah*, and Rabbi Kalir yielded this honor to Reb Isaac the second day. The learned, the just, and the humble, regardless of their origin and occupation, were the most honored and respected, together with yeshiva students and those engaged in charity.

"Proclaim aloud, spare not like the sound of the trumpet, lift up thy voice."

The Rabbi thought, who proclaims, Abba, the words which you write and you dispatch? It is true, Abba, that Chantze wants to risk her life and deliver a batch of your letters to one of the capitals, to a statesman, a philosopher, a writer, to a President, or to a Prime Minister, even to the Pope?

"Declare unto my people their transgressions and to the house of Jacob their sins."

David, you are right, but I can't admit to you or it will shake the very foundation of God's throne, or maybe expose religion in its naked banality; not Judaism, but that of the pretenders who have accepted its scriptures.

"Yet daily they seek me, and desire to know my ways, as a nation that hath done righteousness, and hath not forsaken the ordinance of God."

Yes, Kiva Kagan. Did I ever say it is wrong to share wealth? Did I not approve cooperatives as social justice? Yes, Label Moscowitz. There is a way to attain this just claim, but not through a gangster government.

Paltiel, how distressed I am, I know what is in your heart. Your grandson Reuvke wants to fight his way to the Holy Land. He is militant, like Israel Grodzensky, God bless his soul and the souls of all our fallen sons and daughters. You approve his willingness to risk his life. Daily you see him struggling. He wants to know if it is right to leave his family, to be separated, and to offer himself as a sacrifice. I know this, for my son Judah will follow him. What is there for us to say. Many will be separated.

Father will be divided from son, husband from wife, mother
from child.

"And the eternal will lead thee continually and satisfy thy soul
with heavenly splendor."

No one was a better leader, Paltiel. You succeeded in Suha-
Vali and at such difficult times. So many diverse opinions, so
many contending parties. Not once did you or I ever denounce
the Zionists, our sons; even though religious Jews in other parts
openly fought against Zionism.

And you, Shmuel Leiser and Zeidel Stuzinsky; and you,
Rachel, Zirel and Chantze, you the flower of our youth. What do
you want? Not honor, not wealth, not comfort. You want to build
in Zion a society such as Isaiah prophesied. It is in your names,
under the stress of your desires, that I protest this day to my
God! my God!

Hear ye, hear ye, a voice called out. The great trumpet was
sounded. The angels above shuddered as they beheld their
images. They retreated in fear and trembled as they regrouped
to proclaim the day of judgment. Who goes on trial? The angels
in Heaven. Verily, for even they are not found faultless. But they
came both as defenders and prosecutors. Who comes before the
supreme judge of judges? All the angels and all inhabitants of
the earth.

I Shabsi Shepsel ben Levi Yitzhak do solemnly protest against
the traditional procedure whereby decrees, decisions and final
judgments were rendered and pronounced against the House of
Israel.

Verily it is written in thy book: on the first day of the year it is
inscribed and on the fast day of Atonement it is sealed and determined; how many shall pass by and how many be born; who
shall live and who die. But I, Shabsi Shepsel the son of Levi
Yitzhak, do hereby submit that this procedure be reversed or
suspended. For consider who has usurped thy role to frustrate
life and brutalize death, to rob graciousness from the young and
peace from the aged? What power has surrendered us to this
evil? Who allowed us to perish by fire; to drown by water; to be
shot and to be stabbed? We would have willingly submitted to
the natural adversities man suffers in the course of his days on
earth: hunger and famine; earthquake and plague; death in all
its million forms; wanderings and homelessness; poverty and dis-

ease. But never shall we willingly submit to that which is not decreed by thee, but perpetrated by the sons of Satan, Amalek and Nazidom—they who purged thee from their obdurate hearts.

All afternoon throughout the *Musaf* service, the twilight *Mincha* and *Neilah* evening service, he succeeded for a few split seconds only in lifting the veils that blocked his intercession before the throne. How much he longed to speak with God as Jacob did in a vision, when the angelic ladder descended; or as the barefoot Moses did when he stood before the celestial tongues of fire. But the heavens seemed sealed with silence. Perhaps he had disturbed the serenity of heaven. Why did God not vouchsafe him an answer?

It began as it ended. The Jews confessed, but not their neighbors. Those in the synagogues—like all their brethren throughout doomed Europe—prayed for forgiveness and peace, brotherhood and mercy, love of God and love of men; they asked to be left alone to live their life, to do their work, to raise their families, to teach, guide, and rejoice in *mitzvos* and holiness.

On the way home with his son and wife, the Rabbi again heard hopeful greetings from his people. And he heard his own voice cry in their behalf: "Leave me not, neither forsake me!"

MOSCOW LINES HOLD. SNOW SLOWS NAZI
TANKS. VICHY: NAZIS ORDER EXECUTION
IN FRANCE, 100 HOSTAGES.

*Unchaste thoughts are more dangerous than
transgressions.*

Yoma, 29.

15

FORBIDDEN AGUNAH

Rachel was alone in the classroom when David opened the door.
Her admirers who tarried after class were on their way out,
accompanied by her parting words: "Your mothers will be waiting."

"They seem to like their teacher."

"They are excellent students. By the way, David, did you see
Mr. Dunsky. He has a plan."

"No I didn't. He hasn't approached me."

"Dunsky has some original ideas." Rachel opened the door and
called out, "Abba, will you please come in."

Abba promptly obliged.

"Tell him about your plan!"

"What can I tell him. I spent days and years thinking, and you
want me to tell him in two words! If I don't say it right, you
won't think it's a good plan."

"Who said anything about two words. Take your time."

"I am a teacher," Abba adjusted his glasses by pushing the
frame up his nose, "I am a teacher for over fifteen years. I have
observed that children don't enjoy sitting in cramped quarters.
They fidget. They spend eight hours a day just fidgeting and listening. Passive. Teachers try to make it interesting. But grammar
isn't, and mathematics they hate. Talmud is difficult. Composi-
tion is only for the talented. I therefore have come to one final
conclusion; we need two large classrooms, one for study, the other
for a work shop. We not only need to give them activity but we
have to teach them a trade. Many are taught by their parents, but
not very well. Do you know what happens to our young men in

191

Eretz Israel? They first have to learn how to till the soil; how to be mechanics, even after their preparatory *Hachshara* courses here. Why not combine work and study, and humanize the classes. Yes, humanize the classes."

"Very practical," Rachel said. She thought it would have been true in normal times, whereas now it was a hope.

Right now David and Abba were in different worlds. Only David's was twice as complicated, twice as dangerous. David faced an enemy whose tactics he did not yet fully comprehend, and was concerned about his beloved, whom he did not know how to save from this antagonist.

David stood by the window, charged and immobile with his thoughts and feelings. He felt helpless and somewhat anxious.

Without being aware, he touched her hand. The barrier which they overlooked was there as they walked out of the room, past the hall, into the street.

He could, at last, he was sure, find happiness with Rachel; there was the religious law with its restraint. Could Rabbi Kalir help him to clear up once and for all if Rachel was still married to Zechariah? Maybe the marriage vow was never completed under the *chupa*-canopy? All these years his precious youth was wasted in classrooms and by dim candlelight. At last he found a spark to bring back his almost lost youth and his rapidly vanishing hopes.

They strolled past the market place, down Synagogue Street and stopped on the wooden bridge to behold the last feverish outburst of summer-fall. The dam was fast in place. Streams of water escaped over the barrier. Fish darted out from beneath ringlets of water for their last look at the bright sinking sun. Brown leaves were carried away unknowingly by the stream. Everything was stirring to get away. Even the broken rays of the sun reflected in her face hurried back to another sun, below the horizon. They leaned against the log railing. But they could not drift away like leaves, or recede like the sun's vast rays.

Washing women, in the shallow water on the other side of the dam, began to pound their wash on the water smoothed stones. A stork took off; he became alarmed when the alert sparrows were panicked. Soon the sparrows returned, reassured that the blast of a gun was aimed at some other prey. White bellied swallows circled for a last look at their deserted nests in eaves of barns and houses. Then grouped in V formations high above the trees and winged away to reach their summer homes in the warm countries.

No words were spoken between David and Rachel as they breathed in all this beauty and wonder; all the incredible ways that God endowed to the earth and its living forms. The sky stood still in all its clear blueness, like a silent prayer. While below on earth, everything was moving at different tempos and in different directions, but all together spelling words, sentences and paragraphs of life, despite cavernous rumblings underneath. Even while preparing to break away, the sun was disappearing behind a lingering horizon; at night the crescent moon and the stars would look down nostalgically with their pale light from the serene canopy above.

"Rachel!" David's voice trembled.

"I know—"

"I'm trying to say . . ."

"What are you trying to tell me?"

"That you mean everything to me and I would do anything to prevent you from becoming Von Preissig's secretary."

"Why do you work for him?"

"This is different. I consulted Rabbi Kalir. He understands my predicament."

"David once you get involved with Von Preissig he'll pressure you for more information."

"Don't be silly. He has all the information he wants about this town. But somebody had to be in contact with him. I will try my best to protect our people and see that those drafted for work are neither too young nor too old and are not mistreated. As for my work I'll be assigned to classify the books in the library and do some translations."

"It is still dangerous to help Von Preissig in this field."

"Aren't you in greater danger?"

"Danger?"

"You are a girl, a beautiful girl. Why did he select you? There are others who can type."

"I'll just do my work."

"You'll not be safe."

"If I refuse to work for him I may be sent away to a work camp."

"Rachel, I don't want you to be there."

"David if only . . ."

"You mean everything to me. I'll move heaven and earth to save you from him and from disgrace. We'll both have to escape to Bialystok."

"David, I feel the same about you. I'll never change. But I am not free. How can the two of us just leave town together?"

"I asked the Rabbi about both of us."

"What was his answer?"

"It was negative. But if new evidence is produced everything could change for us."

"I wish I knew what I am."

"Isn't it possible that you were never married, that the ceremony was never completed?"

"How could I remember?"

"You must!"

"Who would believe me?"

"I believe you."

"It is not enough. The Rabbi told me that I am an *agunah*. It is hard on me but I am going to comply until such time as ..."

They walked back from the bridge. The barriers that thwarted their happiness were the lawful and the unlawful. The law was explicit. It could not be changed unless there was new evidence or interpretation. But the shadow of Von Preissig followed and lengthened behind each one in the late afternoon. The quiet and peace was only an interval preceding the storm.

For the first time in many a week David was certain that no dream would interrupt his already troubled sleep. He had already endured the pangs and the joys of his dream by day. It was a dream that could never be surpassed by anything, however strange and revealing in the almost mysterious visions encamping his soul and conscience at night.

Several days later David walked up to the high bookshelf alongside the oven in the rear of the synagogue. He fingered first one book on the shelf below, then another on the shelf above. Finally he removed one leather bound volume of Mishnais. The things he sought must be in one of them. He remembered even the image of the page, the place and the letters seemed to regroup themselves in his memory.

Could it be in *Teruma?* But Teruma deals with the heave-offerings from the fields which Israelites and Levites—from their own tithes—were required to give to the Priests. These gifts to the Priests were for their dedication as teachers of the people in the service of the Lord. Would the subject of womanhood be found in such a treatise? Why not? Marriage is sanctification. Heave offering and a girl's virginity are both sacred. David was absorbed. He kept on saying, "Not here, perhaps on the next page." It was almost before him; then his fingers touched the lines, his eyes scanned an old friend. Koppel did not utter a word. He thrust his palm up toward the book as if to say, "Let me in on this discovery. What is it?"

David understood the gesture. He confidently placed the book on the stand. He opened it and pointed his finger to the paragraph and line; and Koppel began to read: " 'If gentiles said, Give us one of your women or we shall assault all of them, then let them all be defiled rather than hand over to them one soul from Israel'."

"David, you are a young man," Koppel addressed David, with a paternal posture. "You are able to bridge the gap between the old and the new. But youth also means impulsive action—sometimes without authority. Rabbi Kalir is my master. I may know the law as well as my teacher but it is he who renders the decision."

"What decision?" David's face became taut, his dark eyes were afire, as he stood straight against the massive Koppel.

"The law."

"What law?"

"David are you challenging what we consider the law."

"I know the law too. This is exactly what the Mishnah tells us: that we are all responsible to uphold the virginity of a Jewish girl."

"Who threatens her?"

"Von Preissig."

"How do you know?"

"I know him well."

"Then why do you serve him?"

"I don't."

"These are the rumors."

"Are you also a rumor monger? Didn't the committee—and you were there too—approve my day to day contact with the Germans?"

"Yes, but with reservations. I am suspicious of Von Preissig's machinations. One never knows his real intentions."

"Have I not helped the community with food and better conditions?"

"I don't deny your accomplishments. But working for him is too risky."

"You deliberately avoid the fact that I am forced to work for him. I alone take the risk."

"No, you endanger the entire community."

"This is absolutely untrue."

"What is it?" Koppel seared by David's words turned to Burka who walked in excitedly. It was very unusual for Burka to come this early unless he had committed a theft and someone was in pursuit, and he was seeking sanctuary here in the house of God.

"What about the *Mishnah*?" David ignored Burka.

"I was coming to that. The *Mishnah* is clear in regard to a Jewish girl—in this instance Rachel—who must be saved. But your plans to save her for yourself are questionable."

"Why do you twist it your way, the old fashioned way?"

"We Jews believe in King Solomon's words, 'if young men say build and old men say demolish, follow the advice of the older ones'. I read, I understand what goes on in your mind," Koppel continued, "young nowadays means new, vigorous, fresh, dynamic and all the phrases heaped on youth. Old means aged, useless and to be discarded. This is an age of movement and action and old people don't fit, so they are useless. Our laws are mature and sound, but you call it old. If it's old it is assumed to be quaint, to be viewed like a museum—that's all. You must be very careful. Do not act upon your own impulse, whether it is in regard to Rachel or anything Germans request from you."

"This is not an impulse."

"What is it?"

"In regard to Rachel?"

"Yes."

"Love."

"I'm beginning to understand," Koppel shook his head.

"What is wrong?"

"Nothing. In the midst of all this, love? Did you tell this to the Rabbi?"

"Where is it forbidden to love a girl?"

"If she is free!"

"Who is to judge, who knows?"

"There is law."

"What law. Are you the Rabbi's surrogate?"

"*Agunah.*"

"I know this term too. Who appointed you to throw this in my face? All around us savages have taken the law into their own hands. They have abolished all laws. Murder is right, and violence is correct and immorality is proper. I and all the Jews are the only ones upholding any law. I am trying to save this girl from the *"Lumpen!"*

"How?"

"David! Look!" Burka interrupted.

"The Germans are hauling timber in a long row of wagons," Koppel pointed to the window.

"What do they mean to do?" Burka asked.

"They are always moving and restless. Who knows what they're up to." Koppel said. David exchanged worried glances with Koppel as Burka sat down.

Alter stood aside to assay the situation. He recalled that Zaleski the Pole asked him only yesterday to build a shallow partition alongside the wall that separated the house from the barn, occupied by three cows and a sow with a litter of pigs. With its secret trap door from the cellar it would be a perfectly concealed apartment. He could put away surplus grain or hide valuables or who knows what. The Jews were in greater danger than the Poles. What could he and his sons do?

"These logs are not for construction or carpentry," Alter added.

"Nor are they for fuel," Koppel said.

"It could only be for one purpose." David whispered reluctantly to verify out loud his traumatic prophecy.

"It is about three meters long and over two decimeters in diameter," Alter estimated.

"In the last war," Koppel moved closer to David and confided, "the Germans requisitioned such wood from my forest for a stockade, for forced labor at the Okop estate."

"No one can be certain," David said, "but we must find out. The Germans don't start something unless they are prepared to see it through."

"God forbid," Alter protested, and inched closer as the conversation became covert and private.

David moved closer to the door. He wanted to get out and get

away from Koppel whom he now defied. He was determined to
take Rachel along with him to Bialystok. There was no other
way to save her. Reuvke Rosenberg and Judah were waiting for
him to lead them. Would Rabbi Kalir blame David for taking
his son Judah along? He was sorry for the Rabbi. It was a
decision for them alone to make, and not for their parents.

November 1, 8, 9, 20, 1941: NAZIS FAN HATRED LEST
CIVILIANS SOFTEN TOWARD
JEWS. REV. LICHTENBERG, DEAN
OF CATHOLIC CATHEDRAL,
ARRESTED. PRAYED FOR JEWS.
BIGGEST R.A.F. RAIDS OVER
COLOGNE, MANHEIM, BERLIN.
GERMAN TROOPS ENCIRCLED. . . .

Three schemed against the Jews.
Balaam who instigated was killed,
Job who was silent was punished and
Jethro who fled—his descendants
were privileged to sit in the
Supreme Court in Jerusalem.

Sanhedrin, 106.

16

THE INSTIGATORS AND THE SILENT

By the end of November the news, picked up through Potocki, Denikin, and rumors, was neither good nor bad. The Germans were in the Crimea, but were encircled at Rostov. The invader was evidently stalled in his advance on Moscow.

But for the Jews there was no respite from the indiscriminate draft of young boys for the work camps. Arrests and confiscations continued. Quite a few died or were shot trying to escape from those slave camps. When the Jewish leaders complained, they were told, "Get your *Judenrat* functioning and make your own selections."

They tried it on November the ninth when Schwarzhund demanded a hundred boys of all ages to report to headquarters. They were lined up and ordered to march toward the river. Once there, Schrecke mockingly told the boys to swim in the deepest part. When some of the boys began to scream that they were drowning, the order was changed, but not before three were drowned. Later on David found out that this date coincided with the anniversary of Crystal night on November 9, 1938, in Germany. It was the night when the Brown Shirts, as Hitler's

199

storm troopers were known, ran amok, smashing windows and heads, burning synagogues and books, and instituted a reign of terror against the Jews of Germany.

David was up all night brooding about the bitter lot of the Jews and the rumored confinement of the Jews within ghetto walls. He lapsed into an uneasy slumber for a short while, only to be engulfed in a nightmare. It was a different dream; disturbing and yet revealing: there were friends, including Rachel, in its background. Yet several unconnected episodes were depressing.

David woke up before dawn, cold and limp from the peculiar and frightful dream. He decided not to let this nightmarish experience remain something private and hidden but rather to expose it to the wisdom and counsel of the rabbi.

" 'A dream at night is a reflection of one's dreams by day'," Rabbi Kalir spoke slowly as he concentrated to interpret David's dream. " 'No dream is without banality. Neither a good nor a bad dream is ever fulfilled in its entirety. A dream that is not explained is like an unread letter'." The rabbi paused after these quotes from the Talmud.

"Four gates and four roads led to four towers. From the apertures of the towers four doves, each bearing a letter, flew out. A letter was dropped at your feet. The dove represents the Torah, or the house of Israel which called for help.

"The doves tried to find safety in the towers of our civilization. They were pinpointed and expelled by the ravens. These are the religious perversions of some European nations that incite them to violence against each other, and especially against the Jews. The vultures are the prototypes of the indifferent masses and nations, waiting to finish off the struggling victims. Meanwhile, the winged monsters undisturbed by a single raucous call from the ravens and not panicked to flight by the mere wing-flapping of the more numerous vultures and birds of their kind, are encouraged by these silent witnesses to attack the lone defender, the Jew.

"Voices called you and your friends from the orchard. All of us, when young, tried or broke into orchards. Later on this attraction to forbidden fruit changed into a desire for the orchards of learning, where sometimes we were drawn to its off limits, dangerous tree of knowledge. But this orchard in your dream and its forbidden fruit trees of knowledge tried to ensnare you in a trap; especially the voices which you associate with the four leaders who were also tempted by a similar hazardous orchard.

"There were four different approaches to the four gates of the orchard and the four towers inside, by four renowned Jews when Rome threatened Judea and the Torah. Ben Azzai saw only an immediate choice between liberty and death. Ben Zoma formulated a moral struggle against Rome. Acher preached submission to Caesar and Roman culture. Rabbi Akiba rallied his disciples and Jews to join the army of Bar Kochba in a relentless war against Rome.

"The Romans were enemy invaders who tried to conquer the Jews by two methods, by the sword and by conversion to their way of life. Those who opposed them were cut down. We are also confronted by a power, the most dangerous enemy in our history. Again we have to choose: which one of the four roads to follow, which one of the four gates to enter, which one of the skytowers will extend refuge to us, which letter will reach the capitals of the world and centers of religion, who will answer and how will this dove-Keneseth Israel—escape the sinister ravens, the blood thirsty vultures and the satanic monsters? Today we face the monstrous enemy alone, like Akiba and his disciples. We are cut off from Bar Kochba, his army, and our fellow Jews beyond. The Amalekites and Ishmaelites all around us, like the winged monsters have joined the enemy or hover nearby as collaborating vultures. They are about to imprison us in a ghetto. I hope it wouldn't happen. Not far away stand the indifferent silent witnesses, with their backs toward us, deaf to our calls for help. They are like the ravens in their nests, one eye open with an encouraging glance toward the perpetrators while the other eye in range of the victim is closed.

"A dream is only partly true," the Rabbi said after a long pause.

"I saw the invasion and the disrupted wedding and it came true."

"Only God can foresee the future."

"Did not the prophet tell us that young people will prophesy?"

" 'And it shall come to pass afterward that I will pour out my spirit upon all flesh and your sons and your daughters shall prophesy.' Is this what you mean?"

"Yes."

"The second part of the verse explains that, 'Your old men shall dream dreams.' This is certainly not for our age. It is full of fear, and there are two requirements whereby a dream becomes a vision and then a prophecy."

"What are they?"

The Rabbi shook his head and was silent.

"And Rachel? she called me!"

"Are you sure it was—?"

"She called me."

"She is married to Zechariah. You must not even touch her!"

"Was the marriage completed under the canopy?"

"She was married properly, and you as an interested party, cannot contest a solemnized union."

"She is in danger."

"And you intend to save her and violate a law?"

"We love each other."

"She is an *agunah* and love cannot change this fact."

"*Agunah*? Does that mean that Rachel must wait ten years before I can marry her?"

"If Zechariah does not return."

"This is cruel."

"This is the law."

"Even a law can be outdated."

"David, you talk nonsense," the Rabbi said angrily. "When our father Abraham founded the Jewish nation over three thousand years ago, a man would go out to the market place, field, or forest and grab himself a woman, or steal a woman from another man. From the days of the Egyptians and the Romans, when a woman was nothing more than a bondwoman, up to recent days of lingering slavery in Africa, the Americas, serfdom in Russia, legalized prostitution and covert promiscuity almost everywhere, little has changed. I was told of many instances among the non-Jews where men went to war or were taken captive and given up as dead. When they returned to their wives after the war they found them married to other men. There would be chaos and the sanctity of marriage and family would collapse if women rushed to marry other men under such circumstances. God, man and woman are sacred. Whoever violates the dignity of man will also defile the woman and deny God. This is the basic trilogy of bloodshed, immorality and idolatry to which we must never submit, even under threats of death. It is the essence of our Mosaic law which incidentally you upheld when you argued so skilfully with Label."

"That was general."

"And this is something special that concerns only you?"

"The *agunah* law threatens Rachel's life and happiness."

"How?"

"She is in danger without a husband."

"All women, girls and men are in danger. The law cannot be suspended even for one second. By challenging the law you distort the law. Our Torah draws a line between the permissible and forbidden. Nazis, fascists, and communists break the laws of God to pursue their own corrupt ways under the pretext of expediency. We reject their destructive ideologies: that in order to establish totalitarian Nazi, fascist, and communist conformist state societies, thousands and millions of people and even nations and states must be sacrificed on their Holocaust altars. To desire a woman, illegally draws one nearer to the final step—to violate her. It thus leads to immorality like hate to bloodshed, and anti-semitism to idolatry. The Torah compares rape to violence against man thus; 'For as when a man riseth against his neighbor and slayeth him even so is this matter'."

"But how can you compare my love to violence?"

"It is forbidden."

"What kind of a law is it, if it is applied regardless of circumstances?"

"Suppose you come to a great palace and you say, 'Let me remove that stone below the foundation, and no one will miss it, the structure will not be impaired? I may need it to support the wall in my house.' The answer then is that the removal of one stone will weaken the entire structure, because once the breach is made others will remove more stones under the same pretext. One law like one stone, supports the whole structure. Maimonides states it specifically thus: 'If a man about to die sets his eyes upon a woman and the doctors say let him have relations with her, so that he will live, we follow the Torah and say, let him die rather than violate the chastity of the woman or unmarried girl.' Therefore Rachel is still in a state of betrothal and marriage."

"Rabbi, is this . . ."

"David, don't finish! We must wait. But for the present this is my verdict."

"Rabbi, I am troubled by the Kommandant Von Preissig. He hates Jews like the rest and yet perhaps he pretends to like them. He talked to me for a long time, rambled along about conquering the Jewish God. He said the English and Americans control the seas and commerce and that the Jews control God and that all three must be conquered by the Germans."

"Is it only God that he wants to conquer?"

"He is not rational. He said, 'We don't need your God, and that conquest and enslavement is not enough, unless it includes the soul.'"

"He suffers from something."

"Yes. That is why he wants others to suffer too. He talked about a scientific theory to control the minds of mankind to win this war."

"What else?"

"He wants me to work for him."

"Working at what?"

"A library. He asked me to classify, translate and assemble all primary source books of Jewish learning and the classics of our literature. He will give me all the scholars. I told him that I can't become a traitor. He replied, 'You are free to go. We'll treat you as you treat us.'"

"This is worse than I thought. But since you're dealing with one mentally deranged you can pretend to go along up to a certain point."

"What am I to do?"

"You must never collaborate at your expense or at our expense. Translate harmless books. It may take you a year to translate just one. It is not clear, unless to classify means to label each book and in a line or two explain the contents."

"This is probably what I will do, until further instructions."

"Keep me informed of his plans. This whole library project is incredible. Perhaps it is a pretext for the Kommandant to get hold of valuable and even rare books, to sell eventually to museums for profit?"

"I don't know. Suppose I can help the Jews by pretending to help him classify all these books."

"You can only help the Jews by thinking of him as an enemy. He may not seem vicious, but eventually he will obey commands from higher ups. You can help individual Jews, you can help us with more food, you can help us by protecting us from the German and Polish criminals."

"Did not Jews in the past negotiate under compulsion, even with our enemies?"

"No. We resisted their enslavement and survived as a free

people. Freedom cannot be inherited; every generation must fight for it."

"Fight with what?"

"We can't fight with weapons but we are still free. The most powerful tyrant can't and won't make us his slaves. This is a satanic age that rouses all the evil of the ages. Against Satan—if God wills it—we can only offer our 'Shema Israel' martyrdom."

"Martyrdom? Is there no other way?"

"Have you forgotten your own dream? We are surrounded. Ravens, vultures and monsters are pursuing the dove of Israel. David I heard rumors about the bad conditions under which our men are forced to work for them."

"Yes it is true. Over four hundred of our healthiest are engaged on highway construction from Yanowa to Sokolke; on a special project at Novidvor and Dombrowa; and timber cutting near Agustowa. They are demanding more and when we don't provide them they grab anybody, even the sick."

"You cannot compromise with Von Preissig even for one second. Suppose Rabbi Akiba negotiated with Hadrian then. Even the Romans would have said: Hadrian is just and right because an outstanding Jew followed by other Jews negotiated with him. Let us erect a wall of iron between us and the Caesars and even a greater barrier between us and this Satan Hitler. Let us label him, expose him as *trefah*, as *ossur*, as *rosho*. Remember, David, once at a Zionist meeting you said, 'Messiah has to be prodded to redeem the Jews.' Let us first be worthy before we even utter it, even if I commended you then."

Von Preissig was studying Kommandant's Rintzler's order to enclose the Jews of Suha-Vali and perhaps other towns in a ghetto, within a compressed area. He had no choice but to submit to higher authority, including Schwarzhund's psychological steps. He won, however, important concessions: to proceed with his peculiar conversion, library and work projects. Relishing the formidable plans entrusted to him alone in the original, he glanced at the carbon copies labeled: 'Col. Schwarzhund, Capt. Messer.' He reread his own copy, on whose folder was typed in big red letters: Kommandant Johann Kristus Von Preissig. Underneath was the legend of special significance to him: Approved Von Preissig projects XXZ. He felt proud, that only he alone could decipher the meaning of this code which

stood for secret experiment Z under supervision of Alfred Rosenberg. Then followed in outline form the headings for the successive steps. First was the Schwarzhund section on surprise; then
force; then relaxation; then more force, also their implementa-
tion by psychological terror and brute terror. There was a special
section on confiscation of property. The ghetto and its liquidation, underlined in red, was in the second section. All the material was precise, orderly, detailed. It even went as far as to
enumerate the material—wood, nails, shovels, machine guns for
watchtower, lights, barbed wire, additional guns, hand grenades,
German shepherd dogs, and of course special uniforms for the
Polish guards, including leather whips which proved to be a
great morale booster. Nothing was overlooked. Even two sirens
were included.

Assignments were clearly defined on another page. The gendarme of the military were to supervise construction of the
ghetto. But once it was constructed the S.S. would take over. It
was clearly obvious that the military were in charge of general
administration, defense, and supply, while the S.S. had complete
jurisdiction over the Jews—answerable only to Heinrich Himmler, who acted in the name of the Fuehrer. Actual construction
would be assigned to the Jews. After all, Von Preissig mused
half lyrically, the ghetto was for their own protection. "Confidential" was stamped in red on every page. He surmised from the last
pages referring to work camps in Grodno and Auschwitz that it
implied the rumored final solution of bones and ashes. Only before they would be surrendered to the 'fire brigade', as he referred to the gas ovens and other methods in the C. camps, he
would first undertake his great experiment to reduce the minds
and souls of the Jews to subservience. As for their bodies, what
would it matter if the Germans had a couple million of zombies.
Later on, he might do it more easily with the Poles, Russians,
French, English and even Americans. These plans and schemes
added an element of suspense and mystery in an otherwise
dismal assignment. He always kept the dossier under lock in the
steel box of the bottom drawer. He was afraid that Ludke or
someone else whom he suspected would get to it and relay the
information to the Nazi henchmen and they would explode into
violence prematurely.

There would be a few difficulties, but on the whole it would
be carried out. The Jews would be kept in the dark about this

final solution, and by the time they would find out, it would be too late. Von Preissig rose from his chair and assumed a military stance as he continued going over this important episode in his mind.

That day, Friday, December 19, five days before Christmas and thirty days hence, would be perfect—just perfect, to confine the Jews in a ghetto. All Jews would be home, right in the midst of *Chanukah* celebration. The next day would be their Sabbath. They are supposed to rest. They would not protest. War is war—don't Germans suffer? Why should the Jews be exempt? He closed the folder, locked it in the steel box, and felt somewhat relieved. He opened the cigar humidor, and took the last cigar.

Von Preissig felt relaxed even before he held the cigar in his thin lips. It was like a vast military operation or a big engineering project. He would employ ju-jitsu, the Japanese art of wrestling whereby you use the opponent's strength to defeat him with little effort. That must have been the secrets of Hannibal, Caesar and Napoleon. Snow is a protection against cold—soldiers in trenches know it. And ice water is the best remedy for frozen fingers. A backfire can halt a spreading fire.

Let the Jews trust in God and cling to one another. Let them pray and let them even study in their secret books. Anything in a book is not a secret. The more they trust in God the more they'll trust us Germans. That's it. Then these smart Jews will walk into our trap like sheep. We will keep them long enough to squeeze out every bit of their body and soul. The same will be repeated all over Poland and Europe, then later America. Then in one volume, I'll write down the code of the Hebrews as handed down by the best Jews to Kristus Von Preissig.

My two triumphs are David and Rachel. David will translate all the best holy books and codify their laws. Rachel—well I have plans for her; of a noble nature, of course.

Seven days later the orderly informed Von Preissig that a Jewish committee was waiting to see him.

"What do they want? They have their orders. It must be carried out to the full—let them come in for a minute."

Skipping all preliminaries, as if explaining in the terse lan-

guage of the military a plan for attack, he accosted them thus:
"With the erection of the ghetto we shall have more order and
you shall have more protection. From now on you will elect a
Judenrat. I will send for you if I need you or anybody. Now what
is it that you want?" Von Preissig shouted impatiently in his last
phrase.

"Herr Kommandant," began Koppel, "it is about the ghetto—
the time?"

"The time? It must be ready within nine days, ready to move
in on the third Friday evening."

"But Friday evening is the Sabbath," protested Rabbi Kalir.

"I am not interested in your Sabbath. Besides if you are more
industrious you can move in on Thursday."

"Herr Kommandant," David edged forward, "what we are
trying to say is that we have been delayed in the construction.
You gave us only a week. It is difficult, almost impossible with the
cold weather—the ground is frozen—we have no wagons, no
sleds, no horses. How can our men complete the stockade and
string barbed wire, within four days?"

"Nothing is impossible—I would tell you what German soldiers can accomplish . . ." He hesitated. "Those not moving in—if
you can't move in, we'll send you to another ghetto. It must be
finished by Christmas time, before that I mean. I don't disturb
your holidays, don't disturb mine . . . You may leave. Details will
be posted." With these words Von Preissig dismissed the committee.

Now that the order was official, that all the Jews of Suha-Vali
would become prisoners in their own homes and within
a confined space, David tried to help Rachel. She would be in
greater danger, once trapped in the ghetto. He could always
escape. The deadline was four days away.

Raids were now stepped up and Polish hooligans were given a
free hand to rob and beat Jews. This was all a part of the plan, to
convince the Jews that they would be safer from their enemies,
the Poles, within a well guarded ghetto.

Late at night he took along Rachel, after much persuasion, and
together with Reuvke, Judah and Chantze, headed for Bialystok.

The next day Velvke did not heed the warning that the Germans were arresting Jews, and he went to the synagogue. Velvke
pushed the glasses up his thin nose, straightened his luxurious

white beard with his right thumb in the vest pocket. Softly he walked across the worn out boards, lest a loose board creak and expose him. He halted behind one of the posts supporting the gallery and listened. He waited until there was a pause in Elchanan's learning.

"*Sholem Alechem!*"

"*Alechem Sholem!*" The Yeshiva student slowly raised his eyes.

Velvke sat down. He had no right to interrupt him. The seminarian was a blessing for the town. In normal times he would have asked him a few questions but not now. He did notice however that this student Elchanan preferred Chazkel Schneider's house for his lodging and meals, although he was assigned richer homes and readily complied. Was it Chaim his son, the former student, or Hadassah, Chazkel's teen age daughter who attracted him?

For the past several months, due to the war, no itinerant student outside of Elchanan had honored Suha-Vali by adorning a bench in the synagogue and keeping vigil over the Torah far into the nights. Meals, even at such times, and also shelter, were still to be provided, even though the influx of the poor and needy overtaxed Velvke's resources. Velvke's signature scrawled on a scrap of paper was a passport to the most respectable household and even an introduction to a marriageable girl. This had been a tradition for many years, maybe hundreds of years. Young men were sent to study in the academies of Wolozin, Mir, Telz, Radin and Slobodka. If the spirit moved them they returned to their own towns or to another town and staked out a bench in the synagogue; and with a *gabai's* recommendation, settled down and got married.

Trouble was all around; Velvke was afraid that the poor student would be forgotten. But the Jewish people, even under the worst circumstances, never forgot those who illuminated their journey in the darkness with the light of the Torah.

The student strained hard to soar, to rise above, to reach the far away, to propel himself. The earth was full of commotion and strife, but beyond, years back, in the valleys and on the hills of Judea or along the Euphrates, there were robed men sitting on the floor of a barn listening to a master; and two or three and maybe more tillers of the soil and shepherds or even merchants with sandals on their feet girded their loins and sat down with their tired bodies to refresh their minds with a discourse on Torah.

The door flung open and the draft blew out the candle. And then men marched into the synagogue. In his loneliness it came to him like an abrupt shock, the realization that he was not insulated against the naked, shameless, sanctioned crimes. Then the gruff and cursing Murad of the Gestapo hurled him against the splintered window and he crashed down to the floor, cut, bruised and stunned by sudden evil.

One of them shouted: "Your name?"

"Elchanan Stabinsky."

"Where from?"

"Stabin, I had to leave."

"Stabin? Eh! Your papers!"

"We were told to register in a new location."

"Why didn't you register?"

"I'm on the way to Bialystok, I have family there."

"Then why are you here? And why aren't you at work for your own good?"

"I'm a student—a Talmudic student."

"Student, student, you are all students, we have no need for students, nor for books, we need busy hands to feed our soldiers and people. You, old man," he said to Velvke, "now that you have had time to think up something, tell me fast."

"My name is Velvke. I have a general store and hardware."

"Where is your merchandise?"

"It was taken away—taken by soldiers."

"Don't be insolent, Jew, it must have been confiscated as contraband. Both of you are under arrest. A contraband candle and violation of the blackout," he wrote down in a notebook.

"But there is no air raid alarm and no blackout," Velvke protested.

"There is always a blackout for you Jews." Murad said as the two Polish policemen thumped them on the way to the door.

It was late in the afternoon. Von Preissig was busy going over the last details before the Jews were to move into the ghetto within two weeks. The sinking sun cast an eerie light against the snow covered fields. It flooded the window through the hand crocheted linen drapes, picked up for him by the tail wagger Todt from Daniel the brewer.

He looked out through the window. He was well pleased.

There was activity and action. The ghetto was coming up on schedule.

"We've a shortage of long spiked nails," Lt. Schrecke reported.

"Telegraph immediately," he told him.

"We need more barbed wire," the lieutenant added. "Ten rolls are not sufficient, we need more to crisscross."

"If it is actually needed, I'll order it. Personally, I think reassuring words will keep them in better than barbed wire." The lieutenant shrugged his shoulders as Von Preissig returned to the window.

"Good! Good!" he mumbled aside. "The ghetto walls look presentable, not like those of a prison, but more like those of a camp. Good, good! Church Street after the red school house is just ideal, and perhaps Synagogue Street all the way down to the blacksmith shops. Now that will give them two big synagogues and a square. They will not complain."

There was so much to do, he began to use up every page of the calendar for names and notations. When these were filled he began to write in a little red notebook. Now there was one more item; he must order David Sokoloff to proceed with more speed to translate all the basic learning, wisdom and religion of the Jews. He will supply him with a staff and all the necessities. David did not report the day before. Did he escape? How far could he get?

Oh yes, he noted on the memo, the lieutenant and the gendarmes want to move in immediately into the houses vacated by the Jews. The cows, horses, chickens, goats will be removed and placed in custody of the Resettlement Office. After all the military cannot be bothered with the chores required for their care, and the Jews will need all their energies to take care of themselves. A double underlined memo—Schwarzhund wants to eliminate synagogues from the ghetto, they are needed for the military, library and hospital. As for the lower square, to be included inside the ghetto—the western half would be 'convenient' for a cemetery. The Polish guards also want houses, and more things. It has to be done properly and orderly. He is not going to degrade himself into a plundering chieftain. There are rules and regulations, nothing shall be done without his signed order.

His orderly admitted Col. Schwarzhund who, without a greeting rebuked him:

"The walls are too weak."

"Why worry? The damned cannot escape and those who escape are damned."

"It would be a mistake to cuddle them and show them
mercy."

"Col. Schwarzhund, I want you to understand I am not running a penal colony, nor supervising a slaughter house. If they
are to be damned anyway, instead of chaotic looting why not
get something important out of them? Who knows? Maybe the
plans call for their rehabilitation."

"Herr Kommandant," the Colonel was stupefied, "this sounds
like heresy. You are fortunate that I am your associate."

"I think you misunderstand me. I am not acting without authority. Alfred Rosenberg has full jurisdiction over this town. We
are trying to prove something of the greatest benefit for the
German people."

"But our object is to destroy them, this is what the Gestapo
wants, and I represent it."

"There are all kinds of methods. In Devil's Island they are put
in holes, to break down their will to escape. In penal institutions
they are confined and their hopes are crushed. In Auschwitz and
Dachau—they are planning a similar set-up in Grodno—they
are eliminated by various processes. I have a very interesting
plan, you may call it unique. It will satisfy even the Governor
General of Poland, General Frank in Warsaw. My plan is not
liquidation, but rehabilitation of millions, to work and slave for
us—a better grade of slaves."

"I must warn you!" Schwarzhund stood over him, his face was
chalk white and his whole body coiled and agitated. "You are
running counter to orders. You will supervise the ghetto until the
time when it will be liquidated according to our plans."

"A *yeshuah*—a *yeshuah*," an omen of salvation. Velvke the
gabai greeted David upon his safe return from Bialystok, and
grabbed his chilled hand in the wavering dimness of the unlit
New Synagogue. There was no candle light, nor was there fire
in the oven when David found the gabai alone.

"Why?" he pointed to the wood inside the oven, propped over
cold ashes.

"A light, smoke from a synagogue chimney, signals someone is
here and they come to search and usually arrest those who come
to pray. They send them away to work camps."

"And where is Elchanan?"

"Elchanan is still in prison. We were both arrested on trumped-up charges. I was released to tell you, he and others will be held as hostages until you and Rachel report to Von Preissig."

"I must return."

"No," Velvke held him back, "they'll shoot you in the dark."

"What is on?"

"A curfew: they imposed it without forewarning. It is a good thing you came first to the synagogue."

"A few steps and I'll be home."

"There is someone approaching." Velvke stopped with a "shhh."

"Soft steps," David said.

"They wear rubbers or felt over their boots."

"Reb Velvke! David!" they heard a flat voice.

"Abba, you risked getting shot?" Velvke said.

"That's the least. I'm worried about Chantze. It's my fault."

"What fault? You ought to thank God she returned safely." David said.

"Chantze wanted to get my letters out to the outside world. She thought that by going along with you to Bialystok she could manage to smuggle it across frontiers through Zionist couriers. I shouldn't have let her take such a risk."

"God was with us . . ." David said.

"You mean something happened?"

"Almost. Reuvke Rosenberg and Judah Kalir escaped. Chantze, luckily, was away to locate a courier; three boys were caught. We were warned in time that the house of our rendezvous was surrounded."

"It is my fault. I'll stop it—what good are the letters if someone has to deliver himself into their bloody hands?"

"Abba, it is not your fault."

"What is happening on the outside? Are we alone? Are there any good people left? Is God with us?"

"That's the question I heard everywhere in Bialystok," David said. "I don't know too much about God's intentions, and I can't tell you where the good people are. But I can tell you this much. The Jews suffer the most. They don't beg, and don't bow, they don't inform against themselves even when reduced to skin and bones. There is not one informer in our midst. If one weakens after all of this, we must forgive him and blame the perpetra-

tors." David fought against his own tears and said, "There is still
hope. The news from the front is encouraging."

David pressed his face almost to the pane of the window. He
recognized the figure of Kagan.

"Noske is busy with Chanukah candles. He even invited us to
be there. It is the first day of Chanukah, and at such a time . . .
David I . . ." Kagan was startled.

"You thought I tried to make my way to Marseilles. I was
already in Bialystok. It was not right for me to have asked
Rachel to join me. I can't leave my parents behind."

"No one knows what's right to do."

"You said something about Noske and at such a time?" David
felt something was wrong, and turning to Abba who pressed a
hushing finger against his lips, "What are you trying to cover up,
I must know? For God's sake, my parents need me."

"No one likes to be the bearer of such news," Abba apologized.

"What news?"

"There are rumors that we'll be moved into the ghetto today,
one day early," Kagan reported.

"Are you sure?"

"No. But in several towns, they gave the Jews a few hours
notice. We must be prepared for their cruelties. They arrested
Elchanan and your parents."

"Why?"

"They and Elchanan are held in custody until you return."

"I must report immediately to the Kommandant."

"I am going with you," Abba said.

When David and Abba were admitted to Von Preissig's office,
the Kommandant was on the telephone.

"They were shot, eh, for escaping from . . ." He did not finish.
He just said *"Jawohl,"* and hung up without any formal parting
words, as if speaking to a clerk.

"You were gone for several days without my permission; and
Rachel too," the colonel admonished David.

"Rachel was sick, I had to take her to Bialystok."

"Were the others sick too? It's foolish to escape. Two were

shot this morning in the work camp at Agustowa for trying to break out. Why are you afraid of me? If Rachel is drafted by anyone else, she'll really be in trouble. Your parents will be released. You are wise to have come for them."

"Thank you, thank you," David said.

"What do you want?" he turned to Abba.

"Elchanan Stabinsky," Abba stuttered.

"Yes, Elchanan Stabinsky," David reminded himself, "he is innocent."

"I don't know such a name."

"The student from the synagogue," David explained.

"Ah, the Talmudic student; you call him innocent? He was caught with a stolen candle and lit it during a blackout. He refuses to eat our food, mumbles and reads without a book. He is crazy; so take him. But I warn you and the others: Even if one in a thousand breaks out he'll be knifed by the Poles or shot by our men!"

Elchanan went directly to Schneider, for the first time by his own volition. Elchanan had made up his mind long ago that no matter what happened and what was impending, he would not be a messenger of gloom. Did it not say that the *Shechinah*, the image of holiness and the heavenly ambassador of justice, love and mercy, abide only in those who are of a cheerful frame of mind?

"Reb Elchanan," the elder Schneider addressed him with the appellation reserved for sages and scholars. "You'll wait a little while, we'll have some food, if it is ready." The house was more than disturbed. Chaim packed his books, which he kept in his father's house, in deference to the father's pride in his son, the *talmid chocham*, a learned disciple. He wasn't just an ordinary tailor, his son was a Rabbi, who gave meaning to his existence and endless toil. Now he assessed the box of books as one of his worthiest possessions, as valuable as the sewing machine. He thought that if it ever came to a desperate moment where he could save one of the two, he would favor the books.

"Oh *tate*," she lowered her eyes and then brazenly asked her father, "why can't I get married to Elchanan?"

"What?" her father was more distracted than shocked. "This is no time ..." and dropped the subject. In normal times he would have been delighted to entertain the very idea of his daughter marrying a *Yeshiva bochur*. But now, what could he say?

"Chaim, you know the law," Hadassah approached her brother who tied a bundle of books.

"What law?"

"Didn't you tell me once, Chaim, that if there were no ten commandments we would have learned our laws from the conduct of animals?"

"Not all the laws, let's see: the seventh commandment of morality from the dove and cat, the eighth—not to steal—from the ant . . ."

"But the Torah did mention a cat, and a cat is a mother, even in wartime, why can't I become a mother after I marry, even now?"

"Hadassah, please please . . . How do you . . . how can you put your mind . . . ?" Chaim shrugged his shoulders.

Elchanan, who examined a book given to him by Chaim, came over.

"What is it, Hadassah?" he finally half whispered to her in that bashful undertone peculiar of Yeshivah youths. "Is there anything—I mean what do you . . . ?"

"It's nothing, nothing—I wish to God, I only wish . . ." she ran out from the house. He followed her to the rear yard and into the shabby barn. She crouched in the far straw-covered corner, where a litter of kittens huddled, more for sympathy than warmth. Panther, their mother, was somewhere around in search of milk, a rare luxury since the cow was taken away.

He saw her crying, and the tears were not merely for the kittens.

"Yes, our sages understood," the Yeshiva student finally said.

"Understood what?"

"They understood why the prophet Jonah was sent to warn sinful Nineveh: to repent within forty days or be doomed. He reneged; ran away on a ship; and was tossed into the waves, when he was exposed as God's runaway. A whale swallowed him and released him. This time he fulfilled his mission. The people of Nineveh proclaimed national fast day for man and beast. Our sages inquire, why a fast for animals? Those people threatened God: "If you do not have mercy on us, we will not have mercy on them.""

"But we have mercy on animals, so God should have mercy on us, shouldn't he?"

"Yes, it is the other way, if we have mercy on people we have mercy on animals. How much more sinful are the people who have no mercy on people."

"Whatever is first, but we do learn even from dumb animals." "My brother said that we could also learn important laws from animals, like . . . Do you know that pigeons marry? Their couples are loyal to one another just like people who get married. Both of us should get married, honestly . . ."

"What are you saying?" he said, struck by her frank words.

"What I mean . . ." Hadassah stood there unable to utter another word.

"Yes, we must help and have mercy," she finally said. Covering her face with her hands, she ran away, on the verge of tears.

Several hours later he found her in the back yard. She was inside the wide doorway of the barn sweeping away snow and crying when Panther returned to nurse the kittens.

For a long while Elchanan watched from outside the doorway how Hadassah bedded down the cat and her litter on fresh hay. There were so many things on his mind, so many things he wanted to say. For one split second he saw Hadassah as she would appear in a home as a mother. Snow flakes began to touch his face. A sudden draft slammed the door of the barn, and everything was as before.

December 7, 8, 19, 1941: JAPAN LAUNCHES WAR ON U.S.
PEARL HARBOR ATTACKED.
RUSSIANS PUSH WEST OF MOSCOW.

*Normally even a hostile neighbor
becomes a friend after living together.
But the* yezer horo, *imbued with evil,
always desires to destroy his peaceful
friend.*

Tanhuma, Beshalach, 28.

17

D AYS OF INFAMY

It was late in the evening, one day before the removal to the
ghetto, and Sarah Beile had not yet returned from the nearby
village of Olshanke. Rachel was stuffing children's clothing into
potato sacks.

There was great uncertainty as to what they would be allowed
to take along.

Ben Zion, who had come back from Bialystok one day after
David returned, sat uneasily at the table repeating for the third
time, "Maybe if you would tell me whom she went to visit in
Olshanke, I would go to meet her."

"She'll be back, nothing to worry. She went to Franik . . ."
Rachel said and proceeded to pack away even old clothing.
"Someone can use them."

"Still every road on the outside is dangerous."

The last word was a slip of the tongue in the presence of
Rachel and Avreml. Ben Zion tried to correct it, ". . . Unless you
are sure of a friend." His fruitless search for his family and his
failure to make contact with Zionist leaders—these were frustrations he kept within. But what he heard about atrocities, and
concentration camps—these gave him away through Freudian
slips.

Late after midnight Sarah Beile faltered through the kitchen
door with a bag of potatoes slung over her shoulders.

219

"Mamma, you shouldn't have. We were worried."

"You took a great risk," Ben Zion added. "That's for men. What would you do if a German patrol stopped you?"

"I can walk through the fields with my eyes closed. There is no danger in the dark." Danger was always somewhere around, but she was now too busy to be aware of it. "It is almost daylight, what am I . . . ?" She didn't finish her implication.

For the long day ahead pressured her with endless problems. Today was almost tomorrow. What was next? How could she face it? Oh God, Oh God, she wanted to cry out, have mercy on my children.

She cried inwardly with her eyes closed, her face shielded by Rachel, who stood over her. Ben Zion sat near the table lost in his utter inability to do anything. He shifted and moved in his chair; opened and closed the book on the table. He looked at the title. But he could only make out "Wilna", where it was printed. There was a sub-title, "Grodno." It didn't matter. He couldn't think coherently. He was always at his best when facing a roaring and noisy crowd. This was different. There was a snarling sound outside. He couldn't assemble his thoughts. He couldn't remain here as a burden. He must get out and get food. Wasn't he supposed to collect jewels for the Germans?

Sarah Beile was aggrieved and in great pain; she was overcome by a desire to cry. She wanted so much to have her husband at her side now. But she could only sigh against the bosom of Rachel. And she beseeched God, "O, God in heaven. I am a simple woman. I'm alone with four children. Why don't we hear from my husband? The children need a father. And Rachel too is without her husband. The little ones are so afraid. They know, they know. Where shall I turn, O God? Franik can't help me. He is afraid. All the other peasants don't care or are full of hate. The bad ones are flocking to the city. Was it to join the worst on earth in the red house?"

It was uncommon for Sarah Beile, who ventured alone on country roads and carried heavy sacks from distant villages, to feel so dreadful. No task was too hard for her. But an effort in behalf of her family that was frustrated by an overwhelming barrier, made her fall limp from exhaustion on the sofa. Rachel covered her with her blue coat, raised her head and put the beaver muff underneath. It was given to her as a wedding gift

together with the beaver coat by Osher Joel. She sold the fur
coat to Franik in exchange for the potatoes.

To Rachel this night was a reminder of the one under the
canopy. She still was under her own roof, but a storm threatened
to uproot her. No one slept—only the dead-tired were stretched
out, numb with the night's terror.

A cold stiff wind came from across the flatlands and the
swamplands. It whined and whistled over the snow-covered
meadows, beyond the western bend of the river, and alongside
the highway to Fort Ossovetz and Bialystok. It found an opening: the space between the red police house and the rectory.
Down the market square, it whirled violently in a cloud of
churned powdery snow; then it funneled its way toward the
brick synagogue, where it reconnoitered, rattled every window,
looking for a weak spot. It then circled the structure, all around,
up and down, from red tiled roof to basement; through an un-
fastened rear window forced by Skura on the black Sabbath, the
wind slipped inside and flung open the door. A powerful gust of
wind now sped through the synagogue door, speeding from
house to house, down the street. It raced on to jar loose windows
and force doors open. Over the rooftops, into the gardens, across
to the stubbled fields, and into the forest, it swept, out of control.
Dancing a mad dance, a second wind whirled out from the direction of the police station. With reckless abandon, it burst into
every direction.

Rachel listened to the wailing wind lash the window-shutters
against the wall. It rose to crescendo and then was reduced to a
sharp moan, as it burst through cracks in the wood. Victoriously,
it broke through the paneless window of the gable. Muffled and
choked by the very emptiness, it whipped up dust against the
rafters. Rachel heard its tempestuous voice and warning of the
storm that was still gathering.

Abba Dunsky paced from side to side in his room at Abchik
the druggist's. It was still dark. But he heard the movements of
Chantze, and her sister Zirel. Abba was in dress all night. He
tried hard to close his eyes. But something pried his eyelids. He
was not sleepy. Abchik and his son-in-law Kagan were packing in
the next room. It was no problem for him to move his books and

the few belongings, which hung over the door and in the bulging cardboard suitcase on the chair.

He opened his notebook and pulled out a blue-lined sheet, the kind he reserved for correspondence. Smoothing out his pen against his nail, he dipped it in the ink and began to write.

"Honored and respected Jewish leaders of the Jewish Congress in Europe, America and Israel, hear me:

"You may not know who I am. My name is Abba Dunsky, a teacher of the higher classes in the Hebrew School of Suha-Vali.

"I am writing to you of the great danger facing us. Today is Friday and we have been ordered to move into a ghetto. There are now less than 2000 Jews there still alive; there were once 2500. Seventy five have died from hardships and catastrophes. The rest are in work camps, hospitals, in hiding or have vanished. We are being cut off from contact with Jewish communities and cities in Poland and throughout the world. Everything is forbidden. We have to move into the ghetto today, as I already mentioned. The entire population will have to move into four blocks of houses; about four families to a house. They have taken away our household goods, merchandise, cows, horses and wagons. We are prohibited to pursue our normal occupations and cannot earn our bread through the toil of free enterprise. Jewish artisans cannot produce; merchants cannot buy; stores cannot sell. I am afraid that this is not a ghetto, where we are to be segregated, but a concentration camp in our own city.

"If this is allowed to happen here by the indifference of mankind, then the same will be repeated in Stabin, Yanowa, Sokolke, Bialystok and Grodno. The three million Jews of Poland and three more million in the rest of German occupied territories will be doomed in similar ghettos or concentration camps.

"You must do everything to help us. You must help your brothers. Who else will help them? Go to the governments. Refuse to leave until something is done. Get insulted, get thrown out. But remember: what happens to us will happen to millions of Jews.

"We can't wait for the war to end, because we may not be there if nothing is done now to save us.

"We can't believe that the world is deaf to our cries. What good are all these speeches the allied leaders are making? Help us. Save yourselves. Save mankind."

Abba began to turn the pages of the Holy Scriptures to find supporting sources. He read and reread verses and paragraphs.

But he couldn't find what he sought. "Who changed the order of the pages and the verses?" he mumbled to those in the room. "I am coming." Abchik Opteker looked tensely on his wristwatch. He moved from room to room. He had no heart to see his drug store dismantled.

"It is all ready," David reported to Kiva Kagan, Abchik's son-in-law druggist, who handed him the last carton of large colored and labeled bottles. "I think we'll have to cover it with potatoes. This fresh dug out earth would not be recognized."

"These are all chances we must take. Personally, I don't think we can hide too much, if anything. But we've got to try to put away food, medicines and valuables, in several places."

"But these may be outside the ghetto." Label said.

"No one knows their final plans, nothing will be easy." David said in a tired voice. He was drowsy from the sleepless night and weary from the futility of trying to advise and to salvage from the impending disaster something, anything.

Although the two blocks of Synagogue Street, from the brick synagogue to the ancient synagogue, were included in the ghetto, David's, Rachel's, and Hershke's houses, adjacent and opposite the new synagogue, to be reserved for a hospital staff, were to be vacated.

Ber Leib put the books together on the big table, all ready to be saved or abandoned without discrimination. "Ber Leib, its late," Dinah called to him. "Where is the envelope with the addresses from America?"

"I don't know," he kept on saying, still surveying the books.

"Ber Leib, what are we going to do without the addresses?"

"Dinah Elke, why do you need addresses? How are we going to send letters? Through a special messenger? We don't even known our own address."

Dinah was about to start crying once again, when David, his pants covered with clay and straw, appeared. He ran to his drawer and emptied its sheaves of papers, letters and memoranda into the big basket. He selected a few letters and papers and put them inside one of the Talmudic volumes.

"Where is the box of spices and the citrus box?" David was perturbed.

"They're right in my pocket, together with mother's marriage ring, and also the packet of earth," his father told him. David

was glad that this last link with the Holy Land was not overlooked.

It seemed hopeless, as far as David could judge, to select the
few memorable things which they could take along on their own
backs. Franik's loud voice was heard outside. He had come to
move their belongings for safe keeping.

"I'll take this with me." He tenderly held the Talmud with his
correspondence, the citrus box, the packet of holy earth and
spice box. He was on his way to Hershke's basement to put it
away before it was sealed. David reminded his father before he
left to insist that Franik also move the few belongings of Sarah
Beile.

"I hope, may God grant Panie Sokoloff," Franik said, "that the
war will be over, and then I'll return all the things you give me."
Ber Leib wondered and Dinah Elke's face was against the wall.
Jews were giving away all their belongings. A few were selling
them for hard to get sacks of potatoes, loaves of bread and for
worthless Polish currency. Household furniture that was collected during several generations was now dispensed for almost
nothing. It was not their value that mattered, it was the depriva-
tion of the last dignity on earth to possess things and themselves.
For those who slept in the beds and broke bread at the tables,
were less than birds who make their nests and normally create
them without coercion; and even less than ants who will feed
undisturbed in their own chambers.

"Be careful, take care of this chair," Ber Leib cautioned
Franik's son. "And this clock—it never stopped Franik, it kept
perfect time, here is the key, wind it once a week, on the eve of
Sabbath." Ber Leib sighed and reflected. Soon strangers would
enter these houses, David thought. Strange men and women
would make sport of Jewish traditions and toil. They would
carry away holy vessels that made the house a temple and the
table an altar.

It was near the dead line of 3 o'clock, in the afternoon. Drifting flakes began to fall on the dull gray snow. A wind from the
southeast lashed at the barren and naked wings of Hershke's
windmill. It was still and silent, its huge wheel came to a grinding stop. Its sturdy oak teeth gaping at the deserted interior. An
empty sack was suspended below the chute. The key was taken
away and the last wagon with confiscated flour departed.

Hershke sat by the window. Motke, his son and his two daughters, were brushing flour dust on the clay that sealed the trapdoor of the basement.

"You can't bury everything," he said, uncertain of what would happen to the small objects, that were buried in the cellar floor: silver, paper currency, marriage rings and David's spice box and citrus box.

Five teams, headed by David, Abba, Shmuel, Burka and Label began to make the last frantic round of inspection of all Jewish homes, beginning with Koppel's house.

Reb Koppel was reading Exodus. It was now on the eve of a new exodus. The Jews were also making bricks, cutting, scraping and hammering on the split trunks on the frame supports to wall themselves in. For ten days and nights, in shifts, they had been working overtime on the stockade walls. Only three were completed. The western wall would be finished later, when it would be strung with barbed wire like the other walls. Outside, Germans and Poles were waiting, ready to act if there was any infringement of the so-called 'Rehabilitation Requirements.'

They now came into Velvke's house. He was writing out meal tickets for the displaced Jews trapped in Suha-Vali. The Yeshiva *bochur*, who sat on Velvke's right, held on to his battered suit case. The closed Gemara was on his knees and on top the *talis* and *tephilin* bag, his praying paraphernalia. These were all his possessions on this earth.

Shimon the wagoner whispered into the ears of Shmuel Leiser and Burka something about a false wall where not only valuables and food could be stored, but even as many as twenty people could be crowded within. It was on the northern wall of his house next to Koppel's. It was too late, they told him, to move any supplies inside.

German police and Polish militia began to shout orders as stragglers struggled in the deep snow to pull their last belongings into the ghetto.

The guards began to dance, strut, shake and shout as they lined both sides of the street to welcome Rabbi Shepsel Kalir. He carried the Holy Scroll in his hands and his wife Zippora carried a big volume and Codes and a little basket packed with food.

The hooligans began to close in on him, pelting him with snow balls and screaming.

"A farewell present, Panie Rabin."

"Are you human or animals? This is what you do in front of your church? Would you do this to your priest?" Zippora put out her hands to protect Alter and David, who rushed to help him.

"Arrest her!" Skura raged at the Rabbi's wife, "and beat the others," he pointed to the Rabbi's rescuers.

Rachel now ran holding Avreml's hand, while her mother followed with the twins Leishke and Leika.

"Go to Mother and wait for me—don't leave her," she let go of Avreml. She advanced toward a sedan army car. It was guarded by two soldiers with fixed bayonets. The curtained window was now drawn.

"Are you going to let these rowdies and drunks molest innocent Jews?"

"They are not rowdies," said Von Preissig. "They serve the Reich. They just attended Church. They are devout Christians. But why be angry—come into my car and we'll talk this over."

"Herr Kommandant, I have no time for frivolity," she said and left him holding the door for her.

Von Preissig was startled by her audacity. She fascinated him more than ever.

"Let them into the ghetto. We are already an hour behind schedule." The Kommandant returned the salutes of Messer and Schrecke.

Sometime later, Beryl stood waiting near the gate at the head of a cluster of Jews. They were waiting for some one to admit them. No one cared. Beryl was cold and hungry. His wife Bashke handed him a *suchari*—dipped in vinegar and overbaked; he started to pray. But he was worried. Then, somewhat content that he brought along with him the little flour, he uttered *'hasdei hashem'*—the graces of God. He would save it for the Sabbath. The first two *chalah* breads he would bake for the Rabbi. By making smaller forms he could make a dozen or more for the young children. Every bread had to be reported and deducted from the daily ration. Anything unrecorded, even moldy bread and chicken feed, was *Verbotten* under the strictest penalties.

Hershke the miller, alongside him, looked forlornly. His daughters and son covered him with his old coat.

Hershke could see across the bare crowns of his trees, shaking to and fro in the wind. What would happen to his orchard? If he could only raise himself he would also be able to spot the top wings of the mill. Would they know how to take care of the mill? The sails on the wings would stiffen and freeze unless rolled up. Had the clay dried over the trap door to the basement? Both his and his neighbors' possessions were buried there. This anxiety was even greater now that it was clear to him that their trust in his ingenuity was in vain.

The Polish militia began to stir as Skura, accompanied by S.S. Lt. Schrecke, came through the gate. It was well after dark. But to the waiting Jews in front of the closed gate, who were deprived of celebrating Chanuka, ushering in the Sabbath with lights, God's day and night were darkened and profaned.

The voluntary committee, and not the *Judenrat* as requested by Col. Schwarzhund of the Gestapo office, began to assert itself. David, accompanied by Shmuel, persuaded Von Preissig to allow the Jews themselves to administrate their transfer to the ghetto. There had not been too much interference. Von Preissig persisted over Col. Schwarzhund's veiled threats, to try out this 'self governing,' formula. It was a respectable title.

"The results would be the same," he assured him.

The Jews agreed that the role of the *Judenrat* was detestable. Ben Zion expressed it best, "We will not become our own executioners."

The committee now began to make the last round on the outside before the guards herded them inside. They were given ten minutes. They made last minute efforts to find winter coats for those who had none, or from whom it was taken away by the guards.

"Reb Beryl," David stopped to inquire, "are you well, do you need anything?"

"No, no—I have everything." His face was ash gray and his nose was red from the cold. "What shall I do with these?" he pointed to the pile of sacks under him.

"It must be flour," David surmised.

"It is flour, for the children and the Rabbi," he admitted.

"We run a great risk," David said.

"Let's fill our pockets," Burka suggested.

"Good, a very good idea." They began to transfer handfuls into their pockets.

"Have you a place?" David asked Beryl.

"At Moses Der Tucker's."

"That is correct," Shmuel Leiser checked the sheet which the committee had carefully worked out, pairing friends with friends and taking into account all factors which would reduce friction under overcrowded conditions.

"Reb Hershke, you are also there," Shmuel told him.

The final moments were perched on the menacing bayonets of the German guards and Polish auxiliaries. Capt. Messer gave the order to 'seal off' the Jews from the outside world. He acted on final instructions of Col. Schwarzhund who nullified Von Preissig's attempt to allow farmers to sell their products within the walls.

Shmuel Leiser, at a great risk to himself, persuaded Capt. Messer, with the help of several gold zlotys, to extend the time for one half-hour.

As the gate was flung open, the pushing and shoving by the guards even against the infirm and sickly people did not abate. Sages stumbled, women fainted and children cried as they were herded through the gates of sorrow, into confinement.

"Where is your Jewish star—do you want to be shot? Inside the wall you son of a son!" Messer screamed at David.

"What star—we were not told."

"Every Jew must have a star sewn on his clothing within twenty-four hours."

December 19, 20, 1941: EQUAL RIGHTS TO JEWS WILL BE
GUARANTEED IN RESTORED
POLAND.
JAN STANCZYK
MINISTER OF LABOR.
(POLISH GOVERNMENT IN EXILE)

*Against all the Gods of Egypt I will
execute judgment.*
Exodus, 12:12.

*There is no nation which is smitten that
its Gods are not smitten together with it.*
Sukkah, 29.

18

WALLS OF CAPTIVITY

By official permission, the big shed of Bezalel Tepper, the brick
maker, and the barn of Shaike Suchovolsky the leather merchant
were designated as synagogues. The big Old Synagogue with its
pagoda tiers, its adjoining *Beth Medrash,* the New Synagogue
and the red *Brick Synagogue* were deliberately excluded from the
ghetto.

The Germans had promised not to molest worshippers in the
two sheds. But most, in deference to the interned synagogues,
decided in advance to pray in small groups as long as there were
the ten required for a 'minyan.'

They had finished their prayers along the wall and in the corners. It was now time for a bereft meal to these four families in
Isaac Melamed's house. They were crowded from both sides of
the long study table that almost extended from wall to wall.
Rabbi Kalir and the Rebetzin were at one end and Reb Isaac and
his wife near the kitchen end.

Ber Leib was on the Rabbi's right, then David, his head bandaged, and Dinah Elke. Hershke, who with his son and daughter
sat next to them, began in a low voice *"Shalom Aleichem,"* the
traditional peace greeting to the Sabbath angels. His face was

swollen, and his beard covered blue and red bruises. Ber Leib
now raised his voice like one making an urgent request.

"Come in peace, angels of God."

David repeated after him, "Bless me with peace." It occurred
to him—an incisive thought which would obsess him to challenge and to rebel against the accepted—that instead of the singular "bless me" it should have said, "Bless us." He unconsciously
uttered the plural *"borchunu"* instead of *"borchuni."* Rabbi Kalir
acknowledged this departure from the text by just nodding that
he understood his interpretation.

David remembered how this table beneath its cover was rough
and splintered; carved and scratched by bored and playful children. He could almost feel the loose molding, which anyone of
them in a capricious fit would snap with a bang to distract Reb
Isaac's pointed and sharp questions. It was the portion of *'Mish-
patim'*—*"Judgments,"* that condemned slavery, established responsibility for direct injury, an eye for an eye, and indirect
damage by one's ox or fire. When the class was cross-examined
to explain 'an eye for an eye,' Israel Grodzensky replied that it
wasn't enough to pay damages—how much could a poor farmer
or shepherd pay, since there was no insurance.

"What would you do," he was blunt as usual, "take out his
eyes instead?"

"Yes!" Israel countered, "restore his sight through an operation."

"Where will you get an eye?"

"In a laboratory," Israel answered. The class rocked with
laughter.

Then Isaac taught them other important laws of the portion:
the four kinds of damages; mercy for the stranger as well as the
thief; special consideration for the widow and the orphan; to
support verdicts of the majority for good only; dedication to good
deeds; and finally, that God himself would intervene in behalf of
the Israelites for their possession of the Promised Land whose
boundaries would extend from the Red Sea to the Mediterranean
and from the desert (Sinai and Arabia) to the Euphrates River.

Reb Isaac knew they would have preferred stories, or a fight
with snowballs outside if they could get out. He read their
minds very well. He even resigned himself to the fact that some
of the children could not read nor understand the fine print
below the text.

One night they walked out one by one, each claiming some

ailment or illness. "What is happening?" he demanded an explanation.

"Your questions are hurting us and we will sue for damages," they shouted in rehearsed unison from under the window.

But notwithstanding these problems, Reb Isaac believed that his students learned more than the students of the modern Hebrew School. Isaac could never forgive the school committee for not recognizing his talents, and employing him as a teacher in the new system.

"Ber Leib, what does it mean? Fancy glasses, a stiff collar, a teacher shouting commands like a corporal. I'll admit it looks nice; all marching into class, raising their heads like frightened sheep, even wearing a uniform cap. New books, eh—without the commentaries! New stories, eh—new stories without ends—but what about results, eh?" He squeezed his goat-like silky beard. "Results? Can they read? Can they translate the Bible and read Rashi? Are they pious? How many of them come on time to the synagogue on Saturday and pray?"

"But, Reb Isaac," Paltiel had said at the meeting, convened to abolish private schools. "Maybe some of them remember your lashes more than your lessons."

"It says in the Bible, 'He who spares the rod, hates his son.' "

"Please, Reb Isaac. I'm surprised you employ the Bible to cover up your own mistakes. One verse is not the Bible; how about 'educate a child according to its specific needs?' "

"That's exactly what I did—I am modern too. I can trim my beard like Reb Jacob, put on my Sabbath garments on a weekday, will you give me a salary? I can still teach, look at the generations that I raised!"

"No one can deny your accomplishments."

"All mine," Isaac saw his opening and continued at the top of his breath. "There are teachers, several doctors, engineers, leaders in all parties, all mine, I put plenty of my blood into them."

"And plenty of their blood," Paltiel was quick to retort.

"Yes, I made them work. It was worth it. Yes, I lost my temper. But remember they were with me eight to ten hours each day. Remember they were boys: full of mischief. Show me one father who could control himself under such conditions."

"We will find a place for you. You'll help, I mean you'll give extra lessons to slow students," the chairman Paltiel conceded.

"You don't mean to give me all the dumb students!"

"I said slow students who will make up a full class. You will

instruct them in your specialties: reading and translating the
Bible, with the proper quotations from Rashi, Medrash and the
Talmud."

It was pleasant to recall this scene as Reb Isaac with his spare
greying beard, lonely blue eyes and pale face reflected the wisdom and experience so peculiar to teachers who were called
"Rebbi." Generations entrusted their children to his quaint but
proficient *cheder* in the cramped room of the log weathered
house on the clay hill. Fathers knew that when he lost his temper
the angels looked aside. He employed a strap or something
harder to good effect. David remembered a few occasions on
which he went down the line. No one was spared, to show im-
partiality to the toughies who complained that they were picked
on.

Few words were exchanged and most sighs were hidden at the
first Friday night in exile from their own tables. Dinah Elke
would have uttered a long penetrating sigh but Dwoshe began to
cough incessantly, in the same manner that she would have used
to signal Isaac that a parent was approaching, and that Reb
Isaac had better take care of his temper.

Grace was recited in monotones. Only when Ber Leib came to
the passage, "God bless my wife and son," he added out loud,
"and my gracious host and all our people." Reb Isaac was grateful not so much that he was remembered, but that even at such
times, Jews were "observant and correct" as he always said—that
was the prime objective of all learning. The method is rough, but
the product must be refined. Out of downtrodden clay, the finest
of pots is shaped. Even grain has to be thrashed on the floor. The
bee that makes honey buzzes and stings, but the spider who
works quietly and efficiently builds a trap for a helpless victim.

The candle lights were flickering and melting. For a moment
all cocked ears as steps were heard. The door opened and Abba
walked in.

"Aren't you together with the Optekers at Suchovolsky's
house?" David asked him.

"Yes. But Mr. Opteker wanted to sleep on the floor, so I could
have the sofa."

"There is enough room here." Isaac said. "You are a colleague
and a learned man, and there is plenty of room."

"You sleep near me—up in the garret," David suggested.

"Here," Dinah Elke said, "is a pillow and a cot."

"Here is food," Dwoshe coming in from the kitchen, told him.

"Thank you Dwoshe, but I already had supper."

"Come David, let's go up now."

David was well acquainted with the entrance to the garret. It was behind the kitchen door in the hallway. As a former student, he remembered it well as the retreat and refuge, on cold days, when they couldn't go into the garden or barn. They invented all kinds of excuses to go up there. They were either looking for a misplaced book or wanted to drive out a squirrel that made its winter home underneath the ridge of the roof, or were going to retrieve the cat for Dwoshe after they deliberately brought it there. It happened quite often in the afternoons when boredom and drudgery instigated them to find thrills and excitement.

Up in the garret, David moved a few steps toward the far corner to show Abba his bedding for the night. He stopped and began to search in his mind something he had forgotten to do.

"What? What was it," he tried to unburden himself.

All of a sudden David's words were smothered. His numbed lips were stiff and shivering speechless and immovable. It was ordained that "a man must search his clothing on the eve of Sabbath lest he forget and carry out something." He was carrying a burden—a heavy burden.

There was a slip of paper in his pocket. How did it get there? Was it by mistake or the wrong suit? Out of habit he always went through his pockets after brushing his Sabbath suit with kerosene. It was there and he knew its contents—as he fingered it—even the first lines.

"David, there are some things I would like to talk to you."

"You mean about the ghetto, our prison?"

"Yes, that's the word—it is a prison. By locking us up in a big prison they can do with us whatever they want and plan; you don't believe their promises?"

"No, I don't."

"You wouldn't do anything to help them?"

"Abba, you know me."

"Are you sure? Are you free?"

"What do you want me to do? Do you think it is easy for me to work on this plan?"

"What plan?"

"You are ordered to report every day to translate all marked
and selected Hebrew books into German," he unrolled a crumpled sheet of paper, and read: "failure to comply or . . . will be
punished severely. In the first category . . . Bible Mishna,
Talmud . . . commentaries, codes, responsa, ancient, medieval
and modern Hebrew literature."

"Who issued it?"

"The Kommandant himself, here," David flaunted Von Preissig's directive. "There is also a P.S. on the bottom about filming
special Jewish scenes."

"Films? Didn't they . . . ? It means they'll stage incidents,
blood incidents . . . is there no other way?"

"I was warned by Von Preissig, 'You will be responsible if you
don't want any one else to be hurt. There will be swift punishment for any deception. We have ways to check!' "

"I am afraid for you and for all of us."

"Do you think I would ever do anything to hurt or betray my
people?"

"No! But they could use you as a tool."

"What can they get from me?"

"What can you get from them?"

"We have to keep in contact with them. We are forced to
negotiate with this enemy, as we were compelled since the days
of Rabbi Johanan Ben Zacai, Abarbanel in Spain and others, to
communicate with their leaders.

"But those were different people; those were part human."

"These are not human at all?"

"Exactly."

"This is what I have to find out, Why? Vicious animals have
no fears nor consciences, they follow their own instincts. Why do
the Germans act inhuman? Have they no fear of God, law, mankind?"

"Evidently not." Abba looked away.

"Why not? Because no one cares. Religious leaders, humanists,
philosophers, advocates of morality, justice and peace are indifferent. Therefore even the better nations have become sterile
and incapable to act against the sinister plans."

"Then this plan, is something more?"

"Perhaps."

"It isn't just a library plan?"

"No."

"It must be important, if a Kommandant supervises it. Who knows in how many more places they are doing the same?"

"I don't know for sure whether or not they are doing it anywhere else. But this could be the first place."

"How can you tell?"

"Von Preissig told me his whole future and career depended on this outcome and maybe the future of the Germans, if he could only accomplish this. To find out the secret of our religion, to find out what makes us survive."

"What secrets?"

"They are really not secrets. But it is a tempting mystery to the Germans that the Jews, a minority deprived of a home and protection, should have accomplished so much in the world."

"It is the triumph of God."

"But there is something more to this," David lowered his voice. "I can't say what it is."

"You said 'this plan is something more,' and 'sinister plans.'"

"Don't quote me."

"It is preferable to rumors."

"Rumors by whom, the communist Label?"

"We have a right to know the truth. Isn't this library like the transfer of a man's will before he is executed?"

"I must not say anything more."

"Is it too frightening to tell me that they want to learn our secrets before they do away with us?"

David said nothing.

"We ought to call Koppel and Paltiel," Abba said. "It may have reached a point that compels us to seek the advice of our Rabbi. This is too important and dangerous for you to keep it to yourself."

"I know it." David broke off the conversation. He stretched himself out over the grass mat. He moved over so that Abba would have room to sleep beside him.

Hot water and hot milk—even diluted milk would have been fine to restore any pretense of Sabbath dignity. But there was no thought of water or milk. Above the faint echo of a rooster's call, he heard the cries of babies. The cries stopped, then burst out with greater vigor, then stopped. He could almost feel the mother's gentle hand caressing the baby in a strange and crowded hard bed. Then the crying resumed. No milk.

David examined his crumpled suit. He always saved it for the Sabbath. The edges of the cuffs were threadbare, the pants were worn in the seat and knees, but no one else knew it except maybe his mother. His jacket was still in good shape and he felt relieved when he put it on until he put his hand in his left pocket and fingered the notice to report to the Kommandant.

Abba Dunsky, who seemed fast asleep, began to shift on the hard floor. The grimace on his face increased as he made a full turn. "It feels like somebody is rolling stones over my back."

David was startled.

"Did anything happen?" Abba inquired.

"Only the usual sounds of the night."

"Didn't you sleep?"

"I slept, but kept on waking."

"Did you have another dream?"

"Why must I tell you?"

"Because I am beginning to think perhaps you do see visions."

"I saw wagons."

"Where?"

"On the highway to Grodno."

"What has this got to do with us?"

"I saw familiar faces. I was there too."

"You said before that the Germans want to do away with us, and you saw in your dream wagons. There must be something to it."

"David! Abba! David! Abba! To the *minyan*." Shmuel Leiser called.

"Shmuel, I thought you were out on the other side, you escaped."

"No, I couldn't, I had a chance. An underground group asked me to join. You remember the peasant who said he wanted to sell bread? He was a *chalutz* agent who planned to take us through Bialystok then Riga and across the Baltic to England. But I thought of my mother and brother—he hadn't been feeling well, and I thought that to be alive, while they—well, I returned."

The three young men went below to pray.

"Good Sabbath," Abba joined David as they welcomed Reb Koppel and others of the emergency committee for a meeting in the afternoon.

"This is the latest '*Verbotten*,'" David handed Koppel a carbon copy of paper at the *minyan*. There were no details. It was terse and addressed to S.S. Captain Messer.

All weapons, metals and surplus foods are to be handed over to the authorities . . . Severe punishment for hoarding and speculation . . . Committee hereafter to be designated *Judenrat* will be held responsible for delivery of men, boys or women for work tasks in town or for special projects in vicinity . . . Assembly, prayer and study is verbotten . . . Exit from ghetto *streng verbotten* . . . Burial within walls only.

It was stamped. "District Headquarters—Grodno," and initialed by Rintzler, Von Preissig and Schwarzhund.

Reb Koppel reread the last lines in utter disbelief and handed it to Label to pass it on to the others.

"There are ten main paragraphs in this document," David opened the informal discussion. "Here are new ten commandments, only they're opposite of those in the Bible—double in meaning and double-crossing the Jews.

"There are many problems before us. We have to make some decisions. First: Who shall be in the committee? Second: There is the problem of volunteer police. Third: We also face the problem of cooperative and equal distribution of food, clothing and drugs. And then we must supply 400 men every day, also one girl secretary or more."

Reb Koppel said, "It should be remembered that today is the Sabbath. We cannot write anything down, and if we did we would incriminate ourselves. Our assembly is therefore without authority."

"I think it is with authority," David interrupted.

"It is not official and it is not safe. It is therefore my advice to take out a book—so that at least we can say we are studying."

"Reb Koppel is right," Abba seconded. And Shmuel Leiser added, "I think even you, David, will yield this point."

"What is this, a private meeting?" Label, who joined them late, angrily protested. I hope it is not a secret meeting. Well, I'm still on the committee, am I not?"

"You are," Abba replied.

David resumed: "In fact, I think the defense committee can now be activated into the *Judenrat*. The Germans insist on this official name. We'll pretend to call it such, but as far as we are concerned it is still the committee, and not the *Judenrat*."

"Still this is our Sabbath. Study? Yes. Discussion about certain problems? Yes. But an official meeting? No!" Reb Koppel persisted.

"I dare to say we are in a state of *pikuach nefesh*, our lives are

threatened. Therefore this meeting supersedes the Sabbath,"
David said. "We are in great danger. Let us act."

"We are not here to render a decision," Koppel rebuked him.
"this is for our Rabbi to do."

"I always said," Abba said, "let's get in touch with other communities, Zionist and other organizations. Let's appeal to the
world, to the conscience of nations. If they will abandon us to
the enemy, then the blood will be upon their heads."

"Time is short. There are orders . . ."

Label interrupted. "David, you mention orders. You also said
something about activating the *Judenrat*. How do you know all
this, especially the *Judenrat*."

"I didn't say *Judenrat*, I said the defense committee should be
activated into the *Judenrat*. By now we all know that it is official."

"Official from whom?"

"From the Germans."

"Did you know it, Reb Koppel? You Abba? You Shmuel
Leiser? In fact, you are the only one who seems to know. How?
When? Tell us! We'll listen."

David was in a dilemma. He was reluctant to explain his
recent contact with Von Preissig.

"You have nothing to hide!" Reb Koppel said.

"I have complete faith in you." Abba supported him.

"Me too," Shmuel seconded.

"Let him explain!" Label backed David into a tight corner,
and reverting to second person, craftily addressed him, "Explain
in detail if you please."

"You must believe me—I have been drafted to do translations
just like others who have been drafted for other tasks. I am not
the only one, there are perhaps hundreds of others forced to do
this loathsome task," David explained, for he could not believe
that he was the only Jew engaged in this project.

"I have no proof of the hundreds, but by your own words you
are a collaborator."

"You lie, you just lie," David retorted vehemently and
stopped. Koppel warned Label. "This is serious charge," I don't
believe it!"

"It is a false, and I might say a dangerous suspicion." Abba
protested.

"We don't believe it. David is one of us—he is us—and we are he—we are all one," Shmuel Leiser was eloquent in his defense. "The minute we are divided we are lost."

"We should really summon the Rabbi. Zorach, call Rabbi Kalir." Koppel spoke with authority. "This is very serious. You know the severity of the Jewish law about making false accusations. Charges have been made against David. But there are no witnesses; insinuations, but no proof."

After Rabbi Kalir heard all sides he concluded that such a wild accusation was inevitable. For under the relentless pressure of the Nazis one or more had to maintain contact with them. After the Rabbi finished, he nodded to David to speak for himself.

"With the Rabbi's permission, may I? If a woman is accused falsely of being disloyal to her husband she'll be willing to drink the water mixed with the parchment erasures of God's name. The Torah calls it bitter water. Well I'm willing to swallow the bitter words of Label to prove my innocence."

"David!" Rabbi Kalir said, "You need not drink any water, especially bitter water. Now there are nineteen complete blessings in the *Amidah*—the silent prayer while standing. Yet it is called *Shmone Esrei*, eighteen. Do you know which is the nineteenth?" They all nodded as he quoted, "And to the informers, may there not be any hope." Rabbi Kalir swept his eyes toward each as he spoke as if prying into the conscience and soul of each one.

"Now this nineteenth blessing does not refer to an individual Jew being asked to translate Hebrew under threat of death. Suppose you and you and you were forced to translate. What would you do? How can you tell what is their objective? Do you recall in Jewish history how the Torah was translated into Greek by seventy wise men during the reign of Philadelphus, in Alexandria? Of course, the Talmud adds that it was a tragic day—to open up our treasures to people who have repaid us evil for our good intentions. Have not all our holiest of books been translated?"

"As for the contact between David and the Kommandant, we'll have to see and wait. So far he has represented us without any mishap. If he fails us, we'll have time to judge . . ."

"Rabbi, if we allow him to go on, it may be too late," Label interrupted.

"We have said enough—in fact too much. Let us forgive one another and not accuse wildly. The enemy, the danger, is not

within the walls. Here it is the holy Sabbath that has dominion.
Let us cleanse ourselves from evil, thought, talk and deed."

Outside in the late afternoon, after intermittent prayer and
study, some people came out for fresh air. It was too crowded
inside the houses. They braved the jeering Polish guards who
taunted them with *"Do Palestina,"* and mispronounced *"Ver-
pluchte Yuden."*

Undaunted, the Jewish youth turned their faces away from
their tormentors. They distinctly recognized some of the voices
and especially the sneering faces perched above the barbed wire.
The guards looked gruesome, intoxicated with a sickly hatred;
their German overseers took pride in their finished handiwork.

Within the walls was a city in captivity, in subdued mourning
on this holy day of rest and tranquility, David walked along with
Abba and Shmuel. An unseen curtain surrounded them. Abba
said something about the splendid way three and five families
lived together in a few rooms; how older boys and girls collected
books and studied with the young. Shmuel mentioned the plan to
collect food for the poorer families, if necessary by a decree of
the 'committee'. But if supplies are cut off, the money is gone,
and . . ." He did not venture to finish for he knew there was no
end to conjectures and problems facing them.

"THOSE WHO HAVE LAUNCHED THEIR
PEOPLE ON THE PATH OF WAR AND
CONQUEST WILL BE CALLED TO
TERRIBLE ACCOUNT. THEY WILL STOP
AT NOTHING THAT VIOLENCE OR
TREACHERY CAN SUGGEST."
CHURCHILL BEFORE U.S. CONGRESS.

*The (righteous) kingdom on earth is in
the image of the heavenly kingdom.*
Berakoth, 58.

19

COUNTERFEIT MASTERS OF CLAY

Five days later the defense committee met to activate the *Judenrat* at the request of Col. Von Preissig. For a thousand years, Jews exercised autonomous self rule in most European countries. After paying their taxes, serving in the army and obeying civil laws they were governed in matters of religion, education and even in business transactions through their *Botei Din,* Rabbinical Courts. In some countries their community leaders even levied taxes to maintain synagogues, Hebrew schools up to the university level of Yeshivahs, charity institutions at home and in the Holy Land. Between the First and Second World Wars, Europe was convulsed by violent revolutions and upheavals. With the overthrow of Czarist Russia by a communist government, religious autonomy and educational institutions were obliterated in Russia. But until the Nazi invasion this cultural autonomy prevailed in most European countries.

At this meeting, at which David presided, they faced a dilemma: whether to approve the mistrusted *Judenrat* in its dealings with a government committed, as David and others warned, to their destruction, or to maintain limited relations as a committee with the local regime and try to obtain the best conditions from its maverick Kommandant.

During the heated and sharp discussion, Label led the attack

241

against giving the committee an outright mandate to deal with
the Germans. Rabbi Kalir followed every word of the discussion.

"Brothers, it seems that the majority favors this committee,"
Koppel said, "however we have not yet heard the opinion of our
revered Rabbi."

"This is not a religious question. I am against the committee,"
said Label.

"I have already expressed my opinion publicly and privately,
Rabbi Kalir said "I cannot sanction any group or committee to
help this government impose its rule on us. Our sages ruled *Dino
demalchuno dino,*' the law of the government is our law, only if
such a government is reasonably just. But so far we have witnessed only *'rishus.'* We must judge each act and decision on its
merits."

"I am sorry to say that the whole discussion is irrelevant."
David's dark eyes were now aimed at Label. "While we debate our
people go hungry, children are without milk and our men and
women are carted away to slave camps. We need funds immediately to buy food. Shmuel Leiser told me this morning that quite
a few have already contributed money."

"Who authorized Shmuel?" Label asked.

"I asked him to serve, but it is up to the majority to confirm
him."

"You mentioned contributions. Are the rich giving up their
hoarded zlotys and food, and what are we doing to extract it
from them?"

"Label, there are no classes in our midst."

"I voted in favor of this committee," Ben Zion said. "It is not
the name, it is what we make of it. It has to be organized. For
instance I have limited funds and some jewels in my possession
which I collected for *Eretz Israel.* I am turning over both to the
committee.

"He is out of order and without authority," Label interrupted
him. "David is a Zionist, Shmuel is a Zionist, Abba too, and
Kagan is a socialist Zionist; is it a surprise if they appoint secretly a Zionist as collector and controller of our funds?"

"Label, one does not need authority to do a *mitzvah.* Let us
not criticize those who act for our own good," the Rabbi reproved him. "David was right: there are no classes in our
midst. We are all without tags like one people before God."

"What about the Hebrew school?" Abba asked.

"We will do everything we can. We will have to give up some of our rooms during the day," David replied. "Kiva," he called on Kagan the druggist, "have you anything to report?"

"Both Dr. Epstein and Dr. Lev have been released and will be here to examine and treat our serious cases. We are running short of some medicines, but we are procuring some at great expense. The most important problem right now is how to get work for our men, especially for our skilled workers. Those who work on the outside are better fed and in better health."

"I talked to Von Preissig and he promised me that he has a project in mind that will provide us with jobs," David said.

"Can we trust him?" Abba asked.

"If you nominate executives, appoint fund raisers and are about to control jobs, without consulting anyone, what do we need a committee for?" Label persisted in his criticism.

"Is it your communism or is it within you to oppose and disrupt everything," David spoke angrily. "From now on any decision including my chairmanship will be decided by a majority vote."

"At what point," Abba asked, "are we going to stop cooperating with the Germans?"

"We are not cooperating. But if the committee ever becomes an instrument for our own destruction, we will abolish it," David declared.

Rabbi Kalir called David aside before he left.

"Is it as bad as it seems?" he asked him.

"It is worse."

"You are not influenced by any dreams?"

"Rabbi, I am disregarding them, but I see so much happening like in a nightmare."

"The Holy One preserve us and guard us. May he also protect you from the clutches of the 'reshoim' and put an end to this government of tyranny."

Twelve long drawn days had passed since Von Preissig promised to provide work for the many unemployed family providers of the community. But so far there was neither confirmation nor denial of the pledge, only rumors. It was after Chanukah and on the eve of Christmas. The church bells of the twin towers tolled endlessly. Peasants began to arrive early from nearby farms and

from distant villages for church services. Meanwhile those who
attended an early mass returned home to their families, while
others remained to buy and sell.

It was forbidden to barter with the Jews. But the greedy Germans, the Polish Militia and the camp women could not resist
the profitable inducements. Gold wedding rings, earrings and
watches were preferred by Gestapo men in exchange for flour
and cereals. The *gendarmes* settled for silver cups and fur coats.
Skura and his renegades who acted as intermediaries for peasants demanded silverware, cloth, furniture and dresses for their
women in exchange for black bread, potatoes, turnips, and sometimes, for special prices, hard to get cheese or whey. Label protested that the poor had nothing to offer in exchange. David
summoned the committee and it was decided to offer soup and
bread to those who needed it most.

The Jews never complained. Abba Dunsky the teacher summed
it up in a letter, which he addressed to the Geneva Red Cross
for world wide distribution:

> A boy in my class told me that when his father asked for more
> potatoes in exchange for a suit, the farmer answered, "You are
> asking me to give up one feeding of my pigs, this is too much."
> Gentlemen of the Red Cross, you probably know the facts better
> than I do. It takes a few hundred pounds of potatoes to produce a
> pound of pork. After it is cured, salted and eaten, its thirst has
> to be quenched by beer, again using up hundreds of pounds of
> grain. Adding up vodka distilled from potatoes, there would be
> enough food to feed our hungry and starving people by not over-
> feeding the pigs and perhaps not overeating and overdrinking by
> the peasants of even a few villages . . .

Only the young were anxious and fearful. The Hebrew classes
at Suchovolsky's and Bezalel's barns were irregular. They were
too cold and drafty for any duration beyond a few hours a day.
How empty it seemed now that Chanukah, with its delightful
surprises of gifts, lusty singing and endless happiness by the
Menorah lit candles, eluded them. They received a few meager
gifts, paper drawings and potato pancakes fried with linseed oil
which was procured on the black market in exchange for a silver
menorah. They pressed against the narrow cracks of the stockade
walls. Outside they caught glimpses of well fed and well dressed
people going to or returning from church.

It was now midday, the daily delivery of rationed food did not yet arrive. There was little to eat and less to do. Their teachers told them that every day of study was a gift to themselves and every prayer at night was another Chanukah lit candle in the darkness. But what did it mean if they were prevented from skating on the frozen river and could not dash down hill from the brick synagogue on a sleigh. What would be tomorrow, if to-night there were no happy singing boys and girls waving lanterns, and romping over the snow covered streets playfully and free?

They were soon distracted by the late arrival of a wagon with cans that stopped for inspection near the gate. Milk! some one said, water another one whispered. The women and children who were waiting for their weekly allotments noticed that the second wagon that supposedly would deliver potatoes and some-times a little grits, was missing. One gate was half opened. David and Shmuel were waiting to receive it.

"Where is the other wagon, with the food?" David asked.

"The driver went to church," Skura replied with a sneer, and began to stir the whey with the handle of his whip. He repeated the search for hidden tools or weapons in the other two cans; and then kicked a can and shouted, *"Poshol."*

"They are half empty," David complained to the German guard after he helped Shmuel load it on a cart. The German slammed the gate in his face.

Some children scrambled to the top of the wall. Soon Polish boys outside, jeering and shouting, taunted them to climb over the barbed wire strung above. Others began to gesture and make faces, like they used to do whenever they saw bearded Jews or even boys and girls carrying Hebrew books. Avreml was infuri-ated that well fed children could be so cruel to undernourished imprisoned children.

"You are wicked if you do this to us. You sin . . ."

A guard from the watchtower aimed at him fired and missed, as he and others after him dropped down. For a long while Avreml crouched against the wall, too stunned to cry. He re-called previous encounters with Polish boys. They skirmished with stones in summer and with snow balls in winter. But their voices now were more threatening than past incidents during Christmas and Easter.

The next morning the gates of the ghetto were thrown open. Lt. Schrecke accompanied Capt. Messer and a civilian to the

porch of Suchovolsky. David and the committee who comprised
the *Judenrat* were waiting for them. They looked at their watches,
it was five minutes before Kommandant Johann Kristus Von
Preissig was scheduled to arrive.

Capt. Messer and Lt. Schrecke mounted the steps of the porch
and stood at attention as if it was a platform from which they
would review a spectacle. Rabbi Kalir, David and the other leading members of the community, remained standing near the
steps. At precisely 9:30 a.m. the shiny Mercedes of Von Preissig
roared through the gates and brought its wheels to a grinding
stop over the packed snow.

"*Achtung!*" Capt. Messer introduced Von Preissig, flanked by
Lt. Schrecke on his left. A civilian edged forward between
them.

"I have good news for you. You will be given an opportunity
to work for the Reich." He glanced sideways to Rabbi Kalir and
the committee, below on the right. "Herr Gruber will instruct
you in the art of pottery—that is, the fabrication of earthware
from clay." The portly civilian, his small eyes peering from a
masked pallor, half smiled. "You will get all the details today
from Herr Gruber. That is all."

Von Preissig handed the 'order of the day' to Herr Gruber
from Dresden. He snapped his gloves in the direction of the
committee both as his way of greeting and indifference in the
presence of other German officers.

The Mercedes barely started to move on the slippery packed
snow when Herr Gruber, sprite and bouncy, called out,
"*Komitee!*" He asked them to come nearer. He opened an envelope and read from a paper.

"Fifty men and women will be mobilized the first week. You
will supply your own clay. Until potter's wheels arrive, you will
supply your own forms of clay or wood. You may make all plans
today and start working tomorrow. Any questions?"

"The ground is frozen. We have no wagons," David said.

"I expected such questions. You have money. You will find the
means to move the clay. We start tomorrow. You select the
place. I will be there."

It was a relief for once not to be told *pünktlich*. But David did
not like the uncertain hour nor the covert manner of this civilian
Herr Gruber. Was he an instructor, a contractor who came to use
slave labor to make easy money for himself and for the concerns
who sent him, or perhaps something else?

"Rabbi," he turned to Rabbi Kalir who was chilled and shivering in the cold. "I'll meet with the committee immediately. I will let you know the results."

"David, if you need me, don't spare me, don't spare me!" he repeated as he departed.

Early in the afternoon they met in Suchovolsky's living room. Shaike, the host, sat underneath the mounted reindeer head.

"Pottery. Pottery." The worldly Shaike was critical. "Maybe statues they'll ask us to make. Or all of us will become stone cutters, who knows?" He shrugged his shoulders as they were waiting for Bezalel the brickmaker to arrive.

David did not say anything. He was stumped. He could almost read the indignation on the faces of Koppel Magid and the others.

"They're out of their minds. No. It's deliberate cunning. It is a new German method. Insane! Only we are the sufferers. They enjoy being insane," Koppel said. "In Egypt, over three thousand years ago, the Pharaohs ordered us to make bricks from clay, to build tombs."

Abba said, "There is no parallel in history . . ."

A gust of cold air burst through the door as Bezalel stamped in.

"I was fixing the oven for Beryl. He hopes to bake. I heard what this is about. It is impossible to get clay now."

"It is Gruber's order. We must act without delay." David insisted. "You think because it is Christmas tonight, they'll excuse us tomorrow?"

"They'll be drinking." Burka said. "We can't take chances. They can be vicious either way."

"Pesach," David turned to the blacksmith's son, "get us some coal, and you Zorach," his eyes met Alter the carpenter's son, "make a box which will keep the heat in over the coal until the top clay layer melts. Shmuel, get us a sled, spend whatever you must. The Germans mean it. Here is the list of general volunteers. Abba, let us sit down and see if we can get volunteers, if not we'll have to request volunteers. Before you go Shmuel, get a pass, call me if you have difficulty."

"I'll stay with you. I need a big place. I have a few tools."

"You can use my house." Bezalel volunteered.

"No—we need a warm barn. Shaike's barn has some hay. It's roomy," David suggested to the brickmaker. He nodded with his angular face, his brownish beard already reflecting the raw clay color.

Late at night, progress was noticeable as the tired men trickled in from the roaring winds outside. David added up the results to Bezalel, surrounded by the first batch who volunteered for work the next morning.

"Malinoski promised to deliver his sled. He only asked twenty zlotys. No horse. We'll have to pull it. Pesach scraped together a sack of charcoal by making the rounds of every house on the street. Zorach brought in a box lined with tin and an opening for the smoke in the center. Burka reported that almost everybody wants to work. He brought along a few shovels and a pick."

"It's amazing!" Abba said, "do they know what this is all about?"

"It is better they don't," Koppel retorted. "I suppose you'll find something—I mean work for me too. It will keep me occupied," he said to David, who benignly put his hand on Koppel's shoulder. David said 'good night' and departed.

The volunteers were at the clay field before dawn. They stamped their feet and swung their hands as they waited. Bezalel puffed at the slowly glowing charcoal which he put over the top layer of the pit to melt the frozen crust.

"It is soft, now I think we can dig," Bezalel said.

They struggled and punched the frozen ground with the picks until the soft clay responded mercifully to the half frozen diggers. They dumped the brown chunks into half a dozen sacks, bound them securely and began to pull and push the heavily loaded sled.

The guards were still under the spell of Christmas and liquor as they came through the gate. Herr Gruber was waiting. He didn't get angry at them, he only said *"Das ist gut!* Report early, very early tomorrow morning. I'll be there."

The dawn of December 25th was grim, like the reddish-brown clay in Suchovolsky's barn. The bells were hoarse, and their echoes fell like chunks of ice against the ghetto walls. A few stragglers came to church, but more, many more, were still drowsy from overeating or drinking and fast asleep. In the red house alongside the parish, empty bottles and turned over glasses littered the tables. But the guns were stacked neatly against the corners, and though the officers were soaked with alcohol, they were sober enough to remember, even on this day of Christmas, to take proper care of their weapons.

Beryl the baker was alone with Bezalel the brickmaker in Suchovolsky's barn. They had risen early, like they used to do in times of peace.

"Keep warm, sit against the hay," Bezalel prompted him. "Now I'll take this clay, I brought along some warm water. I'll mix it until it becomes soft like dough." He gave him a ball of clay and said, "Just make something, anything you like. We don't know yet what to make."

Beryl the baker's delicate long fingers were at last busy. They caressed and fondled the soggy clay.

"I sought him but I found him not," words came to him from his favorite verses, out of the Song of Songs. "Who is this that cometh out of the wilderness like pillars of smoke, perfumed with myrrh?" He saw always a statuesque maiden, the virgin of Jewish morality in all her beauty. It was a maiden carrying a jug. His dextrous fingers were putting on the finishing touches on a Biblical jug. It was broad at its base and gracefully narrow on top, like an inverted funnel. Its cylindrical lip was like the mouth of a baby.

Beryl had never been a potter, nor were there any in his family. His grandfather related to him that baking was a family tradition as far back as the Levites in the Holy Temple in Jerusalem. He spun the potter's wheel. All that was required it seemed to him, was to mold something which expressed identity. With a spoon handle he outlined an igloo-like brick oven, and in front he shaped a bearded man removing a loaf. He joined them together at the base.

"A fine piece of work," Reb Koppel said. He was the second apprentice to arrive. He was eager and somewhat curious.

"Coming from a master like you, It is a good sign—will they like it?"

"Why not, it doesn't cost them anything."

"I wonder why they gave us only clay?" Beryl asked.

"Adam was made out of clay. It was a beginning. Then Pharaoh enslaved us with works of clay."

"I wonder when we say in our Holy Day's liturgy, 'Behold the clay in the hand of the master, so are we in Thy hands.' If God is the master creator, why does he hand us over in his image to those who are mere clay without a soul?"

"You remember, Beryl," Koppel thrust forward his bearded chin, "God told Jeremiah to go down to the potter's house. He observed that when the vessel which he made out of clay was marred, he made another vessel without a flaw. God told Israel, 'Cannot I do with you as this potter?' May God forgive me, but if we compare nowadays the two vessels, it is they who are marred and grotesque.''

Reb Beryl pretended not to hear Koppel's vigorous protest to God, he murmured, "Out of poor despised clay, beautiful forms."

Jacob Zaban perspired profusely as he struggled with a lump of clay. He wanted to make two books leaning against each other like a gable.

"We are getting back to creation," Reb Jacob said to David, Rachel and Hadassah, facing him on the other side. "There is an old story which tells how mercy and truth met justice and peace and they kissed. Truth, on the eve of creation, begged God not to create man, because he is all falsehood. Peace likewise pleaded against man, because he is all provocation. But mercy and justice defended him. "If truth and peace were opposed to man, and mercy and justice defended him, why did they kiss? Were they not violently opposed? Evidently it was God's intention that there must be a coexistence with man. If truth will prevail there will be justice.

"God said, 'Truth shall always emerge even from the earth.' He thereby cast down truth to roam in our midst. When Cain tried to hide Abel's murder God told him, 'The voice of thy brother's blood crieth out to me from the ground.' But where is truth now?'' Reb Jacob sighed.

Herr Gruber, the instructor, moved over, and all conversation ceased. He unfurled a banner to hang on the wall. It read, *Arbeit Macht Frei*. But it is doubtful whether the instructor felt that this motto meant 'to make one free.' Life meant work, work implied a new interest to live, even to struggle and suffer, not to be humiliated. A Jew was never humiliated as long as he walked with God. In the beginning the Creator had no partners. But when He completed his work on the sixth day and breathed his spark, the soul, into the human clay, it was on the one condition that man preserve the image of God as a partner entrusted with the soul. But Herr Gruber and his anti-God generation had banished the spark of God from their beings and were now trying to reduce all human beings into slaves and lifeless clay.

David kept close to Abba, who was blinking because of the constant strain on his eyes, concentrating on the dark clay. He started out to make an *ethrog* box, but it still looked like a match box.

"I don't like it," Abba called David aside.

"What is it?"

"This is no work project, it's more like a farce."

"Farce?"

"They're at war. They're short of supplies and workers and then find nothing more useful for us than clay things?"

"You are right, Abba, they sent our strongest to Agustowa and other work camps."

"Exactly. Our skilled blacksmiths, carpenters, mechanics, even several engineers, electricians, and students chop down trees and do other purposeless chores."

"It is beginning to make sense. So far they have shipped very little of the wood to Germany. The trains are loaded with plundered food, our stolen possessions and even our own people, along with others forced into slavery or something worse."

"Did you complain, David, to the Kommandant?"

"I did. I even asked permission to work with you. He was vague. Whatever he knows—it is possible that he is kept in the dark—he doesn't tell. I am not supposed to be here, I wish—"

In the opposite corner, Rachel, who was granted permission to work part time in the shed, held her composure and withstood the ordeal well. She fashioned a miniature cradle based on rounded legs. She put it down and it tilted back and forth. Hadassah drew her breath and said, "Wonderful!" David's eyes met Rachel's, and she resumed her work. Hadassah now moved closer to Jacob Zaban and said, "Why are we helpless?"

"We made a covenant with God to abandon bloodshed and murder. All the nations claim they promised the same. Only we fulfilled our obligations much too early. We resorted to peace for the last two thousand years. Their answer was a declaration of blood."

"*Kol anoth* . . . , There is a noise of war in the camp." David gave the prearranged signal.

Reb Koppel devised this biblical quote of the Golden Calf rebellion against Moses as a code to warn of a German's approach. As a precaution, the secondary alert was "*Plishtim olecho*, the Philistines are upon us."

Von Preissig's jerky steps hurried through the yard and into the barn. Curiosity and boredom prompted Germans and Poles, officers and police, masters and lackeys, to be present. The Kommandant even welcomed an audience of rogues.

"*Sehr gut—ach die Juden sind artisten auch.*" Von Preissig was pleased at the industry and ingenuity of shoemakers, carpenters, tradesmen, and scholars making pottery.

"David Sokoloff," he called out, "I must compliment your people. But they have a teacher who I suppose knows his trade." Von Preissig acknowledged Gruber with calculated indifference.

Gruber followed him. "They learn fast—what shall we do with all this pottery? Maybe enough?"

"I'll speak to you later."

"Tell me, David," he deliberately removed his gloves so no one would complain about the cold, "did the Jews make pottery for the Pharaohs?"

"No! They built cities and pyramids."

"Ach! So! Very interesting. Builders, eh?"

"*Ach mein lieber Herr.*" Von Preissig turned to Menashe the inn keeper. "*Was ist das?*"

"Whiskey glasses—I mean a whiskey goblets." Von Preissig was interested in the slender goblet, which could be used for cognac; and the pitcher which was so cleverly constructed that the five goblets could be nested within its base.

"*Ach so mein Herr*—we have the goblets but not the whiskey," Von Preissig muttered.

"Whiskey?" Capt. Messer became alive. "Herr Gruber, you must have some to celebrate this enterprise," the captain prodded the contractor from Dresden.

"Yes, in fact I have it here," Gruber took out a bottle of cognac from his attache case. Von Preissig, more relaxed now after a drink, then said: "Yes! We have everything: food, drink, cigars, victories, even when surrounded by the Russians." He recalled the letter he had received from the Russian front. His uncle, Gen. Stulpnagel who returned from an inspection tour for the *Fuhrer*, wrote: "We are victorious even when surrounded." The last word was underlined with a blue pencil. He understood the meaning.

He was a little unsteady on his feet. It must have been the cognac he drank. Or was it the vodka, Russian at that, that Gruber let him taste? The contractor knew his pottery. But what else did he know or want to know. Did the vodka loosen his tongue? As the Kommandant he must be careful in the company of a civilian like Gruber.

"Ludke, Ludke, my coat and gloves." The orderly helped him with his coat, handed him his gloves and said, "The car is ready."

"Take along these." Von Preissig pointed to the model brick oven which Beryl had kneaded out of clay. He winced when Gruber took Menashe's cognac set with him.

Von Preissig had left Suchovolsky's clay yard. Some German and Polish women, camp followers and entertainers, privately browsed around, in the company of Murad and Skura.

"Cups, cups—strong cups for coffee." a blond entertainer, unsure of her footing, kept on repeating. She walked up to Alter who had made some strong pitchers, like the copper one he used for washing his hands before a meal.

"More color, red and pink!" she said.

"Use your lipstick." Skura roared as he took one.

"Careful." Murad cautioned.

"Oh, it is strong."

"But not strong enough," Murad told the dancer, "to hold your liquor. It will melt before you raise it to your lips."

Murad and Skura shook with laughter.

Moses der Tucker, alone near the wood pile, looked up.

"What are you looking at?"

"At the sun, coming through the cracks to dry these plates and pots."

"You are not looking for your God, are you?" Murad mocked him.

"His God!" Skura joined in, "is hiding under the clouds; let's see what you've got for the ladies."

Moses der Tucker was hurt and deeply humiliated. Murad who collected all der Tucker's produce taunted him. "*Ach du Jude!* Where is your God? Hiding in the synagogue? Shall I go and fetch him?"

This was more than the wood turner could endure. Only a while ago Murad flattered him that Germany could make good use of his skills. Murad even hinted that he could find a market for Tucker's decorative spinning wheels and good profit for both.

"You are Christian. Don't you know that your God was a Jew, that Peter and Paul were Jews?"

"*Ach so*, interesting, very interesting," Murad gibed.

"Your religion was taken from ours."

"What do you say, Skura?" Murad turned to him with a scornful smile.

"Why, the Jew mocks our religion! Arrest him."

"No, Skura, your religion is taken from the Jews. Our religion,

like our God, is German." He switched to sneer at the Pole and
then, turning to Moses said: "You see, what you say is new to
Skura, *nicht wahr?*"

"But they killed our God." Skura was angry.

"You hear, Ludke, their God was killed," he almost choked
with laughter. "But not our God Wotan," he shrugged his
shoulders and burst into a shrill voice. So you see, Moshka, you
must die. Skura is a witness, he testified that you and all the Jews
killed his God. So you must die and you are as guilty as any one
of them."

He aimed his revolver at Moses.

"But how, how can you in the name of God?"

"There is no God, no one will hear you. We made sure."

As all eyes turned in his direction, and everything seemed
frozen with his threats, he suddenly exploded like a laughing
hyena. He fired a shot into the air and put his revolver back into
his holster.

Days sluggishly turned to weeks and months. The hopes raised
by the clay project to provide work and self respect even for a
limited number of imprisoned Jews, dissipated. Not only was
there an overproduction of pottery due to the lack of orders for
export, but the morale of the workers sagged. For they soon
realized that this project was getting nowhere. Even the hardiest
in the barn became depressed.

Surrounded by props and boxes, toward the rear, Label was
almost isolated. He did not wish to engage in any militant de-
bates ever since Lt. Schrecke slapped him, when Label was ordered day after day, in cold freezing weather, to move clay from
the pit in a crude sled. "You talk about ancient books," Label was
tempted to say. "Maybe they are important, but I read Karl
Marx. There is one book I left in my house, somewhere in the
garret. On its last page was our family history; don't forget I
also come from respectable people, a few Rabbis were also my
ancestors. To me, though, the most important record was my
parents' wedding day, and the recorded dates of the children. It
was a Mishnah, I never cared to look inside its pages. But my
father studied it like his father and grandfather, so maybe it was
important enough. Who knows, there were some insights that
even could have been helpful to Karl Marx." There was only
silence, as when one confesses in the presence of friends.

Burka Mazik was direct in unburdening himself. "I never read books, I read very little. But I always touched my mother's prayer book, I held it close to me. For it was all my mother— every page and line. She prayed and cried for her orphans. Because there was nothing to eat. But she cried even more when I returned and brought a loaf of bread or a sack of potatoes. Because she suspected that I stole it or sold a stolen horse to get it."

"We must get some books, we must get them." Abba, who suppressed his great love for books, panted like one cut off from fresh air.

"Books, books, of what use?" Label was dubious. "Unless they can teach us to establish a peaceful and classless society." It came to him easily and well rehearsed.

"Now we are only one class, humble like slaves, waiting for the executioner," David was provoked to retort.

"Don't speak like that. Nobody will chop my head off. I bend to nothing." Burka was defiant. "Once I needed wood badly. I found a horse and a harness in a barn and brought home the load. Next morning I released the horse."

"That I don't believe." Label shook his head sideways.

"The story?"

"That you released the horse."

"We will wither away without books it's food for our souls," Abba pleaded again.

"My soul doesn't eat, but I could eat a barrel of meat," Burka quipped.

"I must find my book ends." Abba walked away.

"Every book you will carry is a passport to death. It will give us away." Label was brusque. "Don't you think so?" he said to David.

"Think what?"

"That Abba exaggerates books?"

"No! The books are to us passports to the Kingdom of God and freedom."

Von Preissig's temporary preoccupation with the clay works, in addition to his library project and films, did not conflict with his routine activity supervised by Col. Schwarzhund in behalf of the Gestapo. There were periodic raids for hidden weapons, hoarded clothing and food. Even books were confiscated, presumably for the library. This was done to placate the Kommandant, who protested about the continuous raids.

Their methods were both subtle and brutal. When Rabbi
Kalir's rooms were searched for books, the pretense was that
they were needed for research. All the Talmudic sets, 'Codes',
Responsa, and other valuable source books were removed from
the Rabbi's shelves. Were it not for David who managed to return to him the 'Code of Laws' (Karu), the 'Code of Maimonides' and his prized rare edition of the Bible, his household
would have become barren of the printed and inscribed word for
the first time in his lifetime and in the history of over one hundred generations of his ancestors.

When they raided Abba's room, the excuse was that they were
looking for communist and anti-German literature, and hence had
to take all of them away for examination.

Meanwhile, David was kept busy at the library. Sorting and
indexing the books was routine, but describing the contents in
the margin of the index card was not only difficult but dangerous. For there was always the ominous threat that other transla-
tors, alluded to by Von Preissig, would check the accuracy of his
summations.

The days were long, the nights were endless, the hours were
chained. Only he, as translator, and Rachel, as secretary, mostly
in her own home, were doing respectable work. All the others,
beside the voluntary committee, teachers and Jewish constables,
were treated as slaves.

David became aware of an abnormal situation. While books
were stacked in the *'Centrale Bibliotek'* as Von Preissig called
the experimental library, the Jews were deprived of their own
library. A few textbooks for the makeshift classes of the Hebrew
school, allowed to function on a day-to-day basis, were all that
were officially permitted. The Jews nevertheless from the Rabbi
to the water carrier, had saved what to them was most precious
—books. He recalled that his house, like all Jewish homes, for
centuries back, took it for granted that books were not only
symbolic of status but a necessity.

There was another reason why Von Preissig's library project
aroused doubts. David alone was singled out as a translator, while
other scholars and intellectuals who were as good or better, were
ignored.

Finally, Von Preissig lost interest in the clay works, and the
project floundered. There were rumors about wagons, sleds and

even trucks that were ordered to pick up these products for shipment. A few crates were shipped away from time to time. But there was no confirmation that this was delivered anywhere. In order to follow up this suspicion of the clay works, David asked permission from Von Preissig to work on certain days at the clay works.

The next morning Von Preissig granted David's wish to spend two days a week in Suchovolsky's barn as a worker. David assured him that he would make up any missed library work in the evenings. He reported before noon in the cold barn. There was nothing to do, for no clay was ordered. They sorted the numerous clay utensils and crude but sensitive individual works of art.

"David, how do you explain these?" Abba pointed to the cluttered-up clay utensils on shelves, in the corners and along the dark walls.

"I don't."

"Then this lack of interest to ship our products means they are not interested."

"Yes."

"I asked you last time, why they waste our skilled men on chopping wood. Did you inquire from Von Preissig?"

"He told me it would be worse if they were shipped to other places."

"What places?"

"He didn't tell me."

"Do you think he is deliberately vague?"

"I don't know. I can only surmise."

"Why were you allowed to leave the library?"

"I asked Von Preissig permission to spend two days a week here."

"What about the project to translate, codify, and classify these books?"

"Everything is in disarray."

"Didn't Von Preissig know that you could never do it by yourself?"

"He did, and expected more scholars, but his higher-ups probably put a stop to it."

December 31, 1941: JAPANESE DRIVING ON MANILA IN
GREAT FORCE. RUSSIAN TROOPS
RETAKE TOWNS IN CRIMEA.

Esau appeared to Jacob as a scholar.

Hulin, 91.

20

THE MASK OF ESAU

Early next morning, David heard a knocking on the door.

"David, they are calling you!" Reb Isaac, half dressed and half frightened, stood before him. Was it a dream? Where was he? At the well with Rachel? Where was Rachel? Something fell in the water—maybe Rachel. They all ran to save her, but more fell and more came to save her and the walls of the well began to buckle and there were commands not to pull and more commands not to save; and finally they were all falling, falling swiftly down into the deep and he tried to grab at something and Rachel held on to him and then there were knocks.

"What is wrong?" Ber Leib asked.

"It's just a note."

"What is it, read it to me." Ber Leib was anxious.

"Report for further instructions," David read.

Below, the large signature of Von Preissig was scribbled. He dressed quickly, ate sparingly after a brief prayer and left for the red house. David passed through the wooden tower and by the hateful Polish supernumerary, who examined his pass and into the office.

David fidgeted in the waiting room. From across the dining room came a clatter of dishes. He overheard a garrulous voice above the noise.

"They are burning them in gas ovens, by car loads." Then there was wild laughter.

"What will happen to the Jews in this town?" a quiet voice asked.

"What do you think," the talkative voice laughed with abandon.

259

It came down upon David like a sledge hammer. He heard these ugly rumors before. Now it came from a German. Still the Jews would not believe him.

It was a siege made possible by the Jewish confidence that man is basically good. Therefore how could Jews suspect that millions of men would organize their annihilation?

The door opened, "My cigars, Ludke," said Von Preissig, who was in a Japanese robe. He preferred this informality instead of calling Ludke. Casting his eyes to David, he chided him in a lower tone but in the same irritable mood, "You came too early."

David did not tell him that '9 a.m.' was written on the pass, and it was already 9:15. Von Preissig closed the door without saying anything.

Ludke was out of breath when he returned carrying a cigar box and a flat package. Von Preissig took one out, put the box in a drawer and lit the cigar as he bit off its blunt end.

After drawing several puffs he was satisfied that the glow was even; he began to read to himself: "David Sokoloff—on special pass from ghetto—directive—library collection and classification —complaint about arrests—request for food—hospital facilities —work—trade..."

He paused before the last phrase and read it in an amazed voice: "Pictures for the Sabbath?" and then added, "I must have forgotten it. Now as for food," his tone modulated as his perturbed eyes met David's. "I have good news, we will not search your homes and cellars for hidden food. You can use it—even share it."

"But Herr Kommandant, we have none; our homes, cellars and garrets were searched." David protested.

"We'll be generous. One pound of potatoes per person each week. You can also buy skimmed milk or whey from farmers."

"Herr Kommandant! We can't get any kind of milk, it is winter, cows withhold milk before and after calfing. We need meat, oil, vegetables—we need it for the diet—for the health of our children."

"Don't tell me about diets. We are also undergoing hardships. Our soldiers come first; our people get what is left. We are responsible to collect and ship all surplus food from here to the front and to the 'heimat.' As for you," again in a mellow vein, "you can engage in a profitable industry—expand from pottery to china.

"The barn is full of pottery."

"No shipments have been made lately. Transportation is tied up with urgent tasks."

"Is this not urgent?"

"The military views things differently. Everything must move to the front, even if civilians are denied certain privileges."

"Privileges? Our people need work and bread."

"The enemy bombs our rails, highways. . . . There is a shortage of trucks and even wagons. They break down in such weather."

"Why don't you return the tools to our blacksmiths and mechanics. They could repair . . ."

"Are you telling me what to do?"

"We have sick people, we need a hospital."

"I have provided that too. Those critically ill, infected I mean —will be quarantined inside the ghetto, for your protection. Of course it must be understood that the *Judenrat* will pay us for this and other services, every Sunday promptly at 9 a.m. It is worked out in detail on this sheet; you may examine it."

Von Preissig left the room, and David began to examine all the headings on the chart. On the bottom was an *'achtung'* which warned: "Any food raised inside ghetto will be deducted from allocations." Further down, penciled in blue: "hospital transfer." Letters—blurred and wavering—aligned themselves into the names of his parents. Surely they needed care. But there were others who needed medical treatment even more. Why were they singled out?

Von Preissig had contrived a scheme quite different from the terror tactics of the Gestapo. He seemed to favor David's parents while actually holding them as hostages. This was to make certain that David, who was allowed certain freedoms, would not run away.

Von Preissig returned after a late breakfast. "I want to say—I must tell you this, David Sokoloff," Von Preissig spoke to him intimately. "I was hungry; I'm not always hungry. I went hunting yesterday on Potocki's estate. His steward Basenko has quite a kennel of hounds, but I wasn't successful. Anyway it is not fun to pursue a helpless animal with all the advantages on your side. In sport, everything should be fair. Give an equal opportunity to the pursued. Otherwise, what is the point, a massacre? I mean an easy victory?" The word massacre would have been a slip of the tongue. Or was it? "Well, that's all, I suppose. You may go."

"You will be taken to the library, it is one project I intend to complete," were the last words he heard from Von Preissig. Several days later, a rather polite German in the uniform of a Wehrmacht officer ordered David to accompany him. His name sounded like **Dr. Himmelfarb.**

David eyed him warily. He was young and correct, and from the corners of his eyes he appeared to David as one who as a civilian put on his rubbers before a rain and wrote a letter to his mother without delay when away. He looked sedate and cool as he guided David into the New Synagogue, converted into a library or "Centrale Bibliotek."

The officer was smartly dressed, his boots were polished, his uniform well-fitted and what was inside was amply fed.

Was this a man or a robot? He could have been a father with cherubic youngsters climbing all over his knees, or a clerk or student. He must have attended church every Sunday.

They were now through the doorway of the synagogue. Dr. Himmelfarb cautioned him *"vorsichtig"* as the hanging door swung back. How courteous and correct he was as he said *"Bitte, Herr Sokoloff."*

"I am from the *'Deutsche Kultur Ministerium',*" he began. "I was appointed for this district by Minister Alfred Rosenberg, to collect, classify and interpret the trends in Jewish books and other special projects." He dropped his voice and swallowed the last words, as if he didn't want its vague suggestion to linger.

"This collection of books is routine all over occupied territory," the Herr doctor explained. "Even books can serve a purpose. Even your books can help—I mean they have to be preserved. Pragmatically speaking, everything can be utilized. After all, we have a war on our hands, and what has to be done shall be done, in whatever way it need to be done. We Germans certainly know how to value books."

"Please sit down," he urged David, who out of habit and training did not dare sit on one of the benches stacked with Hebrew books.

"May I?" David pointed to an empty crate.

"Of course," he replied. "Now, as I said, I'm in charge, but locally under the supervision of Von Preissig, who is especially interested in a certain phase of the project. In the meantime, you will categorize the books as follows." He read mechanically from a typed sheet:

Major Classification	General Classification
I Biblical	VI Hebrew literature
II Post Biblical	a. sacred
III Talmudic	b. apocrypha
IV Post Talmudic	c. secular
V Rabbinical Responsa	d. modern

"Now you'll notice there are six piles." David observed the
Latin numerals on six rows of tables and benches, all covered
with books ranging in size from the Talmudic folios to the new-
est compact publications in Hebrew. "During the first few days
you will classify them. Anything suggestive or novel, put under
the heading "miscellaneous." Mark down title, author, subject and
code number on stickers already attached to binding—in German of course. On a filing card, duplicate the same information
plus a brief summary of contents—in a few lines. The filing cards
will form part of a master index arranged according to the following sequence: class—one of six—chronology, and alphabeti-
cal listings of authors. As for Bible, Talmud and similar origin,
leave author line blank. One of my assignments as a librarian is
to locate in these books anything offensive to the Germans."

"What exactly do you mean?"

"German scholars have uncovered in Jewish books defamatory
references to gentiles."

"You have adopted our Holy Scriptures. What bias did you
find in them?"

"I don't exactly refer to the Scriptures. There are other books:
the Talmud and secret protocols."

"The Talmud was translated into German, and so you can
examine it yourself."

"*Ach so!* What about the Protocols of Zion?"

"The Protocols of the Elders of Zion has been exposed a long
time ago as an anti-semitic fabrication."

"Are you certain?"

"Authentic scholars have verified its distortion. Here is a book
and I'll find for you an important article . . ."

"Don't bother! Confidentially don't you have secret books that
are anti-German?"

"No."

"If you find such a book specifically advocating hate toward
Germans, let me know."

"None of our books ever advocated hatred toward Germans or anyone else. Moses proclaimed 'Love they neighbor as thyself.' "

"Well do you regard me as a neighbor?"

"In the Hebrew text 'friend' is more correct than 'neighbor.' "

"Is this your interpretation?"

"No, the prophet said it better. 'Have we not all one father? Hath not one God created us? Why do we deal treacherously every man against his brother?' "

"I see you are quite informed. I am sure you can help me with this project."

"What do you mean?"

"I'll repeat again, find the source or sources of a Jewish conspiracy against the Germans."

"But this is impossible."

"Never mind. I'll be back. One more thing; Von Preissig asked me to remind you to prepare the Jews for the Sabbath. It is his special project. No acting—just natural—you understand. Goodby," he said abruptly and left.

David went from book to book and noted the slips of papers protruding from the closed books lying flat in piles. He was disappointed that Dr. Himmelfarb was not even curious to inquire about the jottings, so clear in large printed German script. He read out loud from the book markers: "Justice as practiced by the Jews." It was subtitled (a) God's laws—the ten commandments. (b) Rabbinic interpretation of eye for an eye and other laws misquoted by outsiders. (c) The incredible record of the Sanhedrin, one death penalty in seventy years. (d) Strict testimony of qualified witnesses that protected the accused.

On other slips he found Jewish mercy, compassion for the orphan, widow, poor, the innocent. And on another, Jewish involvement. Everyone was responsible for his fellow being and could never stand aside and do nothing for one in distress and even danger. David concluded that this Dr. Himmelfarb was only interested in books as another weapon of bias and distortion.

He was alone and surrounded by books. They were not just pages and paragraphs, but living precepts that require wisdom in their gracious application, and reasonable men who use the law like tools to create new and better designs for healthy living.

He felt alone, facing a speechless vast and sullen white world.

Every sound travelled far before it returned—there was no answer. The sky was a canopy too far above.

Somewhere beyond was a bridge, but here there was no crossing. On the high ground above it was the highway, narrow, forbidden and restricted. Only the river below it flowed endlessly.

David suddenly remembered that he was not free to pursue even this reverie. It vanished when he heard the heavy tread of boots beyond the door. He returned to work.

Von Preissig stood in his custom convertible, a Dusseldorf which was assigned to him by quartermaster division for his special projects. The Mercedes Benz he preferred for more private relaxed moments. The chief cameraman, Gerhardt, was alongside, directing three cameras stationed at different angles.

"No beatings!" Von Preissig's face reddened as he ordered Ludke to calm down the Gendarmes, who raised butts of guns and whips in threatening gestures.

"Beatings will bruise and bloody faces," he explained to Capt. Hans Messer and Lt. Fritz Schrecke from the S.S. detail. This directive, he assured them, was not prompted by mercy and humanism but by practical considerations. "These," he pointed to rolls of films, "will be records—we want them to be—for our benefit, not as evidence against us."

"*Achtung!*" Captain Messer summoned the Gendarmes and Polish police. "No rough stuff. These pictures are for our benefit. Be good. Your time will come. Not now," he winked. "Now go to your task."

Von Preissig called over David and asked him to "marshal all the Jews for a pastoral scene—all going peacefully to attend synagogue services—and the Rabbi too."

"But Rabbi Kalir is not well," David protested.

"He can come out to pose."

David was driven by the command. He was not free any more as he walked into the house of Rabbi Kalir.

"Who is that?" he inquired from the *Rebetzin* Zippora in an almost inaudible whisper.

"David has come to see you."

"Good Sabbath, David!"

"Rabbi!" he said, but did not dare to finish the sentence.

"Don't for one moment hesitate to ask or say what is on your mind. Is your father well; and mother? What is wrong?"

"They are in the hospital. But Rebbi," he struggled to tell him the truth. But how could he summon one from a sick bed?

"May God grant them a *refuah shelemo*, and all of Israel—a *geulah shelemo* of redemption."

"Rabbi Kalir, you'll forgive me."

"What is happening?" Rabbi Kalir raised himself—his silver speckled beard framed a delicate pale face. Only his lips moved. "What are those voices outside? Zippora, my coat, my hat, let me. I'll dress myself."

"But Rebbi, they have assembled to make sport of us."

"Let me be with my people."

Rabbi Kalir wavered but steadied as he held on to David and walked out down the wooden steps from the porch. His eyes blinked as he faced the sun for the first time in weeks.

A deafening shout came up from the camp followers, German and Polish women, who were gathered for entertainment by their masters .

"The Holy Rabiner," Skura smirked his lips. "How long will he remain holy, hey *Chlopzi!*"

"Quiet!" an order came from Murad, as the cameramen began to focus their lenses.

"Once more," the order was directed for Rabbi Kalir and some older Jews, then the girls and children, to pass by the grinding cameras. Chaye the Good gracefully walked past alongside Jewish women.

"Cut!" Von Preissig ordered—"not these," he rejected with a flip of his wrist some older Jewish women who walked slowly as if in a daze; their worried faces lowered almost to the ground.

"Now inside shots—select several houses. *Geschwind und realistisch,*" he emphasized to Gerhardt with a borrowed gesture. "Catch the mood as they are."

Back at headquarters, Von Preissig told his orderly to bring him a mid-day refresher—cognac, biscuits and black coffee. He lit a cigarette, puffed a few times and crushed it against the brass ash tray. He opened the cigar box—but he knew that if a cigarette was bitter, certainly a cigar would give him a splitting headache. The orderly knocked on the door and placed the tray in front of him. He drank half the cognac, put down the glass on the tray and pushed it away. He took a towel, poured water from the pitcher over the basin drain in the corner, mopped his face, neck and patted his forehead. He was exhausted from the excitement and the unexpected.

The pictures would be great. Certain images remained in his mind's eye. David knocked down. Then revived to pose. The Rabbi's face washed off. Not a trace of blood. Though tottering, he had been defiant.

The mother and child haunted him. The mother dragged, fighting, resisting, freeing herself and for a blissful moment she kneeled down to hold the baby, who almost cried "mammi." It summoned to mind the image of other Jewish mothers and other doomed infants.

"We love the Jewish mother and child, yet we almost killed a Jewish mother and child. We kill others; we kill more, more."

"Herr colonel, what are you yapping about. Kill! Kill! Let's have another drink." Captain Messer, accompanied by Lt. Schrecke, barged in.

"Now what is it this killing business." Schrecke's eyes were bloodshot and on fire. "Who kills? Who touches them?"

"Good. I don't want any woman hurt," Von Preissig said and poured more into his glass from a new bottle.

"There will be thousands and millions dying and you bother about one woman?" Messer said unsteady on his feet.

"Shut up, you swine!" Schrecke said to Messer.

"Millions or a few dying does not do us any good," Von Preissig said and moved away.

"And I say it is good for us: we live by millions dying," Messer stuttered between hiccups.

"What's more, your pictures are terrible," Schrecke said after downing a glass.

"Why?"

"Because," Schrecke put down his empty glass, "we portrayed the Jews in the passion play, to look mean and bad. This is the way we were told they must look to Germans, on stage and in life."

"The Passion play of Oberammergau? Why it was a Bavarian beer hall version, not artistic at all."

"It did the job: to make us hate Jews, and this is your job. We'll do the rest."

"Colonel you are drunk and weak," Messer pointed a finger at Von Preissig.

Von Preissig became tense.

"What is more, I am going to slap you."

"You are under arrest!" he burst out trying to control his emotions.

"You can't arrest me. Remember what Col. Schwarzhund said, you must not interfere with us. You said some questionable words about the *Fuhrer* and the Reich."

"Who said?"

"You did, and Schrecke is a witness."

"Another drink and we'll go home and maybe forget," Schrecke suggested to his host.

Von Preissig brought back the bottle, measured out small glasses and raised it in toast to victory.

"To victory," Messer chimed in hoarsely.

"To our victory!" Lt. Schrecke declaimed. Capt. Messer just winked.

Chaye the Good brought Elyeh Schuster's son to Rachel. Skura returned the baby after he was paid for "board". She embraced it and held it tightly to her breast.

"It is good you brought it, it needs care and protection."

"You also need protection," Chaye said. "Maybe—I don't know how to explain it."

"Just for the baby is enough," Rachel said, and tried to put it to sleep in her bed. The baby was restless, as if alerted by a fear it didn't understand and wishing to withdraw after being subjected to the touch of strange fingers and unfamiliar voices.

Rachel sang a children's song but the child kept on crying. She sang a folk song, sung by the school children, but still the baby persisted whimpering and shivering as it turned away.

She tried to sing a bird song, but it lacked the gay and carefree twitter of the feathered songsters. She started many melodies and many tunes without effect.

Finally, she remembered a short tune. She heard its melody from the lonely yeshiva seminarian whose echoes drifted daily to her room, before the tragic event. The baby sighed deeply, its face relaxed, its cherubic lips poised to kiss the one who sang it. It was a lullaby of being wanted and loved in the midst of so much hate.

January 1–February 15, 1942: RUSSIA SMASHES GENERAL GUDERIAN'S ELITE NAZI DIVISIONS. SOVIET PAPER HINTS U.S. COWARDLY FOR DECLARING MANILA OPEN CITY. BRITISH SURRENDER SINGAPORE.

For the pillars of the world are the Lord's and he hath set the world upon them (the just).

I Samuel, 2:8.

When God saw that the just men dwindled and the wicked increased, he planted them in every generation. For the world can survive only because of the just.

Yoma, 38.

2 1

SEED OF THE JUST

Towards the end of January, David, beset by many problems, went to see Koppel in his tiny room at Suchovolsky's. He recounted how Col. Von Preissig demanded more men and boys for the Agustowa and Kirchof work camps. When he and Shmuel suggested that the February quota would be filled by volunteers, the Kommandant replied tersely: "Volunteers? Give me their names and they'll be at the camps this very day. Somebody else in my place would be more severe." It was obvious that the Kommandant wanted to head off Col. Schwarzhund, who loomed as the real power in behalf of the Grodno Oberkommandant Rintzler in charge of ghettos.

Several boys who escaped from the work camp Agustowa and the penal Kirchof Lager; and a few men who were released as useless physical wrecks, told of the barbarous conditions under

269

which they worked. Label relayed a message that he and two
others planned to break out. Judah, the rabbi's son was one of
them. If those who escaped could not be replaced by unreported
dead inmates or volunteers, there would be reprisals.

"Whether the camp prisoners succeed or fail, the Germans will
retaliate against us and the Jews will condemn us as members of
the *Judenrat*," Koppel said.

"Then let's do away with the Judenrat; the majority of its
members want it dissolved."

"And you want my opinion?"

"You already committed yourself against it, in the name of the
Rabbi."

"Why not do it formally?" Koppel suggested.

"Each of us would be charged with treason."

"David, any day they will ask us, through you, to submit a list
of names for the work camps."

"I will not do it, and no one else would take it upon himself to
hand over our people to them."

"I agree. They have been raiding our homes in daylight and
grabbing men whenever they appear on the two block streets
within the walls. Who will say 'no' to these Nazis?"

"I don't know, there are so many things happening, we are
being squeezed into a tight corner. A fire of mysterious origin
has burned down almost every house in Dombrowa: this was the
official explanation for the sudden order to move the Dombrowa
Jews to Suha-Vali on one of the coldest winter days. We'll have
to take them into our crowded rooms and share our food with
them."

"It is becoming impossible . . ." Koppel said.

"We have no choice as prisoners, but we don't have to deliver
our men to their torture camps. I don't trust Von Preissig even in
regard to the library. Likewise, the clay project should make us
suspect their intentions."

"What do you mean, David?"

They are trying to extract our soul—and crush our hopes for
survival as God's chosen people."

"No nation has ever been able to do it to us," Koppel said. "It
cannot be done—what provisions have we to hold out." Koppel
shifted to more immediate problems. "We must have food—how
much money, gold and silver and notes, is within our reach?"

"Very little, and they know it."

"How much potatoes, how much grain?" Koppel pressed for information. "You have the figures. Shmuel Leiser must have told you."

"Shmuel Leiser told me we have only limited quantities of a few things."

For a while they were both frozen by the word 'limited.' For it referred to so many things. The days were numbered. A year was a lifetime. The minutes and seconds were like gifts never to be repeated, this sunny but still snow covered cold day of January.

The sun was deliberately stubborn, defiant as if by design, altering its course. It poured forth warm rays against the frozen blanket for some minutes. The snow began to melt. Across Synagogue Street beyond the walls, rivulets gurgled their way down the cobbled street. All the coldness was challenged by the warm sun and yielding to its caress. But here, within the walls, spring was far away. Its beckoning smile was frowned upon by the cold-fettered deep frozen earth.

And Koppel watched boys and girls returning from an inconspicuous one room school house.

"Isn't it a little too early, Avreml!" David called over Rachel's brother.

"Do you want my sister?"

"No!" David said. "Why so early to-day?"

"Well, you see, the Germans—they ordered us to report for work tomorrow at five in the morning. Our teacher Dunsky was disturbed and angry."

"Five o'clock for what?"

"To take the geese to feed on winter rye."

"I never watched to see if geese wake that early."

"They are not hens, are they?"

"Well that's the order—it takes time to get them across to the rye fields; they have no sense of direction."

"It's because of their goosestep."

As if they didn't have enough problems, the Jews of Suha-Vali experienced trouble some days in trying to find shelter and food for the Jews who were transferred from Dombrowa. David and Shmuel worked for long hours until everything was provided for the refugees in the over crowded quarters. There were wild rumors that the nearby towns of Novidvor Korichin and Agustowa were marked for a similar fate. But meanwhile there

were children waiting for Abba to teach them Torah at Bezalel
the brickmaker's house.

It was *Tov Bishvat*—the fifteenth of the month *Shevat*—the
Jewish Arbor Day or New Year for the planting of trees. On this
day of celebration, the lunar bride waited patiently in her orbit
under an almost cloudless canopy.

In another hour at dawn the younger teacher from Dombrowa
would bring his class, a few children at a time, so as not to
arouse the Polish guards who begrudged even this privilege. The
room was chilly, punctuated by snoring of the sleepers in the
crowded bedrooms and in every available space, nook and corner
of the house. Soon he would have to wake them, especially those
stretched out on the disarrayed matted straw in the living
room.

When the Dombrowa teacher arrived, he called the class to
order. Abba began to explain that since it was Arbor Day it was
proper to make the blessing *"schecheyonu"*—for a new fruit. A
boy interrupted him.

"But how can you make the blessing of *"schecheyonu,"* for a
new fruit, when there is no such fruit here?"

A gust of cold air, a good morning greeting and more children
surged through the door, each in turn stamping his feet to shake
off the snow.

"This class—*ken yirbu* (may it grow)—will appreciate it if you
take over," Abba offered the Dombrowa teacher the prerogative
to join the teachers' staff.

"Not before you answer my question," the last interrogator
reminded him.

"Oh yes, I have something, thanks to Hadassah."

"But Hadassim (myrtles) are twigs—they are not fruit." The
class responded to the pun with restrained laughter.

"I said Hadassah—the girl. You know Hadassah, the sister of
my colleague Chaim Schneider."

"That's something new to make a blessing for a girl," a spunky
boy revived the pun, amid prolonged laughter.

"Class attention, this is serious." Abba regretted they were already too serious.

"You see children . . ." he quoted the sources, but there were
many unanswered questions. Where were the figs, the dates, and
the carob? Where were the snow-white almonds in bloom which
Joseph Zaban and Anna Steinberg described in letters from Is-

rael? There, it was a time for planting. But here, in Poland on the borders of East Prussia, the sons of Cain and Amalek were planting, not trees producing fruit but trees of evil.

"You remember this scrapbook? You remember how the Rabbi sanctioned the preserved *ethrog* for use on Succoth (Tabernacles)?"

"It was Hadassah who had the forethought to save it. And do you know that she also preserved for this day a carob?" He opened the scrap book and displayed the dark-brown, shriveled, but recognizable carob.

"Please, please don't," a boy cried out.

"Don't what?" Abba was amazed.

"Don't eat it, it looks so nice, I mean mounted on the page. I also have a fruit, it's not much, I have it with me from my crab apple tree. A squirrel was feeding on the tree, but he saved an apple for us, for a '*schecheyonu.*' "

"Class, if we can laugh, this in itself is a blessing. I'll take this fruit from you," Abba smiled and turned to the boy. "I am going to make a blessing over this apple."

The blessing was made and the boy winced as he bit the tart miniature apple. Abba handed over the class to the teacher from Dombrowa.

When Abba left to visit Rabbi Jacob Palimer's Talmud class, he found Rabbi Kalir and the committee already there.

"Children, today is a great day, isn't it?" Rabbi Kalir directed his eyes to Gedaliah. Rabbi Zaban was proud of this gifted boy who was skipped from Rachel's class. Abba, over whose class Gedaliah leaped, didn't mind.

Gedaliah's shoulders floated under an oversized grey coat.

Everyone recalled his brilliant comment on the Saturday night test in June: "The Gentiles have books and laws, but these don't count in wartime."

"Gedaliah, do you know this week's portion?" Rabbi Kalir, recalling that night, was eager for another surprise.

"Jethro," he sprang to life.

"Now, in regard to this week's reading, the *Medrash* makes the following comment. "When God gave the Torah (to the children of Israel) no bird chirped, no fowl flew, the ox did not bleat, nor did chariots rumble, the Seraphim did not utter 'holy, holy,' the ocean did not overflow, the creatures did not utter a sound, the

whole world was still and silent. Then came forth His voice, 'I
am the Lord thy God.' What does that mean?"

"Even animals knew that when God is present they had to be
quiet and good."

"Very good! but what about the Seraphim Angels and the
ocean?"

"If you will pardon me, Rabbi," Abba broke in, "my class will
be waiting for you."

"And my class too," the shy Chaim Schneider spoke up as his
pince-nez fell off his nose.

"It would perhaps be best to assemble them all here. But there
is no room, unless by a Jerusalem miracle," Chaim exchanged
glances with the Rabbi.

"Chaim I know what you mean," the Rabbi commended him.
"Jerusalem was crowded with pilgrims from all of Israel yet no
one complained, 'I have no room.' "

After a few whispers, and more nods, the children surged
through the doorway. From the foyer to the front room, to the
living room and into the spacious kitchen, the children filled
every available space.

The Rabbi explained to them the origin of this Arbor Day; the
tree symbolized a faith which stressed the right of men not only
to exist but to develop and flourish through its deep roots in the
Torah.

"But Rabbi, the tree is a tree of life. How can you plant it here
in winter?" Avreml asked. "Why, Rabbi, why plant something in
cold winter when we can wait for spring?"

"The earth is always warm a few feet below the snow and
frozen ground. The earth protects a sapling and seals its buds
until the warm days."

"But it takes years until a tree bears fruit, while a vegetable
grows up in a few months?"

"Trees, like lessons and good deeds, have to be planted for the
future," the Rabbi explained, "and we must take care of them
and preserve them until they ripen. We do things not only for
ourselves, but for the generations to come. There is a beautiful
story about Honi the Circle Drawer. He was at a loss to understand the meaning of the verse: 'When the Lord returned the
Jews from exile, we were like dreamers.' He thought the verse
spoke of the seventy years of Babylonian exile. But was it possible for a man to sustain a dream for seventy years? Man's life

was too short for such a long dream. One day, while on the road, he chanced upon a man planting a carob tree. He asked him: 'How long will it take for the tree to bear fruit?' 'Seventy years,' the man replied. 'Are you certain that you will live another seventy years to eat its fruit?' The man replied, 'I found ripened carob trees in this world. Just as my forefathers planted for me, I too plant for my children.' It seems to me that this Biblical utterance 'we were like dreamers,' means we never gave up hope of returning to Zion. It wasn't a short dream for a few years, but it lasted seventy years, beyond one man's lifetime. We also must have *bitochen* and trust God that the dream to return to Zion and be free again will be fulfilled. May He redeem Zion and us speedily during our lifetime. Amen."

After the children left for their homes, the Dombrowa teacher introduced Abba to a boy from his town.

"This is the scribe's son." Not long ago peasants broke into his house, and demanded money from his father and then from his mother. The peasants could not find anything except parchment and an unfinished scroll. They vented their anger on the holy books and the parchment, which they cut into shreds and smeared with ink. They took the unfinished scroll—the scribe had just finished the twentieth chapter of Exodus—and wrapped it around his body; they bound him and his wife and then they set the parchment afire, then the house. The fire spread to other houses. Mobs of Poles from surrounding towns began to loot Jewish houses. When the Jews resisted, they were shot. Ten died; fifty were wounded. The Germans stood by as the mob looted the houses and then put the entire town to the torch. Only the brick Synagogue remained standing. All the Jews who escaped were compressed into the house of God.

"The next night, five volunteers, representing all the Zionist parties, took this boy to pay a surprise visit. I was one of the five. We stole into the house of the murderer of his parents, who was fast asleep, surrounded by Jewish belongings. He was shaken violently. 'Come with us,' our leader ordered him. 'I haven't done anything, I bought these silver cups from the Germans.' 'And this coat and those boots?' he pointed to the sheepskin coat hanging in the hall and the murderer's own high boots near his bed. 'They are mine, my very own, I'll swear by the crucifix.' 'And these blood spots on them. Are they yours too?' 'I don't know anything,

I'll swear by the crucifix,' he kept on screaming. We took him away to the woods; we told him to say his last prayers; we gave the boy a knife, we told him, 'Kill him; every law tells you to kill him. Here there is no law, so you must do it yourself.' 'I can't,' the boy protested. 'He stabbed your father with a knife and cut your mother's throat.' 'I can't,' he began to cry. 'We'll walk away and you do it yourself, we won't look.' We tried to reassure him. We walked away a few paces. The boy's hand was shivering as he held the knife. I turned only once to look back. After a long while we heard the murderer speak softly to the boy. 'Please don't, you learned not to kill. It is your law.' When the boy hesitated, the murderer jumped up and disappeared into the woods. The boy screamed as he dropped the knife. They pursued the murderer but he was gone."

'Why?' was the only word the leader uttered to the boy. He didn't answer. I spoke to him, pressed him to my bosom. I didn't ask him anything."

On the following afternoon, Rabbi Kalir experienced anxious moments when David informed him that Label escaped from Agustowa. Two other boys also broke out, but it could not be verified. Label was hiding out somewhere around Potocki's estate.

"Isn't it possible to locate Label and also find out who those boys are?" the Rabbi asked.

"Not yet."

"Why?"

David told him the grim story. Zorach and his father, Alter, were doing carpentry work for Zaleski. As a collaborator he was rewarded by Capt. Messer with free slave labor for his rambling farm. He also made weekly trips to Agustowa to pick out for himself and other farmers special skilled inmates. Label hid in the wagon—sleds are not allowed because they can move off the main highway and cannot be checked. But no sooner did Zaleski's wagon roll into his yard when his dogs flushed out Label underneath the straw. When he saw that Label was emaciated and limping he told him 'I have no use for a cripple who can't work for me.' He screamed at Label to get out before he reported his escape. Alter and Zorach begged Zaleski. They promised to work extra hours for the time they used up to take Label to a safe hiding place in the wood shed. "We have to get him out of there before he freezes to death or is captured. We must also replace him before hostages are shot."

"God forbid." the Rabbi said.

"Let's first deal with the first part, how to get him back."

"Shmuel is making arrangements," David suggested, "for a wagon to deliver potatoes for the refugees from Dombrowa and the new arrivals from Novidvor. He asked me to help him. On the way back we'll stop at Zaleski's to pick up Label."

"Master of the universe, what have we done to deserve this, one *tzoreh* (trouble) after another?" The Rabbi paced the floor. His *rebetzin* was sick. He gave up his room at Suchovolsky's and moved to Label's house to make room for new refugees. He refused even the privilege of space. The least he could do was to share their crowded quarters. But Judah, his son, was in the hands of *reshaim*, and he was very concerned.

"Before you go, David, I want to ask you one favor."

"What, Rebbi?"

"I know what happens to prisoners when one escapes. God safeguard Label and all our innocent sons and daughters slaving for the *reshaim*, may their names and beings be obliterated for all the suffering they inflict on us and the house of Israel. But I ask you only this: find out where my son Judah is, I'll take his place."

"Rebbi, what are you saying? They'll force you to work long hours, and if you can't produce they'll shoot you. They don't respect a Rabbi nor any man or woman old or young."

"How can we stay safe inside our walls while all this is going on. Oh God, how can you . . . ?"

"Rebbi, didn't you teach me to have *bitochen* in God?"

"Yes, *bitochen* in God is possible if others—our gentile neighbors also believe in it. But do they? Look what they are doing to our children."

At night, after Alter and Zorach returned from Zaleski's, David and Shmuel accompanied a wagon of potato sacks with Label underneath. The guard at the gate began to inspect the load, when David interrupted him.

"Here is my pass and my permit. I worked late at the library. I am cold and you are delaying the unloading of these rotten frozen potatoes."

Zid, don't be arrogant," a Polish guard advanced toward him. But the German waved his hand in disgust and let the wagon pass through the gate.

They were all around Label. It was all a miracle the way he
escaped from the well guarded work camp in low freezing temperature in Zaleski's wagon, and how dangerously close he came
to be discovered underneath the potato sacks a few terrifying
minutes ago. He was so weak and overwhelmed by the good turn
of events that after one spoonful of broth, he put it aside.

"Thank God and everybody," he spoke slowly. "It is coming,
the good news. The Germans are retreating on the entire front
from Moscow to the Black Sea. Moscow is safe, Russia is saved."

"Label, will Russia ever remember this and be good to us in
the future?" David asked.

Label did not have the will nor the strength to debate with the
Rabbi or anyone else. He was overcome by the sudden twist of
fate where he was saved, helped by one with whom he disagreed
and now he shared his small rooms with the Rabbi.

"Yes, yes!" Label sighed from time to time as he slowly told of
his ordeal. He was seized in the first group of one hundred and
sent to Agustowa. There he found more Jews from surrounding
towns toiling for the lumber firm 'Schweper und Buchla,' under
virtual slave labor conditions. From before sunrise to past evening, they were driven like cattle. They felled trees, delivered
them to the mill where they were cut, sorted, and finally transported across the East Prussian border. Even the healthiest and
the strongest could not endure the sub-zero weather nor subsist
on the meagre rations.

When packages of food and clothing—from their own dwin-
dling supply—were sent by the families, the guards selected for
themselves the choice items from each packet and then yielded
the rest only after getting a money bribe which they cynically
labelled 'Dienst-leistung.'

One day the guards mercilessly beat up a bearded Jew who
leaned against the tree for a few moments of prayer. The victim
pleaded with them that he would work an extra three hours,
which was the usual punishment for those caught praying with
phylacteries before the work day. Praying, it seemed, interfered
with mustering for the work detail.

Label shook his head. He was evidently in pain as he tried to
raise himself. "My feet," he feebly pointed to the heavily bandaged frost-bitten feet.

"Did others pray?"

"Yes, many."

"Were they punished?"

"Many were beaten for the slightest infraction. You could bribe the guards. But this Jew had nothing to give. When I revived him with snow, a guard hit me with the gun stock. I lost myself and ran away."

"David, do you think . . . ?" Rabbi Kalir called him aside and then finished the sentence in a private huddle, "they will come looking for Label?"

"Definitely."

"We'll have to send a replacement immediately. We'll draw lots," Shmuel Leiser said.

"I think you are right," Rabbi Kalir said, "otherwise if we leave it to them, as a reprisal they'll pick up young boys and old men, for a cruel joke."

"Schneur Zalmen, the Chasid, wants to volunteer," Shmuel said.

"He is on his way to Kirchof, David said. "Kirchof is a *Schtraff Lager* engaged in road building near Bialystok, for criminals of all nationalities, including Germans. It is there they sent one hundred of our boys. Burka Mazik, who was sent to investigate a report of beatings, was caught and locked up in a torture cell. Schneur Zalmen came to me with a plan—his two boys were there too. He would pose as a squire from Yashinovke, who would contribute a sizeable sum—to the *schtab kase*—in exchange for using a select group of boys to do some preliminary work on a dairy plant that is to be erected in the spring. I learned that plans for this plant are under way. Zalmen speaks a good Polish, once he trims his blond ear locks and changes his garb, he'll pass."

"It's too risky," Shmuel said, "but then who knows what is best and what is not?"

"How will we get Burka out?" the Rabbi asked.

"We'll select him as the foreman, one experienced in supervising young boys and familiar with a dairy."

"We'll need quite a sum," Shmuel suggested.

"He already raised it. He got it from Daniel the Brewer and Velvke plus a little of his own," David said.

"May the holy one have mercy on him," the Rabbi sighed.

"One more question. Suppose they investigate at Yashinovke?" Shmuel voiced his doubt at the prospect of risking Schneur Zalmen's life in a scheme that if it failed, the Germans would exact severe reprisals against many.

"The squire of Yashinovke is away, Graf Potocki told me, and

will not return for some time to his estate. The actual manager of
the estate, a certain Conrad, will cooperate, for a price."

"Endless blackmail. And then what?" the Rabbi sighed and
closed his eyes. He heard David open the door.

"David! Shmuel stop him!"

"David," Shmuel intercepted him outside, "Didn't you suggest
to draw up lots?"

"I have a special library pass. If caught I have a good excuse. I
came to inquire about hidden books."

"I shouldn't have let him go into Agustowa, a sure fire," the
Rabbi talked to himself.

"Rabbi" he was interrupted by Elchanan, "the old scribe Ezra,
who stays with the Schneiders, needs you." Elchanan was distressed to impose on the weary Rabbi to go out late at night in a
bitter cold and face the risk of drunken guards.

"The boy is crying, the boy from Dombrowa who stays with
his uncle Ezra. It is dark in the house every night. But he has no
candles and Ezra can't write."

"Darkness," Elchanan mumbled; then, aware of the word,
said, "Darkness for the scribe of the Holy Torah? I must find
candles."

"Elchanan, come back!" the Rabbi called him. He was gone,
and the two of them walked under the protecting shadows of the
shameful moon.

They entered the low slung house. Ezra the scribe sat at a
table near a small window. He had just lit the stub of a tiny
candle. He held the quill in his right hand and the fingers of his
left hand pressed a ruler beneath the unfinished line. He gazed
intently at the last letters. The Dombrowa boy was off in a corner, asleep. He whimpered now and again.

"The boy stopped crying a while ago but I can't write," the
scribe mumbled when they entered his room.

"Elchanan went to get candles," the Rabbi mentioned the
item, which he thought would project normalcy.

"It is not the candles; I write only by day, Rabbi," the scribe
seemed in a daze.

"Food?"

"No."

"Strength?"

"My hand can hold the quill, I have ink and parchment, there is sufficient light in daytime. I can't continue," the scribe was now himself.

"Why? Is there anything wrong?"

"Yes."

"Did you make a mistake?"

"No."

"Did you finish Genesis?"

"No."

"I see you are on Exodus, the Ten Commandments."

"I'm still writing Genesis."

"But you have started Exodus?"

"Genesis, Genesis," the scribe repeated with emphasis.

"Is it your—your eyes?" the Rabbi was concerned.

"They are clear," the scribe answered in a firm deliberate voice.

"Your hands?"

"They are firm."

"Your lettering?"

"Perfect."

"Then what is wrong?"

"The *kavanah*; it is not my hand, another hand is writing for me."

"I don't understand, I see no mistakes."

"The letters are all there and in place," he reassured the Rabbi.

"And the spelling?"

"Faultless."

"What is it then?"

"The crying."

"It disturbs you?"

"And those words."

"What words?"

"As soon as I start to inscribe the Ten Commandments, I say to myself, 'Here there is no law. Whatever I write I see only the words from Genesis, 'And God looked upon the earth and behold it was corrupt; for all flesh had corrupted his way upon the earth'."

March 6, 1942:   NAZIS VOICE FURY AT PARIS AREA RAID.
2,500 FROM JAPANESE THREATENED
SINGAPORE REACH AUSTRALIA.

*The preservation of life supersedes every law
except idolatry, incest (including adultery)
and murder.*

Sanhedrin, 74.

22

WILL I EVER LIVE AGAIN?

They stood there shivering in the military courtyard. The
sadistic supernumerary Mikulak kept on swishing the air with a
long whip and from time to time barked at them, called out
"Pshakreff Zid, why do you look so sleepy? Do you want feather
pillows perhaps? Attention!" They stood there rubbing their eyelids, chilled more by the shrill voice than by the cold morning.

They were all young boys who were to herd geese. The older
groups were dispatched across the river to herd the cows around
the hay stacks. Gedaliah huddled at Avreml's side. "Attention!
Left face, right face, march, about face—come on; don't you
understand?" The children fumbled their steps, unaccustomed to
military routine. In Hebrew School they lined up to march into
class. The precision step didn't matter.

At last Mikulak stopped his capricious exercise. He released
squawking geese from the shed. Avreml and Gedaliah, at the
head, led the geese, flanked by boys, through the gate. After
passing the church and cutting across the market square, they
headed east through Yanowa Street toward the snow-spotted rye
fields below the windmills.

A piercing wind raced across the treeless fields. It tore into the
huddling line of boys. They stamped their feet and rubbed their
chilled hands. Avreml drove around the geese, keeping them
within a circle. In the distance, toward the river to his left, a
third group herded pigs who dug up the pale green grass,
awakening from its dead blanket. They excavated with their
snouts, and scooped up roots and bits from the gouged turf.

Beyond the highway, stretching across the horizon like a flaxen cord, a column of smoke was buffeted back and forth by the playful wind.

Gedaliah was already exhausted and the sun had not yet reached the midday mark in the sky. Thank God, he thought to himself, he didn't have to herd the pigs. But he felt bad that other Jewish boys had to do this task. Mammi always said, "Don't rejoice and don't say you're lucky, if it is at the expense of others." I think I'll pray. Praying is as refreshing as a nap when one is tired. I must not fall asleep.

"Gedaliah—don't fall asleep—they'll get angry," Avreml shook him up. "You see, they're eating now. A lot of meat, bread and wine."

"Don't mention it—it is a sin."

"Food is no sin—the Torah tells us to eat."

"But not the way they eat—just to tease us to beg them for a crumb. I have my own bread. But how can you make a blessing and then eat bread in fear?"

"Wait, they'll eat and fall asleep, see—just like those pigs— resting and rolling over in the sun. But be careful."

The wind was soft and he saw his mother standing over him during these anguished minutes that fevered into fantasy.

"Take me away, mammi . . . Forty thieves lurk in the barrels . . . close the shutters. They are murderers—I see a knife. He's got a knife, sticking out from the barrel."

"Child, child, do you hear me?"

"Mammi, Mammi, hold me, I'm so cold."

"What is frightening you, precious one? Say the prayer 'Redeeming Angel'."

"Mammi, Mammi, he is chasing me, a man with anger on his face, and a dog . . . I can't see his face, he is dressed in white . . . What soft grass, what fragrant flowers. There is the river by Olshanke. Is any one there? Let me join the children . . . We will play . . . all in a circle. Let's go round and round in a circle. Today is *Lag Boemer*. On this day long ago our people overcame the enemy. But so many died, lower the flags."

"All in a circle, break your wooden swords and thrust them into the ground." Those voices, those harsh voices. *"Verfluchte! Verfluchte!"*

"Mammi, don't leave me. Reb Isaac, I didn't finish my prayer. Before I give my soul to God, I must finish my prayer. A man with a whip . . . Somebody is hurting me. Mammi, help me, Mammi, help me. Save me."

Mikulak was standing over him and lashing him with a horse whip. When he got winded, he began to kick his limp shivering body with his feet. Blood trickled down his face and over his bruised lips.

"Maybe a soft pillow," Mikulak said. "Over there is a soft ditch, I'll dump you there if you don't get on your feet."

"Please don't, my Mammi will be looking for me."

"You hear, his Mammi will be looking for him. I'll shoot this little bandit." Mikulak laughed. "Come over here. I have a surprise for you, a much better job, how would you like to herd pigs?"

Gedaliah did not move. But when Mikulak raised his carbine and aimed at him, he picked himself up, aching in every part of his spent body. "Move faster or you'll really get a surprise."

Gedaliah joined the boys driving the pigs toward the meadow, around the swamp. A snorting piglet dashed toward the swamp.

"Go get him," Mikulak singled him out. He ran after the snorting piglet who by this time waded into the mud. He walked after him, stopped, started again and fell flat on hands and face. He picked himself up, dripping and shaking all over. The angry Pole now headed straight for him, waving away Avreml and others who came to help him.

"Hey, little bandit, haven't you forgotten something?" he pointed to the pig stuck in the mud. Gedaliah called the pig, waved at it frantically, even got angry at it, but without results.

"Not this way, Jew." Mikulak menaced him with his gun. "Go in and get him!"

He inched closer, he could almost reach it and touch it with his fingers. He reached out and pulled back. The smell nauseated him. He closed his eyes and tried again. He barely got hold of its tail, but when it screamed shrilly, he let go, sprawling in the mud and crying, "No! No!"

"Come here, you bandit," Mikulak lifted him by his collar, menaced him with his fist, "Maybe this is not such a clean job for you. I have something clean and dry. It will keep you warm." He called Casimirski aside and after long whispering to his now hilarious buddy, the orders were shouted. They were marched back to town in the direction of the old synagogue, up to its storage shed in the rear.

"Get the material out from the shed," Mikulak opened the gate.

"You and you and you," Casimirski selected the strongest looking boys, "Pull out the stuff, and pile it up in the middle."

They were stacks of surplus books, Von Preissig already had copies of them in his collection. Col. Schwarzhund told them to collect the last prayer books, and the prized Bibles and individual Talmud volumes which some Jews from Dombrowa and the Novidvor Jews who arrived the night before, brought along with them in preference to the permissible weight of food and clothing. The only Torah which was saved from the fire in Dombrowa, and which was the only parchment left by the martyred scribe, was now unrolled like a length of linen.

"Now what do you see, Jew boy?" Mikulak taunted him.

"It's a Torah, *Hatorah Hakdosha—di heilikeit*, a Holy Torah."

"It looks more like bleached linen to me," Casimirski said.

"He is right, now your feet won't get muddy, step on it," Mikulak gripped his elbow and pushed him on the parchment. "Go on," he cracked his whip over the boy's legs. Gedaliah, despite the stinging whip which felled him, crawled away from the parchment. He saw before his eyes the holy words handed down to Moses on Mt. Sinai. Every Saturday, holiday and also on Mondays and Thursdays, it was lifted up, placed on the *bimah* platform and read. It was then rolled up, covered with a velvet mantle, and as it was carried to the ark, he never missed a chance to kiss it, or touch it with his fingers and then kiss the tips of his fingers. The Jews marched with it for forty years in the desert. It was carried by the Levites and protected from four sides by the other tribes. The Torah, placed in the Ark of Testimony, was the most guarded treasure which they were to protect with their lives. It is the very first thing Jews must save from a fire. As long as it was in their midst, they would be protected against all evil.

"Stand up! Here is a box of matches, light this parchment," Casimirski ordered him. "Make a fire to keep us warm. Put paper underneath and put a match to it." He laughed crazily and began to tear out pages from a book and scattered it over the scroll.

"Let's get it over, burn the stuff," Mikulak flung a pile of books and waited for the terrified Gedaliah to start the blaze.

"No, no. They are God's and we can't," he threw down the matches and bolted. In an instant Casimirski lit the pile.

"Hey, come back," Casimirski shouted at Gedaliah who bounded over the fence.

"Get him and throw him into the fire." Mikulak ran after him and fired several shots.

Gedaliah kept on running. He ran behind the gardens, toward the river and woods. Avreml called after him, but he kept on running.

"Come back, come back, Gedaliah you mustn't, they'll shoot!" Avreml's voice began to recede. He heard only the beating of his heart. Exhausted, he fell against a pine scrub near a garden behind a house in the woods. It was getting dark. As he lay there he heard for the first time desultory gun fire and angry shouts. He saw a pile of hay and crept into it.

He couldn't sleep. Deafening shots and harsh voices rang in his ears. He pushed deeper into the hay but the echoes of explosions and shouts followed him.

Somewhere in the distance a steady firing was heard, *t-t-t-w-e-e-t-e-r*. He heard angry words, 'donner wetter' coming from familiar voices; it shook his jaws, until they rattled one against the other. He tightened his jaws to listen. There was more shooting. It was remote and yet near, this *t-t-a-t*. Whom were they shooting? He strained his ears. Fear could not alarm him any more. He heard barking. Every trunk was a shadow, and every bough shaken by the breeze cast a fear. He began to pray. He heard intermittent barking. He fell asleep.

Beyond the limits of the city, where scrub and sand sloped toward the river, stood the almost sunken house of Malinoski. His only daughter Wanda was fast asleep. But Malinoski listened to the night. He recognized those barking dogs, whose presence he suspected ever since he heard that they were specially trained. To smell out criminals he was told—but who were these criminals? Was it some poor Jew or Pole hunted down?

It was before spring—usually he would have been busy weaving baskets, doing odd jobs before Passover. It was a nice holiday, and he earned enough to support himself and Wanda. He didn't need anything more than a roof over his head, which he had, and food, which was always given to him by the Jews. But now they didn't have it themselves.

"After the bloodhounds come the hunters," he reflected. Bloodhounds don't distinguish between the scent of a Pole or a

Jew and the blood hunter will kill both alike. Many Poles were standing by, hands behind their backs. They thought that the Germans were only after Jews.

Before dawn Malinoski fastened the cords of his moccasins, he thought he heard running steps in his garden. Malinoski stamped both feet as if to make sure that the tightly laced bootikin would give him firm footing. He probed the fog-swept garden with his knotted cherry cane.

He listened carefully. He felt good. Despite his age, his ears were still tuned to the faintest echo and rustle of a dry leaf kept at bay by the snow.

He stopped near the haystack and carefully lifted a layer of disturbed winter-weathered hay with his cane. Underneath, it was green and fresh; and smelled as if it were just cut, and dried in the sun. He bent down and pushed his cane into what he thought was a fox's lair. Sensing that something was there, he brushed away the hay until he recognized first a shoe—then two tiny feet. He knew immediately it was a boy from town. He gently pulled, and then yanked out a sleepy boy, who let out a cold quivering sigh.

He was almost sure of his identity. Then the boy awoke. He wanted to scream. Malinoski clamped his hand over his mouth. "Your mother's friend."

"Malinoski. Your friend."

Gedaliah rubbed his eyes with his chilled fingers. His body was shivering.

"Come to my house. I'll hurry to your mother."

He tucked Gedaliah under his home spun wool coat and brought him to his shack.

"We must be careful. Here is bread and milk. Climb on the back of the stove, cover yourself with this." As he spoke, he handed him a peasant's sheepskin, with the wool on the inside. "Don't move, and don't answer, fasten the door. When Wanda wakes up, tell her; she can be trusted."

Chaye the Good's tense face relaxed for the first time that morning when Malinoski appeared on the threshold.

"Your son is in my house."

"Oh, good God!" Chaye wept as she locked her fingers and raised them to her face as an offering to God, begging forgiveness for not having had complete faith.

"Wait, there is someone at the door."

Burka, who was released through a ruse by Schneur Zalmen, burst in, "I," he began and stopped. "I have an important message," hesitating again when he saw Malinoski's sleeve through the kitchen door.

"It's Malinoski," Chaye answered as if to say 'we can trust him.'

"Shmuel sent me to tell you they are going from house to house and searching every nook and garret for your son."

"I know" she sighed. "They threaten to punish all the Jewish children unless I deliver Gedaliah to them."

"There is Skura! Quick, Malinoski—through the garden, they musn't see you," Burka warned.

As they got out through the rear, Skura kicked open the front door.

"Where is your son?" he asked in a fit of anger. "Who left the house?"

"My son?" Chaye mumbled, "only God knows."

"You impudent Jewess. I'm asking you, not God!"

Chaye's face changed to a crimson. "I don't know! I don't know!" she kept on repeating.

A shot rang outside, as Skura jumped out to investigate, he only heard the 'Verfluchter Peuer!'

"Let him go, he can't go very far." Skura interrupted Murad who aimed with his gun again.

"Very good!" Murad accepted Skura's advice.

Before long, Skura and Mikulak spotted Malinoski limping in haste to his home. At first Malinoski was only thinking of saving Gedaliah by warning him to change his hiding place. But since he was discovered, he knew he would be followed.

"Where are you hiding that criminal boy?" Murad and the two Poles surprised Malinoski whom they overtook near his house.

"He is not here, not here," Wanda retreated in great fear as the three men pushing Malinoski aside advanced, ready to explode the house with their anger. "He, he—" Wanda was so frightened that she couldn't finish.

"Where is he?" Murad demanded in a low—deceptive voice. "We'll do you no harm, but you'll face punishment if you don't cooperate."

"He ran away—right through the door, into the woods. He

screamed, and cried, and ran away." She pointed in the direction
of the clump of trees, behind the wood pile.

"That little boy?" Murad was skeptical.

"He ran away," she insisted.

"Come on, let's go." Murad said in disgust, pretending indifference.

All morning the military police combed, smashed and looted
the ghetto, as they supposedly searched for Gedaliah. They used
their butts not only on furniture but also on the underfed and
emaciated bodies of men and women.

A *gendarme* burst into Isaac's house looking for David. When
told that David was in the library, he banged with his butt on
the floor and shouted: "The *Judenrat* must report to the Kommandant within half an hour." It was relayed to Shmuel who
instantly notified the members of the committee.

Shmuel and the committee reported to Von Preissig's office
ahead of time. They walked through the door and were met with
an avalanche of words from Von Preissig.

"We are going to teach all the Jews to obey us. You have in
your midst a boy who arrogantly defied our military police, and
at this very moment you are hiding him and encouraging him to
resist our law. I am going to hold the entire group of Jewish boys
as hostages. If the boy does not return tomorrow morning, neither will the hostages return alive."

Von Preissig summoned his orderly to dismiss the Jews. He bit
nervously off the tip of his cigar, without lighting it. He was
annoyed that David was not there. No one saw him in the library. The latest excuse that David was sick was preposterous.
As long as David's parents and others were hostages, he didn't
have to worry long. He'll be caught, he told himself. He was
tired. Nothing was to disturb his afternoon nap. He was expecting guests tonight; very distinguished guests from Warsaw and
Berlin.

Rabbi Kalir was ill and stretched on his bed, fully clothed. For
there were rumors that anyone found in bed was to be evacu-
ated, into the hospital, outside the walls. And he would be with
his people.

"Rabbi, how can one live? How can we exist? God, oh God,"
Chaye pleaded. She pressed her knuckles and draped the hand-

kerchief over her face. "Rabbi, they threaten to—I heard about it. Rabbi, I don't want anything to happen to any of the children. What shall I do?"

"I can't believe it! God forbid . . ."

"What does the Torah say? What do the Rabbis say? The Holy Books? Tell me. I will accept your verdict."

"Daughter of Israel—the Torah is all against murder, against men taking the life of a fellow man for any reason. The Sanhedrin executed a man only once in seventy years. We are against punishment, because man cannot be trusted to hold life and death in his hands.

"Woman of Israel, how can we ask you to sacrifice your own son? The Torah condemns the sacrifice of children. Now listen carefully. 'A man was passing from one place to another with Heave-offering loaves in his hand and a gentile said to him, Give me one of them and I will defile it; and if not I will defile them all.' Rabbi Eliezer says: 'Let him defile them all, but do not give him one in order that he may defile it.'

"No man on earth, no son of man that was ever born is good or wise enough to judge that any living creature ought to sacrifice himself for somebody else. Do you see? Suppose two men were stranded in a desert, with only a pint of water between them. If they both drink the water, both will die. If one drinks, he may have a chance to save himself and summon help for his comrade. Ben Petura says, 'let them both drink and die rather than one survive to see the other die." Rabbi Akiba says 'That thy brother may live with thee. Your first duty is to save yourself, and then your neighbor.' God forbids us to offer human sacrifices, be it yourself or someone else."

It was past midnight. Rabbi Kalir's eyelids closed but he forced himself to stay awake. After Chaye left, he called Shmuel and the committee to his room.

"We must appeal to the Governor General," Abba came forward.

"An appeal would never reach Warsaw and the signers would be put to death. It happened in Grodno," Shmuel Leiser informed them.

"We must see Von Preissig, and ask for more time. We have no money to offer. Prayers? Only God receives them. Mercy and justice are our last hope, but they are in the wrong hands," the Rabbi's words trailed off.

"We mustn't waste any time, if we want to see Von Preissig,"
Shmuel seconded the Rabbi.

Meanwhile, Gedaliah slipped through the gardens into the old
wooden synagogue. It was unheated; and had been used only
during the summer for special occasions.

It was getting darker; he was cold, hungry and terrified. He
mounted the steps of the Holy Ark, rolled back the blue velvet
curtain, opened its doors and saw the mantles. Inside it was
snug. A safe hideout. But this was the Holy Ark, a doorway to
God. Suppose he fell asleep and his shoes touched the Torahs.

He stood there, not knowing what to do. He closed the doors.
But, once inside, he could call to God and God would call his
mother. His hands pushed the doors open again. He wanted to
be inside, to be touching the friendly scrolls. They came from
God: his mother and father came from God.

His fingers felt the hand-embossed gold-and-silver lions.
Above their proud manes, the gold embroidered crown, with red-
beaded Hebrew letters "Crown of Torah" on the coronets' band,
glistened in the dimness.

"Blessed God—give sleep to my eyes, and slumber for my
weariness. God of my father and mother, give me peace. Wake
my soul in the morning to praise thee. Hear Oh Israel, God is
one . . . Hear, I can't hear . . . They can't hear—God is one—they
can't hear that God is one . . . The Germans—they are coming.
Blessed be God who gave us the Torah of truth—and the Torah
of life he planted in our hearts," he finished the second blessing.
"My blessings. I have to know them before my Bar Mitzvah. But
I can't, I can't say . . . Some one is holding me. More than one.
My jaws are locked, my feet are numb. I can't cry for help, I
can't cry, Mammi. Where is my father? Mammi, please help me."

"Gedaliah, don't cry. I'm your mother, son, my son. You are so
cold. God help us. Here. Stand up, open your eyes."

"Mammi, what will they do to me?"

"Here, cover yourself," she took off her woolen headdress and
draped his chilled body.

"Mammi, what will they do to me, answer me."

"Oh, Gedaliah, my son, my only son."

"Mammi, I want to live."

"Yes, Gedaliah," her voice trembled.

"I am afraid, Mammi, don't leave me."

"I'll be with you and God will be with you."

"I want you."

"If only they would take me instead."

"Why?"

Chaye took Gedaliah by his hand and led him through the door of the Synagogue.

"Where are you taking me, Mammi?"

Chaye did not answer. She turned to the abandoned synagogue, closed her eyes and mumbled whatever isolated prayers that came to her.

"Where are we going?"

"Gedaliah," she mustered her strength, "we are going back."

"I'm afraid they'll punish me. I'll run away."

"They'll punish the other boys if you don't come back."

"Never, never, they'll kill me."

"Gedaliah, there is no other way."

"I want to live."

"Gedaliah, come with me. Oh God have mercy on him, even if others . . . ," she didn't find her words.

"Mammi, what are you saying? Stay with me. Don't leave me."

"If they would only take me instead of you."

"The boy has been found," Murad announced triumphantly as he knocked lightly on the half opened door and walked in on this pleasant breakfast hour. Von Preissig only uttered "Good!" He was glad that the Gestapo would not reprove him for being soft to the Jews. Especially after refusing to see the *Judenrat* in behalf of the boy. Now it was their responsibility. Of course order must be preserved and justice meted out.

"Where is the colonel?" Von Preissig inquired about Schwarzhund. He finished his coffee and turned to the window facing the yard. At the far end between the sheds and the jail, the boy cuddled to his mother, surrounded by S.S. soldiers.

"He'll be here in five minutes," Murad replied. "He has ordered that the guards around the wall be doubled; and invited the *Judenrat* and the other Jews to witness the 'procedure.' "

"What procedure?" Von Preissig asked.

"The usual Gestapo method," Murad reassured him.

Von Preissig adjusted his tie and cocked his hat to the right, filled his humidor with five fresh cigars, reviewed himself from every angle in the hidden mirror in his drawer, and proceeded to the yard through his private exit.

The committee met in a hurry in Label's house where the Rabbi was now housed. Shmuel, who presided told them about the command to gather all the Jews in the yard behind headquarters. As a precaution they were advised that the young and healthy looking stay away lest they would be drafted for forced labor. They were about to leave when they heard a commotion at the back door.

David, who ran into trouble at Agustowa, returned and was guided to Label's house. His clothes were in shreds and his face was pale and drawn. He had not eaten for the last two days. He told them of his frustration and failure to replace Label. After he failed to get inside the camp because of the reinforced guards and the formidable barbed wire barriers, the next morning he followed a detail felling trees a few miles away. At dusk he joined them and confided to one of them about his plans. He was led to the leader who warned him that his plan was too risky: Label's escape was discovered. David argued that he had Label's identity card. The leader told him that he might get by with the forged identity card, but that he who had dark hair could never impersonate Label, who had red hair. The leader finally told him that there was a daily count in the morning and at night. If he were caught, he pleaded with David, not only would he be shot, but many others too.

"David, they have been looking for you. Gedaliah ran away and is now in their hands."

"I must see Von Preissig."

"You don't understand," Shmuel said, "they'll arrest you. Col. Schwarzhund has brought in many S.S. men. We have to report to headquarters and we are late."

"Gedaliah is in danger," David said.

"You are in danger too, David," the Rabbi said.

No sooner did they leave the ghetto when S.S. men surrounded them. Murad manacled David and told the gendarmes to lock him up in a secure cell. The others were allowed to proceed to the police yard.

Both sides of the yard were lined with Jews, including the committee. Polish police faced them at intervals and at the far end Capt. Messer and his S.S. subordinates flanked Gedaliah and his mother. In the center Col. Von Preissig, with Schwarzhund on his left stood erect, and stared blankly ahead. Colonel Schwarzhund, followed by S.S. guards, stepped forward two paces. At his command Gedaliah was separated from his mother and, led by the guards, stood one pace in front of him. David crouched against the peephole of the bolted door. He failed at Agustowa and failed to save Gedaliah.

"You, Gedaliah Sklar, are guilty of insubordination. Do you confess?" Col. Schwarzhund confronted the pale boy, his taut and terrifying eyes staring at him as from a fiendish skull. Gedaliah was petrified when the colonel nervously fingered the revolver in his holster.

"*Barmherzigkeit,*" Chaye implored. She struggled forward, fell to his feet and begged, "take me instead, please." Two guards thrust her back.

"Yes or no?" Col. Schwarzhund demanded. "*Du schwindler,* answer or I'll," before Gedaliah, in the grip of the inquisitor's searing eyes could even open his lips, Schwarzhund fired at him point blank. Chaye in a desperate lunge, broke through to him.

The boy wavered, toppled and fell in his mother's arms.

"Mammi, I don't live any more." She let out a blood-curdling cry. She cradled his head, blood spattering from his forehead to his face and trickling on her hands and dress. "Will I ever live again? *Shema* Israel." The words came out with his last breath. Chaye fainted and fell alongside the body as his feet kicked the earth for the last time.

The Jews were escorted back to the ghetto. Chaye was clubbed and dragged away by a guard, as she tried frantically to cling to her prostrate son.

Von Preissig was somewhat shaken by the incident. He saw the S.S. and Gestapo move fast, and with a terrifying savagery.

"Our methods always succeed," Schwarzhund challenged Von Preissig. The Kommandant eyed him coldly and departed after a limp salute.

A few churchgoers followed Skura and two of his men, who carried the body of Gedaliah on a bloodied blanket.

"Back up," he waved them away. "Just a criminal Jew. Over there!" He casually ordered his men to dump the body over the fence into a shallow ditch reserved for executions.

The bell in the church tower began to ring and the worshippers disappeared behind the massive doors. Skura and his men washed their hands in the trough, glanced once to the Jewish walls on the left, and crossed toward the church.

The shadows lengthened, as the peasants returned to their villages. Inside the walls, shock and bitterness wedged into their crowded rooms.

And Chaye the Good arose after seven days, changed her dress but wore the blouse with the mourner's tear. "There is no bread and there will be no *matzos* for Passover, let's go to the Rabbi," she called on Reb Beryl.

He put on his coat and led the way from his house.

"The Jewish children are swollen from hunger." Chaye wiped her eyes so that no one, not even in heaven above, would see her tears as they walked along.

"There are not even enough potatoes—peelings of potatoes," Beryl sighed.

"No meat, no milk, no cereal, no bread, nothing—just water and peelings, full of sand." Chaye clenched her fingers more in distress than in anger.

"Only a miracle can save them," Beryl said.

"If a miracle can save them, then God must make it."

"He must," Beryl seconded, "only we don't know when."

"Why, God must make it—now. Not one miracle has happened lately," she sighed. I'm going to ask Rabbi Kalir, he will forgive me," she said as they entered through his door, putting away her bereavement in her heart.

"Rabbi, God bless you," Chaye asked resolutely, "is a miracle possible?"

"Of course, everything is possible with God."

"You see, Reb Beryl, we must have faith," she said.

"But," he wanted to qualify his words.

"And this miracle, can't it be speeded up?"

"It is in God's hands, like the coming of Messiah," the Rabbi said.

"But suppose you want a certain thing at a certain time, like . . ." Beryl searched for an answer to his and Chaye's insistence about a token presence of the Messiah.

"Like what?"

"Like matzos for Passover."

"There is no flour even for bread, I can't bake something from nothing," Beryl said.

"That's why we need God's revelation," she pleaded.

"Children, children!" Rabbi Kalir was in a dilemma. One must not depend on a miracle, but this was an exception. He agreed but how could he force it. "Perhaps, let me see—why shall I doubt it? Yes, I see it. Yes it will happen by the grace of God. It has to happen because . . ." He could have cited one or a hundred reasons. Whatever his germinating differences with God, he would not disclose it.

"So you see, Reb Beryl!" Chaye cried out triumphantly, "It will happen, it has to happen."

The next day a lightning rumor spread inside the walls that there was flour—it came down from heaven.

"Is it true, Reb Beryl?" Label demanded in the company of David and Abba, that he confirm there was enough flour for matzos.

"It could be."

"It could be? Now speak up." Label was indignant. "We are starving, risking our necks to buy at any price. We are giving away our last wedding rings to get flour and you speak in riddles."

"God will give us bread." Beryl spoke slowly.

"What nonsense are you talking? God gives us nothing other than what we buy."

"I say God will give us. Chaye the good has faith in it and Rabbi Kalir has verified it himself."

No one knew how and by what communication, but the rumor that the Jews had bread through a miracle, spread like wildfire from the ghetto to every village and hamlet. The peasants who hitherto sold their hoarded food for exorbitant prices, panicked. Whereas before they demanded gold, silver, and clothing in exchange for their products, especially flour, they now offered it to the Jews, through their contact Malinoski, at deflated prices.

When the Germans discovered that there was bread in the ghetto and they asked David Sokoloff in his cell to account for its sudden and mysterious presence, he said, "It is the presence of God. He sent the bread."

CHURCHILL WARNS NAZIS OF GAS
REPRISALS. HIMMLER AT ODDS WITH
ARMY. ARMY DEMANDS THAT ELITE GUARD
BE SENT TO FRONT AND GERMAN YOUTHS
(15, 16) BE DRAFTED FOR HOME FRONT.
ZIONISTS IN ACCORD: FREE PALESTINE
AND JEWISH ARMY.

Love thy neighbor as thyself.

Sabbath, 31.

*What is hateful unto you, do not to your
neighbor.*

Leviticus, 19:18.

23

TEN THOUSAND TRUCKS

David was awake all night in his cell going over his life: what
might have been and what must be now and after now. He was
imprisoned because Von Preissig considered him the instigator
of the breakouts from Agustowa and Kirchof. This was a major
crime in the eyes of the Nazis. There was also the suspicion that
he somehow undermined the *Judenrat* as a cooperating unit inside the ghetto. The very fact that he was not handed over to
Col. Schwarzhund, who dealt harshly with such violators, made
him feel uneasy.

Evidently the Kommandant had other plans for him. The library project was bogged down in routine labelling of books.
Most of the books were packed and shipped away to Königsberg
for scholars to go over them. There was no way for him to check.
The clay works were almost abandoned. From time to time individual Germans asked Bezalel the brickmaker and a few others
to produce pottery and clay toys which they took along with
them as gifts on their furloughs.

He was determined to escape, but he feared that Von Preissig
would make good his threats of reprisals against his parents and
others. Whatever he decided, Rachel would be included in the

plan. How could the Rabbi insist that Rachel was still legally married to Zechariah when nothing had been heard from him since he was taken away from under the bridal canopy! They never lived together as man and wife. The wedding ceremony was interrupted. Still Rabbi Kalir insisted they were united according to the law of Moses and Israel. In the midst of chaos the Rabbi insisted that he and other Jews adhere in all matters to the strict law.

Rachel must stop working for Von Preissig. They must somehow escape, and others too. How many would risk their lives and bring reprisals upon others? Reuvke's last report was not encouraging. Of the fourteen who escaped from the work camps, Agustowa and Kirchof, ten were apprehended and shot. Reuvke, Burka and Schneur Zalmen were still free. Label and Judah were ill. But all were in great danger of being arrested and executed.

He was slumbering in troubled spasms when he heard the creaking of the opening door. He rubbed his eyes; sunlight and air rushed toward him. There stood Rachel, as in a dream, and behind her the rigid frames of the *gendarmes*.

"Only five minutes," a gruff voice warned her.

"Thank God you have come," and then looking away, "it's better no one else is with you."

"Why?"

"*Beivrith*," he cautioned her to speak in Hebrew rather than Jewish, which Germans could understand.

"What are they doing to you?"

"I can't tell you!"

"What is it—torture?"

"No—but it is even more terrible."

"David, you once told me that we must never withhold anything from each other; trust me," she pleaded.

"They have a plan. Maybe it is to confuse us and wear us down until . . . If they were normal people! Right now Von Preissig is experimenting on me—on us."

"I don't understand."

He began to unburden himself in a low tense voice. "It's better you don't understand. Rachel, you have no idea what they do to people."

"I've heard."

"They experiment with people—mostly Jews—in the sanatorium. Dr. Epstein told me that they even grab visitors and confine them. Please warn our people to avoid the sanatorium. They inject them with all kinds of diseases like they do to mice."

"Your father and mother are there."

"They are sparing them for the present so that I can be useful to them."

"How?"

"Von Preissig appointed me to work in the library. It never produced the results he expected."

"What results?"

"That somehow I would uncover self incriminating evidence to justify Nazi atrocities against the Jews in the eyes of the world. Communist propagandists in Russia have always resorted to quotes from the Bible or any Jewish book whenever they mounted a campaign against the Jewish religion or Jews. Stalin and the N.K.V.D. employed such methods to incriminate any official, general, writer, intellectual, or functionary whenever they wanted to legalize murder and brutality."

"Weren't these falsehoods and lies then and now?"

"This is a foolish and naive world that either believes anything or is indifferent if false accusations are printed, broadcast; and indifferent when the military court authorizes execution of the victims by firing squads."

"Did he demand anything from you?"

"No. He told me that I face grave charges for helping the boys to escape from the work camps and that I neglected my work at the library. But he must have something else in mind by detaining me."

The guard was annoyed by the barrier of language. He swung the key on a big ring in a menacing way. David glanced at his glowering face and resumed, "You must believe me. They are trying to take us apart, to see what makes us unique, why we survive, what's our greatness and how they can take it away from us. While doing my routine work in the library I came across a batch of anti-semitic books labeled: 'Goebbel's Propaganda Division.' Whether it was a mistake or deliberate I don't know. But evidently this dominates the twisted minds of the Nazis.

"They—he or they—at the moment I don't know who is in charge, Von Preissig or Col. Schwarzhund. The Nazi plan all along has been to mislead us, to make us believe that they do not plan to kill us. Meanwhile they are robbing us of our last possessions. Oh, they are cunning. They keep us in the dark as to their

intentions in order not to panic us, lest we go into hiding or
even resist."

"This is why," she tried to explain why she came. But he
poured out his staunch conviction without a stop.

"They are herding us like sheep for the slaughter. The last
thing they want is for us to discover their plans. But nobody
believes me. No Jew can ever believe that the Germans can be so
evil. But it is true, Rachel. You must escape, and all others who
want to join me. I've made up my mind."

"When, David?"

"I don't know."

"You must know. This is why I came here. You must act
now!"

"If we escape what next? How many of us can hide? Only God
knows that there are no places to hide for all. Where? In the
Polish villages? They are full of informers. In the forests and
woods? I don't know the answer yet. Even before Abraham there
was a law not to cut off a piece of raw meat from a live animal
and eat it. They are reviving something more savage than can-
nibalism, they are actually eating us alive. Rachel, you are in
even greater danger."

"David!"

"Rachel, you must believe me. They don't merely experiment
on sick people. They imprison girls of all nationalities and transport them to Germany to be exploited and degraded in homes,
factories and brothels. They trample over laws and morals. You
must get away from Von Preissig."

"You must get out first."

"Why?"

"David, you may be forced to cooperate."

"Is this what you came to tell me? I'd rather die than help
them."

"I want you alive."

"I don't know yet."

"This is what is wrong with you. You hesitate."

"What do you want me to do, be selfish?"

"Rachel, Rachel," he called her but the guard led her away.
He was slow to propose to her. He hesitated until it was too late.
She was free now; not quite. The Jews hesitated too. How aggressive must good people be in order to avoid mistakes? He
made a mistake but not the Jews. Their only mistake was in

believing that the good God in their hearts was also in the malignant hearts of their enemies.

He could neither sleep nor wake.

It never occurred to David that he would be thinking about life as something to exchange and barter. Like all young people, he took life for granted. He knew of death and suffering, but it was far away. It never happened to him. Now that he was confronted with it, he wanted the assurance that it was not in vain.

Now, if he, a Jew, must be ready to give his life rather than be immoral, corrupt and criminal, he must also be given the opportunity to preserve his life, if he fulfills God's law. But how can he, how can the Jews live if debauchery, the worship of brutal force and all out war is practiced and made to look proper by a nation and tolerated by many, many segments of mankind as inevitable.

Oh God, save us—David invoked the personal privilege of every Jew to become involved in a dialogue with God—save the Jews! The Torah without the Jews is worthless! The Scriptures, and holy books—everything from God is in vain without the people chosen to transmit this word of God to the nations. No one can replace them and say we have a new prophet, new priests, followers as numerous as the stars and rituals performed in magnificent buildings beyond comparison. For holy, holy is not always holy; it could be just paper, inked words, chattered prayers, haughty lyrics, vain music and deceiving eyes raised to graven images and illusory heavens.

For their love means hate, their mercy means murder and life means death. They have corrupted the design of creation first by a vengeful and libelous cross and now by rampaging death itself —the infamous hooked cross. They cry law, law; but their only law is a command to destroy that which their beastly instinct cannot tolerate. The vow Bible, Bible; Scriptures, Scriptures, but whatever they read or utter is turned into counterfeit—like those who built a tower to challenge God—a babel of falsehood. They pledge love, love; brotherhood, brotherhood, but their only persisting passion is to satisfy Molech's insatiable pyres for victims, especially Jewish.

Where is God? His cup is overfilled with tears! He was unable to say another word. Twilight shadows began to converge. All

the words he uttered to himself, all the protesting thoughts that
hemorrhaged from his shackled soul were now absorbed within.
He was alone in solitary combat with an oppressive night,
haunted by visions without a dawn and dreams closing in on him
and storming his last refuge.

His dream came uninvited; he was the medium whereby it
could be transmitted and he had to endure its burden. It was
about a ship. There was something about it that intrigued him.
Was it because it is only a shell without a cargo and without a
port of destination? The first time he had seen a big ship was at
Danzig; he was there to guide the first *Chalutzim* group from
Suha-Vali to Israel, after they had completed the *Hachshora*
training at Melech Handler's farm.

That boat—the boat of his dream—was constantly pounding
at the gate of his retrospection. The gangplank was jammed with
passengers—pushed and driven by some unseen force. All of a
sudden, without warning, scowling sailors began to force the
waiting and confused onlookers up the gangplank and into the
holds below. Others began to chase those who jumped over-
board. A shrill whistle and a continuous morbid roar drowned
out the protesting voices of those forced to remain in the ship.
The gangplank was now hastily hauled up. The boat began to
quiver and rock as the grinding motors roared into a deafening
pitch.

Many voices were calling to him; he recognized them. But
their faces were clouded by black smoke belching from chimneys
and exploding balls of fire. He had one last glimpse of his mother
waving a kerchief and of his father's right hand extended, like a
priestly blessing. "Wait for us, we'll return," their faces seemed
to say.

Something held him back by force. He wanted to call an officer to stop the ship before it sailed away so mysteriously. But
there was no one around. The shops were closed. The warehouses were shuttered and the depots were abandoned. Then he
heard from behind him voices of Rachel, Abba, Reb Koppel,
Rabbi Kalir, Avreml and others, "Did you say goodbye to them?
Come, we are waiting for you," someone asked him.

"No, it is too late; I was too late," he kept on repeating, still in
a trance. "Look! Pigeons!" he startled them with an exciting
voice. They were flying from the vanished horizon of the ship, as
they flapped their wings in ever quickening paces as if pursued

by rapacious hawks. "They are my pigeons, I want them," Avreml cried.

Outside his cell, David heard the familiar movement of German and Polish guards. The acrid fumes from the chimney and the taunting frying odors of food prepared for the military personnel in the kitchen, sharpened his hunger.

David recalled the routine within the walls. The committee would meet at least once a week, and sometimes every day, to devise ways and means to acquire food. Shmuel Leiser would report about new contacts made through greasing the palms of greedy Germans. But they demanded more jewelry and more valuables. Barter items were getting scarce and prices for food were exorbitant. The people in their crowded rooms were hungry and starving. Von Preissig, when approached by the committee, for more food and permission for artisans to work in the villages, told the committee time and again, "I have made contact with Warsaw. I expect a response any day. I have connections. The Gestapo double crossed me." At last, Von Preissig, in an unguarded moment, conceded that he was getting nowhere.

The boat in his dream vanished in the hard light of the morning. The ocean was far away. Rachel, her very image, was now the only pleasant longing in a painful world. Abba and Rabbi Kalir shared his dreams, his parents were a part of his life, but only Rachel regulated his heart. It may have been incredible to attach so much to a girl who in the eyes of the Rabbi still belonged to another man. He was willing to wait and survive together with her.

Jewish history, both Biblical and the periods succeeding it, was replete with Jewish leaders inspired by heroines: Abraham by Sarah, Isaac by Rebecca, Jacob by Rachel, Rabbi Akiba by Rachel, Rabbi Meir by Beruria, etc. But was it right for him even if his love was pure and acceptable, to identify his final redemption with marriage? But to him she represented the highest ideal of Jewish chastity and purity.

This was the image he retained of Rachel and everything he loved and held on to during the painful days and dream tortured nights. In this belief he was never isolated. For Suha-Vali, although beseiged by a cruel enemy, was, in the realm of religion, garrisoned and fortified for a long struggle. It was inspired by a man of God, Rabbi Kalir, and led by trustworthy lieutenants. It could even replenish its own supplies. Its sustenance did not

depend entirely on man—grown staples, but on the everlasting
faith of God.

Bread and water were pushed through the door that was flung
open and shut again. David's mind was sprung and food did not
matter. He geared himself again to his irrepressible soliloquy.
Suppose a German division or garrison was cut off, subjected to
the attrition of terrorism, violence and starvation? How long
would it go on before it disintegrated, became demoralized and
was put out of action? How long before it finally surrendered?
Its strength depended on an undiminished flow of supplies,
weapons and cannon fodder. German leaders depended on re-
taining a stance of arrogance; of being always the master, free to
break laws, unrestrained by conscience. Only the Jews could
survive honorably against incredible adversity.

David picked up the slice of bread. It was genuine, unlike the
scarce ersatz bread in the ghetto. He touched it with his fingers
and put it down again. He wetted his lips with the cup of water,
held it close to his mouth until he could not control his thirst and
gulped it down. But the bread could wait. How could he eat
when Jews were deprived of even this bitter slice of affliction.

As the summer months ended and fall drifted in, the jail in the
shed behind headquarters became a cell of cold terror. Whereas
those detained before were dispatched to work camps, the new
occupants were either hostages to be executed or special prisoners like David who were harassed by the Kommandant.

When Abba appeared the guard warned him, "Five minutes,
no more!" Abba stood inside, his back to the door. There were so
many things he had to tell David.

"We received some beans and barley. Malinoski is old, but he
helped us get the beans. He came at night and we bribed the
Germans; those watching the gate. We got the barley flour from
Schrecke."

"Lt. Schrecke?" David was amazed.

"By day he curses. At night he's just a sly thief. He takes
anything he can steal from the kitchen. The farmers won't sell
anything unless they are paid in gold and silver. The Gestapo
wants diamonds and they promise to sell us potatoes. Who
knows—it may be a trick." Abba waited for an answer.

"It is a trick. After we run out of the things they want, what
then?"

"Our women, God bless them, just add more water. And yes, we wanted to start a garden and plant vegetables. They told us, *"Streng Verbotten!"*

"Soon they'll forbid us from growing grass even though it grows by itself," David said.

"I forgot to tell you. No more grass. It was posted on the clay shop wall."

"Why?"

"Why? It may be mistaken as a source of food. Since they provide us so well with food, it is an insult to them, our benefactors. It is not good, David," he raised his head as if to inject the one probable hope, "I have written everywhere; to London, Paris, Washington and to the Pope in Rome."

"The Pope is supposed to be neutral, despite the pressure from Mussolini's Italy to side with the Nazis. A letter to him should go through."

"So far none of the letters I sent through Chantze and Potocki came back from the Geneva contact to the fictitious return address of the old windmill. We checked. What does it mean?"

"Who knows? How do we know that the Gestapo itself didn't establish this contact in Geneva?"

"Why would they do it?"

He took Abba's naivete as another example of Jewish persistence to believe in man's ultimate goodness. David looked around and spoke in a low tone. "The devil has been presented to us going to church, reading a book, kissing a baby, handing flowers to a sweetheart, talking even about progress, justice, freedom and other deceiving words, then why can't he deliver our complaints to a mute world, while inside him a hellish satanic fire will one day ignite him to consume us?"

"Then it could happen . . ."

"What could happen?"

"Nobody believes it David, but it is possible. I have to believe . . ."

"For God's sake, what is it?"

"This happened in the evening, while I was teaching a class in Bible, a few children at a time, in Isaac Melamed's kitchen. Avreml brought in a barefoot frightened girl. She had somehow managed to squeeze through a hole under the wall. A torn dirt-covered dress covered her skeleton frame. At first she wouldn't speak, her large eyes in the shrunken face blinked rapidly.

'Jews?' she finally said and could not continue. I calmed her. Then
she began to tell us a strange story. She was sorting clothing,
that is, from the victims in Kolbasim near the Grodno ghetto.
She stopped talking, she was hungry. We gave her bread and
soup. After a few spoonfuls, she almost became hysterical. Rabbi
Kalir and his wife joined us. She composed herself. 'What were
you doing with the clothing?' I asked her. 'Diamonds,' she
answered. 'They were looking for valuables. The Jews who were
given soap and towels, never came back, never came back, only
bones, ashes remained from the big fires.' She kept on repeating
and crying. But she had no tears. She stopped, stared and continued: 'Then there was nobody left, just the girls and a few
men. Guards gave us soap . . . told us to go to take a bath.' She
could not go on.' I kept on asking her, 'What happened?' 'We
came too early, there was a big oven and drunken soldiers were
shoving live bodies into the fire. We started to run through gates.
Polish and Lithuanian police ran after us. I hid in the woods
. . . I walked two nights. I wanted to go to my people in Sokolke.
I got lost. A peasant woman gave me this dress and flowers and
told me, 'Say you are from Gremnatski, going to town.' "

"David," he sighed, "I have to believe what you always warned
us."

The guard approached, twirling the ringed key over and over
his finger.

"Here, *cigaretten*," Abba gave him one of the last packs,
hoarded like a treasure for such a purpose.

The guard accepted the pack, pulled out one, lit it and as he
blew out the smoke from his mouth mumbled, "Five more
minutes, maybe more."

David was now alone again, but not isolated as a visionary.
Abba's words, "I have to believe what you always warned us,"
verified his revelations that the Jews were threatened by a great
catastrophe. His dreams and interpretations were ignored, just as
the Jewish prophets, whose visions were for all nations and all
time, were spurned. Christian theologians quoted and misquoted,
interpreted and misinterpreted stern but fatherly admonitions of
the prophets to the Jews to justify their biased posture against
Judaism.

David was too beaten down with exhaustion to even think of
his intent to escape. He was aroused by the shock of Abba's visit
to survive only for the sake of telling the world and, particularly

the Jews, to how this greatest of all crimes was being waged against the Jews, and how Von Preissig conceived a mad plan to inherit the Jewish God and the Jewish genius after the crime was completed.

"We'll both have to come to a decision," Dr. Epstein eyed his younger colleague, Dr. Lev, with expectant admiration. Failure to report typhoid cases inside the walls spelled instant execution for both. He could at least claim that he was busy shuttling back and forth between military outposts and therefore not responsible for the typhoid cases. They had just spent the early hours treating the sick in Suchovolsky's garret, before reporting to their sanatorium duties. They were under strict directives to report immediately those infected with this contagious disease. But they were repelled at the very thought of these sick Jews lined up before a ditch, shot, dumped and covered in a nameless shallow grave.

"If I were to report them," Dr. Lev said, "It would be outright murder."

The senior doctor nodded approval by shaking his hand vigorously.

"Before this war," Dr. Epstein recalled, "there was still a semblance of conformity to certain minimum observances of international law, even after periodic orgies and pogroms. When the Turks slaughtered the Armenians and the counter-revolutionary White Russians and Ukrainians killed Jews—both slaughters estimated at a quarter million victims—during and after World War I, the world was horrified and protested. Now the world doesn't care . . . When I started out as a doctor everything was so different."

"How different?" Dr. Lev asked.

"Even war was different. We reverted to the jungle with our faces turned toward civilization."

"And now?"

"Now we are past the jungle stage, down into the cave age . . ." Dr. Epstein searched for something in his pocket.

"Subhuman," Dr. Lev said in disgust, then in a concerned tone, "What are you looking for?"

"Medicine. It is a habit with me, this is the last we can provide for them."

"Don't we have any drugs?"

"We have none," Dr. Epstein said in a note of resignation. Then reminding himself that such words were themselves bad medicine, he corrected himself, "None right now, but I expect supplies."

"From what source?"

"Elsa, Murad's mistress. She will help us bribe him."

"Do you really think so?"

"Let us hope he is more greedy than patriotic."

"Every one of these ailing young men and women," Dr. Epstein called out their names as they lay on mattresses and the bare floor, "I brought them into this world, with a little help from Grune Akusherke. They were once healthy and strong; now after spending months at Agustowa they're just skeletons. Doesn't it break your heart to see them this way? They're lucky to have been released, the flower of our youth."

"We must do everything to help them," Dr. Lev said.

"They became active after their release from the camps until they were stricken. We both agree," Dr. Epstein conceded to his younger colleague, "that the symptoms of fever, nose bleed, chills, malaise, rose spots and loss of appetite indicate that it is typhoid, without any doubt."

"Suppose we write in our reports to the Germans that they have sore throats," the young doctor suggested. "They wouldn't bother the patients, would they?"

"They would dispatch them, sore throats and all, to labor camps."

"How long will it take," Dr. Lev asked, "before they recover?"

"Five weeks is the duration for the disease."

"Let's see, you checked their temperature?"

"Yes, it ranges from 38° to 40° centrigrade plus. I am sure that while I am away, you'll be able to manage."

"I'll have to," Dr. Lev said. "The one thing that bothers me is the syphilis. The Germans sin and come to us to be cleansed."

"I hate it too, but this is the only way we can get by, and obtain a few drugs. I am worried about only two things," Dr. Epstein said.

"Does it concern our responsibility?"

"No, we have settled that, we are responsible only to our own conscience—Jewish conscience."

"This lifts up the Hippocratic oath to the highest level."

"Quite so, but the two things are conditions for their quick

recovery—drugs and our endurance. They are both in shortage,"
Dr. Epstein stated.

"As long as Grune the Akusherke can manage to stand on her
feet and hold together her bones, we will. As for drugs, we'll
steal, scrounge and improvise," Dr. Lev said hopefully.

They washed their hands and now that Grune the Akusherke,
the perennial nurse of Suha-Vali in war and in peace, returned,
they felt free to report to Rabbi Kalir.

"Where am I," Velvke the *gabai* asked. His eyes were glassy.
He staggered and grabbed the head frame of a bed. He had
come on a *mitzvah* errand to visit the sick in the sanatorium.
There was terror in the eyes of the patients. He felt dizzy and
asked for a glass of water. After he drank it, everything around
him was blurred. The patients and doctors, the visitors and
nurses, all seemed dressed in white shrouds.

Dr. Epstein, on his scheduled round, found him delirious. He
felt his pulse, touched his sweating forehead and smelled the
glass from which Velvke drank.

"Only water and now I'm sick," Velvke mumbled. "Or maybe
it wasn't just water."

"Don't go away from here," Dr. Epstein said and looked
around frantically. "I'll get you something to clear your head. I'll
be right back."

He held on feebly to the rusty head frame. Shadows in white
garb were moving nearer to him. His head turned in jolted slow
motion, sideways and backwards. He gasped in panic, he was
surrounded by faceless people poised with injection needles and
closing in on him.

"Don't, please don't," he was fearful that at any moment they
would jab their lethal needles into his flesh.

"This is a hospital, old Jew, to cure you."

"I, all of us, don't need any cure, you need it."

The guard gripped his sheathed bayonet.

"Why don't you kill me like you killed the rest?" Velvke challenged the scowling German. "What happened to the four children? They're gone."

"They had typhoid. Is it not so, doctor?" He pretended that the
orderly was a doctor.

"What happened to the two sons of the blacksmith, the mother
and daughter from Dombrowa, typhoid too?"

"No, a dreadful disease," the orderly acted out his sham role.

"But they were all healthy until they were given injections by the military doctors. Please, doctor, do something.

"Are you sure he's got fever, doctor?" the guard grinned sheepishly, "feel his pulse."

"Go, go to the devil, who needs a crazy man here," the orderly screamed.

"Come back! Come back!" Dr. Epstein ran toward Velvke whom the Germans mockingly pushed out through the doorway.

"He wants air, this crazy man, let him," the orderly told Dr. Epstein.

"But this man is sick. He's got fever."

"If he is really sick I'll get a military doctor. He looks crazy to me."

"Let me take care of him."

"Doctor, you got your patients here, take care of them. I'll see that he gets his wish."

Once outside the guard began to stalk Velvke, who shielded his face from him.

"You don't trust us, old Jew," the guard said to him and grabbed him by the neck.

"It is written in our book that a crime must be investigated— it is a Biblical law."

"What Biblical law?"

"Let me show you, let me . . ."

"Hey *chlopzi*," he called to the Polish guards, "you want to see a funny Jew?"

Velvke became dizzy and faltered.

"Let me," he mumbled, "I must investigate before I die; it says in the Bible," he gulped for breath.

"It says what?" the rollicking chorus mimicked him as he went down on all fours like one searching for traces of footprints.

"A regular bloodhound," they laughed and barked.

"It says in the Bible that if a victim is found, then the elders of the city shall go out to investigate."

"Did you hear that?"

"Now where do we find the elders to investigate?"

"We'll be the elders," they answered in a shrill voice.

"Ah good, very good, *chlopzi*, but you have no beards."

"Es *macht nicht,*" it doesn't matter, the German told them. He directed them to stroke their chins. More Germans and worshippers from across the church gathered in front of the whitewashed sanatorium to join the frolicking.

"I can't see ahead of me," Velvke complained, bewildered as he was hemmed in his crouching position by the hilarious mob.

"Follow the shadow," one of the auxiliary police called out, pointing his gun to the long shadow formed by the church steeple.

Velvke kept on crawling, counting and measuring until he was almost near the massive wrought iron gate of the church. He straightened himself. His fever was like a stoking fire about to burst into flame. He cried, "They shall say our hands did not shed this blood."

"What blood?" one of the rabble asked, as he mockingly clapped his hands.

"What blood?" the chorus repeated as they clapped.

"Rabbi Kalir said," Velvke tried to speak above the frenzied roar.

"*Ach so, der Rabiner,*" the German imitated to the delight of the gallery with a display of pantomime, "very big beard, big head, big belly."

"The Rabiner," the chorus intoned as they stroked their chins. Skura, the cheer leader, began to shout, "Chema Ichrael," in a mocking lingo and tone.

"Stop," Velvke strained his voice. "It hurts."

"You hear? It hurts," the German bellowed and prompted them, "louder now again, Chema Ichrael."

"Stop it, in heaven's name, stop! You are crippling sacred words."

"Not the right word? It's your Hebrew."

"You have twisted our Hebrew, our Holy Scriptures with your poison injections."

"Like an injection?" They asked in unison and rolled with rocking laughter.

"Like an injection of typhoid into my blood. Stop! You do this very painful thing to me every time you mention God's name in vain. You laugh, yes? Your tongues are like those of poisonous snakes!"

"*Verfluchter Jude,*" the gendarme raged and threatened him.

Skura now took his cue and punched him as he gritted with his teeth "Zid."

"Lash him!" a voice shouted.

"Let's burn him," another screamed.

"Bury him in the church yard." They cried fiercely and ugliness began to creep out from under their skins.

"Where am I?"

"In the church," the multitude ranted as they closed in on him.

"Oh God, my God, where am I?" He turned from side to side, scanned their hate-surging faces through his blurred eyes and asked: "What are you doing to me? Call the Rabbi."

"Say it again." They pretended deafness.

"Call the Rabbi," he repeated. "I forgot what he once said."

"Call the Rabiner with the big beard," Skura prompted the *chlopzi*.

Velvke came out of shock. He realized that he faced a barrier that no Jew ever crossed. The mob was about to shove him through the gate of the church. He turned and began to retrace his steps, until Murad, the gendarme, and the Polish police became bored with all this. Firm hands seized Velvke's limp arms and led him back a few paces toward the whitewashed low brick house between the parish and Abchik's apothecary. They would wait until the Rabiner for whom they sent would show up to awaken their ebbing interest.

Meanwhile the crowd around Velvke grew larger. "So good, you came to see me," he spoke to anyone who came near him. Haggard with a burning fever he was under the spell of a delirium. "I'm so sorry that I'm sick." The unruly mob now began to act out its vicarious role according to every directed whim of Murad who took personal charge.

"You must be hungry. I will get money for you." He mistook Murad for a needy Jew. The sergeant winked to the guards watching the sham action.

"You must be helped; I am the *gabdai* who gives out charity and scrips for meals. I have neglected my duties, and all of you are waiting. Where is a pencil and paper?"

Murad pointed to Skura and scribbled with his finger in the air. Skura pulled out a pencil and a notebook from his pocket and handed it to Velvke.

"Good, good, I'll provide each one of you with shelter and

food. You must be poor Jewish refugees from another town. You
are our brothers, and we must help you." Murad the Gestapo
man pressed his finger against his closed lips as the crowd tried
hard to restrain itself from hysterical laughter.

"Now young man," he pointed to Murad, who acted his part
crudely with his deadpan face. "You look hungry—you will go
to Reb Koppel, only two in the house. His sons are away. One is
taking care of lumber interests in the forest and the other is at
the University. You'll get a good night's sleep and good meals for
as long as you want.

"You," he next pointed to the guard, a well fed obese beer
drinker, "you will go to Reb Leib, not fancy meals, but substantial and filling. And you," his eyes blinked at Skura, "Hershke the
miller will provide you with food and even work in his windmill.
You look like an honest man willing to work. Hershke is not the
smiling kind, he likes the decent and those willing to toil. You'll
like each other."

"You, you all need help—help from God. These people in Suha-
Vali are all poor," he hesitated, "poor and hungry themselves,
but they have Jewish hearts and are *rachmonim*—merciful and
kind to the needy. Now go before they close their shutters at
night. There are wolves in the forests and badmen all around,"
his fingers still pointing as he turned to all sides until he sank to
the ground and fainted.

For a moment the mob was quiet. Then word passed from
mouth to mouth that the *Rabin*, as they referred in Polish to the
Rabbi, was on the way. He was spat upon and greeted by jeering,
whistling and cat calls. "Hey Rabin, can you revive him." "Just
in time." "Say the prayer for the dead," the toothless chimney
sweeper howled at the top of his voice. One peasant who recognized him as the benign patriarch of charity, as he became known
among some of the peasants, crossed himself, but was startled by
Skura's *'pshakreff'* and a chain of curses.

"The Rabiner," Murad chuckled, "the Rabin," the mob now
howled and whistled. Some made faces at him as he walked
straight to Velvke and bent over him. As he wiped the perspira-
tion off Velvke's brow, the victim, surrounded by his tormentors,
raised his eyes to make certain that the first kind touch and
benign face was real.

"Rebbi, holy Rebbi, God sent you, it is you—isn't it? I can't
recognize faces any more."

"I am your friend. I want to help you. What are you doing here?" he inquired according to habit, knowing too well what was taking place.

"*Eg-la A-roo-fa,*" Velvke uttered the syllables between gulps of breath. "Where are the elders to find the criminals. You said so, you told me so, it is a law of God," he beseeched his teacher to invoke this ancient law, whereby the elders had to wash their hands to indicate that they had taken no part in the crime. If a man was killed and it was not known who murdered him, then the elders and the judges had to go out and measure the distance between the victim and nearest city. Then the elders of that nearest city offered a heifer for a sacrifice washed their hands and said: "Our hands have not shed this blood, neither have our eyes seen it."

"Very true, Velvke," Rabbi Kalir said, knowing very well who were the murderers of so many Jews without measuring the distance. For the source of the instigation, the murderers, and the wayward elders were all around them.

"Rebbi, you said so yourself," he persisted, "if many are dying, then we have to measure the distance to the nearest responsible city; all the way—all the way to the capitals of the world, to help us find the criminals."

"Velvke, I know what you want to tell me," he was aware of hostile eyes, "but you need help. You'll be yourself again, doing *mitzvos.*"

"How can I rest, how can anyone rest, where are the Jewish elders? Oh, God, forgive me. What am I saying? I am so confused. They, the Jewish elders, are all in prison, but where are the elders of the nations?"

He was now emerging from the harrowing hallucination and conscious of the harsh faces surrounding him and the gracious Rabbi.

"If you add up the number of murdered and the number of measured paces to establish the nearest cities to the crimes, where courts and judges should have investigated the crimes, then their . . ." He was groping for the final indictment. "But since the courts and judges of those cities near where so many were murdered, failed in their duties, we have to do it, measure the distance and trace the tracks of the criminals all the way to Berlin, Rome, many capitals of Europe and even to America and to all countries."

"Emes"—so true—so right, his heart told him. He was so over-come by Velvke's inspired effort to resurrect a ritual from the world of so long ago, that he could not hear the shrill whistles.

"Jude, Jude!" and mouthfuls of obscenities and curses poured out from Murad's foul mouth as he ordered the Rabbi and the shocked Velvke to get up. Then threatening the Rabbi with his whip, he screamed, "Take this crazy man with you, let him die with you."

Rabbi Kalir wondered whether it was a slip of the tongue or a foreboding of something worse. It suggested that they were impa-tient with all this pretense of step by step liquidation of the Jewish problem. They didn't care any more what happened to anyone. It was another crack in the carefully built up facade of the German camouflaged conspiracy of *schreklichkeit*.

Von Preissig was away to a conference in Warsaw to protest the domineering role of the S.S. Colonel, Ludwig Schwarzhund. Col. Schwarzhund gloated with a sense of fulfillment now that he assumed an active role in the affairs of the ghetto. The Kommandant's "crazy plan," to enslave and win over the Jews on the side of Germany, was bit by bit discredited by him. His orders to the S.S. and Gestapo aids were to supersede Von Preissig and revert to the tough policy toward the Jews. He awaited eagerly their committee.

"You are making a black market out of the food business," Schwarzhund attacked—before Koppel, Abba, and Ben Zion, who returned after another fruitless search for his family—could even present their case for increased rations.

"But our people are starving," Koppel said.

"We have to feed the German army. We also need food for our own people. We have allowed you enough food."

"But," Ben Zion restrained himself, "only a few more sacks of potatoes, just one sack of peas and another can of whey per week, that is all we ask for the three thousand people crowded in the three blocks."

"Orders are orders, no extra food for those who don't pro-duce."

"But you won't let us work," Shmuel protested to Schwarz-hund, who looked irritated.

Shmuel said calmly, "We will supply men and women to help the farmers increase production."

"Nobody needs your help," he pressed his itching nose as he exploded with foul language: *"Heraus verfluchte Juden! Heraus, heraus!"* he was impatient to push them out of the door.

"We asked for bread and got insults," Abba said on the way home.

"Maybe we are too patient, too peaceful, too good in dealing with these fascist dogs," Shmuel was bitter.

Toward evening, the committee was summoned to a meeting in Suchovolsky's house. Avreml was sent to call Koppel. There was something going on in Rabbi Kalir's room, something unusual. A German dressed in mufti had just left his house. There were thick flying rumors. Some said he was from the war ministry with a confidential offer; others that he was an official from the Gestapo warning of imminent danger, and that he wanted a committee immediately to discuss highly confidential matters.

Reb Koppel did not respond immediately. "He was looking inside a Gemara, and walking back and forth over the floor," Avreml told Abba, who went now to call him. The leather bound tractate of *Sanhedrin* was on the dining room table. Most of the lower edged corners were curled and frayed, evidence of learning and indulgence by an attentive book companion. He had been there before, in the world of the *Sanhedrin*, many times in the last two days. Men of wisdom and understanding, investigating, searching, checking all evidence carefully to render a just decision when a life was at stake. A sword was always suspended over their heads. If justice miscarried or they pronounced a wrong verdict—then God forbid—it threatened to plunge down into their midst. He hummed his old tune, leaned forward, backward, and sideways. His tempo quickened and he began to sway to the singsong of the words in all four directions. Everything about him fused into this rhythm of learning. The rickety old chair, the groaning table, the creaking floor, the cracked ceiling, all merged their own shortcomings into the faultless song of study. More than mere words and melody, it was a triumph of man over man. For here was ample proof that the voices of the cave and the voices of violent dark ages were superseded by a gracious and old Jew, loving life and man, dedicated to the peaceful ways of God. Outside was the accompanying chirping of birds and schools of crickets, confirming the man who was an ally of a holy book as a fit partner of creation.

Abba was standing in front of him with that peculiar awe before one who mastered such an intricate subject. Reb Koppel kept on intoning, "A Sanhedrin that decreed a capital punishment once in seventy years was called a murderous Sanhedrin, and in our own time more than seventy have been killed in one year in Suha-Vali alone. All these convictions and death sentences carried out without a Sanhedrin; no court, no witnesses, no evidence, no justice—outright murder; do you understand?" Koppel turned to Abba.

"Reb Koppel, the Rabbi is waiting for you at his quarters," Abba interrupted him.

On the way to the Rabbi's house Abba told Koppel that it was something important, about the release of Jews.

"The prisoners?" he asked him.

"No, it concerns all of us."

"Will David be there?"

"No, David has not been released. Since the meeting will be in Label's house, even though he is still hunted, he will also be there."

"Why, why didn't you tell me at once that the Rabbi is waiting?"

There was more than usual commotion at Rabbi Kalir's one room apartment. "It's a trap, I tell you," Label was about to pound on the table, but the awareness that it was covered by leather bound tomes and smaller sacred books restrained him.

"The last time I saw a Japanese," Alter cried out, "was in 1903 in the Russian-Japanese war. I was a soldier and the enemy was Japan. It's crazy, I tell you."

"Japanese, Chinese—we'll even become citizens of some cannibal tribe, if this will get us out," Kagan said. "Maybe they are more civilized. All the cannibals in Africa killed less in a thousand years than Petlura's Ukrainian fascists killed in 1922. What was the figure—fifty thousand, or together with the other blackguards, two hundred fifty thousand—Does any one know?"

"Why go back to 1922?" Label, now fully recovered, was himself again. "Didn't they make pogroms in Europe for the past one thousand years? Didn't the church instigate these massacres? Right now the Germans who added their own nationalist murder propaganda to this instigation are killing Jews all over Europe.

Let's see, since last June we lost about thirty here and forty five
were killed or tortured to death in camps. How many have died
or will die from typhoid and hunger? The cemetery inside the
walls is filling up fast. Multiply this by two thousand Jewish
communities and you have a staggering figure."

"You can add the thousands shot, tortured and still imprisoned
by the Russians as Zionists, under the name of counter-revolutionaries," Kagan countered.

"Didn't the Russians save Jews?"

"We Jews have nothing against the Russian people, but the
Russian anti-semitic leaders and chauvinists since the Czars
made the Jews scapegoats. In Czarist Russia they persecuted
them as Jews. During the Russian revolution the communists
prosecuted them as capitalists, and the counter-revolutionaries
as communists. The Nazis who borrowed from the two Russias,
and from fascist Italy, added their own improved unlimited savagery. In 1939 Stalin gave the go sign to Hitler to do whatever
he wanted with his share of Europe and the Jews. Suppose Stalin
made a point that the Jews be left alone?"

"Did the Pope go out of his way to protect the Jews from these
Christian murderers?" Label asked.

"We have gone over this before," Koppel intervened. "But this
rumor of issuing us Japanese passports and then permitting us to
leave occupied Poland, I don't understand this, Rabbi Kalir!

"Right now I am awaiting more information from the German
agent who came to see me."

"Was it a Gestapo, or S.S. man?"

"They all look alike to me."

"Why Japanese passports," Koppel asked, "why not American,
English or French?"

"Germany is at war with these countries, while Japan its ally is
still at peace with Russia," the Rabbi explained. "By granting
the Jews Japanese passports it would put pressure and strain on
the inept Russian railroads to allow the Jews transit across
Russia to Japanese occupied China. It sounds crazy, but the
German leaders are crazy."

"We could get passports from Switzerland, Sweden or other
neutral countries," Ben Zion said.

"Germany does not respect a neutral, unless it is a power,"
Shmuel replied.

"How about the Vatican granting the Jews passports. It is

recognized by Hitler and Mussolini as a state, isn't it?" Label asked.

"Are you suggesting that the Jews become Catholics?" Paltiel rebuked him.

"No, just citizens of the Vatican State."

"We might just as well ask the Arabs to make us Arabs, just for a while," Ben Zion said.

"In normal times, this would have been a valid suggestion," Abba said. "Historical precedents verify this. The Jews posed as Mohammedans when threatened with death or forceful conversions. But the present Arabs, guided by the Grand Mufti of Jerusalem and other intrigants, terrorized the Jews in *Eretz Israel* and collaborate now with Hitler."

"*Rabosei,*" the soft spoken Jacob Zaban, the Talmud teacher, stopped the discussion. "We could claim to be Samaritans or Karaites, whom the Germans don't consider as Jews, or even pretend to be Tatars. We could only pretend."

"Rebbi, we have waited for this German for more than two hours. Are you certain it is not a trap to arrest some of us?" Label was impatient.

"When we meet, they never bother us," the Rabbi said.

"What I mean ... What are the facts?"

"Someone a Gestapo agent of high rank, is in town with a plan. I don't know details. I met him only briefly. He promised to see me again today."

"If the agent didn't give any details the first time, how can we rely on him the second time," Label asked.

"The Rabbi would not assemble us if it wasn't something deserving our trust," Koppel defended him.

"*Acheinu,* fellow Jews," the Rabbi spoke slowly, "I would go to the end of the earth and so would any one of you, for just a sliver of hope. If any man or group would come to us even from the North Pole or the jungle with a plan to save even one Jew, we would listen to him."

"But where is the proof?" Label asked.

"The agent told me about an unnamed Yeshiva, with its *Roshei Hayeshiva,* students, their wives and children, who, after being granted Japanese passports, were allowed safe passage across Russia to Shanghai and Tokio."

"Could you tell us more details?" Shmuel asked the Rabbi. For they could not understand the offer made by a high official, the

secret Gestapo friend of Von Preissig, to issue to the Jews of
Suha-Vali Japanese passports for exit this time from German oc-
cupied Poland through a neutral country like Sweden across
Russia to Japan or some other place.

"This Gestapo agent was very cagy," the Rabbi continued. "He
had to be, because the Gestapo was against the plan. He had to
grease the palms of the district commissioner. Yes, improbable as
it sounds, this miracle did happen. I recall that over a year ago
the whole academy of the Mirer Yeshiva was granted Japanese
passports for its personnel and transit through Russia to Shanghai. The Japanese counsel was spurred on by the indifference of
western diplomats to the fate of the Jews."

"How could we check it?" Shmuel Leiser asked, "it is impossible, no man could get through alive. How about other towns?
Does anyone know more about it? A special contact man could
be sent to Stabin, Yanowa or even a big town like Grodno or
Bialystok."

They began to disperse. The scanty information relayed to the
Rabbi about the fantastic Japanese passport deal could not be
verified.

"Ben Zion, you travelled through many countries," Abba
wanted to clear up his own doubts on the way home. "Why did
the agent tell the details of this episode to the Rabbi since it was
not verified?"

"I asked myself the same question. Something like this did
happen as the Rabbi told you, in January 1941, I think. But it
was under Russia, at peace with Germany and with Japan. The
Mirer Yeshiva was in and around Kadan, Lithuania, functioning clandestinely. It was an isolated rescue operation. Perhaps
other such arrangements are being made by Gestapo agents, either as attempts to press out money for themselves or for their
superiors. But in order to convince the Rabbi of Gestapo relia-
bility, the Gestapo agent had to propose this fantastic offer."

"I have my doubts," Label said.

"One of us should inform David. It is possible that David will
be released to resolve this issue. He will be in an awkward position no matter what he says. Abba, I'll see him," Shmuel said.

Several days later, after Von Preissig returned from a futile
visit to Warsaw, he received Colonel Gustav Zolenknecht like
an old friend, early in the morning. They studied together in a
secondary school. Gustav was not especially brilliant, but he was

pleasant to the point of agreeing with everyone. Now he was in
the intelligence section of the Gestapo.

"You wonder, Krist," he called Von Preissig by his middle
name, "what I am doing in this uniform?"

"I can understand, practical adaptability."

"You are wrong. I am ashamed of what I am doing. I was
drafted and when I told them I had no special skill nor interest
in any cadre, they put me in the Gestapo."

"Very typical of them. All their leaders were chosen like that;
that's what is wrong with Germany."

"Krist, you must be careful."

"Have I been betrayed?"

"What do you mean?"

"I'm fighting here in this forgotten village to save something
from the wreckage."

"What wreckage?"

"I have just returned from Warsaw. I was shocked at what I
saw and heard. While Governor Frank plays the piano, thousands are dying inside the Warsaw ghetto. As for the front, it is
fluid, you know . . ."

"I don't. We are in Paris, Vienna, Warsaw, Bucharest, Prague,
Sofia, Oslo, Copenhagen, also in Rome, and we were not far from
Moscow."

"As a military man I know only one formula, victory. It cannot
be attained by occupying territories or capitals. We are fighting
an enemy still formidable."

"As a civilian now in service of the Reich I know only one
thing—we have to be loyal and impersonal. *Deutschland über ales!*
Our duty is to obey our superiors and ask others to obey us."

"War involves strategy and tactics; everything is fair and justified for the sake of success. If we could conclude a separate
treaty with England and face Russia alone . . ."

"We would be victorious."

"Exactly. This is very sound. England plus America is too
much for us," Von Preissig said.

"We are going to win anyway."

"And I say you cannot win wars behind the lines with a
Gestapo machine bent on murdering everybody, especially the
Jews. By the way, have you brought a sealed envelope for
Schwarzhund? He awaited that for a long time. Is it about a final
solution of the Jewish 'problem'?"

"Yes, it is true, Krist."

"My plan is—was is more correct—to make slaves out of the Jews. You may not believe it, but my long range strategy would be to conquer their soul and inherit everything they have."

"Krist, let me ask you this, assuming this is only a fantastic theory. Why must we conquer the Jews to be triumphant and not the English, French, and the Americans who have the resources to crush us?"

"We can start with the Jews and apply it to other nations. Because in a war, a victory can be decided in favor of one side by an exclusive weapon: like the tank with which the Allies surprised us in the First World War. If our submarines or buzz bombs were the decisive weapons, the war would have been won. But we are bogged down."

"Where do the Jews come in?"

"Exactly my point. Nineteen hundred years ago there was one small obscure sect within this Jewish nation, in a tiny country poor in resources, poor in everything except in the gift or maybe genius of its people. Now see what they have done, spread a religion—some say the wrong men, the early Christians transmitted only a crippled version of Judaism, all over Europe and the world. Suppose we could succeed now that they are in our hands, with an improved version from them. Does it make a difference how we get it?"

"It sounds visionary to me."

"Isn't the entire Nazi ideology visionary?"

"Not exactly. Let me ask you this, Johann. What would be your place in this scheme?"

"Very humble, I and you, I'll need good men to expand this very German empire all over the world based on the Jewish religion and everything good the Jews seem to have. We have only uniforms, Gustav, but they have something inside them, the way they look at you unafraid of death, refusing to acknowledge us as their masters—they consider us evil people."

"This has never been tried before. It sounds incredible that we, with the iron and blood image, should even contemplate such a scheme."

"We Germans need rehabilitation. We have to be reshaped—made into decent beings; and we could learn it only from the Jews. If we kill them, we kill the only chance to save our souls, before the devil and blood take hold of us and finish us as a nation."

"We have no time for anything which is a dream or a theory. Right now we are hard pressed. You said yourself that in war everything is justified for the sake of success. The civilians, their needs, their rights don't concern us. Whatever happens or will happen to the Jews is beyond us. Right now we face serious problems."

"What is serious?" Von Preissig asked.

"The Gestapo handles all civilians, controls the economy, and through forced labor and slaves keeps going inside occupied Europe. But it is not so good. Our divisional losses are astounding. We lost whole armies on the Russian front, and the western front is now very active. We lack food, copper, oil, rubber and trucks. Why, we even made an offer to the Jews."

"What offer?" Von Preissig was impatient.

"I have it from a confidential source, one of the original Munich beer cellar circle, that for a certain number of trucks, let us say 10,000, delivered to us by Jewish representatives, we'll spare the lives of a sizable number—a hundred thousand or even half a million Jews. The point is that we are willing to save them, before trains transport them to the death camps.

"I am not exactly certain if this plan will work. Even if we get the ten thousand trucks, we have no gasoline for their motors.

"Our intelligence in London and Washington has relayed to us, that our offer to save the Jews has been rejected, which is certain to be publicized. So the Germans will at least have the Allies as accomplices to all their crimes against the Jewish people."

"They tell me there is something going on in the Grodno ghetto." Von Preissig wanted information.

"I don't know."

"Isn't it a marshalling ghetto, the last station and stop for all surrounding ghettos?"

"There are such ghettos all over Poland. I'm not here to investigate what happens. They are being sent to labor camps."

"Old men and children too?"

"Well, Jews are still bound to families and ties. They are inseparable to the last. There is a story how parents, sons and daughters pleaded to be sent away together. Once such a family was separated before they were herded into the crematorium with towels and soap with the excuse to give them a bath; are you listening?"

"I am listening, but please don't finish the story."

"My advice is keep to yourself. As a friend I also advise you not to challenge the authority of Col. Schwarzhund and the Grodno Kommandant Rintzler. By the way, there is a prisoner in your custody, Sokoloff. Speak to him about this offer before you release him temporarily. You may employ your own methods. Regardless of the credulity of the offer, I was asked to transmit it. Do the same."

"What about the final solution in the ghettos?"

"I don't know."

"If there is a solution, which will doom the Jews, then how do you explain the exchange offer to save Jews?"

"It gives us an option to get what we can while they are alive. You'll excuse me, I have an appointment with Rintzler."

"Do come again on your way from Grodno or similar places."

"Keep your health and your peace, Kristus."

Von Preissig stood there as Kurt departed dragging after him cobwebs of nostalgia and deadliness woven by the Nazi spider.

The next day Von Preissig summoned David to his office. He told David that he would release him provided he cooperated. An officer of high rank asked the Kommandant to enlist the aid of the leading Jew or Jews of Suha-Vali to persuade this community, and if necessary other communities, to help the Germans obtain trucks in exchange for the release of thousands of Jews. It was obvious that the Jews would have to give away their last funds and valuables, and even appeal to Jews in the Allied countries, particularly America, to raise such an emergency fund to save their brethren. The most difficult part of the offer involved the procurement of ten thousand trucks from the Allied nations. If David consented and the committee approved, he would be sent to Warsaw where other representatives of cities and towns would assemble to fulfill this project immediately.

Von Preissig made it very clear that this was not his project, but that he was asked to transmit this information and lend his office to expedite this undertaking. David countered that the Jews had no money and that the Allied nations would not allow their Jews to collect such funds. Furthermore they would never funnel trucks to Germany. At a time when Allied bombers had been destroying German railroads and vehicles by this attrition it would be madness on their part to rebuild the enemy's supply system.

Von Preissig replied that Germany on her part would make a solemn pledge to employ these vehicles on the Russian front only. That the Allied nations would never betray Russia was rejected by Von Preissig with the remark, "Diplomacy is the extension of war through its own code." Now that Von Preissig espoused this immoral code unwillingly but nevertheless dutifully, David acted without delay.

He called together the committee in the afternoon at Suchovolsky's shed. He reported in detail what Von Preissig told him. Although they were already well informed about the offer at an earlier meeting in the Rabbi's house, they were shocked by the sinister angle of this incredible plan. Before leaving the office, Von Preissig told David, "Let's see if your Allies will come half way to save your lives." It was obvious that the Nazis would gain something either way: vehicles for their sorely needed mobility if the plan was adopted, and the blame on the Allies for the Jews' catastrophe if the offer was rejected.

David told them that under no condition would he be a party to such a dubious offer and that as far as he was concerned, he had made up his mind to escape with anyone willing to join him. Ben Zion approved David's report with a strong conclusion.

"I have made several trips to Bialystok. I've seen what is going on there and I've heard about the terrible dying and suffering of the Warsaw Jews. Warsaw is not in a forgotten place like Suha-Vali. It is a capital city. There are correspondents and journalists from various countries, including many neutrals. You know not once have Allied planes dropped even leaflets to the Jews of Warsaw saying: 'We have not forgotten you, keep alive, hope, be courageous!' Neither have they dropped leaflets on German cities denouncing the entire nation for the crimes they were committing daily against the Jews. If they would only have done something—threatening the Germans with a terrible weapon for example—then we might have reason to expect some good from the offer."

They remained there for two hours and agreed to make all preparations for the first organized breakout from the ghetto three days hence, on Friday night.

Before he returned to his room, while he still had a pass till midnight, he went straight to the sanatorium where his parents were kept. He found them in the worst condition possible. Like all Jewish patients they were undernourished and without proper care.

"We are going to escape in a few days," he told them. "I'm taking both of you along with me."

"No, David, we'll only be a burden. Why are we better than anyone else to be saved?" Ber Leib asked his son.

"We'll save anyone who wants to join us."

"Son," Dinah Elke told him, "we are not birds. You see yourself we can hardly move."

It was a terrible blow to David to find them in such a state. But he made up his mind before he kissed them goodbye to make every effort to rescue them.

GERMANS HELD IN THRUST 80 MILES FROM STALINGRAD.

How long will the people of God be delivered for slaughter?

Baba Mezia, 83.

24

NO ESCAPE

Friday was a splendid day for the song of songs to be recited before the Sabbath prayers. This Beryl could offer in gratitude for the miracle granted to him to bake a few loaves of bread: the Pole, Zemliak, had sold him some flour for an exorbitant price.

"For lo the winter is past, the rain is over and gone." Beryl walked over to the window and saw those ever shadowy walls dark and gray against the brilliant sun. He moved away to shade his eyes and continued the melody. It was his own commentary of the text. "The flowers appear on the earth." There were only wilted, dead stalks of weeds; the invaders challenged the text. So far the Germans had not given permission to plant seeds or to let the earth bring forth a blade of grass or a daisy. It was strictly forbidden, lest, in desperation, the Jews would accept the humble herbs from mother earth.

"The time of the singing of birds is come."

Birds darted in and out of the garden. They chirped and chattered, but there was no sustained song, for they were frightened away. Once he would scatter enough bread and crumbs to attract flocks of ever-singing sparrows and crows. But now they were gone. They sensed that inside the walls there were fewer crumbs. But now that he baked for the Sabbath, the smoke from the chimney would summon them.

"The fig tree put forth its green figs, and the vines with the tender grapes give a good smell."

The trees were naked and exhausted from the long winter. The fruit trees of the orchard were out of bounds. The pine trees of the forest were far away, and the young firs, beyond reach, whispered alone. There was no one to lie beneath their canopied

329

shade and no excited voices to accompany the pursuit of rabbits and squirrels.

"Arise my love, my fair one and come away. Arise my love," his memory kept on repeating. He must not interrupt his thoughts by looking through the window, for everything was not pleasant to behold. "Let me hear thy voice." Did someone call him, "Reb Beryl?" No, the door was open. It was not locked. Then, why was someone knocking to get in? "The little foxes that spoil the vines."

"Reb Beryl!" someone was calling and knocking. It is only confusion. He must be tired, from too much anxiety, to hear a voice. Yes, there was a face peering through the window and a voice calling him. He had lost the last verse.

"Reb Beryl open—open," he heard a rough voice shaking the door. He unlatched it, wondering again, who closed it? For he never meant to close it. On Friday it was always open to welcome the Sabbath.

"Reb Beryl, what is wrong?"

"It must be the smoke from the oven." He was embarrassed. For the first time in his life, tears intruded during his lyrical chanting.

"It's me, Burka," he announced as he opened the window for the smoke to escape.

"The bread isn't ready."

"I've not come for bread—you must be ready tonight if you want to be saved."

"Ready tonight!—what do you mean?"

"David told me we're getting out to save ourselves."

"How—where?"

"I don't know—out in the forest, any place, away from here."

"God of our fathers! Are we animals? How can we live in the forest? I'll stay here to die."

"These Germans won't let you live nor die in peace. Did you hear the stories about putting Jews to death in Grodno? They starve them, then they burn them or shoot them as it pleases them."

"It can't be true."

"You have no choice. We may escape through your backyard. It is right alongside the new cemetery. There are fewer guards there at night. They will come looking for you."

"What will happen to the Dombrowa families living with me?"

"They are also planning to break out."

"I'll go and tell all who want to save themselves to be ready; don't talk to anyone—tonight at twelve—take along all the bread that you can."

Burka closed the door behind as he left, crouching and hugging the fence cautiously. Something now stood before him amid the shadows. It was a candle in a window that arrested his steps. All his young life had been wasted in pursuit of things belonging to others. Now he saw Baba Zippe raise her hands to funnel the faint light from the tallow candles to her creased face. He suddenly remembered his own mother, waiting for him. He hesitated as he turned around toward the low roofed house. He was almost finished before reporting to David. He must make one more attempt to take along his mother.

The door was ajar, as he stepped upon the loose board of the porch. In one leap he was in the hall separating the living quarters from his barn. He glanced through the barn door where old horse collars and wheels, old reins and ropes hung from the rafters, left alone by the Germans as useless. His eyes focused on the corner where underneath some wood and straw lay hidden some "tools" of his trade: jimmies and steel cutting shears. It was undisturbed. Everything above was open for anybody to behold and possess, but underneath were his own personal belongings, a part of his past of pride and regret. He turned around to examine a leather woven whip with a bent nail thrust through the knotted tip.

"My son," his mother called out in a feeble voice. Both clung to one another.

"I will take you away from here tonight."

"Why?"

"It is not safe. One day they'll drive us from our homes like cattle to concentration camps."

"They can't just steal it from us, and drive us into the street."

"They'll rob everything from us, they have done it already. They are the worst murderers and thieves. I was never a thief like any of them. I never took away one's last bed, coat, or piece of bread."

"Don't say anything. You still believe in God?"

"I do."

"Remember it took me a long time to carry you inside my belly. I once thought that all my pains were for nothing; was it?"

"No, Mama."

"I'll do as you say, son, if this is right."

"It is right, many more—if they want to, will join." Burka was no longer estranged. At last he returned to tell his mother the right thing.

"Be ready tonight."

When Burka crossed the threshold of Suchovolsky's massive house, Abba Dunsky, Ben Zion and Noske, the Schochet, were packing food and Abba was very carefully selecting papers and a few books to take along.

"We leave tonight at twelve sharp," Burka announced. "Don't arouse attention. Two guards are now searching from house to house."

He was on his way to Hershke the miller and then to Alter the carpenter. He planned to check with David for last-minute instructions.

It was almost ten when Burka, his forehead perspiring and his feet swelling inside his worn-out boots, thrust his face into Rachel's doorway after the two quick taps on the handle.

"I'll be right back. I've got to take along a few things."

"Not too much weight," David said in a very determined, but low voice, as he helped Rachel assemble provisions—hard dried bread, a chunk of sugar, a remnant from better times, hidden for an emergency by Sarah Beile. Before she tied the bundle she held up two silver spoons and her wedding ring.

David examined the spoons and stuffed them into the bundle. He put the ring in his small pocket, unobserved.

"We found them wrapped up in old clothing, otherwise we would have contributed them to the fund," Rachel told David.

"You need not apologize, Rachel. Even if we had to give them a million golden spoons, they would still begrudge us one wooden spoon left in our possession. It's late. Who has the time?"

"I have it," came a weak echo from Abba Dunsky, who had just come with Koppel and Ben Zion. "It is 10:20. Still enough time." He began to wind his nickel-plated vest pocket watch.

"Not much time left," Burka said impatiently.

"What time is it going to be?" Abba asked. "Can I take these along?" He pointed to two bulging portfolios and books.

"At what place in the wall will the breach be made?" Koppel inquired.

"Have we enough provisions and clothing?" Ben Zion was concerned.

David did not answer as he laid out an oil skin on the floor in order to see what could be wrapped up in it in the event it would have to be buried or put in a damp place. There was a flask of whiskey, a honey jar, a medicinal tube labelled iodine and bandages. Questions descended upon his ears, but he was in a trance of bliss. He was aware of Rachel and her graceful movements as she and Abba checked on the important items: bread for a day or two, a Torah, and a small prayer book.

"We'll start in a few minutes," he calmed their anxiety. "We leave all our possessions behind, except for a few things. Nobody knows what is important. I asked Shmuel, who worked out this plan, to check the section of the new cemetery bordering on Beryl's yard. Ordinarily this corner inside the wall is guarded at most by two soldiers or police. But since quite a few Jews broke out through this spot recently, we don't know what to expect. We'll have to go through the potato cellar in the yard. It is about ten meters from the wall. We'll dig a trench about two meters deep and go underneath. You'll find two shovels, a pail and a mason hammer and some boards to shore up the tunnel, which I have prepared in the cellar. Also three candles and several sacks of straw."

"What about the Torah?" Koppel inquired.

"I'm putting you in charge of the Holy Scroll—let one who can run farthest carry it. If one falls, you assign it to the next one to carry it."

"Why doesn't the Dombrowa group join us?" Alter inquired.

"Impossible, too many, a panic will result, and tragedy."

"There aren't too many going," Ben Zion said.

"It is true," Koppel seconded. "Rabbi Kalir is sick."

"We'll have to carry him on our shoulders," Alter said.

"They all say it is suicide to escape," Dunsky added.

"We must escape," David said gesturing with a closed fist.

"Escape into what? David, I'm going along, but I have certain doubts," Ben Zion spoke up. "Where can old men, women, children, girls, and starved sick people go?"

"Escape into the forest, the countryside and into the marshes; join the partisans like Label if you wish; assume different names and appearances."

"David," Koppel reasoned, "we have no right to ask Jews to risk their lives in vain. How long will we last in a forest? How many farmers will give us shelter?"

"He is telling you the truth," Ben Zion pressed his point, "we'll be tracked and hunted down by German soldiers and Polish renegades. Most of us will never survive for more than a few days in the cold dampness and hatred surrounding us all."

"And I wouldn't even trust the friendly peasants around here; they're all enemies," Burka said.

"You mustn't use such words. It is against our faith to lose hope. God waits for an evil man to repent, even one day before he dies," Koppel pleaded.

"It is also said that evil men don't repent even before the gates of Gehennam," David said, and turned to Abba: "What time is it?"

"10:30," Dunsky read on the dial.

"At 10:45 the guards will change," David said and wrapped up his and Rachel's sacks, knotted them and straightened himself up. "The night guard sometimes comes late and drunk on Friday nights."

"Let's hope they'll do it again tonight," Burka remarked. "When do we start?"

"I'm waiting for Shmuel. There he is."

"There are Germans with dogs in the cemetery," Shmuel reported, out of breath. "The Dombrowa group that escaped through Beryl's yard ran into trouble. Two were shot; I don't know how many got away."

"We'll have to change our plan," David said.

"We can go through Isaac's or Noske's yard," Shmuel suggested.

"Isaac's garden will give us better cover." David made the decision. "It has a high fence lined with trees all the way to the wall. To get out we'll have to dig only a few meters under the wall."

"It's time," Burka reminded David.

"Let's go," David gave the order. "It is ten fifty. The guards just changed."

On the way to Isaac he went over again with Shmuel the rest of the plan. They were to proceed to Grabetzki because his house was practically hidden in a wooded valley. If they encountered difficulties they would try to find shelter at Franik across the river. They would also seek shelter at Kazarnik and Zemski, with whom they bartered lately. As a last resort they would seek temporary refuge at Potocki's cottage or nearby at the estate now managed by his former valet, the collaborator Basenko, which was frequented by German officers celebrating and fox hunting on weekends. No one would therefore suspect Jews hiding out there.

It was now past eleven. Kagan, the druggist, and his wife Zirel, showed up. They finally found a home for their baby at Adolph Kislo, near Yatvietz. The appointed time of twelve was ticking closer. David was still waiting for Rabbi Kalir when Alter's young son, Joshua, arrived in a disturbed condition. The *rebetzin* delayed the Rabbi, but with the help of Zorach, Alter's older son, she was to join them within a short time.

"Start moving." David signalled with his hand toward the kitchen door and the yard where the earthen cellar was shrouded in a mist. David wiped the window and mumbled, "This will have to clear up. Let me remind you again," his voice was tense, "we will start in about ten minutes. Only don't alarm the guards. Step lightly—no noise—even a cough or a sneeze is dangerous." The pressure was building up.

"We are about ready," David prompted Burka, as he put a blacksmith's pair of pliers into the sack.

"You see this," Burka explained. "It isn't just a tool—it is a weapon. Even a cane is something. Don't depend on prayers. They'll be waiting for us at the crossroads, and even from behind crosses."

"What do you mean?"

"I mean, you can't trust anybody, even one who kneels in front of a cross can betray us; and from behind the cross, they'll watch to see if we kneel down—that's how they can tell if we are Jews or not."

David spotted Avreml and he bristled with frustration. "I said everyone must fight. You're not taking him along?" he said to Rachel. "We agreed, no children." He pointed to Avreml who eagerly followed every move and now began to strap his school bag on his back.

"Avreml, I know you are brave, but first we have to help the adults to escape, before we take a chance with children," David broke the bad news to him as painlessly as words allowed.

"We made arrangements for you at Malinoski's, Avreml,"

Rachel soothed him and stroked his hair away from his wet eyes.

"My son, Avreml, you must be saved," Sarah began to cry.

"No tears, now," David rebuked her, afraid to face her as he turned around.

"We have no right to risk anyone's life, only we have no other way; we'll be chased and if we slow down, just for one second, we'll be lost," he said to Rachel.

"But he is young and strong. He'll keep up with us, and if he can't, I'll carry him."

"I don't care who carries him, he can't come along. You forget, Rachel," he took her aside, "that he can't speak Polish. Everyone we select for the first attempt can shift for himself, and pose as a Pole. Avreml is smart and fleet, but he is too young to endanger his life."

"What about Rabbi Kalir?" Abba asked.

"I am certain he will join us, to demonstrate to others how to escape—even at the risk of his own life."

"Ben Zion, did Label come with you?" David asked aware that he was missing.

"No, he said he couldn't leave his sick wife behind. But he still wants to join the partisans."

"David, you are cruel. See what you have done to him," Rachel said and pointed to Avreml, who broke away from his mother and pressed against the wall.

"Avreml, I want to talk to you," David took him aside. "You will stay with your mother or go to Malinoski with your sisters," he handed him over to Sarah Beile, who hugged him tightly and soothed him.

"No, I want to go with you," he followed David.

"Mother, come with me," Rachel cried out, "I can't let her go back," she appealed to David.

"Do you want to risk the lives of all these people?" David pleaded with her.

"Are you the law? Let's wait for the Rabbi's decision."

"We're all waiting for the Rabbi. Please Rachel, try to understand that we are pursued and hounded by vicious animals. We can't even think straight."

"Mother I don't care what anybody does or says. I'll get you and Avreml back."

"Rachel, you forget I left the twins behind. Don't wait for me. If God wills it, we'll be together again."

"Mamma, Mamma." Rachel cried to herself. She wanted to burst out, like a flood, with tears. Wherever she turned and groped for an answer, a wall sprang up in front of her.

"Let's get going. Ben Zion, go and get the Rabbi; we can't wait much longer. Alter, gather all the provisions; take along only the necessary things. We've got to travel light. Now, Reb Koppel, you know the forest. You will take us through its hidden tracks. We are ready! Reb Koppel, wait a minute." He signalled to everyone to lie down, as a light swept across from the guard's tower outside the wall.

"Something is wrong!" Burka clenched his teeth.

"It is nothing," David said. "The guards have the jitters, too. Everyone go into the cellar and wait."

"Where is Rachel?" he asked. He surmised by the distance she kept from him that she was very angry over Avreml. It was an awful responsibility to decree who should be saved and who should be left behind.

Within tense seconds they slipped out like shadows into the garden. David began to go through his pockets and he looked at his wrist watch. Twice he raised his wrist to his ear to make sure it was the ticking of the timepiece and not his heart. He gave the order to start digging.

"I have come myself," Rabbi Kalir, who arrived all worn out, announced.

"Where is Ben Zion? I sent him to help you."

"He'll be here. Zion," he punned, "will always be with us. We must not wait for Zion to come to us, we must pursue her. This is what I'm going to tell you. Escape to the outside."

Out in the garden, everyone worked or moved lithely and cautiously. There seemed to be nervous activity on the outside. Echoes from the guards' booths moving in all directions made them crouch against the shadows of the wall. Lights went on and off. Somewhere a motor coughed, sputtered and died down.

"How much more?" David asked after half an hour of continuous digging.

"About two meters," Alter, puffing heavily and wiping his sweat, replied, and resumed the digging.

"Let's change hands," David took charge as he relieved Alter and gave Dunsky's shovel to Burka.

The excavating took longer than expected. No one stopped for a moment. Label dug methodically with a third shovel.

"Looks like clay—it's hard to dig," Label said. "We need a pick and more time. We have another meter to dig."

"There is no time, out of the tunnel, quick!" "Let's try the fence." He said to Alter, "find a weak spot." Alter pressed his nose against the pine planks. "Here, this one," he said and pointed to one board that was loose.

"Let's force it," David suggested. He, Burka and Shmuel tried, but they could not knock out the plank. Alter tried next, but his massive body was wedged tight.

"Burka, Shmuel and I will go over the top," David said. "You'll push him from behind and we'll pull him." David and Shmuel climbed over.

"Ready," he commanded in a low tone. Burka took a shovel, sank it into the pile of sand and, with his back towards Alter, he pressed and pressed but without budging him.

"Alter, you must relax," David told him. He signaled to Burka to try once more, while he and Shmuel would pull simultaneously. Burka rammed his body sideways, and Alter fell through, wincing in pain but uninjured.

They waited, outside the wall. There was no one in sight. The moon began to hide behind fast-moving clouds. From the far side of the fence a shadow moved around the corner. They breathed easier when it proved to be only the shadow of a stray cat. A chained dog barked intermittently.

"This way," David directed them to the bushes that extended outside Isaac's barn, "then through the willow trees. We'll move through this cover toward the river and turn right alongside the highway. Move separately."

The sharp rebound of a broken branch frightened everyone. It was quiet until a burst of a spinning motor charged through the air, followed by a motorcycle's explosive blast.

"Move fast," David almost raised his voice, while the motorcycle rolled on with a deafening roar. "Wait!" It was coming around towards them through the new cemetery. They all crouched behind felled trees. David ran ahead, waving them on frantically, as they halted.

"Shmuel, I will return within an hour. Don't wait for me if I'm late. If I don't return, move on into the forest left of the windmills toward the colonies of Okop and then to Grabetzki according to your plan."

"What about you? We can't leave you!" Abba protested.

Without answering, David reversed his direction towards

the breach in the wall. He passed through Isaac's yard across to Hershke's orchard and past his own house, now occupied by Polish police, to the former Branfman stucco house converted into a sanatorium. He was completely exhausted when he reached the whitewashed sanatorium, standing out like a white shadow in the midst of darkness.

"I came to see my parents. They are sick. They called for me," he told the guards who ordered him to raise his hands while they examined his "Schutz Carte."

"This is only good for the day when you work. There are no civilians here. This place is reserved for wounded soldiers. Stay here, I'll check," one of the guards said to him.

Suddenly David felt the cold sweat of imminent danger, as he realized that perhaps the decreed day of exiling the Jews had already begun.

"I must run," he muttered to himself.

"Hey you, stop!" the *gendarme* yelled and fired. A bullet whistled close by his eardrum. He kept on running past the brick synagogue, through the driveway that led to the fields, straight towards the windmill. He kept on running and panting until he reached the shallow sand drifts and sought the cover of the clay pit ridge in front of the windmill. Beyond, the horizon began to change rapidly from grey to a deep, radiant blue. The rear of the group was waiting for him.

"Shmuel, get them moving." David was angry that they had risked their own safety for him. He cocked his ears to sharp barks of pursuing dogs and the whirring sound of motors.

"Don't worry," Shmuel said, "these Germans—the kind in this town—don't like to be disturbed at night."

"I tell you, they are awake," he was annoyed.

"Maybe these are different Germans," Ben Zion remarked. "Are those trucks?" he referred to the running motors.

"Yes, several trucks. They were moving wounded soldiers into the sanitorium. They removed all the sick Jews."

"What does that mean, David?" Abba asked.

"I am not a prophet," David replied, reticent to predict a final exodus.

"You don't have to be a prophet," Koppel said and shook the dust from his boots. "It is not good."

"Alongside the ravine," David shepherded them, "be careful of stones and fallen trees."

"I have gone far enough, David," the Rabbi said. "I am returning to my people."

"Why?" David asked in amazement.

"My Rebetzin is still there."

"We'll take her along."

"No, Zorach would have brought her by this time, she is too
weak to keep pace with us."

"We'll arrange for her to hide meanwhile."

"They'll be coming to our houses looking for you and me . . ."

"They'll not know for some time that I'm gone. Von Preissig
will be embarrassed to admit to Schwarzhund that his only hope
bolted."

"If I do not return, the Germans will come to investigate. They
have been coming regularly since Judah escaped from Agustowa
and joined Reuvke and Chantze on the way to Zion. I have come
to bless you."

"But Rabbi Kalir, you are our captain. How can we save anybody without you, our guide and teacher, the most valuable?"
David interceded.

"Stop this!" There is no such thing as most valuable. Every
Jew and every person in the world, is valuable."

"If all are valuable, then let us decide rather than you,
whether you are worth being saved," Reb Koppel suggested.

"Don't be stubborn. Every Jew is as good as the other. This is
the greatness of our religion. Every man is precious. This is what
we have tried to teach the nations, for several thousand years.
We have no right to classify: This one to be saved and this one to
be sacrificed. The heathen and criminal governments are the
ones who apply this law of Sodom and Amhara; to starve, torture
and kill innocent people by the thousands and millions. All
beings are equal before God and have equal rights on this earth
to live in peace."

David was amazed to hear the same thoughts which he expressed verified by the Rabbi as authentic.

"Rabbi Kalir," David pleaded, "I beg you once more. My conscience, our conscience, will never be clear if we abandon you to
these beasts."

"What about all the Jews?"

"We are saving whomever wants to be saved, and whomever
will follow our example."

"And whomever God wants to save," Reb Koppel added.

"Don't condemn God," Rabbi Kalir dissented. "If evil people destroy us, God is not to be blamed but rather these people who commit the crimes, because God is not in them."

"Let's go!" David ordered. "Everyone within sight must walk or be carried. We are not going to leave behind any hostages.

"If you are ordering me," Rabbi Kalir countered, "I refuse. I'm still your Rabbi, and I still hold my life in my hands; don't feel badly." He gazed at every face and offered prayerful words. "Remember the beautiful Sabbaths, the love of learning from our books, the voices of our prayers. Remember how we walked with God. Even if as human beings, we faltered occasionally, we were still better than our neighbors. We always got up to walk with pride and strength that comes from a pure life." He waited for an eternity of seconds and then realized that it was he who must pray for each.

"Don't cry, Rachel," he spoke kindly and turned her tears into dew upon her face. He continued his farewell by calling everyone by name. He then embraced each in turn. "You too!" he called Burka. "God forgives, especially mistakes, but not the unrepentant criminals who are after us."

He now resumed once more, with a choked voice, "It is dark there" he pointed to the forest, "but across the darkness is the Promised Land. This is what Moses saw in his last moments on Mount Nebo. He stayed behind with all those who could not go to the promised land. These people are worthier than the desert generation, and I cannot even be compared with Moses. Shall I not remain to share their lot?"

Rabbi Kalir began to move his lips in silent prayer. There was what seemed to David a long silence, then he appealed to him:

"Come, Rabbi Kalir, come, I beg you."

"No, David, please David, I am your Rabbi."

"This is different."

"I have not abdicated my authority to any one."

"I am only in command to save, to save your life."

"God alone is in command. I, and all the people who can't escape, place ourselves under his protecting wings. Go now and may God safeguard you to the land of our fathers."

David was bitterly disappointed. He was more determined to save the Rabbi than to save himself.

"I was under the impression," he began to reiterate his dependence on the Rabbi, when the Rabbi cut in:

"That I would go with you?"

"Yes."

"I suppose you think that I'm not consistent. I joined only to encourage those who wanted to escape. I never promised that I would go beyond this point."

"I just can't figure this out," David told him.

"Life, my life, has always been governed by a verdict, a decision. But sometimes there is no decision."

"But law, your world of law, requires a decision."

"Only if there is a conflict between right and wrong, but not when you have a choice of two roads in order to escape from the disaster of the third. Save whomever you can. Wake up the world. Whatever is left. Go to Zion, Messiah—the beginning, the Messiah, occurs when strife and hatred and bloodshed caused by wars comes upon us. You will live, you must live to see Zion's rebirth in the land of Israel."

"I don't understand," David was again dubious.

"If we expect the Messiah, we wait. We just can't run to him. The same if we expect something final, you can't run away from it—you stand by—you face it."

"But. . . ."

"David, you are going to tell me that bravery tells you to risk, to rebel. That is one kind. If I am ready to await my creator, I must also be ready to await anything else. I feel it my duty to remain with these people. They are also brave. It isn't only those who resist with weapons and fight to be victorious over the hated enemy. There is as much, or even more, bravery in those who without weapons and without any prospect of physical victory, defy the abominable enemy, and triumphantly and without fear walk into the valley of death."

The Rabbi backed away several paces. He stopped near a massive oak tree and began to recite the sixty-eighth Psalm.

"Let God arise, let his enemies be scattered; let them also that hate him flee before him. . . ." David stood there fixed as though enraptured by his saintly image in the sunlit reflection. The shadows cast by the swaying trees pointed toward him as he and Zorach turned their faces on the road back to the walled city.

The horizon was all aflame, clear and crisp as if washed after the weary night. It was the first time for most to have been out all night, not knowing what was ahead of them during this uncertain day.

They sat down to rest on a fallen tree. On the moss and needle covered ground, the fog still clung in shrouded patches to the ground. More and more of the sun's rays began to put the darkness to rout. Birds danced up and down on top of bushes and trees. Now was the time for birds to find their food, sing and play during their well-filled day.

Everyone looked tired and hungry. By this time their escape must have been discovered. There would be the alarm followed by pursuit. But there was no time for food as long as they were within barking distance of the town.

"We will have to cross the length of the forest before we get to the Okop colonies," he told them as they stopped for instructions.

Koppel's eyes were always on the alert, for though he was familiar with every stump and huckleberry patch, he knew that brigands and renegades lurked in the shadows of the forest.

"This way," David pointed to his right as they were stopped by a barricade of dead branches and a pile of stones on the parapet. He turned his eyes to the mound of stones. He remembered when he used to go picking huckleberries. He was certain he never saw this pile before.

The morning sun began to bathe the sparse woods, stumps and uprooted trees that formed the rim of the forest. In the distance, the sun, now straightening out toward their faces, began to throw glowing rays that bounced on and off from something in the distance.

Koppel blinked, as he rubbed his eyes, and said, "I can't see it but it must be the Okop colonies. There is Grabetzki's house."

As they came nearer the large estate of Pan Grabetzki, they faced a reception of the dog barking for a cue from his master to wag its tail or tear into them. *Pan* Grabetzki stopped near the well—his wife and children looking on in amazement. The dog bowed in submission, still growling as it gestured with its tail a begrudged welcome.

"*Panie* Koppel," he mumbled belatedly and eyed suspiciously the others, who remained outside the gate.

"We need shelter, *Panie* Grabetzki."

"I have no room."

"We'll pay well, sleep anywhere, even in the barn."

"It is crowded with cattle."

"How about there?" he inquired about the wooden shed astride a luxurious stretch of tobacco land in the rear.

"Neighbors come to look around, it is not safe."

"We'll stay overnight and then move on."

"I can't be responsible, it is dangerous."

"We'll pay. We'll pay for the food and shelter."

Reb Koppel called the group. He and David led them toward
the rear. All around them were walls of trees to give them privacy and protection. Inside were long rows of tall stemmed
tobacco plants that would cover up their presence.

Shmuel and Burka, meanwhile, looked around for sacks. They
found one in the big barn behind the main house. They stuffed it
with hay and brought it to the shed.

David pushed open the door of the shed, creaking on its rusty
hinges.

"Too much sun," Koppel observed.

"It is healthy," Rachel admired the profusion of light.

"Not for us," Koppel said. "It is good in normal times. Anything that comes from above in normal times is good, but now it
exposes us to danger."

"I understand," Rachel agreed. "We can cover the shed with
foliage."

"Yes, let's cover it with pine branches, like a *sucah*. I can also
build a table and benches; there are boards behind the shed,"
Alter said, eager to help with his skill.

"Good, as long as we don't attract anybody's attention," Koppel agreed. He removed his coat, hung it on a spike and went
outside to help.

Alter found one sawhorse and Burka found another under a
pile of wood. They put down three rough planks across the racks
and gave it the shape of a long table. Kagan's wife took out a
sheet and spread it over the top.

"We'll need it for sleeping," Rachel said concerned with its
clean appearance.

"Now we are eating," Kagan's wife said. "One worry at a
time."

Shmuel indicated which food to unpack. He told the women
that there was enough bread on hand for a day, and he was
negotiating with Grabetzki for additional supplies. He did not
explain that it was out of the question to prepare hot meals or
even simple potato and cereal soups. They had neither food nor
utensils, and a fire indoors or outdoors would have given them
away to informers and Germans continually hunting for Jews
who had escaped. Burka, who came back with a bunch of carrots

which he pulled out from the garden, was now the center of attention.

"It's not right to take things by yourself," Koppel remarked. "You remember the *Megillah?*" When the Jews triumphed over Haman and the hordes whom he instigated, Scripture emphasizes: *'uvabizo lo sholchu es yodom,'* they did not loot, although this was usual in all wars. I promised Grabetzki that we would pay for anything we got."

"Pay him?" Burka was indignant. "How do you know his house isn't full of Jewish goods? He and many others have pillaged and robbed our people and you quibble with an ancient verse?"

"Burka, a law is a law," Koppel said. "We are different from the *goyim*, who make and break laws to suit themselves. Our Torah is very strict. Shmuel, what do we have for bartering purposes?"

"Not much."

"Once we start paying with our last precious items, he'll demand more and more and we haven't got it," David said. "Suppose we offer him our properties with a pre-dated bill of sale, but meanwhile, let's honor our word."

"As far as tonight is concerned, we'll have to pay him with whatever we have," Shmuel conceded.

"This is a well hidden place but I don't trust him. We'll find out soon enough when we ask him to sell us food," David said.

They all sat down to the first wholesome meal that they had had in two years. No one knew if they would ever sit again together, but at least temporarily, they were granted a reprieve from the relentless and suffocating siege encroaching upon them everywhere.

Reb Koppel began to say grace, as the last bread slices were carefully wrapped by Rachel and Kagan's wife folded the white sheet. Everything was repacked for instant mobility in case of an emergency.

"Hey you," a boyish voice called from the outside.

"What is your name?" David asked the small boy.

"Jerzy. Why do you hide in this shed? Are you robbers, or thieves from the forest?"

"We are good people, the best," David said. He recalled nostalgically that once this was amusing, now it was a grim exchange.

"But my big brother is a policeman. He has a gun and he said he'll shoot all robbers and thieves."

"Jerzy, get away from there. Go to mother," Grabetzki surprised his son.

"I've come to tell you," he said to Shmuel aside, "that I'm willing to sell you eggs and turnips. But I want real money."

"Zlotys and marks?"

"No good. I can't buy anything with these. I want gold."

"We have no gold."

"Silver, jewelry."

"All gone."

"Then I can't sell you anything," Grabetzki said coldly.

"*Panie* Grabetzki, be good to us, we'll reward you," Koppel said.

"You can keep God's rewards for yourself," he turned away.

"Here, I'll give you my watch, take it. This we owe you for food and shelter tonight. If you let us stay longer, I'll sell you a part of my forest or any other property."

"*Panie* Koppel, I thought you were a smart man."

"I'll give you a bill of sale dated as of 1939."

"It's no good," Grabetzki said and spit on the floor.

"When peace comes, I'll pay you any price."

"No! I want gold, silver and jewelry. Let me know tonight," Grabetzki said and left.

"I heard everything," David said. "Isn't his son mixed up with the Germans?"

"Probably," Shmuel said.

"We've got to get out before morning," David insisted. "Franik is a short distance over the marshes."

"I could find my way to Franik in the dark," Koppel said. Having failed to find refuge at Grabetzki's, he was determined to see Franik. The rebuke by a Pole who was secure from raids in an isolated valley did not discourage him. There must be good people, he believed, unless it is so bad and the world is coming to an end. While David stepped inside with Shmuel to tell the group that they would have to leave their refuge, Koppel started out on his mission.

"Reb Koppel, where are you going?" Ben Zion stopped him on the way to the woods.

"I'll be back," he said, and vanished into the shadows.

July 31, 1942:   RUSSIANS PUSH BACK FOE. STALIN
                 FORBIDS RETREAT.

*The Holy One, blessed be He, said: I cannot
look at the wicked.*

Sabbath, 104.

25

GODS WITH MURDERERS' FACES

The sun was now in all its brilliance when Koppel, slipped un-observed through Franik's spacious garden from the rear. He was tired and thirsty when he came upon the farmer harnessing a horse to a loaded wagon in his fenced-in yard.

"A very beautiful garden!" Koppel complimented Franik, who supplied him for years with grain cereals and vegetables, and with fruit during the summer.

"The apples and pears are all rotting. Nobody wants to buy them. The Jews were my customers, they bought all the food-stuffs—the Germans want it for nothing," Franik explained.

Franik posed the question, "A drink of water?"

Koppel said to Franik, "Please."

"Get inside before my neighbors see you," he warned Koppel. "I'll get through loading." Koppel remembered that Franik's atti-tude toward Jews was determined primarily by his experiences with them as a supplier to good customers. He always thought that Jews, like God, were to be taken for granted; both were hidden, mysterious; Jews were tolerated as customers, envied as artisans and begrudged as shopkeepers, but when it came to religion, it ranged from respect to blind hatred. He thought the Jews got better results from their religion. They were successful in keeping themselves apart with their own laws, schools, lan-guage and religious practices. Their very success served as a pretext for anti-semitic Polish leaders to incite their people against the Jews.

Franik finished with his loading. "I'll plant some and hide the rest of the potatoes in the cellar behind the river. It may rot—but they take everything away. Come with me," he called him

347

into the house. Koppel sat down at the table in the kitchen. There was no-one else in the house.

"They are in the fields," meaning his wife and children. "It's much safer for them to be away from the house. Germans draft all women and men found not doing anything, for work. Sometimes, they send them away, and they never return," he sighed.

"I know," Koppel nodded.

"*Panie* Koppel, you are a learned Jew; you know all the books," Franik twitched his brow. "You believe in God now, too?"

"We always do."

"Then you must ask him why he doesn't fight the Germans."

"We do."

"Then you criticize God?"

"No! We explain God."

"How?"

"If Germans kill innocent people—Jews and others; if Poles collaborate with them and also kill innocent people; and if those who should have stopped it say God didn't stop it, why should we; then we criticize and reject such a God with the face of a German or a Polish murderer."

"*Panie* Koppel," Franik rubbed his forehead, "isn't it written that many shall die?"

"Written, where?"

"In the Bible, in holy books."

"This is all nonsense. Anyone who uses the Bible or its quotations to kill thousands, is speaking evil and nonsense."

"But the Bible is holy, God's word."

"It is holy, yes, if used to save lives. God is God when he is a father, but when God becomes the voice of murderers, then he is no God."

"How do you know?"

"This is what our Rabbi says, and he is as learned and wise as any of your greatest or holiest men."

"The Rabin is a good man, a wise and learned man, but . . . ," Franik was searching.

"You see, Franik," he wanted to put it in the simplest language, "can God prevent typhoid in wartime when soldiers live in dirty trenches, civilians have no food, the wounded soldiers die, and the refugees starve? It happened in your village in the First World War: scores died and the disease spread to our town to kill even more Poles and Jews. Who killed them?"

"Baskets of fish which my villagers caught in the river, ate themselves, and sold it in town. They were spoiled."

"The fish didn't spoil, Franik, they were caught in the water after the corpses of Russian soldiers were dumped in the river. There was plenty of blood. Human blood spread the disease. Is God to blame for that shedding of blood? Is it wrong to criticize a God who is imagined as a criminal by those who are the criminals?"

"No, *Panie* Koppel."

"I must ask you, Franik, if we are in danger, will you help?"

"It all depends."

"We may have to hide in your place. Of course, we'll pay for everything in good money."

"I'll sell you food. Where are you staying now?"

"We need shelter and food," he told him without replying directly.

"Oh, you ran away, I suppose. They must be looking for you. That is different, very dangerous for me."

"For all of us."

"For me, especially. You see the wagon? I'm trying to hide the food myself. They come searching."

"Even here?"

"All the time, searching. You never can tell when they'll come here. Not safe here—maybe another time. I must put the wagon away. Soon my son will come from the field—he doesn't like strangers."

"We are not strangers."

"All Jews are strangers to him."

It was late, toward evening, when Koppel returned to Grabetzki's shed and found the group very concerned after these frustrations. Sarah Beile and Avreml returned, after a narrow escape, together with Zorach and Kagan. She told how Malinoski's neighbors threatened to hand her over to the Germans unless she gave them money. She took the twins to Levandovski, who accepted them on a temporary basis. Then she and Avreml plodded for five kilometers in the darkness along the highway; crouching and lying still whenever military trucks passed through. At Yatvietz, she knocked on the door of Turel, who told her that other Jews were staying at Adolph Kislo's. There she found Elyeh

Schuster's baby son, Ami, in his small bedroom and Kagan and
Zorach in his potato cellar.

"A little trouble," David whispered. Ben Zion looked through
the paneless opening toward the darkening blue over the forest.
Zirel and Rachel were arranging and sorting the few things in
their possession. Avreml was anxious and restless.

"I wish I could do something," he told his mother, as she
prepared a soup from carrots and potatoes.

"Just rest," Sarah Beile kept on saying.

"I rest all the time. I'm tired from resting."

Abba was correcting a letter. Only Burka Mazik had his back
turned to everyone.

"He wants to do something unusual," David told them.

"All I want is to save you from starvation," Burka said grimly.
"A statue wouldn't miss the eye."

"He wants to steal an eye from the Madonna in Church and
exchange its ruby for food," David explained.

"Burka, that's bad," Koppel reproved him, shaking his head.

"What's bad? I have always been told that anything we possess should be thrown in to save even one life."

"Do you know, Burka, this will arouse the hatred of the Poles
even more than now, and they'll kill every one of us."

"Kill everyone for a piece of stone? Isn't one finger worth more
than all the statues on earth? You said it, David, you were proud
to tell it to Von Preissig."

"I did. That is correct. Anything made from wood, stone or
even gold and diamonds should be sacrificed to save even a
finger made by God himself. We Jews believe that life has priority
over any material. But these people have been led to believe that
this statute is holy and therefore more important than the lives
of Jews."

"As long as we have anything left for barter, we'll get food,"
Koppel said.

"What have we got left? Tell him, Shmuel. You are in charge
of all our funds."

"We have only two watches, a ring, and the clothes we carry
on our backs, according to Reb Koppel, who is the treasurer."

"Reb Koppel, from what you told me, Franik was not encouraging. The most immediate problem is to find a place after we
leave Grabetzki."

"I'll find a place," Burka said. "I know a horse skinner. I'll give
him a horse as a gift."

"How will you get a horse?"

"It is not right," Koppel protested.

"You, with your old-fashioned laws again? Do you want to die?"

"Burka, a law is not something written down and forgotten. It must be repeated and enforced." Koppel rebuked him. "We are Jews always guided by God and his laws. You see over there that gully, the yellow sand all washed away? I remember when clover grew there. Trees alongside were cut down and the soil just drifted away. See the edge of the forest—you don't see tall oaks or beautiful, slender birch, or massive poplars, just stumpy pine trees. Yet, they form a protection, a wall, a screen against the wind and rain, protection against storms. They may look old-fashioned, like these scrawny trees, but they do the job."

"Do you want to die?" Burka asked scornfully.

"We live and we die for God's law—the Torah," Koppel spelled out the words. "As long as there is a Torah, there are laws by which we are guided."

"Do all the nations respect such laws?"

"We cannot answer for them—let each nation answer for itself before God. Thus, the German nation bloodied our sacred laws and threw into the gutter their own laws. On Crystal night, November 9, 1938, after a seventeen-year-old Jewish boy shot a German in the Paris embassy, the Nazis instigated mobs in all German cities to an orgy of murder, looting and violence which has not yet stopped. Ever since I remember, Jewish blood was shed on certain Christian holidays; during Christmas and Easter celebrations. Jewish history records many pogroms and even blood libels that took place during these seasons. Now this is going on day after day and night after night. Only God knows the end."

"Reb Koppel, I am going to Kazarnik," David said abruptly.

"Why not Burka?"

"He has made several trips to get food; it is my turn now."

"I could be back before nightfall," David said. "Kazarnik's farm near the Okop colonies is only a few miles through Pokosne, maybe two hours. He was a friend of my father."

"I'll go with you," Avreml jumped up from under a cover.

"It's dangerous for you."

"I can run, and when I slow down, I can walk a long distance."

"Avreml, there are other problems."

"What?"

"You have to go without food for days."

"I can pick fruit from a tree, and green pea pods from the fields."

"You'll have to sleep in the forest, or even in a ditch."

"I'm not afraid. I can crawl into a hay stack."

"The farmers have vicious dogs."

"Not all dogs bite!"

"But all bark. Do you know what it means to hold your breath, and freeze to the roll of every drifting leaf? Rachel, I'm glad you came to take him back. I don't want to say it, but I must. Death will wait with a thousand eyes from behind every bush."

"You are frightening him," Rachel pressed him closer to herself. "He is very determined and unafraid. At the same time, he does not want to be separated from me or his mother."

"The Germans know it too well, that is why they are counting on the fact that few of us will dare to leave their families behind to save themselves."

"But didn't you say we should take along everyone that can walk, run or even be carried."

"Children are a problem. If we take them along, we risk their lives and our lives."

David removed his felt hat and tie. "Burka, give me your peasant's jacket," he asked him, "and watch Avreml."

"I'll stay here for a while. I know how to get certain things," Burka muttered to himself.

David broke off a branch from one of the fallen trees behind the shed and began to make his way through the copse and then through the forest. There was a road on the other side, but there were crucifixes and much traffic of official cars commuting between Suha-Vali and Sokolke, where the district commissioner of occupation resided. He was tired and hungry. He remembered someone's advice never to move without some bread and water in his possession. He sat down to rest on a stump near a water hole. He bent on his knee and began to lap the water.

"Don't," someone cried. "You can't be on the side of God if you kneel and lap like a dog. You have to cup the water with your hand, it says so in the Bible."

"What are you doing here, Avreml?" he was more enraged than startled. "Does your mother know? You are a foolish boy."

"Please, David, I want to go with you. I'll get sick, all these months not doing anything, not learning, no friends. I've got to do something."

"Promise me that you won't do it again."

"I promise, and I'll pray too, except I haven't my own prayer book."

"All right, follow me."

After several hours of walking and avoiding the main road, they encountered their first frightening moments. One kilometer from Pokosne, David suddenly pulled Avreml down and put his hand over the boy's mouth. David saw a head pop up and stare from behind the crucifix on a tree at the bend of the road. Avreml froze. David waited and then by-passed it to avoid trouble.

He stopped in front of the gate. Several dogs raced forward, barking furiously. Kazarnik, his mouth full of food, and his gawky sons, came out to meet them.

"What do you want?" he seemed angry and upset.

"I'm not asking for anything. We'll pay for any favor," he changed to the plural to assure him of available money.

"Pay for what?" Kazarnik was impatient.

"We need shelter for a few nights."

"How many?"

"Just give us a little space."

"I have no room."

"We'll sleep in your barn, in the hay loft, anyplace."

"No."

"You can say that we broke in at night if we get caught."

"No, I tell you, leave this house. The Germans will punish me." Kazarnik walked away.

"Popka," David spoke affectionately to the sandy-haired boy, "This is Avreml—your size—bring him a slice of bread, please."

"I can't."

"Bring him some water. He's thirsty."

Popka shook his head.

"Why?"

"Because they all say. . . ."

"Say what?"

"That Germans are going to kill you, and that we should join them," Popka said, and lowered his head.

Before Popka could raise his head, the harsh voice of Kazarnik summoned him back to the house.

David was on his way back to Grabetzki, without having found another refuge. Darkness was slipping through the fences and gardens of Pokosne and rolling on to the fields and marching steadily through the trees of the forest. Avreml stared apprehensively at the unknown shadows interlaced in the woods. Above, the branches waved like an endless overhanging canopy. A little star glimmered momentarily.

"How do they kill you?" Avreml suddenly broke the silence.

"Let's not talk about it."

"Did the boy say that Germans will kill us? Will they? Will they kill us with an ax?"

"No," he replied without being aware of his answer.

"With a bayonet?"

"No."

"And they don't poison you? Then with what?"

"With words," he found himself saying.

"I'm not afraid of words. I'll say my prayers. You'll help me."

"I thought you don't understand Polish."

"I can't speak it, but I understand enough."

"Let's go." He wondered if it would be safe to remain at Grabetzki's for another night.

Kommandant Von Preissig ate sparingly while his guest, S.S. Colonel Schwarzhund stuffed the food nervously into his mouth. He had come to warn Von Preissig that the last breakouts from the ghetto were a matter of great concern to him and to Kommandant Rintzler from Grodno in charge of all ghettos in the district.

"Herr Schwarzhund, have any of them really escaped?" he countered.

"Are you evasive or deliberately denying the truth?" Schwarzhund needled him.

"In the last six months quite a few of those who escaped from Agustowa and other work camps were never caught. On the other hand, most of those who got out of this ghetto were captured or killed by Poles. There is no escape for the remnant still at large. They are surrounded and will soon be in our hands."

"My men are in action at this very moment," Schwarzhund responded.

"It all depends on what you mean by 'in action.'"

"Whatever you think of them; they arrest and kill Jews."

"I believe in a correct discipline."

"Our strict methods have attained results, while your projects and theories—what have they accomplished?"

"I don't know what you are talking about . . ."

"You are very clever, I must admit, but we do know, from certain channels and officers, about opinions. . . ."

"What opinions?"

"Opinions of rank and file, officers, and those higher ups—we found out. . . ."

"Found out what?" Von Preissig began to lose his patience as he sensed that he was being cornered.

"They can't be trusted."

"What does that have to do with me?"

"You are one of them," Schwarzhund accused him.

"Are you drunk or mad?"

"Drunk perhaps, but not mad. We have all the information."

"You do?" Von Preissig groped for a straw.

"Yes, I do. You owe me your life," Schwarzhund told him bluntly, and threw him a lifeline which he could cut and let him drift or drown whenver Schwarzhund pleased.

The hours of this afternoon had begun to collapse on him. It was like the pill box in which he had found himself in on the eastern front. Everything inside, fellow officers, men, weapons and cement boulders came down as though crushed by the jaws of thunder. He sat there, utterly stunned by the suddenness of events. It was Colonel Stulpnagel who wrote to him long ago from Berlin that the "*Vaterland* is foremost in my heart." What about Admiral Canaris, head of Intelligence? "The Admiral inspires me to go on and hope for a brighter tomorrow, despite all reverses." That's it. It began to emerge. Hitler has not been heard from for weeks. He was supposed to address the Party for the winter rally. His voice on the radio? Must have been taped before last year, or some other time.

By the end of July, Von Preissig became panicky. A visit by Stulpnagel, or by his chauffeur, did not materialize. He received no message, no letters from Stulpnagel, nor from home. The daily snooping became unbearable. Schwarzhund's impudent at-

titude was a brutal warning that his days as the Kommandant of
Suha-Vali were numbered. He had already given up, almost en-
tirely, his master-plan to use Suha-Vali as an experiement to be
adopted by other camps and towns. It was out of his hands. He
conceded that he could do nothing against the over-all Nazi plan
to exterminate all Jews who had fallen into their hands. For a
while the Nazis told the Jews that their final destination was
working camps. But then reports of the death camps trickled
through to the intended victims. The Nazi hierarchy, apprehensive lest the Jews, in desperation, make suicidal attempts to free
themselves, began to speed up the schedule of the ghettos'
liquidation. Although the war industry complex employed Jews
and other nationalities as slave labor, Von Preissig had an inkling
from Gestapo maneuvering around Suha-Vali, from inquiries
about personnel to replace Jewish labor when these would rejoin
ghettos for removal to a final ghetto, that even those in the
employable category were also doomed.

There was nothing Von Preissig could do but wait, uneasily
and even resignedly. The course of the war, despite optimistic
announcements from Goebbels' office, was not going well. Certain
setbacks had been encountered. This was reflected in the contra-
dictory official and neutral bulletins, and in radio broadcasts.

Von Preissig had just sat down for lunch in his living room
when his orderly burst in nervously.

"There is somebody to see you." Through the screen of the
rear door Von Preissig recognized General Stulpnagel's chauffeur
stepping out of a military car.

"Have lunch ready for him," he instructed Ludke. After all, he
had a message from a friend. He needed the interval to check the
authenticity of the uniformed chauffeur.

"The chauffeur is in a hurry, he claims it is urgent, he wants to
present his credentials and message," Ludke rattled off his request.

"Let him come in." He pushed his tray away, and nervously
fingered the outline of a silencer gun in his chest pocket.

"Greetings from General Stulpnagel," the chauffeur saluted
stiffly—a bit too rigidly for a driver. He never had a good look at
the general's personal chauffeur. The identification card, plus a
personal letter addressed by the General to Von Preissig, was
reassuring. There was only one thing wrong with the letter; it
had an uncancelled stamp. The General had cautioned him on

his last visit that he should disregard anything not delivered by a special courier with a scar on his neck.

"General Stulpnagel asked me to apologize for not having mailed the letter first. He was engaged in an important conference." It sounded plausible, but his language and tone were too polished for a chauffeur. His eyes were deep-set, but something sinister seemed to be hidden in their intense staring. He added, after a pause, "The General, upon second thought, since this was so urgent, sent me to intercept it from the post; a letter is sometimes delayed in wartime." The word "intercept" had a strange connotation.

"Yes, of course, I understand. Before you depart, will you join me in a toast." Von Preissig said.

"*Jawohl*, but read the letter. I was instructed to get your written reply." The chauffeur responded nervously and came closer to Von Preissig's desk.

"That's very good. Before I read it, we'll have the toast, I'll get the cognac and the glasses." Von Preissig went to fetch them from the anteroom, leaving the door ajar. His ears were cocked to the crisp leafing of papers. Von Preissig returned and saw that the chauffeur's fingers were on the pages of a folder which he had just removed from his locked drawer in order to check the handwriting of the supposed general with an autographed signature. The chauffeur suddenly pulled his hand back; his elbow pushed the glass from his host, and the cognac spilled on his neck and collar.

"Ludke, a towel!" Von Preissig cried. He began to wipe the chauffeur's neck.

"Let me do it," Ludke was embarrassed.

"No, no, I made the mistake and I have to straighten it out." As he mopped the chauffeur's neck, he neither detected the scar just below the collar line nor the sting to which the chauffeur would react if he was the authentic emissary.

"Your real identity?" Von Preissig pulled out his gun and pointed it at the chauffeur's back.

"Here is my Gestapo identity card," the chauffeur went for his inside pocket, but before he had wheeled half-way around Von Preissig fired twice into the chauffeur's chest. The chauffeur staggered and fell limp over the carpet.

"We'll wait until nightfall and dispose of him in his own car near Potocki's estate."

NINE NATIONS BID U.S. WARN AXIS,
REFER TO BARBARIC ACTS COMMITTED
BY GERMANY IN OCCUPIED COUNTRIES.

*Woe unto the unredeemable, corrupt heathen
nations.*

Rosh Hashonah, 23.

26

SURROUNDED

Colonel Ludwig Schwarzhund followed up his rebuke to Von
Preissig for responsibility in the Jews' escape from the ghetto,
with action. *"Zum Teufel mit zeremonie,"* he told his henchmen
grimly. He sent out three search parties with Polish police attached as guides. Captain Messer, at the head of one group,
pursued the fugitives southeast toward Yanowa beyond the
Potocki estate. Lt. Schrecke hunted for Jews south and west in
the direction of Bialystok. Sgt. Murad closed the tightening
ring by stalking the escapees north among the hamlets on both
sides of the highway.

Grabetzki's older son who joined Skura with Murad's unit,
waited anxiously for the group to get started. Although he resented being called 'Pollack,' he finally began to see results.
Profits from acquiring Jewish property and inherited bias against
Jews lured him to the role of collaborator. Late in the afternoon,
after heavy drinking, Sgt. Murad and Sgt. Todt led the hunting
pack. When they reached the forest, a short distance from Grabetzki's farm, evening shadows crossed their path.

The forest cast an eerie glow over Grabetzki's wooden shed.
Within its cramped quarters, David, who had returned from a
futile search for a more secure haven, slept fitfully. The long
rows of tobacco breathed with ease as their flowering stems and
leaves slumbered beneath the vigilant stars. The moon above
was pale, mute, mysterious and indifferent.

Grabetzki was returning from the Monopol backroom where
he, Skura, Murad, and their German friends celebrated. There
was plenty of money for celebrations in the hands of German

359

and Polish profiteers who acquired Jewish property almost for nothing and resold it for rewarding prices.

The group was now near the bend of the road. They passed by the crucifix. Grabetzki steadied himself momentarily, but his right hand jerked up and then fell limply as he tried to make the sign.

"Why are you stopping here? Is there an inn here?" Murad asked as he hiccupped from excessive drinking.

"No, my friend," Skura replied, "but I have to stop. See the crucifix?"

"Who is that? What is he doing up there—maybe he is a Jew?" Murad asked.

"No, that can't be a Jew. We Poles put crucifixes in our churches, hang them on our walls and on trees along the road."

"What for?" Murad tried to hold on to the fence.

"What for? Like ikons, maybe for good luck. I don't know."

"Maybe bad luck," Murad teased Skura. "You know what they are? I'll tell you; Jews with Polish faces," Murad and Todt laughed convulsively, while Skura and Grabetzki hesitated for a moment and then joined in half-heartedly.

"You know what I am going to do? I'll aim at this one."

"You can't. I mean you mustn't. It is forbidden!" Skura tried to warn him.

"What do you mean, forbidden, you drunken swine?" and then, shifting his alcoholic mood, croaked "You are my pal; we're all pals, but watch, I'm still a good shot." He raised his gun and tried to aim, but he couldn't steady the barrel as he sighted it with his watery bloodshot eyes. He cursed and fired wildly.

"March!" he ordered, "How far are we from your hovel?" he asked Grabetzki.

"Not far."

"We could have come here in the morning. Why did we drink with these swine and then wind up here in the darkness?" Murad said to Todt.

"It was your idea to get the job done."

"Would Colonel Schwarzhund give up a night's sleep to hunt Jews? Why should we do it, we're Gestapo men who investigate and give orders. This is a job for soldiers and Pollacks."

"*Jawohl.*" Todt nodded, "Maybe we'll be rewarded?"

"There is a price on their heads, isn't it so, Pollacks," he turned to both in derision.

"We'll do our part to help you get rid of the Jews," Skura said.

"Good, I'll try again," he began to aim at the crucifix.

"It's dark," Grabetzki was apprehensive.

"Dark? there is the moon above, and doesn't it always show a ring of light above the Jew's head on the cross?"

"It's a son of God," Skura corrected.

"Whatever it is, I'll shoot."

"Don't!" Nicholas said and waved his hands in front of him.

"Get out of the way." Murad made no effort to aim and fired into the darkness. Grabetzki could almost see the weather-beaten gate and silvered crucifix hanging above it.

"You stay here—my people will be frightened—it is late," Grabetzki pleaded with Murad.

"You are correct. I respect people who sleep. Do your cows, chickens, and pigs get frightened, too?"

David, who heard their voices in the distance, was wide awake. When he heard the first shot he awoke Burka. Both roused all the others asleep in their clothing, and ordered them to grab their kits and get out as fast as they could.

Under pressure, Abba began to fumble for his manuscripts and bundle of books. Koppel gave the Torah to Hershke and then nervously searched for the velvet religious bag. Rachel put a warm coat on Sarah Beile and a blanket over Avreml's shoulders.

"This way," David directed Zirel, who carried her only possession, a small embroidered pillow with all her belongings stuffed in the lining.

Burka pointed to the forest with his studded cane, his only memento of a regretful past.

David remained behind momentarily to pack all the food into a sack. He ordered everyone to move on.

"Run for your life, they are coming nearer." He was concerned with their slow movement. For some tense seconds his eyes followed the jerky steps of the Germans trying to keep up with Nicholas. But they suddenly vanished. Still, their presence was felt; the enemy's hunters were many, the collaborators were numerous and the options for violence were unlimited. David, who had caught up with his group, was now ahead. He turned one last glance to the panting single file trying to keep up with him, as he jumped over the fallen trunks straddling the clearing in front. But this pace was too much for Sarah Beile.

"Children, leave me here."

Rachel supported her arm and reassured her, "We're safe, mamma, there is nothing to fear."

"This is not for me," she pleaded.

"There is a friend nearby. I know him well." David prodded her, "only a few more steps."

But Sarah Beile was panicked by the crushing thought of seeing her beautiful daughter, young son and helpless twins hungry, cold, sleeping on the ground, or maybe worse. Her mind worked —her imagination was even faster. That the twins were in the custody of Levandovski, with whom she was out of touch, added to her anxiety.

"Where are we, Koppel?" she asked.

"Where are we? That's the beginning of the oak forest. Not safe here."

Avreml looked all around him apprehensively, for on all sides brooding massive branches and sturdy trunks were overhanging, hiding the secrets of a forest. He heard so many fearful stories about the lurking robbers and murderers. Now he was in the very midst of those tales that stirred many a nightmare during the story-telling interludes in the one-room study of Isaac, the Melamed.

"Only a short distance," David repeated by habit.

"You are not telling me everything," Sarah Beile said, then called her children aside: "Rachel and Avreml, you are young, save yourselves."

"Mamma stop—we are all together in this—"

They marched on. Sarah Beile locked Avreml's fingers in her hand. It was clear that the three needed each other and would cling together. Avreml just couldn't think of existence away, even in a safer place. It was too frightening to be separated.

From somewhere in the distance came echoes of wheels grinding against the sand, and that familiar creaking of the axle, inside the worn out and greaseless hub of a wooden wheel.

"The nearest place," Koppel whispered, "is a shack. A forester used to live there."

"And now?" David asked. Koppel just shook his head. They were moving eastward toward the diagonal shafts of sunshine, streaking through the dense forest. In the distance, they saw a sun-drenched clearing of sand, dotted with stumps. As a precaution, David told them to stay behind. He and Burka pushed through the last coppice, when a sharp commanding voice startled them.

"Hands up! throw down your gun, you!" A raw-faced, limping youngster with two more thugs right behind him threatened Burka with a revolver.

"It is only a cane."

"Throw it down, before we shoot." Two stony faced farmer boys moved forward with guns pointed in their direction.

"We have been following you for some time. Where are the rest of you?" their limping leader spoke again. "Start searching them."

The one with the blond stubble on his chin began to search Burka and then David.

"Remember, we have real bullets in them," he warned again.

"What do you want?" Burka approached him defiantly.

"Stay away," he warned as he took a step backward and pivoted on his good leg, "just one shot and the Germans will be here."

"What do you want?" David faced him.

"That's better, Panie Zid," he spoke derisively. His shaky voice blurted out the words, "Money and jewelry," and then more brazenly, "is it worth your life?"

There were many rumors about these informers and blackmailers who were called, *Schmalchovniks*. But this was the first time they had encountered three of a kind in the flesh.

"Hey, Jews—fast, hand over the *schmaltz!*" He again used a barbed word, to prompt his dull-faced accomplices, who stopped when they heard rustling in the woods behind them.

"Come out or we'll shoot," the talkative one aimed his gun. "Why didn't you tell us there were more of you. What have you got?" he approached Rachel, Sarah Beile and Avreml, and, waving his revolver at Koppel, Abba and the others, "Nice," his eyes wolfishly devoured Rachel.

"Leave her alone," David said and came between them. "We'll give you this," he took out a string of pearls and a trinket from his pocket; dropping his golden watch in his raised sleeve, just as one of them searched him.

"That's a good beginning," the younger one said to his freckle-

faced confederate. The limping one grinned slyly as he walked
over to David and began to pump his hand.

"We're friends now," and then, in an instant, his face was red
and tight as he spotted the watch fall out of David's sleeve.

"No wonder the Germans don't like you—you wanted to cheat
us. Pick it up and give it to me. Get out of our way, walk straight
ahead, before we call the Germans to kill you, you swindlers."

They had not gone very far on the road east to Yanowa before
Burka decided on his own to reverse and follow them. He darted
from tree to tree as he closed in on them. The hoodlums stopped
and made observations of the group. Burka, now that he had an
idea of what they were up to, returned.

"Let's walk in another direction, south, toward Potocki's
estate," he suggested.

"You think they'll follow us?" Koppel said.

"How did you know?"

"I've been around too long in the woods, and I learned some of
the tricks of thugs." He almost uttered "thieves," which he
avoided in the presence of Burka.

"Those dogs," Koppel said, "have our scent, and after them
come worse dogs; a plague always follows an epidemic."

"Rachel," David said to her and pulled her aside.

"Don't you think I know, or ought to know, what is going
on?"

"Rachel, there are certain things. . . ."

"That I shouldn't know?"

"There are certain realities that we'll have to face. Everyone
doesn't have to know them."

"David," she said to him, "whatever happens, I don't care what
you are going to say, remember, we are in it together."

"It is too risky in the forest. Do you know what it means to be
hunted?" she did not answer and he continued. "You and your
mother and brother should be in a safer place."

"Where is it safer?"

"Malinoski could find a place."

"Where? His neighbors would track us down."

"Where are we going?" Ben Zion, who spoke very little during
all this time, asked Koppel the next morning after a sleepless
night in the forest.

"We'll be crossing a dry bed, and then some cleared land." The trackless forest was all like a map in his mind. "We'll bear south, right after that fallen tree."

"And then what?" David asked.

"The Germans will lose track of us," Koppel explained. "We were intercepted north, not far from Grabetzki. Potocki's mansion is south, about fifteen kilometers in the opposite direction. We have to make our way in between, straight east, where it is thick with trees. One more thing, we must know, at all times, where the Germans are."

"The informers, I am sure, told them about us," David said. "They should have come after us. Yet they don't seem anywhere near us. It is too quiet."

"What does that mean?" Ben Zion asked.

"I don't know. Maybe they have given up on us, and went back to drinking, or maybe they are setting up a trap," David said. "As a large, slow-moving group, we always face such a danger."

"Let's split up," Shmuel suggested. "This is the safest way; the Germans can't pursue all of us at one time."

"What happens if one group is in trouble?" Burka asked.

"You and I will head north toward Grabetzki," David explained. "We must find out what the Germans are up to. Meanwhile, you, Koppel, Shmuel and Abba will lead your groups through the forest in a southerly direction. Should we encounter trouble we'll both run in opposite directions: I to Zemski in the swamps and you, a good runner, to warn Koppel and the others."

"Reb Koppel," David sought his opinion, "is there anyplace where Burka or I will be able to find you?"

"There is a place three kilometers from here on the other side of the forest, after the crossroads. There, on a hill, is the abandoned windmill."

"Is there anybody. . . ."

"It is not always empty," he read David's thoughts. "Sometimes shepherds or others stop over. Make sure no one is inside."

"Koppel knows the forest, follow him. Shmuel, Abba, take care of the others," were David's parting words. He walked briskly, bending down only to pick up a dried branch, which he trimmed and shortened into a walking stick.

David soon found himself walking with Burka in the direction of Grabetzki's house. He could tell from the spare birch trees along the way. He stopped to listen for those telegraphic signals

of steps and voices that always bounced around within the
vaulted timber spaces. There were thuds of hammers striking
wood, the see-saw whine of cut trees, even the laughter of children drifted in strangely—not Jewish, he was certain; but not a
trace or an echo of stalking Germans. They were either drunk, he
surmised, or stealthy in their movements. Still he had to be wide
awake and prepared for the worst. It was like passing through a
village with a vicious dog lying in wait to spring at him from
behind the gate or fence.

David could almost see the crucifix near Grabetzki's gate when
his heart began to pound. Burka tightened his grip on the
knotted cane. There, in front, they started to move, were the
three blackmailers in the company of the Germans. They were
unmistakenly coming toward them. It would be easy for him and
Burka to step aside and lie low in the thicket, but the Germans
kept on, they would surely overtake the whole unsuspecting
group he had left behind. They could never escape, even without
a complete surprise. Without a big head start, Reb Koppel would
soon be out of breath. Sarah Beile would never be able to endure
a forced march, once the Germans started to track them down.
David thought quickly. He had to do something to save them
and himself. He jumped into the fir woodlet, with Burka right
behind him, and waited. The Germans' voices were coming
closer. David could almost see the German faces. They were S.S.
men, whom David had never seen before, led by Murad and
Todt. In their smartly-dressed uniforms, they appeared well-
rested and eager for action. Having never been exposed to any
risk, or to any conscientious dissent, they stepped lively, out-
walking the limping thug who led the way. They were almost
past him.

"Look, these are fresh tracks," someone said in Polish.

"Yes," a German spoke, "let's look around."

"Somebody moving," the freckled boy alerted them.

"Where?"

"Over there, over there, a Jew! And another!" the limping one
screamed.

"Burka, wait awhile and then run in the opposite direction,
warn Koppel."

David bolted and ran before they came any closer. His face
was scratched by parting branches. A shot tore through the
trees. It missed him as it whistled past his ear. He stumbled and
fell, more shocked than hurt. He heard cries: *"Verfluchter Jude!*

surrender, stop, or we'll kill." David kept on running deeper into
the woods. At first he was propelled by panic, then it occurred to
him to pace himself in a steady, slower sprint, his folded arms
waving against his chest in alternating rhythm. He ran past a
pond, then over felled trees without stopping. Beads of sweat
began to form over his eyebrows and dripped into his eyes.

His pace began to lag, and soon he would have to stop or he
would succumb. He must continue after a brief rest.

David arrived at the crossroads. The stretch ahead of him
dipped like a bow with the old windmill somewhere over the
hill. He first saw the protruding tops of the crossed wings when
he reached the top, against the darkening sky. The outline of the
windmill, as he moved closer, looked bare, with boards and shin-
gles just hanging on to its skeleton. It seemed strange. There was
nothing around.

To stop and investigate in and around the windmill would
only invite trouble. Beyond where the land dipped sharply
stretched Mazurski's farmlands, grazing pastures, orchards and
warehouses clustering on the far side around his mansion. It was
now pitch dark. Dogs barked somewhere in the distance. David
thought he would crawl into one of the haystacks arranged in
neat rows awaiting a freeze-up and snow before they could be
moved by sleds from the marshlands.

"David!" he recognized Abba Dunsky's voice coming from the
woods. Avreml ran forward, shouting, "David, don't go there. It
is wet, come this way."

"Avreml, be careful, they can hear," David said and pointed to
blazing lights from a truck sweeping the tree-lined highway.
David and Avreml ducked and waited.

"David, we didn't know what happened. We thought you
were...."

"Where is Burka?"

"Burka returned just in time to warn us. We hid in the haystacks."

"Where is he now?" Abba asked.

"He left to find a wagon that would pick up Sarah Beile and
Zirel."

"Where is Rachel?"

"There she is," Abba said. "Alter is not back from Narodni,
there is no food, everyone is well except Joshua is very sick and
Zirel's baby...."

"Rachel." David interrupted the usual bad news, his eyes following her face like moonlight that follows one on a lonely road. Rachel walked briskly toward him.

"Mother doesn't feel well, she is terrified at the thought of the twins being taken away from Levandovski and put into a monastery. The shoemaker's baby, Ami, is with Franik. He has complained to Malinoski that he wants gold and that he wouldn't keep Ami much longer." Rachel poured out the things with which they were concerned and shared the pleasant and the mostly unpleasant.

"Abba!" David said aside, "aren't we too close to the highway?"

"From here we can watch them," Abba reassured him, "instead of them surprising us."

"You are right."

"What do you see, David, over there on the highway?"

"Just wagons and a few trucks."

"Isn't it strange, empty wagons and trucks moving at night in the direction of Suha-Vali?"

"Abba, don't get us panicky; you must believe . . ."

"Believe, believe," Abba intercepted the unfinished sentence. "If it depended on that . . . the Jews are the greatest believers . . . I have written hundreds of letters; and not even one answer." David detected, from his unfinished sentences that this courageous Hebrew teacher and historian was under too much stress to retain his earlier perseverance. Perhaps he appeared that way himself to others. Still, he could never admit that to Abba.

"You wrote to big people, maybe they are busy," David said to Abba.

"Busy with what? Conferences—conduct of war, statements to the press, radio, declarations, pious protests, even prayers in our behalf, but who is even half concerned to save us? Millions of Jews facing—only God knows what."

"Abba, take charge," he said his eyes following the ghostlike glow of lights disturbing the darkness. "When Burka comes back, put Sarah Beile and Zirel in the wagon."

"Where can they go?"

"To Stashek."

"Stashek? He is an anti-Semite. I remember he once threw a stone into the synagogue."

"He was only a boy then. He goes to church every Sunday, even confides in the priest, his mother told us. Zirel," he called to her, "Zirel, come here." He walked toward her as she pressed unfinished knitted booties to her tear-soaked face.

"David," she wiped her face and then let her head slump—her words dropped singly. "I'm calling my baby John."

"John?"

"The baby John will be Jewish, I promise."

"Originally, John was a Hebrew name, *Yohanan*, but they changed everything—our religion, our names—to suit themselves."

"Maybe that will save him. I'm doing nothing wrong, am I?"

"I am not a Rabbi, but I believe you."

"It is not a crime or a sin?"

"Of that I am sure. The crimes and sins are mostly on the other side, where they call babies Ludwig, Fritz, Casimir and even John."

"If a little change will save him. . . . I'm blond and he is dark, maybe the name will help."

"Zirel, you don't have to convince me. Jews posed as Mohammedans in Arabia and as Christians in Spain to save themselves." He did not say anything for a long time. It struck him as something queer to imagine that a human being could save itself by identifying itself with a beastly being by saying, "I'm going to look like you, act like you, even stick on a new name label. You won't devour me now that I am one of your kind."

Burka returned late, after midnight. They were half asleep on the fragrant hay that they had carried across from the hay piles. David was wide awake near Abba and not far away Rachel's head tossed from side to side, curled up alongside her mother and Avreml. From across the swamp, the wind carried a putrid odor of something decomposed or unburied.

"David," he whispered to him, as he slipped in from the shadows, out of breath, "wagons and military trucks are assembling on the market square. It looks like it is all over."

David did not say anything. He clenched his fists like one helpless in pain. Burka tried to head off Rachel, who suspected that something was not right. As she came near, he said to her, "I couldn't get a wagon from Franik, and Stashek has no room for refugees. But there is a good farmer not far . . .

"Rachel, you must know the truth," he started slowly. "A woman, a girl, to us Jews is sacred just like every man and child is holy. But they, the *goyim*, or Christians, whatever you call

them, Germans and some of the Poles and other nationalities of
Europe, they would use the flesh of a woman, or any Jewish
person, for breakfast to satisfy their animal lust. We'll have to
look for a God-forsaken place in the midst of a swamp, far, far
away, where even animals stay away. Far, far from German animals and beasts like them," his voice trailed off as fatigue lulled
him into drowsiness with Rachel close by.

"Someone is moving over there," Burka startled David, and
pointed to the woods from which came a succession of rustling
noises.

"Let's wait until whoever it is makes the first move."

A cluster of needle branches, whining against a sweeping
breeze, drew all eyes in the direction of the low bushes. David
blinked as he strained his eyes to make out a form pushing
through the twigs in the shadowy silvery blue, lit by the half-
hiding moon.

"Get down low," David whispered and gestured to Burka. It
surely wasn't a lone German, he likes company. A Polish informer? He fears darkness. It could only be one trained for stalking or survival.

He signalled to Burka and to the others to pull out from their
prepared bedding of twigs and hay. David covered the rear of
the line at a slow trot. But the older people began to fall behind.
Rachel, who guided her mother, stumbled now, and fell.

"Are you hurt, Rachel?" David came to her side.

"No, David, just a bruised knee, I think. Take care of my
mother, she is tired."

They were now deep in the forest stretching on both sides of
the highway to Bialystok. When the morning rays began to
bounce off the trees, they stopped to rest. Once more, the crackling movement of crunching needles and twigs followed them
from behind.

"Who is there?" Burka lifted his cane.

"That's me," a head that popped up called out.

"Label!" Abba recognized him. David walked up and embraced him.

"I was worried about you, but Ben Zion told me why you
couldn't leave."

"She was very sick, but I got her out the next day. I stopped in
Gremnatzki, I knocked on doors, but nobody wanted to have her.
She got worse. I put her down under a tree and went to get help.

When I returned she was dead. She was my life companion. Now, everything became dark. I wandered around all day, nothing mattered now if they caught me. I wanted to be with her. I stumbled into a shed off the road. I was surrounded by at first hostile and then friendly men. They were partisans and I joined them."

"Communist?"

"Russians and communists; Poles and Jews; we were in hiding in the Bielovesz forest near Bialystok. Our assignment was to gather information of German concentrations, troop and supply movements and to transmit the information to the main intelligence unit in Wilna. We also did some sabotage on bridges and communications. We were doing good work except. . . ."

"Except what?"

"Well," Label paused and lowered his eyes as he toyed with a round pine cone. "One time I saw a group of Jews being led away near the road; and they began to dig their own graves. I wanted to do something. We had guns, enough cartridges and could have surprised the Germans—there were ten and we were twelve. But the commander told us that duty to our unit was more important than saving the Jews."

"What happened?"

"He said to me—'so you're a Jew first.' I did not say anything, but slipped away through the tall grass and caught up with the Germans. I aimed carefully and fired first at the leader, who fell, then on the rest. Most of the Jews escaped seconds before their execution, and I would have been shot by the Russians as a counter-revolutionary or for desertion if I didn't have the sense to get away while the partisans deliberated about my fate."

"I understand you perfectly," David was content to remark, but Burka gloated, "Now you see what a fool you were to have fallen for Communism."

"Communism! I still believe in it. Our partisan leader always talked about aims and objectives. Here I was safe in the forest with armed comrades, but not far, Jews were going to be shot. I didn't care whether they were Zionists or capitalists; they were human beings and we could save them. I thought this was also an objective."

"What have you got there?" David pointed to his bulging blouse.

"A revolver, a hand grenade and a few rounds." Label said.

"We need it."

"I wish, I wish to God we had more. I learned that all ideologies, principles and ideals don't mean anything unless you can defend them or advance them with guns."

"If God, if this is the only way to God. . . ." David said in a tone of resignation. He just didn't have enough energy left to go into a discussion which shook up his entire conception of religion, for he had long ago concluded that in order to attain Isaiah's dream of peace, Judaism, dedicated to this peace, must resist those who would destroy its priests, the Jews and its kingdom. He was concerned that his own ears should have heard God mentioned in the same breath with force. Then, rousing himself, he said: "Label, we must get inside the ghetto, there is something going on there."

"I know it."

"How do you know it?"

"I heard them talk in whispers—my partisan leader and his men. He told them to hold back the bad news from me."

"What bad news?"

"That Hitler gave orders to liquidate all Jewish towns and to transfer the Jews to ghettos and then to transport them to larger ghettos."

"Then what?"

"Only God knows. I am ashamed I never believed that way in God before, but only God knows where they are taking them. They never return. . . ."

David sat down near Rachel. Traffic was heavy on the highway in both directions. He listened to the whirr of the motors and the rumble of the wagons. Things were moving, wheels were grinding; something ominous was in the making and converging upon his people.

"We'll have to move on," he broke the silence and got up. "I have to talk it over with the others," he repeated a phrase which she had heard time and again and learned to accept, either as something perilous or how to plan the next hour, afternoon or the night ahead. With one glance he summoned Burka and Label and then, with a sweeping motion of his hand, called the others to join him.

"We can't move and we can't stay as we are."

"Exactly what is on your mind?" Label prodded him.

"We are too large a group to move together. It will give us

away and slow down our movements and make it easy to track us down. Shmuel already advised us to split our group. Scattered small units would even be better."

"You are both right," Label agreed for the first time with his former opponents. "Small units with liaison are safest."

"Then let us divide ourselves into units," Ben Zion spoke up, his eyes searching for the nods of better times, "each group entrusted with a specific task."

"But we're not the same; we have old and young women," Alter broke in.

"What about children?" Abba pleaded.

"That is why we have to organize ourselves into units," David explained. He couldn't answer all the questions. Could anyone?

"For better mobility, action and safety," Label impressed the group with a new terminology.

"Yes, good mobility," Ben Zion murmured. He added, as an afterthought, "Let us follow Label's suggestion, but we must take care of Zirel and Rachel and her mother, they can't move as fast. . . ."

"Zirel is gone," Alter said.

"Oh God! We'll have to look for her. Kagan should be back. We'll wait for some time until we have to get away from here for our own safety."

"How about Avreml?" Abba stumped them with another question.

"He'll keep up with us," David said confidently.

"Do you think," Label addressed Koppel, Hershke and Ben Zion, "you and you and you will be able?"

"We are able," David retorted to his blunt words, as he bracketed himself with the group. "Some of us—the younger ones—are stronger and better conditioned for running and walking. But it is all a matter of good luck and grace in the eyes of God." He tried to soften Label's harsh words. "Let no one say, 'I can take care of myself, I can run or hide; but you can't run nor hide, therefore stay behind or go anywhere and take your chances'."

"How are we going to split up?" Abba asked.

"I'm going with Joshua to Narodni," Alter eyed his coughing young son. "I hope to find work there," he added.

"I'll try my luck with Zemski," Koppel said. "Hershke, Beryl and Ben Zion," he turned to each one, "You'll be in my group."

"Abba, Burka, Rachel—Avreml will be a problem," David said and turned to see if he was around, "you'll be with me and anyone else who wants to come along. We'll stay close to Potocki's cottage, like in the eye of a tempest."

CHURCHILL CONTACTED SWISS TO
PROPOSE TO BERLIN MUTUAL
CESSATION OF THE MANACLING OF
WAR PRISONERS.

*God's miracles cannot occur under the
regime of an unrepentant wicked ruler.*

Taanith, 18.

27

ALL DOORS WERE SHUT, FOR GOD ALSO

It was midday when Alter reached the massive weeping willows
that guarded the entrance to Narodni's house upon a rock-strewn
rise. Up above, on the main trunk was a splintered shelf, the kind
that supports a crucifix. It was removed or had fallen down.
Alter could not help but reflect, as he walked up to the doorway,
on how shabbily the house was in the midst of so much abun-
dance. There were clusters of tall pines rising like giants above
the low house. Groves of maple trees, oaks and birch were everywhere. Only a few stumps here and there. It was untouched
because it was so deep in the woods that it was inaccessible by
wagon or sled.

"Narodni!" he called out. "Pani Narodni!" he corrected himself, although as a forest watchman looked down upon even by
peasants, this honorific sounded awkward. For there were none
to pay him a wage now that Paltiel, the owner of the forest, was
behind the walls, nor did anyone hesitate to steal timber if he
could move it, despite all the naive protestations of this simple
man.

"Narodni—Gen Dobra," he greeted him.

"Who are you?"

"You don't know me, but I know you. I am a carpenter."

"Carpenter, good man, you not a carpenter now," he chopped
his words and phrases, for in his isolated life and world, extra
words and long sentences were not a necessity.

"I'm a carpenter, give me work," he showed his stubby fingers
and traces of calluses on his palms. "Give me bread. My son,
Joshua, is dying in the forest, more are starving."

"'Dangerous, you're a Jew. *Yezus* save us."

"Yezus was a Jew, too. His name comes from Joshua, my son's name." Alter was brazen, and as Narodni scratched his head, continued, "He was a carpenter, and my son is a carpenter."

"He was God, your son a man," Narodni was confused by the comparison and yet impressed with the blunt utterance.

"Whatever he was or is, it was so long ago, but my son is alive, sick and dying. I fixed many houses. Ask in Pokosne, in Okop, in Long Village. I and my sons made beds to sleep, tables to eat from, strong doors to guard you, windows to see through—now all I ask is work."

"Now different."

"What is different? God has not changed, God is against murderers hunting innocent people. If you worship a Jew as a God why can't you at least save a Jew?"

"I don't know, all mixed up, God and book and law—all mixed up. See cross? I took it down. Jew once stop—he not cross himself, my neighbor he not far from here, he kill the Jew, so I say, this cross no good, he kill." It was an effort, but a relief to unburden himself of the impact of a murder because of a wooden crucifix that hung on a tree.

"My son, Joshua," he implored to this simple man who was so typical of most decent Christian Europeans who were injected with love for the Jew in the apocryphal image of a God, and for the living Jew, hatred as a scapegoat. Out of this confused innocence, paganism, religion and infected hate mixed into a boiling cauldron, was born tumorous anti-semitism.

"I'll work for you and start right now. Give me a stool. All I ask for is food to save Joshua, as good as any Joshua that ever lived—Yezus was born a Joshua, too, a Jewish son."

"No. I'm afraid. Germans want you and him. I am afraid, everybody afraid, Priest afraid too. He tells us to pray. I pray for you."

"Everybody is afraid, the whole world is afraid." Alter stared away from him, "So you'll pray for me," he muttered to himself. "I don't want your prayers, God doesn't want your prayers, God doesn't want anyone's prayers, unless it can bring good. Narodni," he faced him as he spoke deliberately, "You don't stand in the field and pray, 'Rain is good—good to pray for rain' and then go home to sleep. You have to work in the field for the rain to do any good. Your prayer is like rain, and I am like the earth. It needs me to do any good."

"I don't know—all these years, all these prayers, where are they—only for trees?" Narodni came around to the futility of believing and worshipping without being able to help in the only test of a normal religion and a normal God.

"Just this piece of bread." Alter pointed to a chunk on the table. "I'll give you my boots, only let my son sleep this night anywhere, even in the pigs' stall."

"Take the bread, I don't need your boots, both of you sleep there under the pile of wood."

"Now I owe you some work," he was grateful.

"No work."

"I've got to work."

"No work," he said to him in a final tone as he left for the forest.

Alter surveyed this humble kingdom of safety. It was in a forgotten corner. If he could only transfer the entire group, they could live here undetected and unafraid.

He walked a little distance and there, to his heart's delight, he found a woodchopper's hatchet. He placed a length against a log and, with a well-aimed blow, he split it. He continued until after a while he had split all the cut wood. If he could only find a saw, he would cut down a tree. Too bad he had left his axe behind, the only tool he saved from the Germans, in the ghetto. Why not cut down the hard way? He began to hew at the base of a tall pine. He was almost halfway through, when he spied Narodni coming toward him in big strides, glancing over his shoulder like one fearful of pursuit. He spoke excitedly.

"No good, not safe here. My neighbor, he meet me, he say if you here? Who cut wood there? He know somebody here. He come here soon."

"I'll leave you and stay away from here. But if I come in the night, will you help me?"

"I don't know. He go to police."

"I promise you, no one will see me at night, just food."

"I give you food now, but stay away."

"No—no! I can't open my mouth, I can't open my eyes." David's voice was choked, his teeth tight and grinding. A cold sweat was over his brow. Burka stood over him, unable to understand the trance that smouldered inside David's body and soul. Rachel bent over, wiped his face and covered him.

In this nightmare, he was pursued relentlessly by packs of

beasts. Every door was shut. A dog was at the gate. Every window was dark, the unknown was waiting beneath every thatched roof. He awoke. Above was a clear sky, it was a terrifying thought to die alone in the midst of that enchanting beauty of the forest. Sharp simple notes filled the air. Birds were alive and their throats were full of song, because no one pursued them.

Rachel's beautiful face, despite her placid mien, reflected the toll of ordeal and uncertainty.

"What shall we do next," she kept on asking in a subdued voice, so that no one would have to answer. "What shall we do with the baby?" She referred to "Ami," Elyeh, the shoemaker's son left in Franik's care. That was the name Abba called it. "Ami" means "my people"—but she preferred Amile. This pet name was more tender and affectionate to a baby raised in a merciless world.

David discerned from Rachel's undertone phrases and from hushed conversation around him that their concern was not only with his illness but even more with their dispersal. He, who recovered quickly from all ailments, now began to show the effects of endless attrition. Frustrated by inactivity, he listened to reports.

Alter and his son, Joshua, who went to Narodni, did not yet return. Koppel and those with him, were about to try their luck with Zemski. Burka returned without finding transportation for Sarah Beile. Abba asked Label to bring back Ami from Franik and to inform Kagan that his wife had disappeared. Koppel, who was about to leave for Zemski's farm, sat down on a log near Abba, sprawled on the grass. Burka propped up David's head, who was flat on his back nearby. Koppel wanted to digress from the uneasy mood and to say farewell to them. One never knew if the morrow would ever come again.

"A man is like a tree," Koppel kept on repeating.

"Like a tree," Abba agreed.

"A man is like a tree, with roots that go down deep to an origin and source of life."

"Did you know," Koppel said to Avreml, who edged closer, "that every ring in a tree means a year? Now this tree is thirty years old."

"And this one?" Avreml asked.

"This one is about twelve, a young man as a tree goes."

"How do you know, you can't see the rings?" Avreml's face lit up.

"I can tell by its thickness, its bark and height. The very young ones sometimes lean and cuddle to the older ones, but this one stands straight, reaching out for space, to the top, just like a pious man among the people."

"And this one?" Avreml asked and pointed to a sapling.

"This one is young. It needs protection from the blazing sun, sometimes from the wind, but mostly from animals who trample and bend it—or pull it out by its roots."

"You said a man is like a tree, but is a woman or a girl?"

"A girl is like a tree in bloom that must not be damaged by a storm," Koppel glanced at Rachel. "We are all like trees, flowers and grass, we need nourishment to be strong and free," Koppel put his hand on Avreml's head.

Burka's drawn and twitching face turned in every direction. "I don't care for a forest, ants all over me." He scratched his legs. "It's getting colder. We've got to find a house or...."

"Or what?" Abba asked him.

"Or we'll be in trouble."

"We Jews have been in trouble for a long time."

"Too long!" Burka pounded with his heavy knotted cane. "I don't like to die."

"Who talks about dying? We are alive, aren't we? We ought to be thankful to God."

"Thankful to God? I don't believe in a God. Look at all the non-Jews, what do they believe? In letting us rot to death in this stinking forest?"

"Burka, I haven't the strength to argue with you. There is no answer." Abba's voice trembled. "I wrote letters...."

"You wrote letters to a dead world. Nobody cares. We are surrounded by two-legged animals. I am going to get away. I'll live by stealing. Is that a crime? It is written in our books not to starve or butcher people. Do the goyim care about our books? They got guns and bullets and we got the books—and they burn our books and kill us. If God is still around, where are his miracles?"

"Don't blame God," David spoke with great effort. "God was discovered by the Jews. They documented his laws. Do you know why European civilizations and its religions are bankrupt? Because there is no God in their midst. How is that possible, you ask, with so many universities, learning, churches and millions of Bibles and prayer books a few steps away? Because there is no genuine understanding of God in their hearts, nor any true image of God in their books, and when there is no God in their midst, or a wrong God, the miracles that always happened to good people in Sodom, in Egypt, in Babylon, and in the Holy Land where God persevered, cannot happen here.

"One should never depart from his friends without a quotation from the sages. Hershke, get the Torah. I'll be ready after I finish," Koppel said, elated that David paraphrased the Rabbi.

"The Jews," he spoke with a faint slowness, "always refer to themselves as children and to God as Father." He braced his fingers against his right temple, like a scribe over parchment in search of the place and page; then smoothed out his creased forehead and, having located the quotation, slid his cupped hand through his beard. "The master of the universe once reproved the Jews in the desert for calling him 'Father' when they were in distress. They are like the wayward children of a noble ruler, who were beaten, robbed and stranded by bandits who pretended to be their guides. Good people pleaded with their estranged Father to rescue them. 'They are your children, have mercy on them,' they pleaded. 'My children? They ignored my teachings and they resemble more their wayward mother. There is no proof they are my children.' 'We have the proof,' the good people replied, 'because they are the very image of you'."

"We are in his image and therefore are all equal before him in love, mercy and justice. Only cruel people, who defaced their own image declare openly that they have nothing to do with God. Let me finish. They are lower than the most ferocious beasts who do not devour their own kind. Only the supposed human species, without a soul, kills those who are in the likeness of God."

What day is this? David searched with his half-opened eyes. His face was wan and yellowish; and he tugged the coat until his feet were exposed.

Burka and Abba did not want to believe what they suspected.

"Your feet must be covered—that's why you are chilled," Abba unfolded an old worn-out home-spun blanket.

"We must get help, someone to examine him," Rachel approached Abba and Burka.

"Our own doctors are prisoners," Abba said.

"Then we must take him to Basenko."

"I wouldn't trust this scoundrel even to treat a horse. He works with the Germans and he is a woman-chaser." Burka was derisive.

"David is very sick, he needs a bed and medicine. I don't care who he is as long as he'll help David," Rachel spoke angrily.

"We can't start out until Label returns with Shmuel and Kagan."

"I don't need medicine—there is no doctor. A doctor comes to a house, a house with a *Mezuzah*. There are many houses on the street," David gasped for air, "and on the street is a synagogue, and there are people and a Holy Torah, and a Shofar to drive away . . . to drive away . . ." his eyes stared blankly as he raised himself and then lapsed into sleep.

The next day Label returned with Shmuel and Kagan. He brought back Ami from Franik, whom he found in a nasty mood, complaining about not getting enough for boarding the baby and other favors. Shmuel made arrangements with Adolph Kislo to house his brother and the twins. Kagan, whose baby was there for some time, became very depressed when he learned that his wife, Zirel, vanished. He scanned with his eyes in every direction, hoping that she would somehow find her way back.

Abba huddled with Shmuel and Label. It was agreed to start out for the lodge after darkness.

When they finally arrived at Basenko's lodge, he directed them to move David into the shed behind his garden. He made only one condition that they pay his servant real money.

"Where can we get it?" Abba asked.

"I will advance him in exchange for your giving me a predated note that you sold me a good house before the war. The swines are buying them from the Germans for little money or favors. I will take care of your Sokoloff, and even adopt this baby." He stared at Rachel, then touched Ami in her arms. Ami began to cry and huddled closer to her bosom.

"Will you let us decide?"

"What is there to decide? I'll send my servant for him and for the baby. One of you can come along to take care of him."

"I'll go, if you give shelter to a few others," Rachel said.

"Very well, I accept your offer, but only temporary shelter for a few." Basenko was satisfied that the very desirable Rachel was the price that fell into this innocent trap.

"Have you noticed anything unusual about Basenko's conduct?" David asked her after being there a week.

"So far he has been helpful. He even promised transportation for my mother."

"Helpful? He has been attentive to you more than anything else."

"You are foolish in saying this. Have you a better place? Find us one."

"Rachel, we have no choice in regard to location. But we must suspect Basenko. After he gets what he wants, he may surprise us any night with raiders."

"David, there is no other way here," she said after a long pause.

"There is only one way to test a scoundrel," he said.

"What is it?"

"I'll just tell Basenko that I am going to leave. In the meantime, keep an eye on this hunter." After going over his plan with Abba, David came to see his host. A servant admitted David to Basenko's den.

"My master will see you soon. Please wait."

After some time the door opened from the terrace fronting the garden. He expected him from the library connected by a foyer with the den. But even his servants were not privileged to know his whereabouts at any time. Basenko, with a frown on his face, greeted him in a manner more masked than formal.

"How is your health?"

"Much better, thank you," David bowed politely. "I still feel a little weak, but I can walk on my feet."

"Is there anything you need?" Basenko was impatient.

"We wish to leave," David sprung the words, "and to thank you very much for your help."

"Of course, of course you can leave," then changed his tone, "except that according to laws you must stay in quarantine."

"Why?"

"Regulations against spreading of typhoid."

"What regulations?"

"The Germans'," Basenko was surprised by David's question, and then, recoiling from his first anger, spoke deliberately, "I am responsible to them—they'll see to it that it is enforced," he made a veiled threat.

"But how will the Germans know?"

"You would be surprised. They have ways and connections."

David wanted to ask him how the Germans would even bother about quarantine, when Jews were simply condemned to die outright. He was very uncomfortable in the presence of Basenko and left.

"Rachel!" David spoke softly, lest Avreml overhear. "I don't want to frighten you, but if I tell you that Basenko does not want me to leave, will you believe me?"

"I don't understand it."

"He said I will be quarantined because of typhoid which is contagious. All of us will be kept as quarantined prisoners."

"But you have no typhoid." She thought that the evidence against Basenko now added up. "David, you were right about his intentions to me. He even suggested last night that I come to see him. I didn't want to tell you. I was afraid to lose this refuge. But I admit that I was wrong."

"We will leave at night," he told her.

"But to-night is Friday night."

"It is better, he will not suspect us."

Dogs were barking; David heard it before, but this was different. It was lusty and continuous as if coming from a pack. He remembered that the hunting lodge was the boast of Graf Potocki, who entertained high society, generals, bankers, and it was even legendary before the war, even kings stopped over for a night or longer during the hunting season. Now there were no wolves around here, maybe in the massive Bielovesz forest. But this was so far away.

It looked like there would be some kind of a hunt, but what? One always had to be ready and prepared. What were Basenko's intentions? He must have some kind of a plan as to what to do each day. The kitchen chimney was going full blast, that was quite obvious—there were guests to be expected. What guests? Surely not survivors from Suha-Vali, Grodno, or from other communities, who have been in hiding and now are seeking better accomodations.

David watched for some time from behind Basenko's kennel. The dogs were fed chunks of meat, he could almost see them leap in lustful delight and excited growl. It would be quiet until the hunt. What hunt, geese, rabbits, foxes, wolves? It was now late into fall. The wild geese had long departed to warmer climes, the rabbits were in hiding from the foxes, who were wary of the wolves, who, pursued by hunters, deployed in packs to their lairs. Was this the proper time? What is time, anyway, when nothing is proper?

The old servant was carrying something and nervously looking behind her like one being followed.

"I brought you eggs," she said. "They have plenty of meat tomorrow, big hunt, big feast, I'll bring something more tonight." she added.

"What hunt?"

"They say big hunt, lots of soldiers."

The mere mention of meat would have ordinarily stimulated painful secretions, but eggs were good enough for the Sabbath. Only her words, so openly relayed, were a timely warning of danger.

In the distance on the steps leading from the terrace, Basenko, in riding habit, boots and spurs, fondled his whip. He was now coming in the direction of the shed.

"The wagon is here. Should you need me, you'll find me in my den."

"Thank you, thank you," she said to Basenko, who lingered for a while, and then left.

Rachel did not believe her eyes when she saw the wagon and the driver. She told her mother that at last she could see her children at Yatvietz.

"I'm torn between two worlds," her mother began to cry, "how can I leave you and Avreml behind?"

"Mother, Avreml is better off here. You and others who want to join you will be safe there."

"I don't know. Oh, God I don't know. I'll bring back the twins with me. This is all I ask from God, to be together."

"Remember!" she whispered into her ears as she embraced her, "Don't tell the driver where you and the others are stopping. Get off a distance from Yatvietz."

"God be with you and Avreml and safeguard you and all the Jewish people," she waved as she and four other older people joined her on the wagon, all dressed in peasant garb.

Several hours later, after Rachel blessed the Sabbath, David walked over to the slab in the corner and blew out the candles.

"What are you doing? It's Friday night, Sabbath."

"Let him think we have gone to sleep. Besides, the shadows and lights give away our movements." According to logic, lights would have indicated their presence. But he found support for his action in a Mishnah.

" 'If one snuffs out a candle on the Sabbath because he is in fear of murderers, he is absolved.' We must get out of here, gather everything fast!" he called out in his familiar, clipped syllables, when others were in danger.

He had learned it well in the *Hachshara* movement, to be responsible for the safety of those under his command. They were now on the move. He carried the treasure box, a Bible, the baby's blanket and some food. Rachel held the baby and Burka held Avreml's hand. Abba embraced two books and some letters.

They were now well beyond the estate. The dogs now burst out in a staccato of deep-throated barking. Through the thick woods, they could see one light after the other from the direction of Basenko's mansion, spraying the darkness. No one had yet uttered a word as they stumbled over fallen branches and scraped their skins on thick brush.

"We'll have to get across the hills to Okop," David spoke the first words.

"No, to the right, beyond the river." Burka insisted and led the way. David and the rest followed. Rachel's dress was being ripped by littered dead branches. Abba fell hard but he got up, saying, "It is nothing." Avreml bounced back fast whenever he stumbled. Soon the hunter and the pack would be in pursuit. Their scent was all over the place. If they could get beyond the river, they would be safe for a while.

*Have we not all one father? Hath not one
God created us?*

Malachi, 2:10.

*Are we not brothers of one father and
one mother? Why are we singled out for
inhuman oppression?*

Taanith, 18.

28

BURNED PARCHMENT AND
INDESTRUCTIBLE LETTERS

A few miles away to the left, Koppel Magid, who left the group
two weeks before, was alone in a clearing. He recognized his
own timber, felled but never moved since the war. He had
trudged his way from Zemski, who intimidated the group, after a
ten days' stay, with a possible raid by Germans. Reb Koppel,
shocked by successive refusals and his arthritis getting worse
now that the light snow had fallen, collapsed. He was in no
condition to search for another dubious friend. His old friend
gave him shelter in a shed near a pig sty for a week.

"You can't stay here any longer. The neighbors will find out.
You must go," Zemski told him one night. His food and strength
were gone. He was now wandering aimlessly trying to rejoin
Hershke, Ben Zion and Beryl. It was not hunger that bothered
him, but the loneliness of the soul more than of the body.

What has happened? The trees murmured—there are birds in
flight resting on our branches. Where are the people?—the nests
on our sturdy twigs are half empty. Where are your singing
daughters? Where are your sons with echoes of hope in their
chanting voices? Our roots are strong and the sap is an offering
of incense. Once you told magic stories to young and old beneath

387

our shaded canopies. Will your beautiful and joyous singing children march again in triumph beneath our sylvan arches?

What is it? Koppel asked himself. I only want to rest beneath this tree—only to rest and fall asleep. I'm not asking these questions. The wind carrying echoes from far away, is asking these questions. Once I asked God many questions. Let someone take my place. Now I'm tired.

Then came echoes, it sounded like it came from beyond, no, from the trees. Where are the keepers and the guards? Where are the judges? Where are the protectors? There is no one to help you—only empty sounds and false echoes. Bells are just brass voices and the voices of men are like the hisses of snakes.

Only God is true. Only God in heaven sees all this. Why—you ask—do we, who have been silent for thousands of years, speak up now? Because the world is deaf and mute. Because no one is coming to save our people. As long as we are on earth—we will reveal this secret. God will give us a voice to tell. Reb Koppel, the time has come for you to find tranquillity. A deep sigh swept from tree to tree. Then a merciful pine tree, guarded by oaks, fanned to slumber and eternal sleep the part time innkeeper and timber merchant, who was a full time wise and learned man. A beautiful feathered bird flew high above the trees, the wispy clouded sky opened its blue canopy for a soul and a prayer that were delivered to the throne of God.

It was a colorful procession that started out from the gate. Graf Potocki was never more resplendent than his former valet and riding master, Basenko, now masquerading as a noble, in a similar red-blood outfit of cap, vest and coat. The breeches were green-lined with a wide red seam like those of the Cossacks. Graf Potocki only hunted foxes, but his underling, Basenko, a parvenu who conspired to drive him away and then hunt him down, was an innovator; he was admired by Captain Messer, who was right behind him. Even Lt. Schrecke, who despised him, respected his cunning. The Kommandant, Von Preissig, rode alongside Basenko. Von Preissig, who did not exactly relish this sport, especially the company that normally would have repelled a Prussian Junker, reluctantly joined the mixed pack.

Up front, Messer was impatient, "I enjoy riding early in the morning, but where are the creatures?"

"We'll catch up with them soon," Basenko assured him. "They

can't run and can't hide like foxes." He coughed as he tried to restrain his laughter.

"You rascal, I salute you," Lt. Schrecke now pulled alongside him. "You certainly pulled a fast one on Denikin. How did you do it?" He began to press Basenko to reveal how he got rid of his rival who schemed to replace him as the manager of the Potocki estate.

"I don't like to boast about it, the Ukranian was a tricky character. He sold food to the Jews, and helped those we hunted the last weekend to escape."

"You are the first smart Pole I've met," he flattered him. "I can learn something from you."

"It was simple. I came across a Jew hiding in the forest. He was the size of Denikin. A brilliant thought came to me. In exchange for a suit, I gave him food. I took the suit with me. It was almost new, in fact it resembled Denikin's own suit. He didn't like to put on the suit when I offered it to him as a gift. I gave the suit to my servant, except the vest, who put it in his closet, and took away the other suits. All this happened while I entertained him with a bottle. When he complained in the morning that his riding outfit and other suits were gone except a dress suit, I told him that my suits were also taken away to be disinfected against typhoid. My explanation quieted him down since I was also dressed in a civilian suit. As soon as he left I went to the kennel, rubbed the Jew's vest to the dogs' noses, and as I unleashed them, commanded them to go get him."

"What happened?"

"They got him. It was a little dark. The leader of the pack was new. I luckily got him a day before and he went right after Denikin, who wore the Jew's suit.

"You lucky dog." The Lieutenant smacked his lips.

They were now close to the river and the bloodhounds broke out into a maddening yelping as they waded into the water.

"Come back!" Basenko ordered them. "You'll only wet your noses and lose them. We'll go up the river where there are logs for crossing," he explained to Captain Messer.

The lead dog raced ahead, sniffing and growling. He was joined by the others, and the horses galloped behind them. They were on a sure trail this time. After a spirited chase, Basenko spied the dogs circling in their triumphant manner after bagging a victim. Basenko was the first to dismount and, after him, the Germans.

"That's only a dead Jew," Captain Messer cried out.

"There must be a treasure nearby," Basenko ignored their remarks. "I think I recognize him. He owned this forest. He must have hidden a treasure."

"The dogs can't smell it, but you can smell a treasure, eh Basenko?" Schrecke winked and Messer joined him in laughter.

"It is here! I found it!" Basenko cried out as he began to uncover a sack from underneath a mound of branches.

"What is this? Kommandant, you are an expert on such things." Messer derisively addressed Von Preissig.

"It is a scroll, a Torah, the Holy Bible on parchment."

"So that's what it is." Schrecke laughed. "It is not even worth a pound of tobacco."

"Maybe we can make something out of it," Messer suggested.

"That's a very good idea. Pocketbooks, or maybe we'll wrap it around him and burn the two."

"Will it burn?" Captain Messer asked. "It looks damp."

"It will smoke," the Lieutenant chuckled. "Have you a match, Basenko?"

"Yes, I have."

"Then light it, and now let's go back for a good dinner, but remember, Basenko, you owe us another hunt." Lt. Schrecke jabbed his finger at him.

They were on the run from midnight to morning and now they were tired and spent. David was stretched out behind a fallen tree. Rachel was in a sitting position, half chewing on a piece of bread and then pushing it toward the baby's lips. He sucked at it for a while, then fell asleep, shivering at intervals. His little fingers gripped her sleeve tightly. Abba looked away, trying to figure out whether he was not a burden to the others. He had made up his mind.

Avreml stood ready to move on. He was now a frightened boy, too young to endure the mental torture of being hunted like an animal, and too old to escape into the make-believe world of children. He longed to be with his mother, and was ready to follow her wherever she went. But he hated to be cooped up in a farmer's house, especially when he had to go down the dark cellar whenever neighbors visited.

Burka sat in dejected silence. The only thing that seemed to instill into him a fatalistic determination to hang on stubbornly, was his own substantial role in the group's survival. He remembered the days when there was a stigma attached to his family. As the bread-winner he was always one step ahead of the police, and the last one to be recognized in the community. Now it was different. He shared with them the same hazards and responsibilities. They even followed his advice.

"Burka!" David called him, "We'll wait till nighttime and then we'll go to town."

"Are you crazy? You'll be caught dead on the spot."

"If you can move around and take chances, why can't I?"

"I'm different, I can look like them, curse like them, roll like a drunk—besides, Von Preissig is on the lookout for you."

"We must find out what's happening to our people."

"This one disappeared, this one was shot, and this one was arrested, and this one died—that's all we hear."

"Burka, I must do something."

"Can you be a peasant? Can you cut up somebody with a knife? Crack a bloody whip over a swine's face? I can do all these things."

"How long will your luck hold up, and mine too?"

"I'll be back before darkness, then we'll decide what to do next." Before David could reply to him he was beyond the thicket.

David sat next to Abba, who was now reading again the same letters he had so laboriously composed and, even now, ready to correct.

"It is finished and ready to be mailed or delivered," he said to David. He rolled them up, wound a string many times around and finally tied it with a double knot. It was the first time that Abba did not use the bow knot.

"What do you mean?" David did not grasp the full meaning of the last part.

"I want this to become a record, like those used in Jewish history, that is all." There was no use to press him for further explanations. It was better for each to think that the other implied something else.

"David," Rachel called him.

"What is it?" he asked her.

"I'm terribly worried about mother and the twins." She was now fully recovered from the shock of flight by night. "How do we know Basenko's wagoner did not betray them?"

"Rachel, dearest." It was a long time, perhaps the first time she had heard it from him. It was always in his eyes and in all his words spoken to her. But she wanted to hear it like all happy girls or women hear it from the one beloved, especially in the open and in the presence of witnesses. Was there anything new, did he finally resolve that she was his legitimate beloved; were there two witnesses who could verify what, exactly, had happened to Zechariah, or maybe he had made a firm decision to ignore the strict *agunah* law which imposed upon her a waiting period of ten years before she could marry him. Maybe it was a sin even to think about it while the relentless enemy and death were stalking every living Jewish survivor within and without the walls. "I promise you," he continued "we'll find out without delay."

Several hours later Avreml thought he saw something moving in the distant woods.

"Somebody is over there, coming our way!" Avreml alarmed David.

"Sh—don't be frightened," David crouched and cocked his ear to the ground. "It's Burka."

"How do you know?"

"We once made up for anyone approaching to tap twice on the ground and a third time on the bottom of the trunk. We have signals like prayers for all occasions."

They waited and then Burka's shiny visor, at a rakish angle over his face, was unmistakable.

He hissed in that special way, which only he knew, not quite a whistling sound and much stronger than a puff of air.

"Burka, we must leave immediately to find Sarah Beile, and also to find out what is happening to those we left behind inside the walls."

"Yes, we'll do it. But there is a *mitzvah* we have to do first."

"What *mitzvah*?"

Burka was sweating and excited as he told in half sentences how he had overheard a peasant on the way to town describing a dead Jew near the old oak trees. It was probably Koppel with whose group they lost contact.

David told Burka not to tell anyone about the body. They left together without arousing anyone. They found the damp smoldering parchment over what seemed Koppel's body. Maggots were crawling over his bruised face. He must have offered resistance to the killer who thought that the parchment in the sack was a treasure. They wondered what happened to the others who were with him.

They lifted his body and carried it to an old uprooted oak in the midst of young pines. Half its roots still clung to the gaping hole on the bottom, while the ones above were clustered like the insides of a giant. They scooped out with twigs a shallow grave, cradled the pit with pine branches, and placed the body in it.

They then collected charred bits of parchment, ashes and the two *atzei chaim* trees of life, from the Torah scroll. David deposited blackened and burned parchment and ashes on one side of Koppel. When Burka lifted the trees of life upon which the scroll is rolled, David was astonished to see strips of parchment and scorched Hebrew letters and words still clinging to them. The words were legible. His lips read:

"Do not stand by when the blood of
thy brother is shed . . . . .
Justice, justice shalt thou pursue . . . . ."

"Look, I see the ten commandments there," Burka said and read haltingly some words on the burned parchment in the grave.

When David put down the trees of life on the other side of the body, the ethereal letters soared upward.

"Burned parchment and ascending letters," meaning burned bodies and liberated souls, David quoted Rabbi Chanina Ben Tradyon, who was burned alive by the Roman tyrants. The Jew and the Torah were indivisible and indestructible in life and in death.

After covering the grave with earth, needles, cones and boughs, they recited, in unison, the Kaddish, with only heaven, earth and the trees as witnesses and responding echoes:

"Extolled and hallowed be the name of God,
In the world which he is to create now,
And to revive the dead
And to restore them to a better world."

Burka stopped. David looked around, then continued.

> "And to liberate Jerusalem,
> And to restore the holy temple,
> And banish the evil of idolatry,
> And re-establish the heavenly kingdom on earth."

"I hear barking dogs and voices of hunters. Finish, David." He begged him, then cried out, "We are surrounded from all sides."

When David and Burka failed to return after a day, Rachel was alarmed. She was remorseful for having let them go in search of her mother. She wrapped the baby in her shawl, tied a babushka on her head and told Avreml:

"I'll be back in the morning. If I, or David, do not return, tell Abba to take you to Potocki's cottage. Remember, to Potocki's cottage before the gate is closed and the dogs are unleashed inside the grounds."

Towards evening she stumbled into Malinoski's house. She found Clara on the floor, crying over the body of her father.

"They killed him, Skura and his gang. They said you deal with the Jews, you must have a lot of money. They beat him. When they didn't find any money, they stomped him to death. They'll kill you too, get away from here, hurry."

Rachel walked only a short distance and then sat on a pile of leaves near a fence. She softened a piece of bread in her mouth and gave it to Ami. She munched on the rest herself and fell asleep.

When Rachel awoke there was heavy traffic towards the center of town. She realized it was Sunday. If she were to go in the opposite direction, toward Olshanke, and try to get help from Levondovski, she would surely be stopped. She decided that her best chance was to pretend she was one of them on the way to church with her baby. Once there, she could find a friend or one who would help her to get to Yatvietz, where the only decent Pole, besides Potocki, lived now that Malinoski, the friend, was murdered.

Rachel hurried with all her strength over the wooden bridge, alongside the ghetto wall which cut through the middle of the street. She bit her lips and closed her eyes past the desolate new synagogue in the rear between hers and David's house, now occupied by Polish guards.

Rachel envied the peace of all these men, women and children. Babies were carried proudly by mothers to be baptized and this Jewish baby Ami, where did she carry it, to life or to death? She envied them. Was not the baby as beautiful as any? Was she herself not as good as any of them? Before she even realized it, she was surrounded by curious and hostile eyes. One man stopped and said something. Another asked her:

"Why isn't the baby dressed in warm clothing?" Before he could engage her in conversation, she walked away. She was now in the midst of the unhurried strollers to and from the church; and to their favorite inns and stopovers, in the former Jewish houses, now occupied by Poles, Baltics and Germans. Rachel's anxiety mounted with every step. She must control herself, she thought. Ahead and sideways were surprised stares, and behind the unknown. She hugged the baby as if to protect it from a pursuing fiend. She patted and reassured Ami as his eyes surveyed the unfamiliar faces. It was like being followed and tracked down. His big innocent eyes reflected the forest, the sky, an horizon that divided and challenged heaven and earth; a world which flowed in his blood and to which he longed to return.

On the east side of the square, directly opposite the walled church she saw a crowd near Rabbi Kalir's house and other abandoned houses, appraising their worth and utility. She wondered if anyone inquired about its former occupants. What was once familiar was now distorted. Memories began to play on the strings of her heart. Everything around her seemed strange and terrifying. She lost her sense of direction. Blank faces were closing in from all sides. Some showed hate, others lust and passion. Panic seized her. She was now in flight, hurrying past faces until she found herself being whirled by the crowd.

Young Poles stopped to gaze at the beautiful girl with the baby in her arms. She was fair and dainty—so different. She seemed dressed for Sunday, but she didn't look like an ordinary peasant girl who came casually to church, while her main interests were elsewhere. Kruschetzki, whose daughter consorted with the Germans and thereby managed to buy Koppel's house for a bottle of vodka, followed Rachel closely. He caught up with her and called her, "Zidovka!" and then tensely, "Chlopzi, quick, call the Nemzi."

Now the stolid faces seemed more hostile. She recognized Anna from Olshanka.

"Anna, Anna!" she cried. But there was no answer from the girl she had befriended ever since she came to make up in her house on Sunday. She caught a glimpse of the multiple beaded combs in the red hair of Francesca from Ledinchine.

"Francesca!" she called out. Francesca turned to look at her and took off in the direction of admiring men. Unfriendly voices began to close in on her. The baby now began to cry. Kruschetzki and a woman, with the mob behind them, were in pursuit. Helmeted German soldiers pressed forward shouting "Swines, out of the way!" Someone screamed, "Stop her, kill the Jews!"

Rachel bolted and lunged forward, while clutching tightly to the crying baby, toward the packed mass frantically forcing its way through the gate. She froze and recoiled from the strange sounds, the dimly lit candles, the rigid statues and somber shadows that confronted her from the interior of the church. The baby's crying roused her from the momentary stupor. She turned and ran to her left where the figure of Aaron, the high priest, was in high relief on the front wall. She continued toward the rear of the court, where a Madonna and Child on a low pedestal guarded the entrance to the sacristy.

Polish guards now began to elbow their way toward her. The Germans were right behind them. Rachel was surrounded. The Polish guards pinned her arms to the wall opposite the Madonna.

"What are you? Beasts like the Germans?" she faced her pursuers.

"You love your own mothers, then why would you deny me motherhood? You love your children, why would you condemn this baby to death? All of you are mothers and fathers, why do you let our mothers and fathers be destroyed and their children starved before their own eyes? You would give your gold and sweat to erect in stone such a child and mother," she said, turned and pointed to the statue behind her. "You wouldn't let anyone touch or damage a statue of clay, yet you have with your own hands—some of you—killed and maimed innocent Jews."

No one moved nor stirred. No one could answer.

"Remember, it is God you are killing and torturing, not just Jews. How will you ever face God to atone for your sins?"

"Blasphemy!" a maddened voice broke the spell.

"God save us!" a woman called out and leaned against the wall in shame.

"We are lost!" an older man spread out his arms and a woman nearby began to cry. The German soldiers led her away. On the verge of collapse, they dragged her past the sculptured image of Moses pointing with a scepter to the ten commandments on the right front of the church. The baby, carried by a Polish policeman, cried violently above the mournful tones of organ music coming from the church.

Von Preissig glanced at the list of those under arrest. Most names were already crossed out, presumably shot. He blinked with his bloodshot eyes at the unmarked names: David Sokoloff, Rachel Novor, Burka Mazik and a few others. He was shorn of all authority; neither empowered to order their executions nor to commute their sentences to a slow, painful death via Kolbasin, Grodno and Auschwitz. Colonel Schwarzhund, now in full command, was under orders from Kommandant Rintzler to keep everything under the lid—even delay executions—until the final order came through.

Time was catching up with him. Within a few days or a week every living and starving Jew would be removed from the ghetto. As to his own future, the prospects seemed bleak. His last hope was his uncle if he could get here in time to outwit his mortal enemies.

He was very concerned, ever since a telegram came from General Werner von Stulpnagel on October 16th, that he would stop over at Suha-Vali. He re-read the telegram again: "FLYING EAST. STOPPING OVER." It was cryptic in its brevity. He examined the envelope and the seal. It was in order; that was his style. This was wartime and anything could happen. He was coming from the front. The nearest airfield was in Agustowa and from there he could get to Suha-Vali by car. What was wrong? He was always a trouble-shooter, ever since he expedited the completion of the Siegfried Line facing the Maginot Line. His subsequent intelligence data on the vulnerability of the formidable French fortification system advanced him to a high rank. No, he couldn't be in trouble after all his achievements. Or maybe he could. He was different, original and resourceful.

There was a grand hunt at Potocki's estate. Rintzler, the Kommandant from Grodno, would be there, and others. He wanted to be there, yet he was repelled by the cruel and bizarre manhunt, which was, of late, its main feature.

A week later—the final solution of the Suha-Vali ghetto was set in motion when a unit from Grodno was dispatched to oversee the "operation." The soldiers were lined up, inspected and told to lie down on the other side of the highway, screening them from any view of Suha-Vali. It was a special company of S.S. men, plus a contingent of polyglot mercenaries of Latvian, Lithuanian, and some Polish and Ukranian volunteers. They were well equipped for their task.

The swaggering Hauptschlak was in command. He was once a prison guard, then served well in Auschwitz and was rewarded for his "zeal and thoroughness" by being promoted to "Field Apteilung" in charge of transferring the Jews to distant ghettoes and liquidations according to the blackprint plan.

At last, Colonel Schwarzhund arrived in a car, accompanied by Captain Messer, Lieutenant Schrecke and Sergeant Murad. After a while, Hauptschlak took out papers from a portfolio. With quick glances, they checked last population figures, speed of property seizures, time-table for "transport," and "special" problems. The last two were underlined with triple red lines.

"Any corrections?" Hauptschlak asked.

"Everything is in order, except that we'll have to start within days on project Z, as the final and revised liquidation and transfer of all Jews to Grodno was designated only a day before."

"Why so early?"

"You see, we had a little incident. A German sometimes becomes as sentimental as a girl over a poem and then he is no good," Schwarzhund hissed.

"I don't understand."

"Some Jews escaped, but most were caught. Very few will get away alive. There is a Von Preissig who is the Kommandant of this town; he's an intellectual. He is sentimental about Jews."

"I see. You expect any other breakout?"

"No. They are well guarded—but we would like to surprise them. We are successful with the Jews only because they never know our intentions. Would you believe it—they don't expect us to be so strict and unemotional?"

"This Von Preissig—a Junker, I presume—is he meddling?"

"I don't really know what he wants. A strange German—but it

is better if we surprise him, too. I can see him in his pajamas at five A.M.," Schwarzhund chuckled.

"Herr Schwarzhund, you are a good Gestapo man. You think of everything. I'll recommend you for promotion. How would you like to be next in command of the Grodno ghetto? I also have connections."

"Something more exciting!" Schwarzhund stamped with his foot.

"How about Medaynek or Auschwitz?"

"Auschwitz—that's my ambition," Schwarzhund was delighted like a boy being initiated into a gang.

"Before I forget, all soldiers will bivouac in a Polish village. I know they don't like the smelly huts—but there is plenty of pork and cabbage in their cellars and potato mash—powerful like Russian vodka. They must awake at four. *Aufwiedersehen.*"

When Schwarzhund returned to the red house with Hauptschlak as his guest, he called in his aides for special instructions.

"You have wives, you have children, you have sweethearts," Schwarzhund hooked his thumb over his belt, "you know what to do? You'll get full details and instructions about the exact time tomorrow. Meanwhile, these are the essentials for you to remember: All occupants of the ghetto will be transferred to Kolbasin and the Grodno ghetto, and from there by railroad to other places for work and resettlement. I repeat, work and resettlement! Remember these words. Let them take bundles—five pounds for each person. All copper and metal utensils are to be taken away from them. All who possess money, diamonds, gold watches, are to surrender them for safekeeping. Remember the word 'safekeeping.' Houses are to be left in good order—no panic—in custody of the state, until they return. Those criminals who escaped will not be given any work; they'll be treated according to the law of sabotage and destruction. Don't speak to anyone, not even to Polish guards. Assemble them for routine patrol. Lt. Schrecke, you will arrange transport, about eight hundred wagons, we can't spare trucks. You, Capt. Messer, will be in charge of personnel, and you, Murad, Todt and Ratten will be responsible to me. Any questions?"

"What about hidden diamonds and gold in their teeth," a guard asked as they responded with laughter.

"Germans, this is serious. If you find them, collect them—don't search them—that will be taken care of in Grodno."

"What about women and children?" Murad inquired. "Will they go along? If we separate them, they'll get suspicious. Most of the old and sick are gone."

"What about the girls?" Schrecke, who had a hunch, followed with another question.

"You'll find your answers in the special booklet—*'Transportation und Arbeit,'* as for you, lieutenant, leave the girls to us. You are an actor, why don't you put on an act for the Jews?"

"You mean, dress myself as Santa Claus, put on a mask and laugh at the Jews, Ho! Ho! Ho! and throw poisoned candy to the Jewish children? The Jews wouldn't be here by Christmas. But we can celebrate Christmas now!" The room exploded with bursts of hyena laughter.

As they walked out through the door, Schwarzhund shook hands with every man, happy and exuberant that at last he would be able to prove his ability to carry out such an important project for the Fatherland.

Across the hall, Von Preissig was alone, almost isolated. No one came to see him or consult with him. Schwarzhund had ordered Ratten, the cook and undercover Gestapo man, to watch Von Preissig's movements.

"Everything is sealed," Schwarzhund gloated as he stretched out on the sofa. Suha-Vali was doomed.

WAR PRISONERS IN CANADA FOUGHT
SHACKLING. ITALIAN PRISONERS
WELL OFF IN INDIA. CONVERTED
BULGARIAN JEWS EXEMPTED FROM
WEARING STAR OF DAVID.

*The righteous man perisheth and no one
cares . . .*

Isaiah, 57:1.

*The righteous man is doomed because evil
is rampant.*

Taanith, 10.

29

WHO WILL TELL THE WORLD?

Johann Kristus Von Preissig was now more than ever aware that everything sacred to him was on the verge of collapse.

Germany faced disaster. The religion which he professed was exposed to him as empty and inept in the greatest crisis it faced. His own young son asked him in his last letter if "Love thy neighbor as thyself," applied also to Jews and other nationalities. He asked this himself in his own conscience, and he hoped—if it was not too late—that all Christians should ask this themselves. How can we atone for all these uninterrupted bloody wars against each other and unforgivable crimes against the children of Israel, who are God's witnesses on this earth to judge us and condemn us? How can we ever face them again, we millions of Cains murdering millions of Abels?

It was all in vain now he thought to change himself or avert catastrophe. The Germans were trained to fight, hate and invoke bloodshed needlessly. Something very vicious was permeating everything German. The entire society was therefore responsible for this heinous crime of genocide against the Jewish people. The way he saw it the soldiers pretended that they obeyed the commanders, the officers executed orders decreed by the generals who sold their honor and souls to the mad Austrian corporal. The judges, clergymen, writers, executives, teachers, bankers, capitalists, workers, rich, poor, men, women, all who voted, approved or remained silent and indifferent were guilty participants in these unheard of bestialities.

He could only think about it but as a good German, he thought it was of no consequence to proclaim it openly. Right now he was apprehensive about his uncle General Stulpnagel. Was he one of the very few officers who plotted to eliminate Hitler, by violent means? Could the very few change a whole society at this late date when everything seemed lost?

He relaxed his clenched fist and straightened out the crumpled dispatch from Stulpnagel, and reread it for the third time:

> Do not disclose this to a soul. You were right in disposing of the last message. I am dispatching this with a trusted aide who is risking his life and ours. Remember the date, tomorrow midnight I will meet you at a point seven kilometers eastward to Yanove from your office. The chauffeur will simulate a flat tire, at that point. No lights.

Before dusk he drove the car himself. His eyes darted frequently from the road to the mirror. From a distance he recognized the general's car; the chauffeur was on his knees removing the flat tire. He stopped the car, got out and saw the general waving to him from a clearing to his left. After formalities, they both sat down on the massive trunk of the uprooted fallen tree.

"Don't be afraid, I have taken care of all eventualities," he calmed the fears of his nephew Von Preissig. When the roar of a motorcycle raced nearer, to investigate, the usual breakdown on Polish roads, he had an excuse ready.

"I suppose you know what has to be done," Von Preissig complimented him for anticipating even the pretense to be wounded.

"It is all routine," he shrugged it off.

"What have you uncovered about Todt?"

"It is very simple, I have with me several of his incriminating letters. I will place photostats of these in the hands of Col. Schwarzhund, no, still better in the hands of Murad, who I learned is an overseer for the Gestapo to report on your efficiency to Kommandant Rintzler from Grodno, who in turn is responsible for the liquidation of all ghetto inmates within the

Grodno district. Murad will take care of him anytime you set the date. As for Col. Schwarzhund, that's another matter."

"How?"

"He is above you in authority. His orders come direct from Himmler's office, through Rintzler. You are probably aware that he collects loot through his subordinates which he shares with higher ups. His power depends on pay offs. I have discovered his secret bank accounts in Switzerland under an assumed name with a transfer account in a South American country. His demise will hardly cause a ripple among his confederates who will now be in line for bigger cuts."

"*Die Lumpen,*" Von Preissig said with contempt.

"Col. Schwarzhund, I learned will be promoted and transferred to Auschwitz. He is very anxious to close the ledger in this town."

"When?"

"Any day," the general paused, "I think by the end of October or November, the men want to go on furlough for Christmas and get through with it without delay."

"You have to eliminate him before he does it to you," the general advised him with the furtive cold look in his eyes that disposed of enemies—anyone condemned was labelled an enemy —whenever necessary.

"How?"

"Every man has a weakness, and a day when it can be exploited against him."

"He drinks."

"We all do."

"Moderately," Von Preissig was on the defensive.

"Any vices?"

"He likes women."

"It is quite proper in our army."

"He boasts, and is very inquisitive about military secrets."

"I have checked into that. Anything unusual or abnormal?"

"Almost none, except glass, he breaks glass."

"This is interesting, tell me more."

"He once related how he enjoyed shattering windows of synagogues and plates of Jewish stores on November 10, 1938."

"Yes, that was one of the shameful nights about which we did nothing."

"Oh yes, I think I told you that at a hunting party last fall, I found him standing before a broken pane of a kennel. The dog broke out and was attacking him but he was entirely under a spell of masochism."

"It is a fixed phobia. This paranoiac mania will do, when do you go hunting?"

"I don't—the victims are mostly human beings, Jews, Poles, Russian captives. I stay away."

"Join them. Prepare German police dogs to bid your command. I will arrange it, they have a whole kennel at the Kolbasin station, to herd Jewish inmates into the box cars on the way to Auschwitz."

"What is the plan?"

"Get him aside on a pretext and draw him to the hut where the dogs will be waiting to be released by a broken glass."

"Wouldn't the dogs be cut?"

"After you wave his shirt or something of his, they will disregard their own bleeding and bound away like lightning after the scent."

"Will they attack a uniform?"

"They'll attack anything if you label it as an intented victim, just like human beings."

"Suppose his personal guards rush to save him?"

"Are they loyal to him?"

"I don't know."

"The success of a conspiracy depends on several factors."

"General, are you personally involved?"

"Of course I am, that's why I am here!"

"I mean something of a national scope."

"I have no comment. To know something in which you are not involved would only be a weapon against you."

"I understand."

"I hope nothing goes wrong here or anywhere. But if it does it would be a black prophecy for our nation."

They bid farewell to one another. As General Stulpnagel walked to his car, he looked back to his nephew and to the loneliness which stretched between them.

The general signalled to his chauffeur. The response came momentarily, the motor turned over with a coughing and then burst from a deafening roar into a smooth whir that chugged slowly and then faster on the way to Sokolke.

Von Preissig started his own motor, switched on the lights.

Before he made the turn he leaned out through the door to look back to the distant beams of the General stabbing with profusion and then vanishing into the blackness. He turned his wheel in the opposite direction of the darkness ahead.

Von Preissig could not sleep, he was neither exhausted nor tired. The carefully plotted plan of his uncle General Stulpnagel worked to perfection. Everything followed the script. Sgt. Todt, once the photostats of his correspondence with his wife were submitted to the Gestapo, was finished. After all it was not too difficult to persuade—with the help of the intelligence office— that both he and his wife with their silly complaints about the bombings of Bitterfeld near the strategic Luna Werke, were actually informing an agent who was able to intercept such mail. They found hoarded jewelry and other valuables which Sgt. Todt collected in Suha-Vali, again evidence of a payoff. It was very clever to send such information through supposed letters of complaint.

The Luna Werke which furnished precious synthetic oil for the air force in the midst of critical shortages, was finally crippled right after these letters were uncovered. The accusation against Sgt. Todt was plausible. With Todt out of the way he also had to eliminate the other Gestapo watchdog, Murad. It was so simple, he wondered why he didn't think of it before. All he had to do was to invite Murad who liked hunting to come along.

But the ingenious scheme to get rid of the very cunning Schwarzhund, the pseudo-colonel, excited him the most, despite the wariness of his uncle. It was so masterful a stroke and beyond suspicion. The days were perfect. Schwarzhund himself, was in a good mood; he had important mail, and was only surprised why Von Preissig, the erstwhile snob who despised hunting at the Potocki estate, now in the cold days of November with the first flurries of snow in the air, became a hunting enthusiast.

Without difficulty the Kommandant persuaded him that it was nerves. Everything was coming to a close. The ghetto would be liquidated. He once had plans about his own method to deal with it, or rather experiment with it. His plans were rejected. He had to obey, and now what, what of the future? He needed meanwhile a bit of relaxation. He couldn't drink alone. Would Schwarzhund mind if he joined him? Of course he didn't. It was good strategy not to show his hand yet, against Von Preissig.

The next morning the Kommandant manuevered his prey
adroitly.

"What about that kennel, why aren't the dogs after the scent?"
he intercepted Schwarzhund ready to dash off with the second
wave of hunters. From behind the glass window of the kennel
upon which was marked "Intelligence" and a warning "do not
tamper," the howling shepherd dogs strained to get out. Only a
while ago, he had removed Schwarzhund's shirt and Murad's cap
from cellophane bags and left it in the kennel. The dogs who had
a good dosage of their smells were now straining to get out. Von
Preissig led the curious Schwarzhund straight to the kennel. At
once he heard the pleasant tinkling of broken glass, that of the
oversized window of the kennel. Immediately after that came
the blood curdling cry of Schwarzhund who was attacked by the
vicious, well trained dogs, whom he released by his chronic
mania to break glass. Several of the pack who picked up the
scent of Murad raced in his direction. Everyone was running;
and he ran crying for help, for the dogs were right after him too.
But in an instant he saw Ratten and other Gestapo men who
swarmed in from the woods to save Schwarzhund. Murad however was torn to bits before the enraged dogs were clubbed into
submission with the help of Basenko and others who came
fast.

"What happened," they asked Von Preissig, "you were with
him?"

"I don't know, mad dogs attacked us." He stopped short as if a
ghost passed by when he saw Schwarzhund still alive carried off
in his bloodied and ripped hunting uniform.

Schneur Zalmen Sanzer did not dare wake the Rabbi. He
waited by the door. The rebetzin said, "It is cold outside, come
in I'll see . . ."

He waited patiently and he recited meanwhile all the Halle-
luyahs—the special hymnal praises of King David.

"Baruch Habo" (blessed of God), the Rabbi greeted him.

"Rabbi, I came to see you about a matter that requires your
immediate consideration."

"I am your disciple. But before I came to this town, I was also
a disciple of the Lubavicher Rebbi."

"A great Rabbi. Continue."

"During an emergency he visited the resting place of his father. It behooves you that at such a time, you could—you should likewise visit your father of blessed memory, that is his resting place on the *Beth Almin* (house of eternity).''

"I had every intention to visit my parents of blessed memory, regardless of the risk, and offer a prayer for their intercession before the Almighty."

"What I mean . . ."

"Yes, go on!"

"Among the pious *Chasidim* it is done."

"And we *Mithnagdim* are not pious?"

"God forbid, only *Chasidim* are not ashamed to speak up, to petition God through a pious man."

"Am I that pious?"

"You are—and in this opinion I am not humble. Write your request on a *mezuzah* parchment, and bring it to his grave. I'll go along and call upon eight more to constitute a minyan."

"Good, if God wills it, good, summon volunteers," then in a reversal of tone, "No, no, I myself will go there."

"Why, we need a congregation."

"It is my verdict."

"I don't understand."

"It is forbidden by the decree of the *zedim* to visit the old cemetery ever since they designated a plot within the ghetto as the last resting place, *Olam Hoemeth* (world of truth). I cannot risk a single life."

"What about your life?"

"No one can take another's life, by design or risk, not even his own."

"Then why, if it involves your life, take this risk?"

"My life is not my own—it belongs to every one."

"As soon as Schneur Zalmen departed, Rabbi Kalir left for Von Preissig's office.

"You cannot see the Kommandant now, the orders are strict," a Gestapo man told him. The harsh face was one of a group he had never seen—not that he wanted to remember their images—but he couldn't help but notice that there was something peculiar about them. Their hard looks could not conceal the seething hatred reflected in their eyes.

"I must see him, please," he pleaded with the gruff black uniformed Gestapo man.

"Officer, he is an official of the community, admit him!" Von Preissig intervened.

"But I have orders."

"As long as I am in this office I will give the orders," he glared at the Gestapo man.

"What do you want?" Von Preissig asked the Rabbi.

"I am asking permission to go outside to my parents' resting place."

"On the cemetery?"

"Yes."

"What for?"

"To offer a prayer."

"To whom?"

"A supplication to God in behalf of my people."

"Is God to be found there?"

"God is everywhere to those who want Him."

"Well you can go to the graves of your parents at night. I will send an escort, but if you are caught, you are on your own. Pray for me," Von Preissig said in an undertone.

The escort—Ludke the orderly in the black uniform of the S.S.—was at the Rabbi's door promptly at 2 a.m. A car was waiting outside.

"Take along a white sheet," he advised him to blend with the snow blanketed ground, and with this he unrolled a gray peasant robe. "Cover yourself now to make you less noticeable."

After showing a forged signature of Schwarzhund and stating underneath "to recover buried articles" the guard waved the car through the opened gate. Within minutes Ludke stopped near the entrance. The wall that once surrounded the *Beth Almin* (house of eternity), was breached in many places. The stones, some overturned, others smeared and desecrated loomed through the gaps.

"I'll wait across in the woods," Ludke indicated. "If cars pass by, lay low. Not more than fifteen minutes," he checked his wrist watch. "Staff cars from Grodno are to arrive within half an hour." He had an idea that they would come to arrest Von Preissig who would sooner or later be implicated for his abortive attempt on Schwarzhund's life.

"Help us, O God, the Rabbi supplicated from the confessional as he stood in awe before the modest stone of his father inscribed:

> To the memory of this pious saint
> Father of Torah, teacher of Mitzvoth
> The light of God, the soul of our life.

He continued: "The pious man is gone. Truth vanished from the sons of man. If not for Thee, Oh God, when evil men rose against us, we would have long been swallowed up by their wrath.

"Did you not say," he departed from the Hebrew text, "that a father and son shall not be slaughtered on the same day? Did you not make a covenant of life between thee, the Torah and Israel? Did you not vow that never again shall there be a flood nor a lawless generation? Did you not command that the children of Israel are thine to serve thee, but not to be enslaved by slaves? Is not the whole dedication of thy people Israel—chosen for this purpose to contain evil, to stop *Bnei Bli Yaal*—the Godless, the merciless, the soulless—then why do you allow *reshaim, zedim*, sons of Satan to blot out your holy name from the face of the earth?"

"Hear us, open thy eyes and see our desolation in thy city," he returned to the text. "For it is not because of our piety that we implore thee, but to redeem thy name."

Rabbi Kalir paused, then instinctively offered an intimate prayer to his father in Yiddish:

> Heiliker tate, reis auf di himlen
> (Holy father, rend asunder the heavens)
> Treisel auf dem Kiseh Hakoved
> (Shake up the Throne of His Glory)
> Tumeh lozt nit durch unzer tefilas
> (A vile Tumeh intercepts our prayers.)
> Wer ist dos wos steht in veg?
> (Who is it who bars our way?)
> Wer vertreibt di Shechineh?
> (Who is it who exiled the Holy Shechineh?)
> Tate Zadik, hob rachemones auf unz
> (Fatherly saint, have mercy upon us)
> Rateve unz, weil keiner, keiner—
> (Save us for there is no one else)
> Zeh ich leg awek a tefilo zu Got.
> (Behold I am placing a prayer to God.)
> Brang es zum Kiseh Hakoved
> (Bring it before the Throne of Glory)
> Es is durchgewekt mit unzer treren und blut
> (It is drenched with our tears and blood)

Sei mispalel far Mashiach und die Geluah Shelemo
(Offer thou a prayer for Messiah and final redemption).

It seemed so strangely quiet in the snow blanketed expanse
that held back darkness. Young firs swayed over faintly lettered
tombstones and their glazed needles shivered in the chilled dim
moonlight that glided in and out of clouds to the echoes of his
ascending supplications. Silvery phantom beams bounced off the
bare wilbert, chestnut and willow trees that kept company with
generations who departed to another realm through this tranquil
garden.

The mounds of earth were still fresh over the graves of the
starved, killed and tortured from the forced labor units outside
the walls. The frozen grass peered through the snowy crust over
the graves of Gedaliah Sklar, Israel Grodzensky and others who
joined the ranks of the thousands and millions of a two thousand
year history of Jewish martyrdom.

"Forgive me, God," he whispered, and he remembered that
there in the women's section beneath a lonely birch, its white
paleness glistening in the elusive moonlight, was his mother, and
he had not yet said anything to her.

Mame, geh und wek auf unzer muter Rachel fun ir kever
(Mother, go and wake mother Rachel from her grave.)
Zol sie aufweken die Avos und Imohes
(Let her rouse the Patriarchs and Matriarchs)
Und ale Zusamen dem getlichen Nevi Haneviim
(And together the Godly prophet of prophets (Moses))
Zolen zei ale zuzamen fihren dir und mein tate zum Kiseh Hakoved
(Let them all guide thee and my father to the Throne of Glory)

The veiled moon did not reveal to him, that time was ticking
away in fatal sequences. At last he rolled up the parchment upon
which he inscribed the formal prayer in Hebrew—the very one
he had just uttered in Yiddish, and pushed it through the crust of
frozen snow that covered the grave of his father.

He recited the psalm and intoned:

I will say to my God, thou art my refuge and my fortress.

He stopped to reflect its meaning. The *reshaim* who denied
refuge to God, destroyed the Jews' fortress.

Do not fear the terror by night
Neither the deadly arrow by day

> Nor the pestilence that spreads in darkness
> And the holocaust that ravages at high noon.

In normal times a Jew feared God and not these terrors, who were kept at bay. But now that these demons were in the hearts and minds of their enemies they emerged as Satan.

> He who establishes peace in heaven
> May he also establish peace on earth
> For all and Israel, Amen!

As the Rabbi concluded the Kaddish, Ludke was furious.

"Come on, before you get me into trouble."

At headquarters everything was in high gear that night for the final solution of Suha-Vali. Col. Schwarzhund, his forehead bandaged and a deep open gash on his cheek, finally sat in Von Preissig's chair. Black uniformed S.S. officers and Gestapo men in civilian garb were moving in and out like ghosts. The sagging front in Russia, the hard blows inflicted by the allied air force on German cities, factories and military installations were all forgotten. Col. Schwarzhund was full of rage. He felt that Von Preissig defied him once more by allowing the Rabbi to leave the ghetto on the very night of the last exodus.

"Von Preissig will be transferred to Grodno within half an hour, Capt. Messer reported. I have denied him food and water, but so far he has not confessed."

"Good. Put a heavy guard on him. Have you found out anything about Ludke?"

"We shadowed him to and from the cemetery. Shall I bring him in?"

"Not yet. It is eleven now. I'll be up till midnight. Soldiers and guards must be up at four. All in ghetto must be up at three."

"Isn't that too early?"

"It is never too early for them. It is very effective to surprise your enemy after midnight."

"What about the wagons?"

"We must not tip them off. The wagons must be on the square at five sharp. The Jews who will be lined up by that time must be on the wagons by six. Bring in Ludke!"

Von Preissig's devoted orderly showed welts on his face and his uniform was stained with blood.

"Where did you get the pass to escort the Rabbi to the old cemetery?" the colonel fired at him the question.

"From Col. Von Preissig, and it had your signature."

"Did you know it was forged?"

"No!"

"What have you done with the jewels you dug up at the cemetery?"

"I didn't dig and have no jewels."

"Why didn't you report when a general came to visit Von Preissig?"

"I was only an orderly. I obeyed the Kommandant's orders."

"Unless you tell us more details about Von Preissig's conspiracy, you will be executed."

"I told the truth."

"Truth? Only that which serves us is truth. Guards, take him away. Stay here," he turned to Messer, "at last I have learned to drink," he said and took out a cognac bottle and glasses from a drawer.

"Herr Kommandant, a toast to your success," Messer emptied the glass into his mouth.

"A toast to our success," the colonel responded.

"What will happen to a man like Von Preissig?"

"Rintzler will extract from him a confession to implicate others, who don't fit into our scheme. Then he will be executed, and we will live happily long after. This is our world. We dispense life and death, just like God."

"Some God!" Messer burst out with laughter. The new Kommandant unable to laugh because of the bruised cheek, almost cried in frustration.

Rabbi Kalir who had plodded home alone after the nervous Ludke escorted him through the gate, stood forlorn near the window. Snow flakes floating down to the previous grey layers gleamed faintly through the darkness outside. Tiny lights flashed on and off from several front covered windows. Lonely voices of the night escalated into blood chilling screams and moaning cries. Harsh voices and explosive shots were followed by an eerie quiet. He was tired, sick and crushed by the endless lamentations. What he had feared—the final expulsion of the Jews to an unknown fate—had now reached the bitter end. Zipporah, who had been waiting for him, removed his coat and boots, and helped him to his bed. The room was crowded with his faithful people.

More were waiting ouside for a farewell blessing, perhaps the last.

"Rabbi, please rest," the gracious Velvke who girded his ebbing strength as he pushed to his side, pleaded.

"As long as I have strength . . ." For a moment everything seemed blurred, then as the Rabbi looked straight into the benefactor's gray but twinkling eyes, he concluded, "I must speak to them."

"Rabbi," he heard a voice from one who raised his head slowly. It was Label, in whose house he sojourned this last night. He who differed with him in ideology, and who was despondent after his wife died, scorned at any further attempt to escape in the midst of so much hostility on the outside. The Rabbi put his hand on his shoulder in a gesture that said: I understand. You have returned, you were never far away. What else is there to be said. I bless you.

More pushed forward. The Rabbi raised his limp hand to anoint with a greeting, a phrase that swirled in his memory and a blessing that hung on his lips. Then his hand dropped down with only a nod, a sigh and sad eyes to look from behind a slowly dropping curtain.

David, who saw the coming of this disaster in his visions, now returned himself to save his parents—find Rachel and himself. His parents were gone. The Jews in the ghetto, though they awaited their doom stoically, challenged to the very end this judgement at the hands of the contaminated creatures. They clung with their last hope to anything that would redeem their age old belief that they who were always miraculously saved from tyrants, murderers and Satans, would also be redeemed now. Even David, who saw the fulfillment of the worst, still sought, like Jeremiah, the only sign that makes even the most disastrous of prophecies true—the hint of a redemption.

"He is here," someone shouted, and the doomed stirred from their own fettered agonies.

"Who?"

"David."

"He is—he just came in with Shmuel Leiser."

"Call them in."

"David, Shmuel," he greeted them warmly, but visibly shaken.

"Is anything? . . ." he wanted to add, "wrong," but such a word would accomplish nothing.

"David." His voice could not formulate the next word, as if

speech was useless or forbidden. He looked aside, not daring to
tell the two young men what was locked inside his heart. You
should not see me this way, going into a dark exile and I should
not behold you—the flower of our youth—going to waste. Why?
Where is the crime and where are the judges? What a foolish
world. I am tired and will depart from this wicked world without
regrets.

Only one thing bothers me, he seemed to be saying as he
watched David and Shmuel tie the two bed sheets, which held
their last earthly possessions. Who will tell the world? Who will
live to tell the world and our brothers what we endured?

Rabbi Kalir was tiring. He sat down on the table near the
window. He saw only the listless shadowy movements, the last
frantic errands by children who with their last strength injected
simulated normalcy. There was a commotion outside. David
opened the door and saw at the gate Abba leading a boy, it
looked like Avreml. What could it mean? Only more bad news.
For to return within the walls meant only one thing, that outside
it was even worse.

Very little was said between David and Abba on the way to
the Rabbi in Label's house, where he would also stay. It was
only a matter of hours before all of them would be taken away. It
was hopeless to escape from so many bestial enemies stalking the
Jews everywhere. It was even more horrible to surrender after a
long persistent struggle.

"David, I had to come back . . ." Abba released the pent up
painful words.

"I know," David conceded that it would be cruel to expect any
one to escape, without the slightest chance to survive against
vicious people, hunger and the lonely misery of being hunted
day and night by murderers.

"After you left, Rachel went looking for her mother and you.
We finally went to Potocki, as she instructed us, if you or she
didn't return in a few days. One morning we heard dogs barking
outside the gate. "Germans!" Clara roused us and took us
through the back door of the garage below. She took us to a
recluse in a nearby hamlet. Avreml cried continually. Also, the
neighbors bothered us."

"Come to me, Avreml," David said to him. "I am not going to
question you. I can guess," he tried to imply. But at the same
time, he was eager to find out for himself how he fared.

When they came inside, the Rabbi raised himself to welcome them.

"We found him shivering near the gate," David told him. "The guards were kind; they said, "Let him go inside among his own people." But David did not tell the truth. He didn't have the heart—that Skura snickered and said, "Let him die inside, there are enough Jewish corpses outside."

"Avreml, come nearer," the Rabbi called him.

"Rabbi, I couldn't stay there. I couldn't sleep at night," Avreml began to sob.

"Did you get food over there?"

"Yes, except the meat—I would not eat it."

"Then what was it?"

"Every night kids, neighbors, came near my window and screamed, "Jew, we'll kill you.""

"But they left after their screaming?"

"Yes."

"Then why couldn't you sleep?"

"There was a picture in my room."

"You mean an ikon?"

"Yes, he held a cross, and his eyes looked very angry. I dreamt every night that he wanted to kill me with the cross."

"Avreml, don't cry."

"No, I don't cry, it only hurts."

"Give him the best food you have, Zipporah," he called to his wife.

"Where is Rachel?" David asked.

"She is safe," Velvke said.

"Safe? Where?"

"She was arrested and will be released to-day," Velvke reassured him.

"Why didn't you tell me? It is my fault. I shouldn't have left her alone."

"David," the Rabbi interrupted, "no one is at fault. This happened to so many of our people. What could any one among us have done to prevent it? It is they outside this wall who are the guilty."

"Where is her mother?" he asked Shmuel.

"Her mother is with the twins in Yatvietz. They went to get some assurance that the young children handed over to Christian families would not be converted."

"There are nuns there. They have to get permission from the priest to make such a promise in writing," Shmuel explained.

"Even if it is promised, there is no guarantee," Abba added.

"In time of distress, they all plunder and tear from us away not only our houses and possessions, but our own blood and flesh," Abba said in a voice choked with emotion.

"Rabbi bless me and my son," Alter and Joshua approached him.

"Where is Zorach?"

"He has not returned."

"God protect and safeguard him and all of us."

"Joshua, here is a knife," Label called him aside and handed him a shortened kitchen knife sheathed in leather. "I'll even give you my revolver. We'll teach you this craft of Esau to live by wits and weapons. You'll have to learn to defend yourself and even kill."

"It is needless to sacrifice him," Rabbi Kalir, who cupped his ear to catch the conversation, protested. "We are dealing with vicious animals, we must not provoke them. They'll be looking for any pretext to shed our blood. How could we have made the mistake to imagine that the spark of godliness—even a tiny particle—was in *reshaim*. We were endowed with ability to discover God. Why did our wisdom and instinct fail us to uncover the fiends walking this earth in the counterfeit image of human beings."

He was unable to go on: he was probing too deeply into the restricted limits of the mystery. When one asks a question and believes that God has the answer, this is piety. But, when one also knows the answer, it is a challenge, why? Why did God allow it to happen? Maybe God himself regrets and will eventually rectify it. "A baby," he explained his answer, "has no fear of animals. It smiles to them, because it was nurtured by a loving mother and tender experiences surround it all the time. Oh, my people, my Jewish brethren, my children ..."

"Label, come here. No, I am not angry. There is nothing to say, I only want to leave something with you. Once an atheist taunted a Rabbi: 'If God does not approve the worshipping of the sun, moon and stars, why does he not destroy these.' He replied, 'Shall God destroy the world because of the maniacs?' "

"Rabbi, please rest!" Reb Velvke came to his side again.

"My *siddur, talis, tephilin* and some of my books." He enumerated religious items in his velvet bag and the books within the five pound limit like one preparing on a long unknown journey. "The rest," he said in a regretful tone, "we will leave behind; they are of no use now. Don't forget," he said as an after thought, "prepare food and clothing for the children, the mothers, the sick, and others who need help."

Rabbi Kalir got off his bed. Zipporah, who was busy with Chaye salvaging what they considered as portable, now rushed from the kitchen.

"Reb Shepsel, wait," and handed him his coat which he put on himself and then adjusted his velour hat over the velvet skull cap. He walked up to the bookcase where his great treasures majestically lined the sturdy shelves on both sides of his table. The deluxe leather bound sets of the *Talmud, Shulchan Aruch* codes, Maimonides, and rabbinical response towered above the more compact editions of the Biblical exegesis, classical Hebrew and Yiddish books, as well as foreign language books in German, Polish, and Russian added by his sons. Some stood straight, others leaned, sprawled or rested on piles of rabbinical magazines and Hebrew, Yiddish and Polish newspapers—all of prewar vintage.

Reviewing in his mind the vast learning and wisdom stored inside them, recalling the long years of exhilarating companionship and happines which they shared, he fondled them with his fingers as he passed along. A volume was now in his right hand. He cradled it and then opened it and glanced to the page that recited itself, "Charity and loving kindness are as important as all the other precepts; and loving kindness supersedes charity." Putting it back in its place, he glanced longingly to friends with whom he must part, "Pleasant Fields," "Forests of Honey," "The Crown of Torah," "The Great Luminary," "The Roar of a Lion,"—"Outlines of the Mishnah," and other rabbinical classics.

It was a last embrace, like heaven and earth kissing at the advent of the Messiah to come. Was this the last legacy, the last time? . . . He could not control himself; words came slowly. "My fellow Jews, you wonder what happened to me. I just can't collect myself. I feel we are being encircled by a river of fire and hate, *Sambatyon* 2. We must break the chains of the Messiah to deliver us from the *reshaim*." The Rabbi stopped; he heard undertones.

"How long have we waited for the Messiah! But the *reshaim* hold him back."

Velvke felt frustrated because he could not get enough food for the poor, especially students.

"*Amalek, Amalek,* has returned from *Gehennam*," Alter sighed.

"God's kingdom," Isaac pointed upward, "will not allow *reshaim,* he will convert them to good people. He promised so."

"You are right, everyone of you, we don't deserve the *Gehennam*; but I can feel its hot fire coming closer."

"But Rabbi," the feeble voice of Isaac demanded, "why are we threatened by this fear of Gehennam, why must we die to be resurrected?"

"Why?" it swept like a reverberating echo to the ends of the earth, "Why?" I don't know. I can't know everything. God did not disclose it."

Zipporah had just put away in a corner a German book with revulsion and fingered a Polish and Russian book which she hardly understood, when Rabbi Kalir called out as he wrapped his Torah and manuscript in his talis, "Where is my letter?" It was the last letter to his son Judah that he wanted to give to David. "It is in the Torah," he pointed to the books.

"What is going on here, Juden?" Messer's gruff voice came from behind a flashing light while others at this side, threatened with their guns.

"The Rabbi," Velvke gestured, "is very sick."

"No medicine, much fever," Chaye added.

The S.S. men checked and even pretended to examine him. Ordinarily, they would order the transfer of anyone sick to the sanatorium—not to heal—but as a counter measure for being off the work detail. But now with the "final solution" not far away, Messer told them to leave things as they were warning only, "Remember, what our new Kommandant told you: that everything must be left in good order." Annoyed that such a fuss was made over books spread out over tables or stacked away on shelves, he grabbed a soldier's gun and angrily knocked down books, including the family Pentateuch from the Rabbi's book stand.

"Clean up the house, and leave every room in good shape."

David and the others returned after the Germans left. He picked up the Bible and the sealed envelope that fell out from its pages. He put it back, and gave the Bible to the Rabbi. "Maybe they expect us to leave them a hot breakfast on the table," David lowered his voice as he tiptoed away from the Rabbi.

"And bake fresh bread," Chaye said bitterly.

"And collect our best silverware and tablecloth from the peasants," Velvke said with a deep sigh.

The door opened. "Zorach!" Alter ran to his older son who vanished on the way to Narodni. He told how he was handed over to the Germans by peasants, sent to Agustowa, from which he escaped and arrested when he returned to town. He was released with others to join the exile caravan to Grodno.

"Rachel has also been released," he said to David.

"Where is she?"

"Go and find her, David, tell her the baby is here," Chaye said to him. When she returned to the Rabbi, she saw him slumping near the bed. They helped her put him on his bed.

When David returned with Rachel, they were alone in a corner. He was too overcome to say anything. He had come to the end of his resources and strength. From all his inquiries about his parents, and a futile visit to the sanatorium, he expected the worst. All his plans failed: as a visionary his dreams were not taken seriously; the repeated attempts to escape from the ghetto which he inspired were mostly unsuccessful; the Rabbi did not sanction his courting of Rachel; Kommandant Von Preissig, a probable conscientious objector of the German atrocities against the Jews was arrested, transferred to Grodno and probably executed; and now he himself returned to the ghetto to find no trace of his parents, only Rachel and whatever was left of his shattered hopes.

"We must never be separated again," she whispered to him.

"Never again," he said, took her hand and led her into the Rabbi's room.

"David, I found the letter." David did not answer.

"The letter to my son Judah, take it and Abba's letters and deliver it to somebody on the outside. Why don't you answer?"

"Yes, the letter," David mumbled.

"David, my time is drawing near. The great Sanhedrin is summoning me. Before I close my book . . . ," he was breathing with great difficulty, "your problem with Rachel is an unfinished page. When you survive this vale of agony—you must escape from here now to tell what happened—you will present yourself before a rabbinical court to grant you the *heter* to marry Rachel. It will be verified whether Zechariah is or is not among the

living. The singular circumstances of Rachel's marriage would
be in your favor, I have so indicated in the second part of my
letter.

"Yes, yes, only . . ."

"Only what?"

"I had a dream."

"I've heard enough of your dreams, may they revert to our
enemies," the Rabbi employed the seldom used prerogative during a catastrophe which implores God to strike back at the Jews'
tormentors.

"But this dream . . ."

"All your dreams were fulfilled. Only a Satan could have
wished them upon us."

"This dream is about the Jews becoming an independent nation in the liberated Holy Land and rebuilding the Beth
Hamikdash in Jerusalem."

"Are you certain?"

"I swear . . ."

"Don't swear, only tell the truth!"

"If I lived to tell you only this then everything is not lost."

"No, it is not lost . . . Yes, yes," he searched through the glowing chapters of prophecy. "Yes it is somewhere. What prophet?
What chapter? Grant me, O beloved and holy Father in heaven
this one wish, revive my memory that is failing me now because
of all these *tzores*, before I depart from this foolish earth. Yes,
yes it is there, it is clear as day. David you have finally been
vindicated. Now that your nightmares have been visited upon us
I am certain that your hopeful dream of a liberated Israel will
definitely come true. For God revealed to Isaiah our great
prophet that Uriah's prophecy of disaster must be followed by
Zechariah's prophecy of Zion's redemption.

"When the patriarch Jacob, in his last ebbing moments wanted
to reveal the coming of the Messiah, his prophetic vision was
blurred. Moses who penetrated into the most inaccessible mysteries of God, could not transmit it as he stood for the last time
on Mount Nebo. King David's legacy was that his son Solomon
build the Temple according to the word of God.

"How strange and how comforting that we—all these just
people—shall not live to see it, but you and others will yet see
God's solemn pledge to Israel fulfilled."

It was not Rabbi Kalir who was on the deathbed, although he

was ready to meet the creator whenever it was ordained for his soul to depart from him. Mankind was dying in Europe and critically ill all over the world. It was to this afflicted humanity that the Jews brought with them the Torah, the tree of life. These precepts, laws, commandments, if they would have been accepted by the nations, would not only have insulated the Jews against the contagious diseases of evil, crime and violence, but would have maintained a reasonable balance of sanity among the nations.

The world was dying; Rabbi Kalir wanted so much to reveal the last days, but somehow God did not sanction it. It was cut off from his vision as if it were a scroll he was reading to them and it was suddenly snatched by a violent force and carried away in a pillar of fire up to heaven. And in the last burst of fire a blazing scroll lit the sky to reveal a flaming Menorah upon the darkness below.

POLISH GOVERNOR HANS FRANK
DISMISSED AS "TOO HUMANE" WITH
THE POLES. VICHY GIVING AXIS 35
MERCHANTMEN. ROMMEL IN FULL
RETREAT.

*My soul shall weep in secret places for
your pride. Because the Lord's flock is
carried away captive.*

Jeremiah, 13:15.

*God cries alone in a secret place because of
the nations who suppress Israel.*

Hagigah, 5.

30

GOD CRIES ALONE

A thousand terrors converged upon the ghetto. Uniformed
demons were poised to strike the last fatal blow: to uproot them
from their congested confinement and dispatch them on a journey of no return. Alarmed cries of babies pierced the desultory
stillness of the night. Sages uttered their plaintive prayers in
remembrance of Jerusalem, and its holy temples which were
stormed and burned down. Like their fathers for centuries, they
lamented at midnight the two historic disasters. That the third
Beth Hamikdash temple, symbolized by the Jewish people, was
also doomed, even at this late hour seemed incredible.

The floor clock in Chazkel Schneider's house shivered and
convulsed as it struck for the last time two strokes. Elchanan the
Yeshiva student bumped into it as he fumbled for his candle on
the high book case near the wall. The men and women who were
awake all night now began to pack the restricted few belongings
and food for two days.

Outside, whirring motors, barking dogs, and gruff voices
seemed to be moving closer. Elchanan fumbled for his candle
and Gemara book. He moved closer to the window through
which the snow reflected a faint light. His sallow cheeks came to

423

life when he uttered a blessing of gratitude. Water for purification; where could he find it? He touched the frosted window pane. The floral etchings once the harbingers of spring in the midst of winter's long siege, were now mute witnesses.

Hadassah in the back room heard Elchanan's wistful syllables. "Elchanan," she called him in a subdued voice. He was gone. He thought he heard a cry and he went to investigate.

"In shule arein," (to the synagogue) a lamenting cry startled her. Then it was quiet and she resumed her breathing. The door opened slowly.

"Elchanan, what was it?"

"Kakiami," he said in a somber tone. Then he looked away as if there was something portentous in the simpleton's role as a town crier.

"Stay with me," she tried to hold him back.

"The Rabbi is dying," his voice trailed off.

"Wait," she followed him.

Down the end of the block, in the bricklayer's house, Paltiel the builder who was down to his last suit, walked back and forth in his tight corner. Newly arrived refugees from Koritzin crowded every inch of space in his room and in the big shed to the rear. Now that he was like all the Jews, an inmate awaiting the worst, he reflected over his greatest mistake. He and many more could have found refuge in Israel. But now how terrible it was even to think of what awaited them. Did the Germans really intend to resettle them in a new territory? He didn't trust them. Ertez Israel was the only place where they wanted to go, he was certain. Even a letter from the Holy Land was sacred. He took out the letter which his son who settled in Ekron sent him a few years back.

"It reads like a chapter from our holy books." He read out loud:

"Last night the Arabs attacked our colony, but thank God our people, especially the youth, have guns and know how to shoot. We lost the watchman, a fine young boy from Wilna, but our defenders chased them away to the shadows. We found three dead Arabs in the morning, nearby in the grove. If you could only come over! Sell everything. Your life is never safe. Remember, can a Jew in Poland ever possess a gun without being arrested? In all these countries in Europe they talk about emancipation. A nice word. Ah, the right and freedom. But the right to be free

and to defend yourself belong only to Christians. Tell me more
about your family."

"I almost wrote that I'm coming," Paltiel kept on saying.
"Heraus," a voice shouted.
"I'm coming."
"What have you got there?" a German confronted him.
"Just this," he showed him a picture of the Western Wall which
he took.

Meanwhile at Yatvietz, Sarah Beile had to make a grave decision, whether to go back to the ghetto and be with Rachel and
Avreml or to find first a refuge for the twins. Adolph Kislo was
one of the very few Poles who wanted to help. Several Jews were
being sheltered and fed in his exposed potato cellar behind his
house. But with prying neighbors around him, it was hazardous,
as Kislo explained, for children to stay there. He also told her
what he heard from Polish guards: that all Jews were to be
transferred to Grodno any day.

Now in desperation she took the twins and knocked on doors
late at night. Doors opened and doors closed. One man told her
he would accept her as a servant but without the children. Another wanted Leishke but not the girl. Still another offered to
take the girl. "She has blue eyes," he told her, "and with a cross
on her neck, she'll be safe."

"A cross? Never!" Sarah Beile was indignant. If it were any
other symbol, a flower, a star, even a fish, she would have consented. But the mere suggestion of her child wearing a cross,
marrying and raising children who would also wear crosses, and
then being incited by the same cross to hate and kill Jews, was
repugnant. She sat down on a stoop and cried alone, until an
angry voice told her to go and do her crying somewhere else.
There was no one to help her. She decided to return to Kislo and
take her chances.

Schneur Zalmen the chasid gathered his family in a corner, he
kissed his wife on the forehead, and then his two sons on their
cheeks.

"Do not be afraid of sudden horror nor from a band of
brigands. In vain are your councils," he challenged the *reshaim,*
"your words are nought because God is with us," he kept on
repeating, *"ihr hert teire kinderlach, emanu el."* He made the

last inspection of their chasidic garb, adjusting their wide
brimmed black velvet hats and tightening the silken belts on
their long chantung caftans. He rubbed his sleeve to remove the
last spot and glint from his lapels. He was now ready to be
received by the Kings of Kings. He glanced once more to his wife
whose face reflected the same serenity with which she welcomed
the Sabbath queen. He was ready with his regal family to
present himself to the King of the Universe or if need be wherever destiny ordained. "I'll be back in a few seconds," he told
them, don't move without me. I'm going to see the Rabbi."

When they carried out the Rabbi he was in a coma. His eyes
were half closed, his breath was heavy and his face was wan. His
last wish to be with his people even in adversity was fulfilled.
Shimon the wagoner and the others lifted him into the wagon.
For a few fleeting seconds his people surrounded his wagon until
the angry voices drove them away.

How could the Torah be abandoned Reb Jacob Zaban reflected. To him the Rabbi was the Torah. The Torah was a person, and a person was the Torah. Both were inseparable and
futile without the other. Reb Isaac walked with great effort as he
went back to his own bare walls. Guards were pulling apart his
spare furniture and finally the old clock that ticked and marked
the hours of instruction for so many years. The long table stood
bare, the magic of stories by a dim candle light was now snuffed
out by screaming guards who pushed him and all the others
out.

Reb Jacob Zaban, the instructor of Talmud, and Abba Dunsky,
who waited for him now rejoined him. They were shoved with
others unceremoniously toward the gate. *"Zu Torah vezu se-
chora*—is this the reward for our Torah?" they uttered in unison.

Shimon the wagoner kept his stare toward the empty spot on
the wall in his room from which a mirror was removed. Menacing and reviling shouts came nearer to his door. A wagon and a
horse were part of him all his life. In fact it was like the other
half of his life—the first half was his home and family. He had to
attend to the daily feeding and watering of the horse; brushing
him and after that hanging up the reins and the collar on the
wall. It was like a being for whose daily food and water he felt
responsible. But these *reshaim* didn't allow the Jews even to pro-
cure their own food during all these days.

"Jude steh auf," a threatening German with steel cold eyes and thin lips stretched over a cavernous face, shouted at him.

They want me to go in a wagon—but it is not mine—it is not mine, he pounded on the table. They want to take me and all these good people and my family on an endless journey. I always travelled with Shkape to bring things, so life could go on and work benches hum, and children delight with joy of books and candy. But now—no! He suddenly rose and began to strike with his clenched fist. The startled guards closed in to escort him through the door. The one with the gaunt face backed away and moved the German and the Pole aside. He lunged forward with his fixed bayonet, but missed. The second German came from behind and struck at his cheek bone with the butt of his gun. He slumped down to the floor, blood coming out from the raw wound spitting out blood, but still defiant.

"*Reshaim*, what do you want from us? O God, destroy the *reshaim* because they are killing you too."

The Pole now kicked him with his boot in the groin, and then the German with the contorted face plunged his bayonet into his midriff. Shimon desperately struggled with his choking breath. "Shemah Israel, *Adonoy* (God). . . ." They are killing you too. His bloodied body stiffened into silence. The night before his son told him, "I am going away before morning." Shimon covered his face, sighed, and in a choking voice said:

"You are young and can escape. What will happen to your mother, your sister and me? They say that only parents with working children will be spared."

"Don't say this, I'll stay with you." He embraced and kissed his father and mother. He sat in a corner, wracking his brain before he made a final decision. He tip toed to the crowded room where his parents and sister slept, and stopped. He put on a shabby suit over a good suit, wrapped a chunk of bread in a kerchief and opened the door of the bedroom. After kissing in turn his parents and sister, he slipped out of the room.

"I am not asleep, I saw and heard everything," the mother whispered to the daughter who sank her face into the pillow. "God bless him and be with him."

After a little while, shots split the darkness.

"What happened?" his sister was concerned.

"Oh my son, *Gotenu*, help him!" his mother cried. Shimon who

was also awake, gasped when gendarmes crashed through the
door shouting:

"Heraus banditen!"

"Hey you what have you got in there?" a German confronted
the simpleton Kakiami blocking his doorway, and began to beat
him.

"Tate is sick, you can't wake him, and mama too," he protested
as Mikulak pummeled him with fists.

Grune Akusherke, the practical nurse who helped the sick,
ran to the aid of Kakiami, the simpleton.

"Please stop," she pleaded to Mikulak who was beating him.
"I'll give him something to quiet him down."

"The only thing that will quiet him down is this," Skura raised
his revolver, to which Mikulak promptly responded by butting
Kakiami's skull with its flat side.

"Stop, he is bleeding," Grune wedged in between the sadist
and the victim, but she was not spared and sank to the ground.
Now Bashke Galanti, the good soul who did what she could although she had temperature, confronted Skura.

"Is this right, Panie, in front of the church, to hurt innocent
people and shed their blood in vain, shame upon you."

"Shame yourself." Skura's face turned crimson. "You disobey
the law; the law is to go on the wagons, they want to give you
work, and you Jews delay," he concluded with insults, obscenities and curses. Before he could make the next move Murad took
over. He sized up what was going on and began to pull Kakiami
by his torn jacket. He struggled and cried:

"Prayer, yes; mitzvah deeds, yes; work, yes; but why go into a
wagon? Crazy murderers are after me. Mammi, help me and all
the Jews. The world is going crazy."

Elchanan was back. He was coatless and shivering. He held on
to his candle and *Gemara* folio. A cursing Pole jumped him and
pulled him by his jacket. It was torn and came off him in his
frantic struggle to get away. He faltered and walked aimlessly.
From a nearby doorway a sobbing mother and three boys
brushed by him. He opened the door. A gust of windblown snow
followed him. On the wall a family picture swung crazily. He
steadied the picture. He gazed through the rear window, but
ahead was only a massive wall and rusty strung wire. For a few
seconds there was a dead stillness. He was alone, cut off from his

sing-song melody and the real loving kindness world now being battered down and razed to the ground. What words, what verse, what prayer could he offer? He tried, he leafed the pages of his memory. He swayed to intone, but he couldn't utter a word. Every move was a protest against the abandonment of his people. His voice quivered, his benign facial expressions now tensed around his burning eyes. He straightened and uttered, "Shemah Israel!" do you hear, Israel? Yes, Israel hears but no one else. Holy, holy, holy, everywhere is holiness, shemah Israel, only where Israel is present. But beyond, crazed maniacs were destroying God and the people of God.

Elchanan, Elchanan, he thought he heard a high pitched voice calling him.

Several houses down the block, Hadassah's hands moved nervously as she glanced at a pile of books and family portraits. She found the family album and turned the mounted pages. A class picture of the First World War, a row of little girls on the floor, two rows of serious smiling, and pensive girls standing behind. In the middle a star of David. Chaim and the staff on the side. Another class of boys. Rabbi Zaban in the middle. A long line of children on a Lag Beomer march to the forest, the Rabbi, the teachers, youth leaders.

"Dasale, Dasale, you must go, they are coming," her mother called. She turned the last pages the impressive groups of handsome boys and girls, the Hachalutz, Hashomer Hatzair. A picture post card from Israel, a pioneer with a gun slung on his back ploughing the soil. On the last pages were her own pressed flowers. She pressed the page to her heart and cried.

"Dasale, Dasale, don't cry!"

"I'm not crying. No, mammi, but when is a girl not a girl, I mean. . . ."

"Hadassah, my Dasale, it is not important."

"But mammi, I want to know."

Her mother began to pray, to swallow her tears and above all to avoid her daughter's questions. If there is no reply from there above, how could a mother answer it, she dared to probe in desperation.

"Will I ever be a mother?" she asked, coming through the gate behind the Rabbi and Elchanan. Hadassah's eyes swept from her mother's kerchief covered forehead to her father and then to Chaim. For a long while she looked intently at the Rabbi and

Elchanan for an answer and finally looked up to the gray skies,
through which the sun began to emerge, somewhat tepidly.

Now that the gates were closed the German and Polish police
began to check the wagons and lists of people, each with his
assignment. The eastern side of the square was to be cleared of
all traffic so that the wagons now waiting on the square in the
freezing cold would at last get started. Snow ploughs cleared
Synagogue Street all the way to the highway. The highway to
Grodno was already cleared. Kommandant Rintzler now intervened to stop all movement on the highway except urgent military traffic and vehicles with wounded in order to expedite the
final exodus to "work camps." Since the military was short in
trucks and gas was needed for the airforce, Col. Schwarzhund
worked overtime to conscript the eight hundred and fifty wagons
required for the movement of about three thousand Jews, survivors of Suha-Vali, Dombrowa and Novidvor.

A gutteral order sounded "Attention!" Nothing moved. Everything was frozen. A few frightened sparrows flew away and a
crow lost a feather which drifted eerily from a tree top. It was
frightened away by a German cracking his whip over somebody.
The crow darted down a second time, seized it and flew away
with it to its nest.

Col. Schwarzhund now inspected the twelve guards standing
in the first row, and the two lines of supernumerary Polish,
Ukrainian and Latvian guards lined behind them. Two military
trucks, filled with regular soldiers armed with sub-machine guns,
led the procession of the wagons as they fell slowly into line,
until their wheels rolled in the same sandy tracks from the
ghetto gate through the market place.

The lead wagons followed the trucks and halted in front of the
church opposite the military headquarters. A motorcyclist raced
up to the command car and handed Col. Schwarzhund a dispatch.

On the open veranda, a few soldiers and camp followers, men
and women, watched the procession with great curiosity. Peasants who strayed into town looked glumly, as they do at a sky
aglow from a fire in a distant village, concerned but not disturbed. The church bell started to toll for morning mass and
then stopped abruptly.

The column rumbled steadily down Synagogue Street, the

wheels dipped one after another into the snow holes and ruts deepened by the heavy ersatz tires of the lead trucks ahead. The sky was wistful and clouded and above it all seemed so pure and free. Beyond was the highway. The rickety wagons groaned under the heavy loads. The soldiers ordered the men to get off the wagons and walk, before crossing the shaky wooden bridge. The long column moving toward Grodno was now past the water mill, past the cemetery and near the white birch trees penciled with black ringed lines, garbed in the colors of the prayer shawl which, in this world and the world to come, unites Jews with God.

"More wagons," somebody whispered. "Another transport is joining us from Koritzin and also Jews caught in the forest." Many were brought in because a bonus was offered to the peasants. Two pounds of sugar or tobacco for every last Jew caught alive and delivered to the authorities, or executed before ikon, cross, and proper witnesses.

Along the highway opposite Pokosne, Pesach the blacksmith's son lay shivering in the snow. Every time an auto passed by he pulled the white sheet over his head lest its probing lights expose him. It was five kilometers to town and he hadn't eaten for a day and a night. This was his second night since he escaped from Kolbasin. It would take him several hours to get to town. His hands were frozen and his feet were numb. If he could only stop over for the night in Pokosne. One of the family's friends lived there. Any Pole would be ready to rob and kill a Jew, he was warned. But surely this friend would at least let him rest for a few hours and give him some food. He had nothing with him, just a leather bound compact prayer book, presented to him by his wife as a wedding gift three years ago. She would be overjoyed to see him alive.

Pesach waited for a brief lapse in the traffic and began to run the bare stretch to low lying houses in Pokosne. He recognized the friend's house with the tile roof. No sooner did he reach the fence of the last house when dogs began to bark. He heard the door open. Someone called him.

"Where are you going?"

"To a friend of the family," he answered.

"Who is it," a man's voice called from behind a door.

"It is Pesach, the blacksmith's son."

"What do you want?"

"I need help." He waited for several minutes before the peasant opened the door.

"Where did you come from?"

"From a town." He did not want to tell him that he got away from a death camp, to which he was sent after his escape from Agustowa.

"Something is going on in town," the peasant said.

"What?"

"They are going to move some of them to another place."

"Take me into town in a hay sled. I'll pay you when I get there."

"Well, it is dangerous now. Stay here, rest and even sleep a few hours till morning. Then I'll give you my suit and coat and you'll look like one of us."

"But you say they are taking the Jews away."

"I didn't say that. You are saying it. It may take several days or weeks. Germans don't tell us their plans. Here, I'll fix up the sofa in the room behind the oven. You'll be dead asleep before you know it."

"But I mustn't fall asleep. I have to go there after a while."

"Take my advice. I'm a religious man. There is a cross and an ikon in every room, except where you'll sleep. You can trust me. Go to sleep. I'll wake you up myself." Presently he bedded down some wool cloth and then gave him a sheepskin great coat to cover himself.

Before his eyes loomed the Gehennam stoked by satanic demons in German uniforms. The nightmares he had witnessed at the three gates to Gehennam: Kolbasin, Grodno and Auschwitz, reeled before his eyes: Masses of people driven by sadists and drunkards into Kolbasin.

"Why don't you sleep?" the host asked Pesach who was startled by his presence in the room. "You move around too much."

"I can't. My wife is all alone."

"Go to sleep," he told him angrily.

Pesach opened his prayer book. He could only guess in the darkness that somewhere on its pages was a prayer, asking God before going on a journey, to safeguard him from enemies, thugs and murderers waiting in the shadows. His fingers opened the prayer book and touched its pages. There were so many prayers

there. The Jews must have gone on long and dangerous journeys
before. There were always *mazikim* and *demons* everywhere.

He closed his eyes to say his night prayer, "Shemah Israel."
Noises of the night—no, steps moved closer and closer. He
opened one eye. He thought he saw a hand holding something
long and shiny and the other hand grabbing his wrapped up
prayer book. Pesach put down his hand on the prayer book, the
very instant the peasant clutched it in his hand.

"It's only a prayer book," he told him.

It must be something the way you hold on to it," the peasant
remarked. "I have a cross made out of gold. Is this book valuable?"

"Yes, very valuable," he said. He was too tired to explain to
him the value of prayers.

Pesach now slept fitfully, his hand in the prayer book. He
heard steps again. He saw the peasant with a knife in his hand.
Before he could cry out, he felt a sharp blow over his chest.
Blood choked his breath and it became very dark.

Everything was coming to an end. The last Jews—the sick and
the dying—were removed from their last moments of rest and
pain on this earth. David and Rachel who were holed up in a
corner in Isaac's yard waited for a safe moment to get out. They
waited too long—to find out the whereabouts of her family and
to trace his parents—and miscalculated. They thought that the
guards would vacate the desolate ghetto. Instead some returned
to search for hidden treasures. As they crouched near the fence
underneath a pile of wood to the rear of Isaac's house, they
heard the shattering sounds of smashed drawers, ripped closets
and demolished double walls. Frustrated because they could not
find much, they began to wield axes and crow bars.

After a while the demolition stopped. David observed that
guards were still around. He looked at Rachel. She only
glanced at him. They and a few others were the last Jews in and
around Suha-Vali. Some half frozen wandered aimlessly in the
woods, others hungry and terrified were turned away by hostile
faces and the very last ones were pursued by blood hounds and
blood enemies—Germans and Poles.

They crawled on their bellies underneath the wall, and were
now out in the open. Dressed like peasants they would pretend, if
caught, that they came to look around and do some "shopping."

David had on him the last letter of the Rabbi. It would give
him away. He would therefore read its contents before he was
forced to throw it away:

My son, I am going on a long journey. I would gladly say my last
prayers. But how could I close my eyes, when all this is happening.
Since the days of Noah, and the tower of Babel, when the
generation became corrupt and revolted against God, the world
has not experienced so much *rishos*. Remember the story about
Sambatyon, the river from beyond the dark mountains, that
explodes with fiery waves for six days of the week and rests
on the Sabbath? But this river of hate Sambatyon 2, never
stops, and a sinful mankind stands by and does nothing. Without Israel, what is the Torah, and without the Torah the nations
will revert to *tohu vovehu*, chaos. The Jewish people must return
to the promised land of their fathers. The Beth Hamikdash must
be restored. The Amalakites whoever they are and whenever they
emerge to threaten God and man, must be defeated . . . The *ketz*
is near, very near . . .

Once more the angry S.S. officer shouted the command to
move on. Babies—the last babies born before the war—hugged
their mothers beneath flimsy coats. Their bare heads and frightened eyes looked out to the bleak snow covered fields on either
side. The naked trees shook and shivered. The skies were covered with grey clouds and chilling winds blew from all sides.

It seemed as if every one disappeared from sight. Some were
in church, others were peacefully drinking in the cafes, that
mushroomed in former Jewish houses. No one was in sight. Not a
sound, not a signal, only the tolling of the bell, like the whining
of the wind, and the vain cawing of the raven into mute space.

For it was all winter and a white blanket covered everything,
and the voice was drowned by the wind, and its sighs were
scattered by the sharp piercing of the air by bullets, whose
echoes died quickly against the sky.

People—they were peasants who came and now returned
empty hearted—they did not cry and never let out a sigh. Everything was quiet and dying. Not a sound, not a signal, only the
tolling of the bell and the whining of the wind and the black
raucous crows settling down for the night, a black night.